Lisa Hartley lives with her partner, son, two dogs and several cats. She graduated with a BA (Hons) in English Studies, then had a variety of jobs but continues to write in her spare time.

Also by Lisa Hartley

Detective Catherine Bishop

On Laughton Moor
Double Dealing
From the Shadows
Home Fires Burn

Detective Caelan Small

Ask No Questions
Tell No Lies
Time To Go

Lisa HARTLEY

HOME FIRES BURN

First published in the United Kingdom in 2020 by Canelo

Canelo Digital Publishing Limited
31 Helen Road
Oxford OX2 0DF
United Kingdom

A CIP catalogue record for this book is available from the British Library.

Print ISBN 978 1 80032 133 5
Ebook ISBN 978 1 80032 117 5

Look for more great books at www.canelo.co

Printed and bound in Great Britain by Clays Ltd, Elcograf S.p.A.

Dedicated to the memory of Jack Dolan.

Cé nár casadh ar a chéile muid, tá tú liom i mo chroí.

Prologue

They'd told her to take some time; in fact it had been an order. She had been burned out, exhausted, ill. Close to breaking down altogether.

The first month had passed in a daze as the medication kicked in and her body began to work with it. She spent most of the time in pyjamas, or jogging bottoms and a T-shirt if she was having a better day. She tried to read, dragging from her bookshelf all the books she'd promised herself she'd devour when she had the time. After staring at the text until it merged into one black blur, she would give up, replace the book, open another. She never read more than a chapter. The words made no sense, either individually or in a sentence. She couldn't bear noise, even music. She drank tea and stared at nothing, wondering if she'd ever feel right again.

She had visitors who came and went, smiling, kind and concerned. Frightened for her. Whispered conversations about her health in the hallway, questions asked too brightly, the desperate desire to help grating against her nerves.

Sometimes home could be its own kind of prison.

But Isla did help. She sat quietly, saying nothing, her presence, her warmth, a comfort. Sometimes Catherine clung to her, unable to find any words, but with Isla, there was no need. Everything they needed to say was already in the room with them.

And Jonathan Knight helped. He too was unobtrusive, undemanding, walking into the room with his shy smile and his quiet concern for her. He talked softly about what was happening at work, and didn't ask how she was feeling because it was obvious.

The second month was clearer. She went to the supermarket with Isla, and though it was too busy, too bright, too loud, Catherine was glad she had gone. The world was still out there; she just needed to wait until she was ready for it.

And by the end of the third month, she was. No longer cocooned in do-nothing clothes and a blanket, able to read, to chat on the phone. To be herself again, just about. Two weeks' holiday in the sun tacked onto her sick leave, and she felt as though she'd been put back together. Well enough, anyway. Ready to be a police officer again.

1

He never meant to hit her.

Sometimes he cried afterwards, begging her to forgive him. Swore he'd change, promising their lives would improve.

It had happened again that morning. He'd arrived home at six, tired after working all night, resenting her for being there at all. He'd wanted a cooked breakfast, and a few hours on the PlayStation before bed. She'd spent the last of the money on nappies and when he'd realised, he'd gone berserk. Her fault they had no money, her fault they had two kids, a tiny house and a shit relationship.

As if he'd had nothing to do with any of it.

Now, she stood in the bathroom again, her hands shaking as she held a cold flannel to her cheek. She'd bathed it a couple of times, hoping it wouldn't bruise.

He was getting careless.

He'd shoved her the first few times, pushing her away as if trying to eject her from his life altogether. She'd made excuses, but when the first slap landed, she knew she had to act. She had promised herself if he hit her again, she would call the police.

Why hadn't she?

At least he'd stormed out, gone to McDonald's for a breakfast with his last few quid. Hopefully he'd have calmed down by the time he came home. Hollie had taken the kids around to her mate Lucy's house, just in case. She didn't want them in the house if Andy went off on one again.

Lucy was always up early with her baby and she'd helped out before. For thirty quid, she would have them all day, understanding when Hollie asked if she could wait for the money. Also, Lucy could be trusted to keep her mouth shut. The last thing Hollie needed was people talking.

She soaked the flannel again under the cold tap, explored her cheek with her fingertips before pressing it to the skin. It wasn't too bad. If there was a mark she couldn't cover with make-up, she'd have to come up with some excuse to stay inside for a few days. She'd done it before because she couldn't let her mum and dad see. If her brother found out... She shuddered. No, best to text them, say she had a cold. Couldn't say it was a stomach bug – they'd assume she was pregnant and it'd be like last time, all fake smiles, and rolled eyes behind her back talking about her, how thick she was. Take a pill once a day, Hollie, it's not difficult. Use a condom. Laughing at her, at him. At them. They might as well wear T-shirts saying: 'Told you so'. And they had over, and over. Leave him, come home. Bring the kids, poor little sods. Not their fault. Her choices, her life.

Her fuck-ups.

She squeezed the water out of the flannel, dropped it into the basket which held their dirty washing, shitloads of it. How was she supposed to get it dry? The weather had been crap lately. She'd had a wire clothes horse, but he'd booted it across the living room one day when his favourite shirt had been too damp to wear when he wanted, and that had been the end of it.

4

Sometimes, he'd bring her flowers. Picked from someone's garden in the right season, then wrapped in a few sheets of newspaper. Daffodils, chrysanths. Whatever was cheapest, if he had to buy them. He knew how to make her feel special all right.

She'd loved him once. When they'd first met, four years ago now. In a pub in town, she, pissed on cheap cocktails, he, watching her over his pint of lager. A wad of notes in his pocket. They'd dried up quicker than his affection had. Now he was stuck here. She'd trapped him, like a fly in a spider's web. She was a pathetic bitch, a useless cow. Fucking nothing.

Nothing.

Hollie turned away from the mirror and her own stupid face. His words, not hers. She went down to the kitchen and filled the kettle.

Then the front door slammed, and she turned to face him again. He stood in the doorway, leaning against the frame. His eyes flicked to her cheek, but Hollie could see he wasn't going to apologise. She risked a smile.

'All right?' she said.

'Where are the kids?' He spoke quietly, but she wasn't fooled. Her mouth was dry, and she felt sick. She hated the power he had over her.

'They're with Lucy.'

Andy nodded but didn't move, just watched her take a step towards him. As she halted, her hands fluttering by her sides because she didn't know what to do with them, he smirked. 'Saw a mate of yours while I was out.'

Hollie licked her lips, suspecting a trap. 'Did you? Who?'

'Emma Gibbs.' He was watching her face, and Hollie knew she couldn't allow her expression to change,

5

couldn't give him the excuse he was looking for. Not this time.

'Yeah? How is she?'

'Fine. Looking good, you know?' His smile widened, and he slid his hands from his pockets, folding his arms across his chest. 'She told me she'd seen you.'

Hollie swallowed. Here it came. 'Yeah, I bumped into her in the supermarket a few days ago.'

'You never said.'

'Well, I...' I don't have to report back to you every time I leave the house. She didn't say the words, wouldn't dare, but he guessed what she was thinking. His face darkened.

'Who else did you see?' he demanded.

'What? No one.'

'No one? You went into town, all around Tesco, and you saw no one?'

'Come on, you know what I mean. No one I talked to.'

He pursed his lips, tilted his head, making a show of thinking about what she'd said. 'Sure? Because Emma says differently. Emma says there's a bloke in Tesco you seemed very friendly with. Joe Hudson? From school?'

Hollie gulped, watching his hands. 'Yeah, I said hello to him, but that's all.'

'And what did he say to you?'

'Nothing, I swear. Just asked how I was, what I'd been up to. You know, friendly.'

'Friendly?'

Then he was beside her, grabbing her hair in his fist. He yanked her head back, and Hollie fought to keep from crying out. Don't, she told herself. Don't make it worse.

'Did you think I wouldn't find out?' His mouth was next to her ear, his saliva spraying over her cheek as he

6

yelled at her. 'You don't talk to anyone, understand? From now on, I do the shopping, you get that?' He wrenched her around, shoved her so she fell to the floor. 'Fucking chatting blokes up in Tesco, laughing at me behind my back. Who the fuck do you think you are?'

Hollie scrambled onto her knees, scrubbed at her eyes. Get away, she told herself. Find your phone. It was on the worktop, and she pushed herself to her feet, holding up her hands in front of her as she took a few backwards steps. 'Listen, please, it wasn't like that, I promise. I spoke to him in passing, but that's all. You've got to believe me—'

His nostrils flared as he lurched towards her, grabbing her forearm. 'Got to? You telling me what to do now?'

'No, of course not, I'm...' With her free hand, Hollie scrabbled on the worktop, found the phone and held it up, breathing hard. 'Let go of me, or I'm calling the police.'

He stared at her, began to laugh. 'The police? Yeah, sure you will.'

She lifted her chin, pressed trembling lips together. 'I will. Hurt me, and they'll take you away.'

'Away? It's you who'll be going away, you crazy bitch.' He snatched the phone from her hand, hurled to the floor and stamped on it. 'Who are you going to ring now?'

She screeched, her eyes wild, hand still searching the worktop behind her for a weapon. He came for her again, froze when he saw what was in her hand.

'Now, what are you doing with that?' He raised his hands, opened his arms. 'Listen, I'm sorry, all right? Come on, let's talk. We'll watch a film, cuddle up on the sofa. Put it down, Hollie, before someone gets hurt.'

She was beyond listening, her gaze fixed on the blade. He stepped back, hands still in the air in a gesture of submission. She stumbled towards him, the knife in her fist.

'You want to talk?' she hissed. 'Want me to listen?'

He took a step backwards.

'Of course I do. I love you.'

'Love?' She gave a scornful laugh.

'I do, I swear I do.'

He watched uncertainty bloom in her eyes, saw the blade dip, and sprang for her.

2

Detective Sergeant Catherine Bishop slouched low in the passenger seat. 'Why are we here again?'

Beside her, PC Natalie Roberts drummed her fingers on the steering wheel. 'You know why.'

'Because we were expecting someone to show up. Well, he hasn't.'

'Not yet. We've only been here half an hour.' Roberts leaned over Catherine's legs and opened the glove box. She rummaged around, brought out two Mars bars. 'Here, this'll cheer you up.'

They were parked on an industrial estate on the outskirts of Northolme, a market town twenty miles from Lincoln. Catherine had been based there since joining the force after university. There had been rumours and muttering about the Northolme station being closed, or at least no longer having a CID presence, but so far, it hadn't happened. Catherine knew it might only be a matter of time before she had to think about a transfer. For now, she was part of a surveillance operation that so far had proved fruitless. Tearing open the wrapper, she bit into the chocolate.

'This is ridiculous, you know,' she mumbled. 'Why would he come here?'

Roberts gestured towards the windscreen, waving her Mars bar in the direction of several dustbin lorries parked across the road. 'These are the kind of places he's been targeting. This garage services all the council vehicles, so there's always plenty of trucks and vans around. He'd probably think sending a bin lorry up in flames would be a good laugh.'

Catherine kept chewing. 'You reckon?'

'Last night, he torched a Transit and a couple of trucks. Over a hundred grand's worth of damage, one of the firefighters told me.' Roberts smirked. 'We had a good chat, actually. I asked for his number in the end.'

'You're picking men up at crime scenes now? Smooth.'

'What can I say?' Roberts pretended to preen. 'Not sure if it's the hat they find attractive, or the stab vest.'

Catherine finished her Mars bar, scrunched up the wrapper and pushed it into her trouser pocket. 'I need a drink now.' She looked again at the vehicles, trying to imagine herself sneaking up to them, smashing the windscreens, chucking some petrol and a match inside and making a run for it. 'I don't see what he's getting out of it.'

'Who?'

'The arsonist. Any arsonist really. Power?'

'Dunno.' Roberts stuffed the last of her chocolate into her mouth. 'They reckon it's sexual, don't they?'

Catherine squinted at her. 'What is?'

'Arson. Gives the person with the matches a thrill they're not getting anywhere else, if you know what I mean.' Roberts favoured Catherine with a leer. 'Not a problem you're having these days, Sarge, so I've been told.'

Blushing, Catherine laughed. 'Mind your own business.'

'Whatever you say. About that drink – garage down the road's still open if you fancy a stroll.' Roberts held out a few pound coins. 'Get us a coffee, would you, please? They've got a machine.'

Catherine screwed up her face. 'Why do I have to go? I'm the sergeant here.'

'And I'm the driver, got to stay with the car. You know how it is.'

Roberts flashed a winning smile, and Catherine shook her head as she opened the car door. It was a mild April night, but she was glad of her jacket as a cool breeze whipped past her. She pulled out her phone as she walked, made a call.

'Anna?'

'Sarge? Anything happening?'

'Apart from Nat sending me out for coffee, no. You're at the bus depot?'

'Yeah, parked up nearby with Emily. Everything's locked up though; I don't see how he could get to any of the buses.'

Catherine pursed her lips. 'Me neither, but you know how it is. We need to be seen doing something, even if we're achieving nothing.'

Anna laughed. 'Thanks for the pep talk.'

'Any time.' Smiling, Catherine ended the call as she pushed through the glass door of the petrol station.

She was walking back towards Roberts and the warmth of the car when her phone began to ring in her pocket. In the distance, somewhere over the other side of town, she could hear sirens.

'Bloody hell.' She was holding a cardboard cup in each hand and was forced to put one down on the pavement so she could wrestle the handset out of her pocket. As usual, Detective Chief Inspector Keith Kendrick didn't bother with pleasantries. She might have been out of action for more than three months, but she could rely on Kendrick not to have changed.

'Catherine, there's a shitstorm brewing on our favourite housing estate,' he said. 'Can you get over there?'

'The Meadowflower? What's going on?'

Police officers were summoned to the warren of streets and blocks of flats almost daily, wrestling with public disturbances, theft, brawling or drug dealing. Every town had its trouble spots, and the Meadowflower was one of theirs.

Kendrick was still talking. 'A neighbour heard a baby crying. After it had been going on for a several hours, disturbing their evening in front of the TV, they finally decided to report it.' He paused, and Catherine imagined him sitting in his office, phone under his chin, his huge brogues up on the desk. 'But as we know, there's more community service than community spirit around the Meadowflower. I shouldn't be surprised. On second thoughts, I'll pick you up myself and send someone else to keep PC Roberts out of mischief.'

Catherine frowned. 'I don't see—'

'Why we need a CID presence up there?' Another pause. 'The parents are in the house, but they're in no state to care for their children.'

'You mean they're out of it? Drugs?'

'No, Sergeant. I mean they're both dead.'

3

Slowing the car as he guided it over one of the Mead-owflower Estate's many speed bumps, Kendrick sneezed, fumbling to pull a wad of tissue from his trouser pocket. 'I'd like to know who's given me this bloody cold.'

Catherine turned to look out of the window beside her, hoping his germs wouldn't make their way around the car.

'Sounds as though you should be in bed,' she told him.

He blew his nose with one hand, while the other held the steering wheel.

'Believe me, I'd love to be at home with a Lemsip and the football on.' He flicked on the indicator and turned the wheel. 'But we need to see what's been going on here before I can even think about it.'

'What do we know so far?'

'Our officers arrived, heard the children bawling as reported but couldn't gain access. After they'd booted the door in, they found the bodies. Mum lying in the kitchen, dad on the bathroom floor.'

Catherine closed her eyes for a second.

'Where were the children?' she asked.

'Their bedroom. The baby's only a few months old, her brother a toddler. Hopefully they'll be too young to have known much about what went on, even if they might have been able to help us had they been older.'

She knew she had to push the thoughts of the children, alone and no doubt terrified, out of her mind. At least they were safe, even if their parents were beyond help.

'Do we have a cause of death?'

Kendrick wagged a finger.

'Come on, you know better than that. Jo Webber's on her way.' He leaned forward, peering through the windscreen. Further down the road, a crowd was gathering. 'Seems word's already out. Look at this lot.'

Catherine could hear them. Fifty or so people standing at a junction, craning their necks, talking, speculating.

Kendrick tutted. 'Beats a night in front of the TV, I suppose. Two dead bodies found on your doorstep – they probably think it's some kind of reality show.'

He bumped the wheels up the kerb and turned off the engine. Catherine climbed out, tucking her hair behind her ears as the wind whipped it around her face. Kendrick was already shouldering his way through the crowd, and she hurried after him.

'Is it true there's a body?' a man shouted as they pushed past. 'Is it Hollie? What about the kids?'

Ignoring him, Catherine kept moving. A cordon, the blue and white tape stretching from one lamp post to another and guarded by uniformed officers, was preventing anyone from getting any closer to the house they were heading for. Catherine peered down the cul-de-sac, noting the liveried Lincolnshire police cars and white vans belonging to the forensic support parked at the far end. She could see several white-suited figures moving around – forensics were getting started.

Kendrick stopped by the tape, standing hands on hips, glaring at the crowd of rubberneckers.

'Why the hell are these idiots bothering to wait around? They can't get near the house.'

Catherine lifted her shoulders, let them fall. It was the same at any crime scene, as Kendrick must know.

'Won't stop them trying,' she said.

'I've asked Anna and Dave to get over here. We need to get the house-to-house started as soon as we know what we're dealing with. They can get that sorted.'

Catherine nodded. In an area as well populated as this, there might be eyewitnesses who could help them piece together what had happened here. Whether they would be willing to talk was another matter.

Kendrick strode over to the nearest uniform, who straightened his back and stuck out his chest as he saw the DCI approaching.

'Good evening, sir,' he began. Kendrick held up a hand.

'Is DI Knight here yet?' he demanded. 'I've not seen his car.'

The officer shook his head.

'Not as far as I'm aware.'

'All right. Scene of Crime or whatever we're supposed to call them today are already on site, I see?'

'That's right, sir.'

'They must have flown here.'

The officer stared at him, uncomprehending.

'Sir?'

'They're based miles away now, in...' Kendrick shook his head. 'Doesn't matter.' He ducked under the cordon. 'Anyone got a scene log started?'

Another officer hurried forward with a clipboard, and Kendrick took it.

'Get a car over here so we have a rendezvous point. I assume we have an inner cordon set up too?'

'Yes, sir. Inspector Dhirwan is around; he put everything in place.'

'Good.' Kendrick handed the clipboard to Catherine, and she filled in her name, the date and time.

'What about a common approach path?' Kendrick asked the uniform.

'You're free to walk down the street, sir, as long as you keep to the designated area. I could get a CSI to come and show you?' She looked up at Kendrick, eyes wide, keen to help. Catherine tried to place her, but knew she wasn't from their own station. Had reinforcements been sent in already? From what Kendrick had told her, she had been expecting a nasty domestic, the result of an argument turned violent, maybe a murder/suicide. They were taught not to make assumptions, to go into every case with open eyes, but you also needed to be prepared. What were they going to find at the crime scene?

'Please do.' Kendrick watched the young officer take a step back and turn away. He looked at Catherine. 'Not one of ours, is she?'

'No.'

Kendrick frowned as he took out his phone. He stabbed at the screen, his thick fingers scrolling.

'Apparently we've been sent a van load of constables from Lincoln. She must be one of them.' He looked at Catherine. 'How nice.'

'How come they were here before us?'

'Headquarters knew we had most of our officers on the stake-outs tonight. They probably thought we need all the help we can get, and sent them straight over when the initial call came in.' He pushed his hands into his coat pockets. 'And, depending on what we find inside, we might do.'

It was Catherine's turn to frown. What was he talking about?

'But I thought—'

Kendrick held up a hand as the young officer turned back to them. 'What's your name, Constable?'

She smiled. 'Jenson, sir. Sophie Jenson.'

He nodded. 'Did you get hold of a CSI?'

'Yes, sir. The Crime Scene Manager is on his way.'

'Is it Mick Caffery?'

Kendrick bounced on his toes, and Catherine knew why he was asking the question. They had worked with Caffery many times before, and in a major investigation, having people around who you knew were the best in the business was invaluable.

'Yes, sir,' said Jenson. Catherine smiled at her. Kendrick in full flow could be a daunting sight, but the young constable didn't seem fazed. Kendrick rubbed his hands together, peering over PC Jenson's shoulder.

'Here's Mick now.'

A white-suited figure was making its way towards them. Mick Caffery had removed his face mask, gloves and overshoes, and as he reached them, he held out a hand for Kendrick to shake, then offered it to Catherine.

'Good to see you both,' he said. He spoke gravely, and Catherine knew why. The respect they had for Caffery and his approach to his job worked both ways. There were two people lying dead nearby who, under whatever circumstances, had lost their lives unexpectedly. This was not the time for a chat.

'I'm told we can approach the house?' Kendrick said.

Caffery nodded.

'We've placed footplates on the pavement. Possibly unnecessary, but we've no way of knowing which way our assailant went. Stick to the plates, and you'll be fine.' He held out bundles of protective clothing.

As Catherine stepped into the white suit, pulled up the hood and fastened the mask over the lower half of her face, she wondered how many times she had done this before. Too many to count. She pulled on the overshoes and a couple of pairs of blue nitrile gloves, the familiar mix of crawling dread and tingle of anticipation began to course through her. Early in her career, she had felt guilty for the rush of adrenalin she had experienced at crime scenes. Before long though, experience taught her that what she was feeling was not simple excitement or morbid curiosity, but a sense of determination to learn all she could from the victims and their surroundings. She had learnt to compartmentalise the horror, the fury, and her reaction to the events that had already unfolded. She could not give the victims back their lives, but she could play her part in bringing them justice.

'What can you tell us?' Kendrick asked Caffery as he led the way, stepping onto the first plastic footplate just beyond the cordon. 'Good work, Constable,' he called over his shoulder. PC Jenson straightened her back, still clutching her clipboard, and spoke into the radio clipped to her shoulder. Catherine smiled to herself as she followed Kendrick and Caffery. Jenson had impressed Kendrick – no mean feat.

'Mick? Anything you can tell us?' Kendrick repeated as they stepped carefully from plate to plate, making their way quickly down the street. The plates were designed to allow people to move around the area safely, and without disturbing or contaminating evidence.

'Nothing I'd want to commit to yet.'

Caffery kept walking, didn't look back at Kendrick as he spoke. Catherine wasn't surprised and doubted Kendrick had been expecting any other reply. 'Well, I'll wait for Jo Webber.'

'Not clear cut then?' Catherine asked.

Caffery didn't reply. They were almost at the end of the cul-de-sac now. The rest of the road consisted of a few pensioner's bungalows and houses built in blocks of four. Here, at the bottom of the street the houses were built in pairs, standing around a wide area of tarmac as the road became a turning circle. Peering around Kendrick, Catherine saw the red and white tape that signified the inner cordon – the area where the bodies had been found, and the place they could expect to find the most physical evidence. She knew they would have to sign their names again before entering the house, and sure enough, another clipboard appeared under her nose. She listed the protective clothing she wore and checked the time, scribbling the details down.

Waiting for Kendrick to fill in his own details, Catherine was struck by the silence. Most of the houses had a couple of lights on, but there was no one around. No doubt all the residents had been warned to stay inside. There were a couple of uniformed officers standing guard, but she doubted anyone would be daft enough to need shepherding back inside their property. Generally, even in a trouble spot like the Meadowflower Estate, if a police officer gave an instruction, people tended to obey.

Caffery was pulling on a fresh face mask, overshoes and two pairs of gloves.

'Okay. I'll take you in,' he said.

From outside, the house was unremarkable. The blue front door had paint flaking from it, and the glass in it had cracked and then been repaired with brown tape. Catherine wondered how the damage had happened. There was a patch of grass in front of the house and its neighbour, no wall or fence between the two. The grass had been cut but not collected, and it lay in small piles. As Catherine watched, a clump was lifted by the breeze and scattered across the road. The curtains in the front window of the house next door moved slightly, and Catherine imagined the resident standing watching what was happening on their doorstep. Were they afraid? Shocked? Unsurprised? Soon, they would need to find out. Perhaps the neighbours would have some answers, but as yet, they had no idea of the questions they would need to ask them.

Caffery led the way down the path. As they walked, Catherine took a few deep breaths, calming her nerves and readying her senses. First impressions of a crime scene, as in other areas of life, could be vital to understanding them. Sights, smells, observations all had to be noted and considered. Every scene was different, and until you were there, you had no idea what you were going to find.

'Ready?'

Caffery turned to look at them, and Kendrick nodded, his suit rustling with the movement.

'Pathologist's here,' someone called from behind them. Catherine turned to see Doctor Jo Webber raising the hood of her protective suit as she walked towards them. Catherine raised a gloved hand as Jo nodded a greeting.

'I'd say it's good to see you, Catherine, but...'

'You too, Jo.' It wasn't, not in these circumstances.

The front door opened from inside, and Mick Caffery led them through it.

'Keep to the footplates please,' he said.

They filed into a tiny hallway, with doors leading off it left and right.

'Kitchen first.' Caffery kept walking. The kitchen was tidy, the worktops clean, the floor covered in cheap-looking laminate. 'This is Hollie Morton. We can't confirm her identity yet, of course, but that's the name of the female tenant.'

There was a moment of silence, each of them taking time to gaze down at the body on the floor, heads bowed. A few seconds of reflection, of respect. Then they would push their feelings aside and concentrate on the only thing they could do for her now – find the person who killed her.

The dead woman lay on her back in the centre of the room. She was young; Catherine guessed in her early twenties. Her blonde hair fanned out behind her head, dull grey eyes staring up at the ceiling. Catherine guessed immediately how Hollie had died but knew she would have to wait for Jo Webber to confirm it. Knowing Jo, that wouldn't be until after she had completed the post-mortem.

One of Caffery's team crouched on the floor, placing a yellow plastic marker next to a small pile of smashed metal and plastic. Kendrick peered at it.

'What's that? A mobile phone?' He leaned closer, his white suit straining at the seams. 'And a knife?'

Caffery nodded.

'There's one missing from the block on the worktop there. Obviously, we'll bag it and run the tests.'

Kendrick looked around. 'Can't see blood anywhere though?'

'Wait and see,' Caffery told him.

Catherine looked at the body, the mangled phone, the knife.

'We're thinking this could have been a domestic?' she said. 'The couple have a row, Hollie's phone gets smashed, her partner loses his rag, grabs her around the throat and she stabs him?' She glanced around. 'It can't have been much of a wound though, even if she did. Like the boss says, the only blood I can see is on the blade of the knife.'

'Unless someone else did it and cleaned up after themselves,' Kendrick said.

The pathologist was bending over the body.

'Bruising to her throat, petechial haemorrhages… Nothing I'm seeing so far contradicts your suggestion that she was throttled, Catherine.'

'But you're not going to commit to anything?' Kendrick said.

Jo stood, rubbing the small of her back. 'Correct.'

'When did she die, Jo?' Kendrick held up a hand. 'And before you say it, I'm not asking you to tell me to the second. Give us your best guess.'

She turned away. 'You know that's not how this works. I've barely had a chance to look at her yet.'

'A rough idea then.'

Catherine heard Jo sigh from across the room.

'Very loosely, mid-morning to mid-afternoon. I'm saying no more until I've examined her properly.'

'The parents died over twelve hours ago?' Kendrick screwed up his face. 'No wonder the kids were screaming. Poor little buggers must be half-starved.'

Mick Caffery cleared his throat.

'Would you mind having a quick look at the male victim now, Jo? I know you've not finished with Hollie, but a glance should do it.'

Jo turned. 'What do you mean?'

'You'll see.'

Catherine stared at Caffery, trying to place the tone in his voice. It was unusual for him to interrupt Jo during her preliminary examinations. Kendrick had his hands on his hips.

'What are you getting at, Mick?'

He didn't reply, just led the way out of the room. Jo Webber followed him. Kendrick looked at Catherine, eyebrows raised, before disappearing up the stairs. Catherine hurried after them, careful to stick to the plastic plates again.

The landing was small, square. Kendrick stood blocking what Catherine assumed was the bathroom door. Caffery looked at Jo.

'Best if you put on a different suit, I think, if you don't mind,' he said.

Jo studied him for a second but didn't comment. She stripped off the suit, gloves and overshoes she had been wearing, and replaced them with fresh ones. Caffery held out evidence bags for her to drop the used ones into, then stood across the landing, arms folded, while Jo passed Kendrick and disappeared into the room. The only sound was the rustling of Kendrick's own suit as he shuffled his feet.

Soon, Catherine heard Jo give a low whistle.

'See what I mean?' Caffery called to her.

'Yep.' There was a pause. 'There's a belt around his throat. Can we turn him over? You'll have seen the blood on the toilet seat and the floor beneath?'

'We haven't taken a sample yet, but it's been photographed. I'd rather wait to turn him if we can,' said Mick.

'All right,' Jo said. 'I'd like to have a look at the back of his skull though.'

'You're thinking he fell and cracked his head on the toilet?' said Kendrick. 'What about the belt?'

'There's a plaster on his arm – maybe a cut, considering the knife we saw downstairs? The blood could have come from that, or another injury we haven't seen yet, though if he was cut downstairs and his arm was bleeding that much, I'd have expected to find traces through the house as he came up here. Of course, this blood could be unrelated, not his at all. It could be menstrual blood, for example.'

Kendrick shifted, clearly growing impatient.

'Bit of a mess to leave though. What about the belt?'

'I'm not seeing anything immediately consistent with strangulation. The belt could have been left to try to make us think that's what happened.' Jo's voice was tight, as though she was controlling her temper. Catherine could understand why. Kendrick was demanding answers she had no way of providing yet.

'Well, what *can* you tell me?'

Jo didn't reply. Kendrick leaned forward, and Catherine tried to see around him. She could see a pair of trainers, but the rest of the body was hidden by the DCI's bulk. From the position of the victim's feet, it was clear he was lying on his back.

'We're assuming this is the body of Andy Nugent. He lives, or lived, here with Hollie and their two children,' Caffery said. 'Notice anything?'

'Let's not keep playing silly buggers,' said Kendrick. 'Tell us what you mean.'

Caffery nodded. 'Well, we said downstairs it was possible each victim had killed the other, didn't we?'

Jo emerged from the bathroom, stepping past Kendrick and coming to stand beside Catherine.

'And?' Kendrick demanded.

'Look at him, Keith.' Jo pointed into the bathroom with her thumb, and Kendrick clumped into the room. 'You've seen enough bodies to know. This man died much more recently than the woman downstairs.'

Catherine's stomach lurched as she took in what Jo was saying. She backed away as Caffery and Kendrick came out of the bathroom.

'You're sure, Jo?' Kendrick was asking.

'As sure as I can be at this stage. Rigor's present, but not complete. Whoever killed this man, it wasn't his partner. She died hours before he did.'

4

Outside, drizzle had begun to fall. Kendrick scowled up at the dark, murky sky as he pulled off his protective clothing. A CSI materialised with some evidence bags. He held one out and Kendrick dropped his gear inside.

'Looks like Jo's estimated time of death has buggered our assumption this was a domestic,' Kendrick said, pinching his lower lip between his forefinger and thumb. Catherine pulled off her overshoes, unzipped her own suit and stepped out of it. Once everything was bagged, she watched the CSI hurry away.

'Maybe,' she said. 'But it could have started out that way.'

'We can't take for granted Andy Nugent killed his girlfriend either. For all we know, one or more unknown people killed both of them.'

Catherine nodded, knowing he was right.

'We'll have to wait for Jo's reports after the post-mortems,' she said.

'There was no sign of a break-in. If Nugent was killed by someone from outside, he either knew the person, or he invited them in for some reason.'

'Or the door was unlocked, and the killer walked straight in.'

Kendrick hunched his shoulders.

'We need to confirm the identities of our two victims and contact their next of kin,' he said. 'I want us talking to the people living in the house next door, the ones who called about the children crying. You and Anna can do that now. I need to talk to Raj, find out what he knows, and he's done so far.'

Raj Dhirwan, the uniformed inspector, had been the first senior officer on the scene. He would have spoken to the first attending officers, established the cordons, and taken all the other steps necessary to set a major investigation in motion. Now it was up to Kendrick as Senior Investigating Officer, and Catherine and the rest of the team, to find out what had happened.

'We need to move quickly.' Kendrick said. 'We've already got reinforcements from Lincoln cluttering the place up. If we hang around, we'll have EMSOU treading on our toes as well.' He raised his eyebrows at Catherine. 'Can't have that, can we?'

Catherine blushed. The East Midlands Special Operations Unit worked across Nottinghamshire, Derbyshire, Leicestershire, Northamptonshire and Lincolnshire, providing support and expertise to the five police forces. A few months before, Catherine had been drafted in to work undercover, helping the EMSOU Major Crimes unit with a case in the city of Lincoln. One of the officers she had worked with, Detective Sergeant Isla Rafferty, had been prickly and difficult, at least at first. Then, Catherine had realised the reason for Isla's unfriendliness, and their relationship transformed. That relationship, still so new, felt precious and fragile, as though it could be shattered at any moment. She would do anything to prevent that happening, especially now Isla had seen her at her lowest and hadn't walked away.

Isla turning up with her team to work in Northolme now wouldn't be ideal. She wasn't surprised Kendrick knew about her and Isla. She knew her boss had been concerned about her over the past six months. He would have been keeping his ears and eyes open. Theirs was a close-knit team.

'Isla's not the only officer EMSOU have,' she told Kendrick.

He smirked.

'No. But I want us to solve this ourselves.' Striding away, he called over his shoulder. 'Go and talk to the neighbours. I'll give Jonathan a call. God knows where he is.'

Catherine turned away, heading for the top of the road. The crowd was still there, and there looked to be even more people hanging around than when Catherine and Kendrick arrived. She saw one of their team, DC Chris Rogers, wearing casual clothes and standing towards the back of the group. She didn't acknowledge him, knowing what he was doing. There was a chance the murderer was still in the area, hanging around to see the effects of his or her handiwork. Another possibility was that they were horrified, terrified, and were watching to see what the police were doing before planning their own actions accordingly. Either way, they could still be in the vicinity. It was much more likely the perpetrator had fled the scene, but it was always possible they hadn't, and Chris would be watching. Catherine sent Anna a text, asking her to wait at the outer cordon.

As she ducked back under the blue and white tape, cameras flashed, and she blinked, dazzled for a second. Then a digital voice recorder was shoved into her face.

'DS Bishop. It's been a while,' said a voice Catherine recognised. 'What can you tell me? Is it true there are two bodies?'

Catherine lifted her chin, staring the woman in the eye. Helen Bridges was a journalist, one she had clashed with in the past.

'I can't tell you anything,' she said.

Bridges snorted. 'Can't, or won't?'

Catherine tried to walk away, but the journalist blocked her path.

'Just a quick quote. I won't name you. Trust me.'

'Trust you? You're joking. Why should I?'

Bridges tipped her head to the side with a smile. 'We both know the answer to that. I haven't forgotten.'

'Forgotten what?'

Catherine's hands went to her hips. If Bridges thought she was going to be bullied into making a statement, she was wrong. She took a few paces away, looking for Anna, but Bridges followed.

'I'm surprised you don't remember. Your fling with a woman who turned out to be a murderer.'

'You think it would still be front page news?' Catherine curled her lip. 'It was months ago, Helen.' Thinking about Claire still hurt, but she wasn't going to allow Bridges to see that.

The journalist's eyes gleamed. 'And now there's another suspicious death on our patch.'

'No comment,' Catherine said.

'Either way, the relationship one of the investigating officers had with a woman who killed two men and attempted to murder a third would give an interesting slant to the story, wouldn't you say?'

Catherine straightened her shoulders, determined to give Bridges nothing.

'You reckon?' she said. 'I don't see how. There's no link whatsoever.'

Mocking laughter. 'You're the link. I'm sure I could pull something together.'

Telling herself to remain calm, Catherine leaned closer, speaking calmly.

'Whatever you think you know, forget it. You'll get an official statement when we're ready to make one. Until then, stay away from me.'

She turned, wanting to put as much distance between herself and Bridges as possible. Anna was hurrying towards her, concern clear on her face.

'Sarge? What's wrong?'

Catherine took a breath. 'It's okay. Just our friendly local journalist making her presence felt. Let's go.'

–

Anna knocked, her identification ready. Catherine stood back, seeing movement behind the glass, hearing the rattle of a key in the lock. The woman who opened the door leaned out, peering over their heads towards the house next door. She wore a fleece jacket in a violent shade of pink, grey jogging bottoms and slippers on her feet.

She nodded at Anna and Catherine, hands on hips. 'I knew we'd have the police knocking one day, asking about that pair next door. The day they moved in I knew they'd be trouble. I said as much to my husband, and I was right.'

I'm sure you usually are, Catherine thought, flashing the woman a smile.

'Mrs Irene Spence?'

Her suspicious expression didn't change. 'That's me. You are from the police?'

'Yes, ma'am, DC—'

Irene Spence ignored Anna and kept talking. 'You may as well come in. When they said some detectives would be coming to see us, I didn't expect two young girls.'

Catherine raised an eyebrow at Anna as the woman stepped back.

As they reached the hallway, the stairs directly in front of them, Catherine realised the layout of the house was the mirror image of the one she had just left next door.

'Shoes off, please.' Mrs Spence stood with her arms folded across her chest. 'I hoovered earlier.'

Knowing better than to argue, Catherine stepped out of her boots, bending to place them neatly on the doormat. Anna did the same, and Mrs Spence nodded, satisfied.

'That's better.' She opened the door Catherine knew would lead into the living room. 'Des, the police are here.'

The room was crammed with furniture. A dark wood sideboard took up most of one wall, with a sofa and two armchairs arranged around the fireplace. Family pictures covered most of the rest of the available wall space – two boys and a girl as babies, toddlers, children and adults. Then more babies. The gas fire was on, the room stifling hot.

In the armchair closest to the fire, a man struggled to sit up, having seemingly just woken. His face was gaunt, his hands trembling as he took a pair of glasses from the chair arm and put them on. He used a walking stick to heave himself to his feet, his navy jumper hanging loose, his trousers folded at the front where he'd had to pull them in tight with his belt. He had obviously lost a considerable amount of weight quickly, and Catherine realised he was seriously ill. Mrs Spence watched him shake their hands.

'We'd usually have been in bed hours by now,' she said. 'Tea?'

When Catherine and Anna accepted, she bustled off, leaving the doors open. Catherine realised she'd done it deliberately, so she could listen to what was said. She smiled at Mr Spence, introducing herself and Anna.

'You can sit down,' he said. 'I don't bite.' He chuckled, then lapsed into a long and painful-sounding fit of coughing. He pulled out a handful of tissues, pressing them to his mouth. 'Sorry about that. Come on, have a seat.' Catherine sat on the sofa, close to Mr Spence's chair, and Anna perched at the other end. 'What's gone on then?' he asked.

'We're hoping you can help us begin to make sense of it,' Catherine told him.

'You'll have to speak up; he's deaf as a post,' called Mrs Spence from the kitchen. They heard the tap running, the clattering of cups being removed from a cupboard. Desmond Spence rolled his eyes.

'I'm not; I just ignore her most of the time. She's trying to earwig, the nosy old bat.' He winked to show them he was joking. 'What do you want to know?'

Catherine smiled. 'Firstly, if you've heard anything unusual today. I think you've been informed about an incident next door?'

He pressed his lips together. 'Depends what you call unusual. We're used to hearing them argue, if that's what you mean. Shouting, swearing. The kids making a racket. I mean, you expect a certain amount of noise in houses like this, but earlier... The baby was screaming for hours.'

'And you decided to call us?' Catherine wanted to ask why they had waited, but she knew there was no point in sounding as though she disapproved this early in the conversation. Spence might clam up if he thought his and his wife's actions were being criticised.

'Well, Irene said we should ring. I wanted to go around there to speak to them, but...' He shook his head. 'I'd tried before and got a mouthful of abuse. I'm not feeling my best and I... Well, we thought it would stop eventually. It usually does.'

'You heard the baby crying a lot?'

'Not really. More than you might expect, but not enough to make us worry, if you know what I mean. It's not like they were hurting it.'

You can see through walls, can you? Catherine wanted to say. She watched Anna make a note.

'Have you ever been inside the house?' she asked. Des Spence looked surprised.

'No, never had the pleasure. I've spoken to the bloke on the doorstep a couple of times when I went to ask them to keep the noise down, but never set foot inside.'

Catherine nodded. 'What time did you first hear the crying tonight?'

He looked at the carpet.

'I'd have to check with Irene. Maybe eight thirty?'

'And you called us at...' Catherine looked at Anna though she already knew.

'Just after midnight,' Anna confirmed.

There was a silence, Catherine allowing it to stretch.

'I know it looks bad.' He seemed almost tearful. 'But you have to understand, it's happened so often that we've learned to just turn up the TV and ignore it. No way was I going around there to complain again.'

Mrs Spence came in with a tray of mugs and handed them out.

'Des is right,' she said as she made herself comfortable in the remaining armchair. 'They go on until all hours, bellowing at each other, the kids shouting and screaming.'

'Isn't one of the children less than six months old?' Catherine couldn't help pointing out.

Mrs Spence sipped her tea.

'They can still make a racket at that age. When we had our three, we made sure they didn't disturb anyone, but these days…'

'What about the parents? Did you heard them arguing today?' Catherine remembered it was after midnight and that really she was talking about the previous day, but none of them had been to bed and to ask about 'yesterday' might confuse matters.

Mrs Spence nodded.

'This morning, yes. Before we went to our Matthew's, wasn't it, Des? About ten?'

Catherine looked at Anna. This could help pinpoint Hollie Morton's time of death, if Mr and Mrs Spence's account was reliable.

'Is Matthew your son?' Catherine asked.

Irene Spence nodded. 'Our eldest. He's off work, just had his appendix out.'

'Can I just make sure I'm understanding you correctly, Mrs Spence – you heard your neighbours arguing together at around ten o'clock this morning?'

The woman stared at Catherine. 'Yes, like I said.'

'You definitely heard each of their voices? You heard both Andy Nugent and Hollie Morton?'

'Yes, love,' Mr Spence put in. 'The two of them yelling at each other, as clear as day.'

'You're certain it was them? It couldn't have been one of them arguing with someone else – a visitor, a relative?'

Mrs Spence was emphatic. 'It was them. We've heard them often enough to know what their voices sound like.'

'All right, thank you. Could you make out what they were saying?'

Mr Spence was shaking his head. 'No, like I said, we put the radio on, or turn up the telly. We're not nosy.'

Catherine held up her hands. 'I'm not implying you are. But sometimes you can't help overhearing.'

'Has he killed her then then?' Mrs Spence sat forward, her tea forgotten. 'Can't say I'm surprised. I told you he was knocking her around, Des, but you didn't believe me.'

Her husband flushed. 'You can't make accusations like that without proof.'

'Yes, well, looks like they've got it if he's killed her.' Mrs Spence pursed her lips with a self-satisfied nod.

'What about later today?' asked Catherine. 'What time did you arrive back from your son's house?'

'Well, we stayed for dinner. About two o'clock?' Irene Spence looked at her husband, and he nodded.

'I reckon so, love,' he said.

'Was there any sound from next door then?' Catherine asked. Both shook their heads.

'Nothing. Didn't hear a peep until later on,' Mrs Spence said.

Again, Catherine shared a glance with Anna. 'What did you hear later?'

'He had some of his mates round. Playing their computer games or whatever you want to call it.'

Catherine frowned. 'You're saying there were visitors next door tonight? What time was that?'

Mrs Spence looked at her husband. 'About six? Two lads from the estate. Laughing and joking, making a row. We had to turn the news up.'

'They play some sort of shooting game. Bombs and guns going off at top volume. Disrespectful, I call it. Young lads playing war games when they've never done so much as National Service.' Mr Spence sipped his tea, his disapproval clear.

Catherine blinked a few times. 'You're saying Andy Nugent had friends round at six this evening? You're sure?'

She found it hard to believe he had invited mates into the house with his partner lying dead in the kitchen but anything was possible, as she knew only too well.

The couple stared at her.

'Yes, as we told you. We're not senile yet.' Mrs Spence fluffed her hair.

'Do you know how long they stayed?'

Catherine didn't look at Anna, but she knew she would be scribbling furiously.

'I think they left around eight p.m. – it all went quiet then, at any rate, until the baby started up.'

Catherine flashed her a smile. 'Thank you. Did you recognise them?'

Mrs Spence laughed. 'Of course I did, I've known them since they were at nursery. I used to be a dinner lady up at the local primary school. I know a lot of people around here, watched them grow up. They don't live on the estate any more, but I knew who they were.'

'Did they leave alone, or did Andy or Hollie show them out?'

The couple exchanged another glance.

36

'I'm not sure,' Mrs Spence said. 'I didn't hear any good-byes, but we didn't jump up to see if anyone was waving them off either.'

Catherine thought she probably had but wasn't going to say so. Not yet.

'Could you give us names?' she asked. 'Tell us where they live?'

Mrs Spence frowned, her expression apprehensive. 'They're not going to be in any trouble, are they? I mean, they made a bit of noise, but they're decent lads.'

'We'll need to speak to them.' Catherine wasn't going to promise anything.

—

Outside, the rain was heavier, the breeze whipping it into their faces. Back on the pavement, Catherine grimaced, pulling up the hood of her coat. They needed to update Kendrick. She squinted at the house, lights blazing, crime scene investigators visible through the living room window. Was he inside? She decided to try calling him. It would be quicker than searching for him and getting in the way. He answered immediately, and she told him what the Spences had said.

'You reckon Nugent killed Hollie then left the house?' Kendrick whistled.

'Or sat and panicked quietly, horrified at what he'd done. Jo said Hollie's body had been moved, didn't she? What if he killed her in the living room or somewhere, then dragged her body to the kitchen later?'

'If Andy Nugent killed his girlfriend then left her lying there for hours while he played video games with his mates… Well, he must have been a cold bastard, is all I'm going to say.'

'Especially with the kids upstairs,' Catherine reminded him. 'But if Andy did kill Hollie and then leave until later in the day, you'd have expected the kids to have been screaming their heads off well before the Spences came home at two o'clock. Surely they'd have been crying all day? Mrs Spence just said they didn't hear the baby until eight thirty.'

'Maybe he took the kids out with him after he killed their mother,' Kendrick said. 'Sounds like father of the year. Social services have taken the children for now, but they could go to the grandparents eventually. They're going to send an officer trained in interviewing young children over from headquarters to speak to the boy in the morning. It's a long shot, given his age, but you never know.' Kendrick sniffed, and Catherine heard him coughing.

'Hollie's relatives do have a motive – Andy's violence. One of them could have discovered her body and then killed Andy Nugent in a revenge attack?'

'It's a possibility. Officers are with her parents now, so we'll see what they say. The different times of death bothers me. You don't think… No. Jo's never been wrong before.'

'It's not as though she said they died at similar times, where there might be some confusion. She was talking about hours between the two deaths,' Catherine said.

'I know. We'll have to wait until she's done the post-mortems. Jonathan's around, by the way.'

'Okay. What do you want us to do?'

'Your thoughts?'

Catherine turned so the rain was blowing against her back instead of her face. 'We need to speak to Nugent's friends. Either the Spences are right, and Hollie Morton was killed after ten o'clock, tying in with what Jo said, or she was killed earlier and her boyfriend was arguing with someone else this morning.'

'Or it wasn't Andy Nugent she was rowing with. It could have been Hollie and a different man altogether,' said Kendrick.

'The Spences didn't think so.'

She heard Kendrick sucking his teeth. 'I know, but it wouldn't be the first time a witness has been mistaken. I've no doubt they'll back each other up, swear on the Bible the voices they heard belonged to their neighbours, but we can't be certain. Let's keep an open mind.'

'These mates of Nugent's might be able to confirm it either way.'

'Or they might muddy the waters some more, especially if they killed him after he beat them on some video game.'

'But Jo said Nugent has only been dead for a few hours.' Catherine rubbed her forehead. This case was already proving to be confusing.

'I know,' Kendrick said. 'Nugent might even have left the house with his mates and returned later.'

'Maybe he disturbed someone who came to the house hoping to see Hollie?'

'Who found her dead, then murdered him realising he'd killed her? Again, it's possible, but we don't know, and we need to speak to these two friends of his. Go and see if they're awake. I know it's late, but they might be willing to talk. Call me when you've finished. They're setting up an incident room back at the station and I want to get over there. So much for that Lemsip.' He rang off.

As Catherine pushed the phone into her pocket, she saw Detective Inspector Jonathan Knight walking towards her, his head down, his hair already soaked. As he reached Catherine and Anna, Knight looked up and smiled.

'Lovely evening.'

'Have you been inside the house?' Catherine asked him. He nodded.

'Tricky one,' he said. 'You've spoken to the neighbours?'

They filled him in. Knight ran a hand across his face, trying to wipe the rain away.

'Jo says she'll start the first post-mortem at seven tomorrow at morning. That's in about' – he checked his watch – 'five hours.' He smiled. 'She should get some rest.'

Catherine knew there was little chance of any of them getting much sleep.

'Could you find out whether either of the two blokes we're going to drag out of bed has a record please, Anna?'

She nodded and hurried off.

Catherine turned back to Jonathan Knight. 'They're not going to be impressed. I think we should leave talking to them until the morning.'

'Keith's got a bee in his bonnet. Thinks the case will be taken from us if we don't crack on.'

Catherine snorted. 'I know. He's already given me an earful about EMSOU stealing it.'

Knight smiled, understanding immediately. 'How's Isla?'

'She's fine, not that I've seen much of her. Living in different towns and both being police officers isn't helping.'

'Understood.' Knight's phone was ringing. He wrestled it from his pocket, hunching his shoulders against the rain. Catherine watched as his expression changed.

'What?' she mouthed at him. He held up a hand. She knew from his face that the news wasn't good. Knight began to walk, beckoning to Catherine, still listening to whoever was on the other end. She followed him, not knowing what else to do. Knight headed up the road, towards the outer cordon. The rain had driven most of the crowd indoors now. Catherine glimpsed Helen Bridges sheltering under a huge black umbrella, her phone to her ear, and avoided eye contact. She was surprised the journalist had the time to hang around since the local newspaper she had previously worked for had folded, and Bridges was apparently having to make her living as a freelance.

Knight stopped at his car, opened the door.

'Come on. That was Keith,' he said.

'The DCI? But I've just spoken to him.'

'He didn't know then,' Knight said. 'We need to go.'

'What about Anna? I need to tell her—'

'Keith's going to talk to Anna. There's not much more we can do here until the morning anyway.'

She jogged around to the passenger side. As she fastened her seatbelt, Knight reversed, turned the car around.

'What's going on?'

'Another fire,' he said.

'The arsonist?'

She knew it was a stupid question. Why else would they be speeding away from the scene of what could be a double murder?

'So much for our surveillance,' Knight said.

5

They could see the orange glow against the night sky as they hurtled down the hill towards the town centre.

'It's another business premises,' Knight said. 'The used car dealership by the bridge.'

Catherine knew the one he meant. 'They must have thirty or forty vehicles parked up there.'

'Several are already burning, as well as the office building.'

'There's a petrol station across the road as well,' Catherine said, picturing the scene.

'I know. Let's hope the fire brigade manage to contain it. The houses nearby have been evacuated as a precaution. A local church has opened its doors to them and volunteers are already serving hot drinks and bacon butties.'

'Lots of people having their night disrupted then, as well as another business going up in flames. Our arsonist will be delighted.'

'No doubt. And it's not one of the sites we had officers watching, so we're none the wiser about who's doing this.'

Knight braked as the traffic lights in front of them changed. A man wandered across the road, his slack expression and unsteady gait giving them clues about how he had spent his evening. He waved in acknowledgement as he lurched past them. Catherine raised her hand.

'Someone's going to have a headache in the morning.'

Knight pursed his lips in response.

'He won't be the only one,' he noted. 'Detective Superintendent Stringer called Keith to tell him about the fire herself. She'd asked Control to inform her if they got a call about another blaze. You can imagine how impressed she was when he told her we were watching half a dozen other properties but not the one that's actually alight.'

Catherine clicked her tongue.

'If the Super's got a crystal ball, I wish she'd share it around. How are we supposed to know what he's going to fancy torching next? Even in a town this size, there are loads of potential targets.'

Knight guided the car across a roundabout, the smell of burning already beginning to seep into the car.

'She's threatening to come over and take charge herself.'

'The Super is?' Catherine tried to imagine Jane Stringer sitting in a car for hours on end to keep an eye on a load of dustbin lorries, but failed. 'I thought she never left Headquarters these days.'

They were close to the scene of the fire now. The road ahead of them was closed, a couple of marked cars parked across it and plenty of signage.

'Looks like we're walking from here.' Knight pulled in at the side of the road and they got out.

As they turned onto the next street, the air seemed thicker. The smell of burning rubber clung to them, acrid smoke making their eyes sting. There were three fire engines, firefighters scurrying around, and several of their own uniformed colleagues keeping an eye on things. There was a small crowd of onlookers: an elderly woman leaning on a walking stick, seven or eight men with cans of beer in their hands, a kid in a hoody leaning on a bike. A

43

constable approached them, no doubt to take down their details. Catherine saw PC Natalie Roberts standing by one of the POLICE ROAD CLOSED signs and lifted a hand to her. Roberts nodded, her expression serious for a change. Catherine and Knight headed over to her.

'How long have you been here, Nat? What can you tell us?' Catherine asked.

'About ten minutes. Seemed daft to leave me sitting on the industrial estate when the action's down here, I suppose. As you'll see, they've managed to put out the burning vehicles, but the building's still on fire.' Nat nodded at one of the firefighters, who was gulping water from a metal bottle, his face covered with a sheen of sweat. 'The bloke I told you about, Jimmy, the one whose phone number I got? That's him. He reckons it's definitely arson, though no one's said so officially yet.'

'No surprise there. At least no one's been hurt,' said Catherine. As she spoke, a shout went up. Jimmy, the firefighter Nat had pointed out, dropped his bottle and ran. Knight and Catherine looked at each other.

'Let's find out what's happening,' Knight said.

He was already on the move. Catherine followed, though she had no desire to get any closer to the flames. Fires were frightening, unpredictable. She knew her firefighter colleagues were perfectly capable of controlling the blaze and keeping them all safe, but even so, the heat surging from the burning building, the eerie glow and the strange popping and cracking sounds all set her on edge.

As they rounded one of the response vehicles, a firefighter saw them and shouted to them.

'Stay where you are.'

'Police,' Knight called back. 'What's going on?'

The firefighter's face was grim.

'There could be someone inside,' he told them. 'One of our guys thinks he saw a figure in there.'

Catherine's stomach lurched as she stared at the flames engulfing the small office building.

'Can you get in?'

She didn't see how. Didn't know how anyone could even attempt it.

He pulled a face as he turned away. 'We're working on it.'

Knight took a step back, then stopped. 'Why would someone be in there at this time of night?'

'No idea. Let's hope it's a mistake, and the place is empty,' Catherine said.

They watched the firefighters near the building.

'Imagine going in there.' Knight shuddered. 'I know we have to deal with some crap, but this...'

'They'll rescue whoever's in there, won't they?'

The alternative was unthinkable. Catherine imagined cowering in a corner, lungs choked, mind spinning, wondering if the flames would kill you and hoping the smoke would claim your life first. All they could do was wait and hope their arsonist wouldn't be responsible for the loss of a life as well as for thousands more pounds' worth of property damage. The person or people responsible might never have meant to hurt anyone, much less be expecting to be facing a manslaughter or murder charge, but setting these fires was putting people at risk, whether it was those living nearby or those whose responsibility it was to douse the flames.

Knight was staring at the blazing building as though mesmerised. Gently, Catherine took his arm.

'Come on, let's move away. We're not helping by standing here.'

They headed back to where Nat Roberts stood rubbing her hands together and stamping her feet.

'I'm freezing, which is ridiculous when I'm this close to such an inferno.' She pulled a face, clearly trying to lighten the mood, but when she saw their expressions her manner changed again. 'What? What's going on?'

They told her there was a chance someone was inside. Nat stared at the ground, chewing her bottom lip. Catherine touched her arm, and Nat managed a weak smile.

'It's probably a mistake, don't you think, Sarge?' she said. 'Why would anyone be in there at this time of night? It's not as though it's a house.'

Knight was checking his phone.

'The owner of the business is called Scott Greaves. Officers are at his house now. Hopefully they'll find him tucked up in bed.' He glanced at Catherine. 'The DCI's gone back to the station. Scene of Crimes are still at the house, uniforms taking statements, but he's sent Anna, Dave and Chris home. He's going to do the morning briefing alone tomorrow, because he wants us both at the hospital first thing.'

Catherine knew what he meant. Attending post-mortems was part of the job, but not one any officer she had ever met looked forward to.

'Okay. What about tonight?'

Knight sighed. 'We've also been told to go home and get some sleep, but I can't imagine you're going to leave, are you?'

'Without knowing if someone lost their life here tonight or not? No. Are you?' Catherine already knew the answer.

His face was grim. 'No chance.'

Nat shivered.

'Looks like we're all here for the night then,' she said. 'Don't suppose you fancy doing another coffee run, Sarge?'

–

Catherine's eyes were scratchy, her head aching. She and Knight had taken refuge in one of the squad cars to try and grab some sleep. It hadn't happened. She had curled up in the back while Knight slumped in the passenger seat. She caught up on a few emails, sent Isla a couple of texts, but she didn't think she'd actually nodded off. She checked the time. Three hours had passed. She sat up and looked around. Two of the fire engines had gone and the area where the building had stood was little more than a soggy, smouldering mess. Catherine leaned forward and nudged Knight's shoulder. 'Jonathan, what's going on?'

He started. 'What? I don't know.'

They both almost leapt through the roof as knuckles hammered on the window, and the scowling face of DCI Keith Kendrick appeared. Catherine rubbed her eyes as she stumbled out of the car, almost colliding with Knight as he staggered towards the DCI. Kendrick was waiting, hands on hips, as she and Knight blinked at him.

'What the hell are you two playing at? I told you both to go home.' He sniffed, fumbled for a tissue. 'We've got three deaths to investigate and two of my officers are having a sleepover.'

Catherine swallowed. 'Three deaths?'

Kendrick blew his nose, then pointed over his shoulder with a thumb towards the office building.

'The poor sod whose body they found over there. Scott Greaves.'

47

Catherine's head dropped. She must have fallen asleep after all.

'You didn't know?' Kendrick shook his head as he pushed the tissue back into his pocket. 'Well worth the pair of you camping out here then. Nothing official yet, but it's a pretty safe bet it's him. He and his wife separated a fortnight ago. Since then, Mr Greaves has been sleeping here.'

'Oh shit.' Catherine ran a hand over her mouth.

Kendrick stared at her. 'Eloquently put, Sergeant. As you can imagine, Mrs Greaves is feeling extremely guilty. She's in no state to be questioned further at the moment.' Kendrick paused. 'She also has to explain to her three-year-old twins why they won't be seeing their daddy again. All in all, our arsonist has a lot to answer for. We need to find him.'

6

Entering the mortuary always provoked the same feelings in Catherine. She was going to witness the dismantling of a human being, and that was never easy to accept. However respectful Jo Webber and her team were, and Catherine knew they treated each body they received with care and compassion, the procedures they had to perform were intrusive and clinical. If the person had died as a victim of violent crime, the post-mortem was yet another assault on them. But then, how else could vital information about the cause of death be confirmed? How could trace evidence be discovered and captured? Hopefully, the samples Jo would take and the conclusions she would draw would provide some answers.

Hollie Morton lay on a nearby table. Catherine told herself it was time to detach. She had to temporarily think of Hollie as 'the body', not as a person. It was the only way she could get through what was to come. She wondered if Knight and Mick Caffery, who was also present, did the same. It was impossible to be unaffected by the sights, sounds and smells you experienced during the procedures, but it was essential to try to protect yourself as much as possible. It was just as important as the gown, mask, gloves and shoe coverings they had to wear whilst in the mortuary. Maybe she should talk to Isla about it, see if she handled attending post-mortems any differently.

Catherine knew Knight and Kendrick were keeping an eye on her. She was taking her medication and seeing her GP regularly, but she knew their concern was justified. She was feeling better, but the shadows remained.

Jo Webber entered the room and moved to stand by the body.

'Are we ready to begin?' She spoke quietly, and Catherine had the impression she was asking Hollie herself for permission. She felt Jonathan Knight shift beside her. He and Jo Webber had been together for a while now, and Catherine wondered how it felt to watch your partner performing these procedures. Unsettling, at best, she imagined. You would definitely need to leave your job at the door when you came home.

Once the various samples required had been taken, including scrapings from beneath Hollie's nails and her fingerprints, the body was photographed, washed and photographed again. X-rays were taken, and then Jo began to examine Hollie's body closely, working from head to toe. She noted the Caesarean scar on Hollie's abdomen and for Catherine it was a reminder of the two orphaned children who would one day want to know how their parents had died. The answers might be difficult to hear but she imagined they would need to know the truth.

Now, Jo focused on Hollie's throat.

'There's definite bruising, as I mentioned at the scene.' Jo spoke without emotion, but Catherine was sure she would be feeling it. 'As you saw, I managed to collect samples from her fingernails. Hopefully she'll have been clawing at the hands of her attacker, and we'll find enough to pin down who killed her.'

'I didn't see any scratches on her partner's hands,' said Knight. Jo looked at him.

'Let's wait and see.' Jo spoke in the same calm tone. She was far too professional to allow personal relationships anywhere near her mortuary. Knight seemed to realise he had strayed too close to the line and Catherine imagined he was blushing beneath his face mask. Jo had already turned back to the body.

The rest of the post-mortem was fairly routine, if the procedure could ever be described like that. Hollie Morton had been in good health, as could be expected for a woman of her age. Jo found bruising around her upper arms, a few days old, consistent with being grabbed and held. Inside her cheek there was a cut, which Jo said could have been caused by her teeth as a result of a blow to her face. Both of these points added weight to the deduction Catherine had made when speaking to Mr and Mrs Spence – that the arguments between Hollie and Andy Nugent had, on some occasions at least, turned physical.

When Jo had completed the post-mortem, she went to clean up, and Catherine and Knight went to her office to wait to hear her conclusions. She hadn't elaborated on the observations she had made, and Catherine wanted to hear her thoughts on the time of death in particular. She wasn't expecting it to differ much from what Jo had already said, but there was always the chance.

As they reached Jo's office, her secretary waved them inside and asked if they wanted tea or coffee. Catherine smiled at her.

'It's okay, thank you. I'll go, I know where the kitchen is.' She looked at Knight. 'Do you think Jo will want tea, Jonathan?'

Knight nodded, started to speak, but Catherine hurried down the corridor before he could offer to help her.

The kitchen was as dingy as she remembered, the walls painted green, the floor covered with scruffy carpet tiles. The tap dripped, and the cups had all seen better days. As she filled the kettle, Catherine took out her phone. Isla answered on the second ring, and, surprised, Catherine couldn't help smiling as she spoke.

'I wasn't sure if you'd be able to talk,' she said.

'You've called at the right time. I've got a few minutes.'

Catherine could tell Isla was smiling too.

'What are you up to?' she asked.

'Going to talk to a witness. Adil's driving.'

Catherine pictured Isla's colleague, DC Adil Zaman. 'How's his daughter?'

'Malia? She's doing well. It's her birthday next week.'

'Hope you've got her a present.'

Isla laughed. 'Of course.'

Catherine removed four mugs from a cupboard. She would be willing to bet six months ago Isla wouldn't have had a clue what Adil's daughter's name was, much less known the date of her birthday. When Catherine first met her, Isla had been guarded at work, so reserved she had sometimes appeared rude. Now at peace with herself, Isla had allowed her colleagues to see the person she really was, and Catherine was delighted.

'What are you up to?' Isla wanted to know. Catherine pulled a face as she picked up a spoon and scooped the tea bags from the cups.

'I'm at the hospital.'

Isla groaned. 'The post-mortems. Sorry, you did tell me.' Catherine had texted the bare details of the double murder and the latest arson attack to Isla sometime in the middle of the night while she waited in the car for news.

'It's okay.' Catherine found a bottle of milk languishing on the bottom shelf of the fridge. She peered at it suspiciously then splashed some into the cups, relieved there were no lumps. 'When will I see you?'

She didn't want to sound needy, and making plans was probably pointless since her team now had three deaths to investigate. She would be lucky to have a few hours to herself anytime soon, but after hearing Isla's voice, Catherine was desperate to see her.

'Soon,' Isla said softly. 'I'll text you. We're hoping to make an arrest today. Listen, I'm sorry, but we're almost at the address.'

'Okay. Speak soon. Say hi to Adil for me.' Catherine ended the call, disappointed. She knew Isla was busy, but she could hear in her voice she felt the same as Catherine did: they missed each other. They had known their relationship would have to come second to their careers, but Catherine hadn't realised how difficult it would be.

She picked up the mugs and headed back to Jo Webber's office. As always, work had to come first. For Catherine, it always had, but she had never before resented her job the way she found herself doing lately. What did that mean? She filed the thought away. Now was not the time.

Jo was coming down the corridor to meet her. She took two of the cups from Catherine's hands with a smile.

'You made tea. Perfect. Thank you.'

Caffery and Knight were chatting, but they fell silent as Jo pushed open her office door. Once the drinks had been handed out, the pathologist sat behind her desk.

'I wanted to discuss the first post-mortem before we move on to the second,' she said. 'There's not much to say at this stage. Hollie Morton was throttled – her death is due to asphyxia. Her hyoid bone was fractured, as was her larynx and cricoid cartilage. Whoever killed her... well, they used considerable force.'

'Can we assume whoever killed her is male?' Knight asked.

'It's probable, but not definite.' Jo paused for a moment. 'Apart from the strength needed to subdue Hollie and kill her, the body was moved – she didn't die in the kitchen where her body was found, so considerable strength would have been needed to lift her, even to drag her. Time of death – between ten a.m. and two p.m. I mentioned collecting scrapings from beneath her fingernails. Hollie's nails were fairly short, and she may not have been able to put up much of a fight considering the force her throat was grabbed with. What I'm trying to say is, she might not have left marks on her attacker even if she did try to defend herself.' She took a mouthful of tea, swallowed a couple of times. 'It would have taken at least two minutes for her to die.'

Catherine's mind filled with images of those final moments: Hollie gasping, choking, her assailant holding tight, possibly staring into her eyes as she lost consciousness. Catherine shivered. The fact that Hollie's murderer had used his bare hands to kill her somehow made her death all the more horrific. Using a weapon meant a degree of separation, but to use your own hands to kill, to have to be so close to your victim you were almost in their arms – it was unthinkable. And yet, this was the third time in Catherine's career she had heard a pathologist describe such a death. One of those deaths had occurred during an argument between two brothers, the other when a father had grabbed his young son by the throat.

Jonathan Knight said, 'Then we shouldn't expect to see scratches or bruising on the hands and wrists of the person who killed Hollie.'

Jo spread her hands. 'There might be there. There might not.'

Mick Caffery was fiddling with an iPad he had removed from the briefcase he had brought with him. He held it up. On the screen were photographs from the crime scene, showing the body of Andy Nugent. 'One of his hands is clearly visible here. I can't any abrasions, bruises or marks at all.'

Jo set her mug on her desk. 'Well, his post-mortem will be completed shortly. We don't need to speculate.'

Her tone was mild, but it felt like a reprimand. Catherine watched Mick shove the iPad back into the case as if annoyed. She could understand if Jo was irritated, because in a few hours she would be able to give them some of the answers they needed, but Mick had been trying to help. Jo was probably tired, but they all were. It was unlike her to be anything other than totally professional.

'Are you doing the PM on Scott Greaves too?' Knight asked.

Jo leaned back in her chair. 'Yes, as a priority. Detective Superintendent Stringer insists.'

'Straightforward smoke inhalation, isn't it?' Knight risked a smile, but Jo ignored it.

'You know I'm not going to comment yet, Jonathan.' Again, she spoke politely, but the bite was unmistakable.

Jo pushed back her chair, glancing at the clock on the wall. 'Let's go and see what Andy Nugent can tell us, shall we? You'll have my full report on Hollie later today.'

She strode out of the room, and they scrambled to follow her. As they went down the stairs, Catherine saw Knight lift his hand as if he was going to place it on Jo's back, then hesitate and change his mind. This was Jo's domain, and she was very much in charge here. Socially, Jo was warm, friendly. Here, she was clinical, almost cold. She had to be, of course, but even to Catherine, she didn't seem herself. Watching Knight hesitate to touch her, she wondered if the problem was personal.

–

Back in the mortuary, on another steel table, the naked body of Andy Nugent lay exposed. The preliminaries were over, and Jo was studying the back of Nugent's head. She was silent for what seemed like forever, but they all knew better than to interrupt her thoughts.

Eventually, she straightened, frowning, lips pursed.

'Interesting.'

'What?' Knight spoke at the same time as Catherine.

'As we thought, he wasn't strangled, regardless of the belt around his throat.' Jo leaned over the body again. 'I think the blow to the back of his head killed him. There's no bruising on his face, so I doubt he was punched there. Maybe someone pushed him in the chest or moved towards him quickly and he lost his balance and fell.' She and her assistants laid the body back down. Jo bent closer, studying Nugent's right arm. 'As you can see, we've removed the plaster and there's a cut, a recent one. At first glance it does look like a knife wound, but I'll have a closer look.'

Knight cleared his throat, and Catherine knew what he was going to say. 'Are there signs of scratches or abrasions on his hands? I can't see any from here.'

Jo picked up Nugent's right hand and studied it, turning it to look between his fingers and then at his palm. She laid it gently back down, walked around the table and examined the other. 'No, nothing. As I said, Hollie may not have had a chance to fight back.' She paused, blinking. No one spoke, the mortuary assistant watching Jo as though waiting for his cue.

It didn't come. Catherine heard herself cry out as, seemingly in slow motion, Doctor Jo Webber collapsed onto the floor of her mortuary.

7

The incident room in Northolme police station was packed. Uniformed officers, civilian staff and some of the CID team were busy sifting through statements, manning phones, and staying out of DCI Kendrick's way.

'He's not happy,' DC Chris Rogers told Catherine.

She leaned against the nearest desk. 'I don't suppose Jo planned to faint halfway through the post-mortem.'

'No, but it means a delay, doesn't it? We'll have to wait for one of the other pathologists to have time to it fit in, and you know how Kendrick is. He trusts Jo.'

'Come on, Chris. He can trust the others.'

'I know that; you know that… He's muttering about Knight too.'

'Because he's waiting with Jo while they check her out? What does he expect? If Kendrick's wife had collapsed, wouldn't he want to be with her?'

Rogers raised his hands. 'I'm not saying I agree with him, but we do have a double murder to investigate, plus the bloke who died in the fire.' He lowered his voice. 'And the Superintendent's been on his case.'

Catherine swore under her breath. 'Great. All we need. We're not going to have any reports from Forensics for a while, so let's concentrate on the house-to-house enquiries. We need to understand who's visited the house today, and who's left it. They're ongoing?'

'Yeah. Nothing useful has come to light so far.'

'What about the Scott Greaves enquiry?'

'Again, nothing useful. There were a few people hanging around the scene and we got most of their names and addresses, though there was a young kid who rode off on his bike before anyone could speak to him. They couldn't tell us anything, just out having a nosy. Some of the people who lived in the area had been asked to leave their houses, and spent the night in a local church hall. Again, nothing useful came from talking to them.'

'This kid – I saw him,' Catherine said. 'He was there when we arrived at the scene.'

Chris nodded. 'Dark clothes, bright green bike? Probably mid teens, going by his height and build?'

'That's him.'

'Can you add to the description?'

Catherine shook her head. 'He had his hood up. I didn't see his face.'

'Of course he did. Bloody hoodies should be banned.'

'We need to try to trace him though.'

Chris blew out his cheeks. 'We're trying, but no one's being much help. The older lady was focusing on the fire, and the group of blokes had been drinking and were struggling to focus on anything. We were lucky to get the few details we have. We were told a few people who were at the church slipped away before anyone could speak to them. Any of them could be the arsonist, but how we'll find them, I've no idea.'

'The usual – door knocking and CCTV if we have it.'

'And it all takes time.' Chris gave a tired smile. 'We need more bodies – and I don't mean dead ones. The arsons were bad enough; now this bloke's been killed as well.' He glanced at her. 'The DCI mentioned EMSOU.'

'He's worried they'll be brought in.' It wasn't a question. Catherine knew Kendrick's views on the subject.

'Wouldn't be the worst thing in the world though, would it? We're stretched here. Nice for you too.' He winked. Catherine ignored it.

'I'm going to speak to Hollie Morton's family again,' she said. 'We need to know more about her relationship with Nugent.'

She turned and walked away, irritated. Why was everyone so obsessed with her relationship with Isla? It wasn't as though she would allow their relationship to affect her work, even if Isla did end up working temporarily out of their station. As she scanned the room, looking for Dave Lancaster, she told herself to forget what Rogers had said. The only person dwelling on her past was Catherine herself.

Lancaster scrambled to his feet as she approached him. He smoothed his hair, grinning nervously at her.

'Did you want me?' he said.

'Hollie Morton's parents – you've already spoken to them?'

Lancaster's mouth turned down at the corners. 'I have.'

She looked at him, the memory of it clearly causing him distress. 'You all right?'

He swallowed, looked down at his shoes. 'Her dad could barely speak, and her mum…' He shook his head, met Catherine's eyes. 'She was pale; she looked ill. I thought she was going to collapse. They were destroyed, completely destroyed. I wanted to help, but I think I made it worse by simply being there.'

Catherine sympathised. As a police officer, you couldn't give everyone what they wanted, and it could be a hard lesson to learn. She and Lancaster had had conversations like this before; he was young, relatively inexperienced, eager to please. She saw his compassion as an asset for a detective, but she knew others would disagree, regarding it instead as weakness. 'Listen, Dave. When we arrive at a scene, whatever's happened is out of our control. All we can do is provide answers for the family, and justice for the victim. You know that.'

'I do, I understand, but...'

He looked wretched. This time, Catherine reached out, squeezed his shoulder. 'But it's hard to put on the mask. I know. Come on. Let's see what they can tell us.'

When Catherine knocked on the Mortons' front door, she expected the Family Liaison Officer to answer it. The house was in the middle of a terrace, on the other side of town from the Meadowflower Estate. She knew the officer assigned to the Mortons was female, but when the door opened, a man stood there, leaning against the door frame. His eyes looked sore, swollen. He held a mug of tea, which he cradled against his chest. Dave Lancaster stepped forward, his face grave.

'I'm sorry to have to disturb you again, sir,' he said.

Eric Morton glowered at him. 'Then don't.'

Catherine held up her ID and introduced herself. 'I'm so sorry for your loss, Mr Morton. We've some more questions for you and your wife. We won't inconvenience you for any longer than we have to.'

He sneered. 'Really. Then can't you just leave us in peace? We found out last night our daughter is dead. What more is there to say?'

'We wouldn't be here unless it was absolutely necessary. It shouldn't take long. We want to find the person who murdered your daughter, sir.' Catherine sympathised with Morton, but she wasn't going to let him intimidate her. Dave had already taken a step backwards.

'I'll tell you who did it, the bastard she lived with.' Morton spoke quietly, his fury unmistakable. 'We were always telling her to come home, but she wouldn't listen.'

'You were concerned about her relationship with Andy Nugent?' Catherine didn't want to have the conversation on the doorstep, but at least Eric Morton was talking, even if he'd made no move to let them in.

'Of course we were.' Morton glanced over his shoulder as they heard a door open. Behind him, a woman appeared, her blonde hair lank, her face pinched.

'What's going on?' She took a deep drag on her cigarette. 'The police again?'

'Yes, Mrs Morton,' Catherine said. 'We've a few more questions for you, I'm afraid.'

'Let them in, Eric. Let's get it over with.' Michelle Morton shuffled away, and her husband, obviously reluctant, opened the door fully.

'My wife's devastated,' he hissed as Catherine and Dave took off their shoes. 'I'd appreciate you remembering that.' Without waiting for a reply, he marched off and they followed him to the living room. The house was cold, and smelt of cigarettes and coffee. The Mortons sat side by side on a red sofa. There was a TV on the wall above the fireplace, turned on but muted, a cricket match being played somewhere warmer than Northolme.

In the doorway that Catherine assumed led to the kitchen, the FLO hovered. She raised her eyebrows and Catherine flashed a quick smile. It wasn't a job she envied.

'You might as well sit down.' Michelle Morton spoke in a monotone. Catherine nodded Lancaster into the armchair, preferring to remain on her feet. She paced over to the fireplace, noting the framed school photographs of Hollie, her brother, and her sister. There were also pictures of a baby and a toddler – Hollie's children, Catherine assumed. Eric Morton noticed her looking at them.

'How are the kids?' he asked. 'They could have brought them here, you know. We'll take them in; we've said that already.'

'They're fine, they're being well cared for.' Catherine turned to look at Hollie's parents as she spoke.

Michelle curled her lip. 'By foster carers? Why can't they come here, to their own family?'

'It's not my—'

'Department? Yeah, strange that. No one wants to take the responsibility. They should be here with us.' Michelle was scowling.

'It's not my decision.' Catherine made sure she sounded calm. The Mortons were shocked, grieving. Their world had been blown apart, and Catherine knew the animosity wasn't personal. 'I'm sorry to intrude, but we need to understand what happened yesterday.'

Michelle Morton's eyes filled with tears. 'Our daughter's boyfriend murdered her, that's what.'

'You're aware Andy Nugent was also killed yesterday?'

'We are.' Eric Morton stared at Catherine. 'I know you shouldn't speak ill of the dead, but I doubt there's many people mourning him.'

Catherine said nothing, holding Eric's gaze until he looked away. She hadn't needed to remind him that Andy Nugent's parents had lost a child too.

'Look, love, you can ask your questions, but if you're expecting us to go into mourning because Andy's gone,

I wouldn't hold your breath.' Michelle stubbed out her cigarette in an ashtray that was balanced on the arm of the sofa beside her. 'Ask what you need to, and then please, leave us alone.'

Lancaster sat forward in his chair. 'We need to establish the movements of everyone connected to Hollie and Andy. Can we start with you please, Mr Morton?'

Eric's head snapped up. 'What did you say?'

Catherine took a breath. Maybe Lancaster should have waited or worded the question differently – too late now. 'It's a question we'll be asking everyone who knew Hollie, Mr Morton,' she said. 'Where were you at eight yesterday evening, for example?'

'Where was I? Are you kidding? What, you think I killed Andy? Maybe I even murdered my own daughter?' He bared his teeth, then made a visible effort to calm himself. 'I was at work all day, which the rest of the team will confirm, and at home all night. Michelle will tell you the same, as will my son and daughter. We were all here together.'

Michelle was nodding. 'We had fish and chips with our son Ross – he picked them up on his way home from work. Chloe got home about half seven, I think. Then we all sat and watched TV together until bedtime, though the kids were looking at their phones half the time.'

Catherine pressed her lips together. This was how they were going to play it then. 'You're saying the two of you, as well as your son, Ross, and your daughter Chloe, spent the whole of yesterday evening together?'

Michelle lit another cigarette, blew smoke out of her nose. 'That's exactly what we're saying. And before you ask, I worked from nine until five, then I came home. Just a normal day, until we found out our daughter had been murdered.'

Eric made a sound of distress, and Michelle reached for his hand. 'Is this necessary?' she said, quietly. 'Please, we...' Her voice disappeared.

Catherine nodded. 'I'm sorry. I know this must be incredibly difficult. Just a few more questions, I promise.'

'Did you see Hollie yesterday?' Lancaster asked gently.

'No, but I spoke to her on the phone.' Michelle's mouth was working, her chin trembling. 'Just before nine in the morning, when I was driving to work. Hollie was worried about the baby, thought she might have a temperature.'

'And she wanted some advice from her mum?' Catherine risked a smile. It wasn't returned.

'She usually listened to me.' Michelle gave a tiny nod.

'But not about her boyfriend?'

A tearful snort. 'No. No, not about him. She wouldn't hear a word against that bastard.'

'Why were you worried about her relationship with Andy?' Lancaster asked.

Michelle glared at him.

'Because he knocked her around. Any idiot could see that, never mind people who've known Hollie all her life. We warned her, said he'd really hurt her one day.' Fumbling to set her cigarette in the ashtray, Michelle let her husband's hand go and covered her eyes. 'Seems we were right.'

Eric slid an arm around his wife, pulling her close. 'If you're asking if any of us murdered him, no, we didn't. We thought he was a waste of space, and he needed teaching a lesson. But it doesn't mean we'd have hurt him.'

'We'll need to speak to your son, Ross,' Catherine told them.

Michelle shook her head. 'It's nothing to do with him.'

'He's been arrested a couple of times over the years. For fighting, mainly.'

Eric was half out of his seat, snarling, jabbing his finger at Catherine. 'Don't you dare come in here and start blaming my son. Young lads, throwing a couple of punches after a few pints? Doesn't make them murderers, does it?'

'Listen, love.' Michelle was speaking to Catherine as she laid her hand on Eric's arm. Her voice shook, but she was back in control of herself. 'Our daughter's dead. We're the victims here. Do you get that? We didn't kill Andy Nugent, we don't know who did, and we don't much care.'

'I wasn't accusing your son of anything.' She wasn't going to apologise, not for doing her job, however much they were hurting. 'We have to keep all avenues of investigation open.'

'Christ,' Michelle spat. 'Spare us the jargon.'

'Can you tell us about Hollie's friends?' Dave asked.

'She didn't see anyone,' Michelle said. 'He saw to that. Banned her from speaking to her mates, tried to stop her having contact with us. Well, we weren't having that. We're her family. We were her family.' She blinked, her lips trembling. Catherine wondered if she was pushing too hard, but however much of a bastard Andy Nugent had been, someone had killed him, and his treatment of his girlfriend gave her relatives motives.

'Are your son and daughter here?' she asked.

'No. They're at work.' Michelle stared at Catherine, as if daring her to disapprove.

'Work?' Catherine tried not to sound surprised.

'You think they wanted to go?' Michelle shook her head. 'They had no choice. They're terrified of losing their jobs. Not easy to find employment around here, you know.'

Catherine did. 'Then could you give me the addresses of their workplaces please?'

Eric's face was red. 'You're not going to disturb them now?'

'I'm sorry, I have no choice, Mr Morton. I have a job to do, the same as them.'

Michelle sneered. 'Except my kids' work doesn't involve poking their noses into people's lives.'

'Hollie's dead, that's all we care about. We've told you who killed her, and as far as we're concerned, we can't help you any further.' Eric folded his arms. 'I realise you need to catch the person who killed Andy, but it wasn't any of us. You're wasting your time and ours if you think we did. I'll say it again – we can't help you.'

Can't, or won't? Catherine stared at him. 'Don't you want us to find the person who killed your daughter's partner? Your grandchildren's father?'

Eric and Michelle exchanged a glance. Catherine wondered what it meant. 'Not particularly,' Eric said eventually. 'Though if you do, I'd like to shake his hand.'

–

Chloe Morton worked in one of the chain pubs in the town centre. It was busier than Catherine had expected to find it on a weekday. Lancaster watched a waiter place two plates of sausage, fried eggs and chips down in front of an elderly couple, who tucked in with relish.

'Have we time for…?' He looked at Catherine hopefully, like a child in a sweetshop.

'Afterwards, but we'll go somewhere else,' she said. They had to eat, but doing so in a place where their victim's sister was working would be completely wrong. Catherine couldn't have done it, and Lancaster nodded his understanding.

'Sorry,' he said, reddening.

Catherine went to the bar, asked the nearest member of staff for Chloe Morton. A man in a shirt and tie overheard and hurried towards her. He had gingery hair and a goatee beard. Catherine watched him look her up and down, his eyes appraising. He smirked at her.

'Chloe's working, she can't speak to you. I'm her manager, and I don't appreciate people distracting my staff when they're on shift.'

Catherine lifted her chin, held out her warrant card. 'It's not a social call. Could you find her for me please?'

He stared at her. 'Police? Why? What's Chloe done?'

Catherine stared back, blank faced. She wasn't going to tell him anything. If he didn't know Chloe's sister was dead, hadn't recognised the distress she must be in, he wasn't much of a manager, even less of a person.

'If I find out she's been stealing—'

'She hasn't. Please, sir, could you tell her I need to speak to her?'

'It's not on, not in work time…' He marched off.

One of the young women behind the bar moved closer to Catherine and spoke quietly.

'Chloe's not in trouble, is she?' she said. 'He'd use any excuse to sack her.'

'Sack her? Why?'

68

'Because she stands up to him, sticks up for other people, and he doesn't like it. He's a slimeball, always trying to chat us up, standing too close, making excuses to touch us. You know how it is.'

Catherine filed the information away. 'What's his name?'

'Bryce Turnbull.'

'And he's the manager?'

A nod. 'In theory. Though he never does any work.'

'Don't worry about Chloe. And make a complaint to head office about your boss.'

She snorted. 'They wouldn't listen, and I need this job.' She looked around. 'Wouldn't be here today otherwise.'

'Try them. Speak to the others, do it together.' Catherine saw Turnbull reappear through the crowd around the bar, his hand on the shoulder of a young woman. She walked in front of him, her expression showing her discomfort as he guided her as though she was a pet. Catherine felt her hackles rise further. Turnbull stopped in front of her with a sickly smile.

'Here she is. Hope she hasn't been a naughty girl.'

Catherine shrugged. 'She punched a bloke who tried to grope her in a bar. We're here to take a statement because we're going to pursue a conviction. His, not hers.' Catherine smiled at him. 'Teach him he can't go around touching people whenever he feels like it. When he's out of hospital, anyway. Hard to answer questions when your jaw's wired together.'

Turnbull reeled, taking a backwards step. Biting her lip, Chloe looked away, the woman behind the bar turning a laugh into a cough.

'Well, I'll leave you to it,' Turnbull managed to say.

'Why did you tell him that?' Chloe asked once he'd scurried away.

Catherine smiled. 'I've heard he's the type. Was I wrong?'

Chloe shook her head. 'No, I've wanted to punch him a few times.'

Catherine looked at her properly, seeing the resemblance with her sister. Her face showed signs of strain, of grief. Shadows beneath red eyes, pale cheeks. Her fingers twisted the hem of her black shirt. 'Is this about Hollie?' She struggled to say her sister's name. Catherine saw Turnbull watching from across the room and glared at him.

'Let's get you out of here,' she said.

'But I'm working.'

'No, you're taking your break.'

'Bryce won't be happy about this,' Chloe said as they left the pub.

'His choice,' Catherine told her. 'Tell him to give my boss a call if he wants to complain.'

She glanced around, saw a café across the street. She wanted Chloe to relax – at least as much as was possible – and to talk to them.

'Fancy a coffee?'

Chloe gave a faint smile. 'I'd love one.'

At the counter, Catherine bought the drinks and led Chloe to an empty table, watching the younger woman's hands tremble as she picked up her cup. Lancaster sat down beside Chloe with a clatter. He picked up his coffee, nodding his thanks to Catherine.

'You're probably wondering how I can come to work,' Chloe said. She sipped her drink. 'I just… I didn't want to be in the house.'

'Why not?' But Catherine could guess.

'Because of Mum and Dad.' Chloe sniffed, swallowed. 'I get they're devastated. We all are. But they're so angry too. All they can say is, they warned Hollie about Andy. On and on, like it's Hollie's own fault she's dead.' She set down the cup, scrubbed at her eyes. 'Why do you want to speak to me? It's obvious who killed her, isn't it?'

'Is it?'

'Andy did.' Catherine didn't speak, and Chloe stared at her. 'Didn't he? You can do tests, can't you? Forensics? I've seen it on TV.'

Catherine was vague, not wanting to give too much away. 'We can, but it all takes time. We need to speak to everyone who knew your sister and her boyfriend.'

Folding her arms, Chloe hunched her shoulders. 'It was him, I know it. He kept hurting her.'

'What did you think of Andy?'

Chloe took her time, seeming to think about it. 'He was nice enough at first. Bought Hollie things – he got her a new phone the first month they met.' She managed a smile. 'Turns out it was so he could keep an eye on her. He had some tracking app on it. I don't understand how it worked, but it doesn't matter. He controlled every-thing, from the clothes Hollie wore to the money she was allowed to spend.'

'What about when the children were born?'

'Oh, he loved the kids. Never laid a finger on them, Hollie told me. Even though...' Chloe paused, chewing her lip.

'Even though?' Catherine prompted.

'Well, people started saying May wasn't Andy's.' Chloe's gaze was fixed on the table.

Catherine said nothing for a few seconds. This could be important, but she knew she had to tread carefully.

'May's the baby?' She already knew the answer, but she wanted Chloe to keep talking.

'Yeah. When she was born, maybe even before, the rumours started.'

Catherine nodded. 'What did Hollie say?'

Finally, Chloe looked up. 'She denied it, of course. When was she supposed to have cheated on Andy? Even if he wasn't at home, he was texting or ringing her constantly. There's no way. It's like she was his prisoner.'

'Have you any idea who Hollie was supposed to have been seeing? Did she tell you?'

'No. She wouldn't even speak about it.' Chloe met Catherine's eyes, willing her to understand. 'Hollie wasn't like that, even if she'd have had the chance. Andy treated her like shit, but she wouldn't have cheated on him.'

'Okay. But people kept talking?'

'Yeah. It was all over town, there were whole conversations about it on Facebook. Andy was fuming, even though he knew it was all bullshit. He was too arrogant to think it was true, believed he was so much in control of Hollie that she'd never even think about it. And he was right, but he didn't like being talked about, so... Well, he took it out on Hollie. We didn't hear from her for a week. I went around theirs in the end.' Chloe swallowed. 'He'd locked her in. She came to the window, could barely stand. There wasn't a mark on her face but I think he'd battered her ribs. She wouldn't tell me. She never said a word about what he did to her, but we knew. Mum and Dad were furious about it, but they knew they couldn't do anything for Hollie unless she let them.'

'Did you speak to her about it? Try to help?'

Chloe closed her eyes. 'Of course. She wouldn't listen. When I got my job, I told her we should find a house

72

together. I wanted to get her away from him, but it was like…' She waved her hands, trying to find the words. 'Like he had a hold on her. She said he would always have to be part of her life, because of the children.'

'But that didn't mean she would have to stay with him.'

'I know. I said the same thing, but she shook her head. Told me I didn't understand.'

Catherine drank the last mouthful of her coffee. 'Understand what?'

'I don't know. I don't… I don't know.' Chloe looked wretched. 'It doesn't make sense to me.'

'Do you think Andy had other girlfriends?'

'Don't know. Not sure anyone would be daft enough, except for Hollie.' Chloe was weeping now. Catherine reached for her bag, handed over a tissue. 'Thanks. Andy has… had a reputation, you see. Everyone knew he was a psycho. Even my brother, Ross, wouldn't mess with him. He was always saying he'd sort Andy out though.' Remembering who she was speaking to, Chloe's eyes widened, and she clapped her hand over her mouth. 'No, I don't mean that. Ross has a temper, but he wouldn't kill anyone.'

Not intentionally, perhaps, Catherine thought. 'When you say everyone knew Andy was a psycho, what do you mean?'

'What I said. I know people who used to hang around with him at school, but he lost all his mates as he got older.'

'Why?'

Chloe blew her nose. 'He picked fights. Borrowed money. Drank a lot. He used to be a laugh, then he turned into a prick.'

'Was there a reason? Why did he change?'

'No idea.'

'Did he have a drug problem?'

Chloe's eyes slid away, and she hesitated. 'Not that I know of. Hollie wouldn't have been with him, if he had. There's no way she'd allow the kids to be anywhere near that kind of stuff.'

'All right.' Catherine wasn't convinced, but they'd find out if Andy had had any drugs in his system when the results of the toxicology tests were known. 'Can you give me any names, people Andy used to be friends with? We've got his phone, but any help you can give us would be appreciated.'

'I don't know any. Andy and Hollie were older than me, I'm not sure exactly who they were mates with back then.'

'Okay. Were you at work yesterday?'

Hollie nodded. 'I started at ten, serving breakfasts. I finished at seven.'

'And in the evening?' Catherine asked.

'I got the bus home after work. Dad offered to pick me up, but I said not to bother. It wasn't as though it was a late finish.' Chloe managed a smile. 'Turns out it wasn't me he should have been worrying about.'

'What time did you get home?'

'About seven thirty. I had a bath, some food, talked to a couple of my mates and went to bed.'

Catherine smiled. 'Had your family saved you any fish and chips?'

'No, I just had beans on toast.' Chloe pulled a face. 'When you've been working in a pub all day with a menu like ours, the last thing you fancy for tea is fried food.'

'Good point.'

Chloe pushed back her chair, shaking her head. 'I've told you all I know. I need to get back to work. Thanks for the coffee.'

Lancaster moved as though he was going to stop her, but Catherine shook her head and they watched Chloe hurry through the door and dart across to the pub.

'Why did you let her go?' Lancaster asked.

'What were we supposed to do, arrest her?' Catherine began to gather their cups together and set them back on the tray. 'We know where she lives, where she works. We can easily find her again if we need to.'

Lancaster nodded. 'What did you make of the idea Hollie had cheated on Andy?'

'If there was another man involved, he might have had a motive for killing Andy, especially if he discovered Hollie's body. But then he could also have killed her himself.' Catherine rubbed her eyes, a headache beginning to push at her temples. She took out her phone, fired off texts to Anna Varcoe and Chris Rogers. 'I want to know why Andy changed when he left school.'

'You think something happened to him? Something we don't know about yet?'

Catherine left a couple of pound coins as a tip on the table and got to her feet. 'Let's face it, Dave. At the moment, we don't know anything at all.'

8

Ross Morton was a scaffolder working on a building site not far from where the fire had broken out the previous evening. When Catherine and Lancaster arrived, he was sitting on a stack of pallets, eating his midday meal. Even sitting down, it was clear he was a big man. The sleeves of his overalls were tied around his waist, his tight grey T-shirt showing off his gym-toned body. He watched them approach, digging a blue plastic fork into a polystyrene tray of food.

'Fish and chips again, Mr Morton?' Catherine raised an eyebrow.

He took his time chewing. 'I know, twice in twenty-four hours. Shocking. Against the law now, is it?'

'You know who we are.'

'I know *what* you are, you mean.' He shovelled more battered fish into his mouth, his eyes on the ground. Catherine moved closer, nodded at the food.

'They look good. Which chippy?'

Now he looked at her, the skin around his eyes appearing bruised. 'If you've got questions, ask them. Don't play games.'

Catherine held up her hands. Ross was expecting them to ask where he had been the previous evening. Either he'd already spoken to one of his parents, or he'd guessed the police would suspect him of killing Andy Nugent. 'I'm sorry about your sister,' she told him.

His Adam's apple jumped in his throat. 'Thanks. It's not her you're here about though, is it? Someone killed Andy.' He snorted. 'What a shame.'

'Whatever you thought of him, we need to find the person who did it.'

He scrunched the polystyrene tray in his fist. 'Why? So you can give them a medal?'

'You didn't like him.'

Ross pulled a bottle of water out of his overall pocket. 'No. Funny, isn't it? I couldn't stand the bloke who kept beating my sister up. You would've thought he'd have been top of my Christmas card list.' He drank, wiped a hand across his mouth. 'And now he's murdered her.'

'We don't know that—' Catherine was tiring of hearing herself say it.

He laughed. 'You don't think it was him? Come off it.'

Catherine ignored that. 'Did you know Andy at school?'

'Knew of him.'

'We've been told he changed once he'd left. Would you agree?'

He frowned. 'We all change when we leave school, don't we? We get jobs, have responsibilities. We grow up.'

'We heard Andy was popular at school, well liked. Now, though, no one has a good word for him.'

'True colours came out, didn't they?'

Catherine nodded at the crushed tray, still in his hand. 'Which fish and chip shop did you get those from?'

'The Blue Whale.' He looked up at her. 'Same as last night. Speak to the staff, they'll tell you. Talk to Abby. She works there.'

'Abby?'

He nodded as he got to his feet. 'My girlfriend.' He glanced around. There were several other men nearby, some standing chatting together as they ate their own chips, others sitting on the half-built walls with their phones. Ross lowered his voice. 'I'm a suspect then?'

'We're speaking to everyone who knew your sister, and Andy. Asking questions, establishing their movements,' Catherine said, expecting the jargon to antagonise him further.

'In other words, you'll be hassling us all, even my mum and dad, asking where they were when their daughter was being murdered?' He let a hard breath out through his nose. 'All right, here you go. I worked here from eight thirty until five thirty yesterday. I stopped for fish and chips on my way home, ate with my family, watched TV, went to bed. That was it. Boring as shit, but that was my day.'

Catherine nodded. 'Can you give us your girlfriend's number?'

He took out his phone and read it to her. 'You're wasting your time. Andy killed Hollie – case closed.' He looked at his colleagues again. 'Break's over. Can I get back to work?'

'We'll be in touch,' Catherine said. Ross sneered as he walked away.

–

Catherine tipped her head back against the headrest and closed her eyes as Lancaster started the engine. Having no sleep was beginning to catch up with her.

'This has been a waste of time,' she said.

'Not totally.'

Now she looked at him. 'Go on then.'

'You don't think the idea of something happening to Andy Nugent that affected him is worth following up?'

He hesitated, blushing. Catherine waved a hand, wanting to encourage him. 'Come on, Dave, tell me what you're thinking.'

'He worked at one of the local scrapyards, didn't he?'

'Apparently. We were told he worked permanent nights, but we're trying to verify that because it seems odd. Why would a place like that need to be open twenty-four hours a day? Even if he was supposed to be providing security, why would you bother? Who's going to want to nick a load of smashed-up cars?'

'I don't know, there's money in scrap metal.' Lancaster glanced at her. 'Do we know when he started?'

'What? When he started working there? I don't think so. We don't even know where it is yet.' Catherine frowned. What was he going on about?

'I was thinking... what if after Nugent left school, he got involved in something dodgy? Maybe unintentionally, maybe someone brought a car in they'd used for a crime, and Nugent saw something he shouldn't have? Something he was still caught up in?'

'You're thinking he was paid to keep his mouth shut?' Catherine said.

'Well, yeah, or maybe he was blackmailing someone. I know you said we're already looking into the place where he works...'

'You're assuming he was killed by someone we don't know about yet, and not one of Hollie's relatives? Even though they say they spent every minute of last night together, quickly providing each other with alibis?'

'They're grieving, shocked, probably frightened they're going to be accused of Andy's murder. They'll know we always look at the family first.' The blush deepened. 'I just thought…'

'No, I'm not saying you're wrong. We need to keep an open mind.' Catherine frowned, thinking about it. 'You're suggesting Hollie's death and Andy's might be unrelated?'

Lancaster changed gear, applied the brakes as a traffic light changed in front of them. 'I know it seems unlikely, but it's possible, isn't it? We know Andy invited some mates over last night.'

'The Spences say he did, but we can't take their word for it.' Catherine checked the time. 'We need to talk to those lads today.'

—

The house stank of fags and farts. The living room curtains were drawn, the room cool. Cal Dobson tugged the curtains open, blinking in the daylight, turning to stare at them with his arms folded across his bony chest.

'You woke me up.' His voice was high pitched, making him sound like a ten-year-old. 'I didn't get to bed until late.'

Catherine sat in the centre of the sofa, pushing a discarded pizza box out of the way first. Lancaster stood against the wall, chin up, back straight. He didn't speak, but Cal was throwing him anxious glances. Catherine crossed her legs, made a show of relaxing. She didn't want Cal to see her as a threat.

'Sorry to disturb you, Cal. What were you up to until then?'

His face was blank. 'What?'

'What were you doing until late last night?'

'Working.' He smiled, proud of himself. 'I was at work.'

'I see. Where do you work?'

Cal named a takeaway in town. 'I deliver food for them.'

'How? Not driving, are you, Cal?'

He shook his head, pulling a face. 'Not allowed now, am I?'

'You've never had a licence, meaning you were never allowed to drive – that was the problem. That, and the fact you took a wrong turn at some roadworks and ended up ploughing into a lorry full of chippings.'

He pouted. 'It was an accident. Anyway, Jamie drives me around when I'm working.'

'Your brother, Jamie?'

'He doesn't mind. He's glad I've got a job.'

Catherine exchanged a glance with Lancaster. She was pretty sure Cal was harmless, but you could never be sure. 'Do you know Andy Nugent, Cal?'

He moaned, pressed his palms against his cheeks. 'Andy's dead.'

'I know. I'm sorry. Was he a friend of yours?'

'A friend?' Cal's eyebrows almost met as he thought about it. 'Yes.'

'When did you last see him?'

'Yesterday.' The reply was immediate, and Catherine knew he would tell her the truth. Making up a story would be beyond him.

'Played some games, had a few beers.'

It was a new voice. Catherine looked up, knowing who she would see. Jamie Dobson almost filled the doorway, his hands on his hips, wearing boxer shorts and nothing else. He sneered at Catherine, looking down at his own body as

81

though he expected her to be impressed, or intimidated. Catherine smiled. She was neither.

'Afternoon, sir. You'll catch your death in just your pants.'

He laughed. 'I'll take the chance. Let's see some ID.'

Catherine held out her warrant card, and he examined it.

'All right. Now we've been introduced, mind telling me why you're here? I heard Andy's name mentioned.'

'Are you aware he's dead?'

'Knew first thing this morning.' Jamie moved to sit down, and Catherine moved across the settee to give him some space. He smelt of beer and sweat. 'No secrets around here.'

'You were at his house yesterday. What time?'

He rubbed his jaw. 'Not sure.' He glanced at his brother, who had wrapped his arms around his body. 'No point asking Cal, he can't tell the time.'

'Come on, Mr Dobson.' Catherine frowned at him. 'This is your mate we're talking about.'

'Mate? What are you talking about? The bloke was no friend of mine.'

'Then why were you at his house?'

He exhaled. 'Listen, Andy was a knob. I hadn't spoken to him for ages, didn't like the way he treated his girl-friend. Yesterday, he phoned me out of the blue, wanting me to look at his boiler. I'm a plumber and electrician, but I'm having a few days off because our mum's in hospital.'

'She's going to die,' Cal said morosely.

Jamie glared at him. 'Anyway, when we got there, I realised Andy lived in a bloody council house. Some of the houses on the Meadowflower are private rentals, but not theirs.'

'Meaning he wouldn't need you for repairs. The council would sort everything out,' Catherine said.

'Exactly.'

'Then why did he call you?'

'He said it'd take the council days to send someone out and with them having young kids they needed hot water and he'd rather pay someone to fix it quickly. I might have been sent there myself in the end anyway – I do some work for the council sometimes. When we got there he said, he'd had another look at the boiler himself and managed to sort it, but we were welcome to come in for a beer. He had loads of new games and a massive TV, so I thought why not stay for a while? We'd been at the hospital all day, and...' He blinked. 'Well, we needed to relax.'

'I'm sorry about your mum.'

He saw Catherine was sincere, and nodded. 'Thank you.'

She waited, then asked, 'Could you check your phone, see what time Andy called?'

Jamie pushed himself to his feet. 'Important, is it?'

'Could be.'

'All right.'

He left the room.

Cal shifted nervously. 'Cup of tea?'

Catherine accepted, mainly to keep him occupied. His reliance on his brother was obvious, and Catherine wondered how their relationship worked. The house was clean, nicely decorated, even if they needed to open a few windows and pick up their pizza boxes and beer bottles.

Jamie came back in, now wearing jeans and a T-shirt. He remained standing, scrolling on his phone.

'Andy rang me at five twenty-three. He asked how Mum was, then said they had no hot water. I knew they've got young kids so I said I'd do him a favour, even though I wasn't supposed to be at work. We'd have got there about ten past six.'

'Thank you,' Catherine said. 'And when did you leave Andy's house?'

'About ten to eight. Then we went into town and drove around delivering crappy pizzas for four hours. We only made three deliveries, spent the rest of the time sitting in the car outside the shop.'

Catherine knew they would need to check. If business was as slow as Jamie had claimed, the Dobsons could have nipped back to kill Andy Nugent between deliveries. 'And after midnight?'

'We came home with a couple of free pizzas, which is about the only perk of the job. We had a few beers, watched the football from earlier. Went to bed.'

Jamie spoke easily, without any sign he was lying.

'And when you left Andy just before eight, he was okay?'

'Yeah, he was fine.' Jamie frowned. 'He didn't have a knife sticking out of his chest if that's what you mean.'

Catherine ignored the comment. 'How was his mood?'

'His mood? Normal. Just… normal. He chatted a bit about the kids, about Hollie and her headaches, but we were concentrating on the game. None of us said much.'

'And did Andy receive any phone calls while you were at the house? Did anyone knock at the door?'

Jamie looked perplexed. 'No, I didn't even see him look at his phone. No one came to the door. It was just us and Andy, kicking each other's arses on the PlayStation. Nothing weird happened – no masked gunmen kicking down the door or psychos turning up with machetes.'

'All right, thank you. And how did Andy sound earlier, when you talked to him on the phone?'

He frowned at her. 'What do you mean? He sounded like he always did.'

'You said you hadn't spoken to him for a while.'

'Yeah, but I've known him for years. He sounded the same as always.'

Cal brought in two mugs of tea, handed one to Lancaster with a wary glance and held the other out to Catherine. She smiled at him and he returned it, looking for approval.

'Thank you, Cal.'

'No biscuits?' Jamie raised an eyebrow at his brother, and he scurried back into the kitchen. Jamie looked at Catherine. 'Got to keep him on his toes.'

'Do you really drive him around when he's delivering food?' Catherine had to ask. Jamie blushed.

'Yeah, well. He's never had a job before, and I wanted to encourage him. This thing with our mum has knocked him for six. I don't think he really gets it. Anyway, he can't exactly take the bus to deliver food, can he? The hours are a pain in the arse.'

'When does he work?'

'Six thirty until midnight, three nights a week. Last night was slow. They phoned while we were on our way to Andy's and told Cal not to bother coming in until eight. They've done it before; they treat him like shit to be honest. Why?'

Catherine lifted her shoulders, let them fall. 'We're piecing together Andy's last few hours. It seems you were the last people to see him alive.'

Jamie dug his hands into his jeans pockets. 'Except for the person that killed him.'

'Except them,' Catherine allowed.

Cal was back with a packet of chocolate digestives and a mug of tea for his brother. He offered the packet to Lancaster, who dug in, though Catherine refused because she wanted to continue asking questions.

'Did you go into the kitchen while you were at Andy's house? Or any other room?' she asked. Jamie moved to sit back down beside her. 'No. There was no need.'

'What about you, Cal?'

He shook his head. 'No. I went upstairs to use the toilet, but nowhere else.'

'Did Andy go into the kitchen while you were at the house?'

Jamie stared at her. 'No, I don't think he did. Not that I remember anyway. He'd brought the drinks in, some crisps. We were sorted. Everything we needed was in the living room.'

I bet it was, Catherine thought. The realisation Hollie must have been lying dead a few feet away from where Andy and the two brothers had sat playing video games was horrifying.

'Was the kitchen door closed?' she asked.

'What the hell is this? Yes, the door was closed. Jesus.'

'What about Hollie and the children? Did you see them?'

'The kids were in their bedroom,' said Cal. 'The door was closed, but I heard them when I went upstairs.'

'Were they crying?'

He pulled a face. 'A little.'

'And Hollie?'

'She was in bed,' said Jamie. 'Andy said she had a migraine, but...' He shifted in his seat, running a hand through his hair. 'Well, I wondered if they'd been arguing.'

'Why would you think that?'

'Because she didn't come downstairs. We know Hollie, and it seemed a bit weird she didn't come down to say hello at least. Then again, if she was ill... Migraines can be a bastard, I know.'

Or she'd already been dead for hours. Maybe they didn't know about Hollie's death? It seemed unlikely, given they were aware Andy had been killed. Granted, Jamie was speaking about Hollie as if she was still alive, but Catherine knew it meant nothing. It took people a while to get used to someone no longer being around. Feeling callous, she decided to keep asking them questions. If they were still unaware of Hollie's murder, she wouldn't have this chance again. 'Did Andy tell you they'd had a row?'

'No, but he shouted up the stairs to her, and she didn't reply. He said she must have been asleep, but I thought she was probably just ignoring him. Couldn't blame her, to be honest.'

Catherine was sickened. It was looking likely Andy Nugent had asked his friends to come to his house in a pathetic attempt to provide himself with an alibi. He'd pretended Hollie was ill in bed, even going so far as to speak to her, all the time knowing she lay dead in the kitchen.

Then Jamie's expression changed. 'She was already dead, wasn't she?'

'Mr Dobson—'

He was on his feet, fists clenched. 'Bit late for pleasantries now, isn't it? I suppose you thought you were being clever, did you, stringing us along? Made you feel important, did it?' His face was red, saliva spraying from his mouth as he bellowed at her. 'She was dead all the fucking time we were there, wasn't she? I want the truth.'

87

Lancaster stepped forward as Catherine stood up. 'I can't discuss the details of Miss Morton's death,' she said, sounding prim even to her own ears. 'The investigation is ongoing, and we're—'

'Yeah, blah blah, fucking blah.' Jamie took a step towards her, his face thunderous. 'You're looking for the person who killed that piece of shit Andy, but forgetting about Hollie? She was worth a million of him! If you coppers had done your jobs and arrested him…' He threw himself onto the sofa, his head in his hands. Bemused, Cal reached out a hand, unsure whether to offer comfort or not. Catherine could sympathise. She had encountered enough grieving people to know the line between despair and fury could be a blurred one.

'Why should we have arrested Andy, Jamie?' Catherine spoke gently, not wanting to provoke him further.

He raised a tear-stained face to glare at her. 'Because he spent half his life beating her up. Any idiot could see she was terrified of him. But no, you lot didn't want to know.'

'We can't act unless we know something's wrong. Did you ever report the violence?'

He bowed his head. 'No. What would have been the point? I didn't know for sure. You wouldn't listen to rumours and guesswork, would you?'

'We would have—'

'No. You wouldn't. Are you leaving now?' He looked up, met Catherine's eyes. 'I need to explain it to him. Please?'

Catherine saw Cal's uncomprehending face and nodded. 'We'll be in touch.'

9

DCI Kendrick sat behind his desk, arms folded across his chest. The end of his nose was red, sore-looking.

'We need the full post-mortem reports,' he was saying. 'I want to know whether Hollie Morton was killed by her boyfriend, or by someone else. We've spoken to everyone who lives nearby now, and no one saw anyone at the house other than the Dobson brothers. No suspicious vehicles, nothing out of the ordinary.'

'But Hollie was strangled, and Andy probably died after sustaining a head injury. It's not as though whoever killed either one of them would have been covered in blood,' Catherine pointed out.

'We don't *know* that's how Andy Nugent died though. He could have a heart attack and hit his head as he fell. We've no confirmation yet, because his post-mortem isn't complete. We don't even have a time of death.'

'Jamie Dobson said he and his brother left Nugent around ten to eight last night. The officers who responded to the Spences' call about the crying children arrived at Hollie and Andy's house about twelve forty-five, and found them both dead,' Catherine reminded him. 'Then Jo examined the bodies at around two thirty a.m., meaning Andy must have died between—'

'Eight p.m. and midnight, give or take,' Kendrick interrupted as Catherine hesitated. 'Dobson could have killed him then taken his brother to work and gone about his evening just as he said he did. It just makes the whole thing more complicated.'

In the chair beside Catherine's, Jonathan Knight checked his phone. 'Jo's been checked over, and she's fine. I left her in her office. She just sent a text to say she's starting the report on Hollie.'

'Good.' Kendrick managed a smile. 'You know how much I respect Jo, and the last thing I want is for her to be ill, but we need to crack on.'

'They checked her heart, ran some tests. Everything looked fine. She'd had a late night, no breakfast, and she fainted.' Knight shook his head. 'Seems even doctors don't always look after themselves properly.'

He was still concerned though; Catherine could hear it. Kendrick was moving on, flicking through a pile of paperwork, pulling a pair of glasses from his shirt pocket and polishing them on his tie.

'As I said, the house-to-house has given us nothing so far, though it's ongoing. Mick and his team are still at the house, so we might be lucky and find some physical evidence.'

'Mick said he'd found no sign of a break-in. Has he said any more?' Catherine asked.

'You mean has he discovered a smashed pane of glass with fingerprints and traces of blood on it?' Kendrick shook his head. 'Unfortunately not. If the Dobsons did do it they were already in the house anyway, but if not, it's still looking as though whoever killed Hollie and Andy was either invited in, or they just opened an unlocked door and strolled inside.'

'But no one saw any visitors, apart from Jamie and Cal Dobson.' Knight was frowning.

'Or they don't want to say they did. The neighbours are closing ranks; you know how it can be. People don't want to get involved,' said Kendrick.

'You'd think people would be sympathetic towards Hollie at least,' Knight said. Even as he said the words his frown deepened, and Catherine guessed he was realising it wasn't necessarily the case. Someone had strangled Hollie Morton. It hadn't been an accident, like Andy's death might have been. Someone had deliberately choked the life out of her, and they had to think about why.

'Everyone's sure Andy killed her, and it's only a matter of time before we reach the same conclusion,' Catherine said. 'It follows they won't be too bothered about who then killed him.'

'But we haven't reached that conclusion, have we? At least, not yet. We need evidence.' Kendrick's hand was on his stomach again. 'Hollie's family's neighbours couldn't, or wouldn't, tell us whether the Mortons had been in all evening like they said they were. We could check their phone records, see if any of them went walkabout, but we've no real justification for doing so yet, or for searching their house.' He put the glasses on, blinked at them. 'Over twelve hours into the investigation, and we've made no progress at all.'

'Well, we've raised a few more questions.' Catherine waited for Kendrick to explode.

He didn't. 'You've spoken to several of the people we have to consider as suspects. Impressions?'

Catherine was prepared. 'Irene Spence is nosy and doesn't miss a thing. It sounds as though Hollie and Andy weren't the most considerate of neighbours, and the Spences say they were definitely both alive and screaming at each other at ten o'clock yesterday morning.'

'And you believed them?'

'We've no reason not to. The Spences went out soon after ten a.m. and didn't return until mid-afternoon. We need more witnesses, people who saw or heard from Hollie or Andy any time yesterday. The staff in the chip shop confirm Ross Morton did call in and buy enough food for his family as he claimed, but that doesn't help us. He could have gone anywhere after that.'

Kendrick folded his arms. 'Everyone's probably glad to see the back of Nugent. You said Hollie spoke to her mum on the phone at nine yesterday morning?'

Catherine nodded. 'We'll need to check with the network, of course. We've already requested his and Hollie's mobile records, and the handsets are with the techies. But Jo said Hollie didn't die until late morning or early afternoon anyway.' She paused, wanting to get the facts right. 'Jamie Dobson received a call from Andy Nugent just before five thirty.'

'So he says,' Kendrick grunted. 'He must know we can check.'

'You mean he could have killed Andy, then phoned himself from Andy's phone to try to invent an alibi?' Knight was frowning.

'I don't think he was lying. Even if he was and he did kill Andy, why involve his brother?' Cal's face came into Catherine's mind – the bemused expression, the nervous movements. 'Cal would be a liability if you were trying to hide a murder, not an asset. He means well, but he'd be bound to say the wrong thing.'

'If Jamie Dobson gave Andy Nugent a shove, making him fall back and crack his head on the toilet, he'd have panicked. If he didn't plan to kill him and it was the result of an argument that got out of hand, it wasn't premeditated. That would fit with his brother being there too. If he'd planned to kill Nugent, Dobson would have gone there alone.' Kendrick pinched his bottom lip between his thumb and forefinger. 'I reckon he realised Nugent had killed Hollie and went for him. Maybe Nugent had gone upstairs to use the toilet or to check on the kids, Jamie Dobson had wandered into the kitchen to look for more beer or food, found the body and snapped.'

'It's possible.' Catherine remembered Jamie Dobson's tears, his anger. If he and Hollie were just friends, was it an overreaction? Maybe. Maybe not.

'Maybe it was the same scenario, but Cal did the pushing,' Knight suggested.

Catherine knew Knight was right, though she didn't like the idea. Then again, it was possible. If Cal had found Hollie's body, she could imagine him lashing out like a child, furious, emotional and confused. 'Yeah, we have to consider it.'

'What about the rumours? The whispers the youngest child wasn't Nugent's?' Kendrick bounced in his chair.

'Hollie's sister, Chloe, said it was nonsense. She told me Hollie wouldn't have had the opportunity or the inclination to cheat on Nugent,' said Catherine. 'She seemed genuine, but we need to check. She couldn't know for sure, or she could be lying about it.'

Kendrick drummed on the desk with his fingertips. 'What if Chloe and Jamie Dobson are in it together? Dobson found Hollie's body, killed Nugent, and went to Chloe asking her to help him cover his tracks?'

'Or Chloe tried to contact her sister, couldn't get hold of her and went to the house. If she caught Nugent off guard, it's possible she could push him over, isn't it?' Knight looked at Catherine.

Catherine spread her hands. 'Probably.'

There was a silence, eventually broken by Knight.

'If Jamie Dobson was expecting his brother to have to start working in the town centre at six-thirty, why did they go over to see Andy Nugent at all?' he said. 'I didn't think of it at the time, but it would have meant that, if Cal had had to go to work at his usual time, they'd only have had half an hour or so at Nugent's house if we factor in the travelling time.'

'Good point.' Kendrick clicked his tongue a few times. 'Catherine?'

'Jamie Dobson was told there was a problem with the hot water at Nugent's house,' she reminded them. 'He was expecting to call in, have a quick look at the boiler and then be on his way. Andy only asked Jamie and Cal to stay longer once they'd arrived, and Jamie said Cal's employers had called and told him not come in until eight. We'll check that too.'

Kendrick nodded. 'Please.'

'Maybe Nugent was trying to provide himself with an alibi,' said Knight. 'He'd killed Hollie but wanted the Dobson brothers to come to the house so he could pretend Hollie was upstairs, and everything was fine.'

'Ifs, buts and bloody maybes,' Kendrick said. 'We need to know whether Nugent was the baby's father. Let's check both kids, to be sure. We'll need the grandparents' consent, as the children's next of kin. I think we'll need to ask the Nugents as well as the Mortons, but better not mention to anyone that May might not be their grand-child after all. The samples will be destroyed immediately because of the kids' ages, but it's a tricky one. Better ask Mick about it.'

Catherine made a note. 'I asked Anna to find out if there were any CCTV cameras near Hollie and Andy's house. I know there are some outside the community centre, but...'

'It's at the other end of the estate,' said Kendrick. 'It's useless. There are no cameras anywhere near the house, either council-owned or private.'

There was a silence.

'I think Jamie Dobson did it,' Kendrick said eventually. 'Nugent killed Hollie, then Jamie Dobson killed Nugent later.'

'If Dobson had attacked Nugent, wouldn't the neighbours have heard them fighting?' Knight said. 'There were no bruises or cuts on Nugent's face. Did Jamie Dobson have any?' He looked at Catherine.

'No. No damaged knuckles, bruises, nothing, and he was hardly dressed when we first arrived.' She thought about it. 'It could have been deliberate, I suppose, showing me he didn't have a mark on him. But if Nugent was in the bathroom, Dobson could have stormed up the stairs and shoved him. If he fell and hit his head, Dobson wouldn't have had time to punch him. He'd already be on the floor. There wouldn't have been a fight.'

'And then Dobson realised he'd killed him. He panicked and fled the scene, like we said before.' Kendrick cracked his knuckles. 'I think we need to talk to Mr Dobson again.' He looked at Catherine. 'We should speak to the sister again too? Sounds like she was more help than the parents?'

Catherine nodded, looking at her shoes.

Kendrick glared at her. 'What?'

'It's...' Even in her head, it sounded naïve, not something an experienced DS should be thinking. 'Well, their

95

daughter's been killed. I can understand them not wanting us poking around.'

'We have no choice. Sometimes we have to trample over people's feelings. I don't like it any more than you do, but it comes with the job. We have to be objective, Sergeant. You know that.' She did, of course, but it never sat well. For once, Kendrick was speaking quietly, rubbing his stomach. Catherine saw the movement.

'Are you okay?'

He winced. 'Indigestion. Serves me right for having a fry-up this morning. Not that I could finish it. My wife always cooks enough for an army.'

Catherine wondered when he'd found the time, since he'd barged onto the scene of the arson before most people were thinking about waking up. She exchanged a glance with Knight, who lifted his eyebrows.

'What about the Scott Greaves case?' he asked Kendrick.

The DCI scowled. 'There's another pathologist scheduled to do his post-mortem this afternoon. I'm going to attend. The Superintendent insisted.' His mouth twisted. 'I'm doing all I can to make sure we hang on to both cases, prove we can handle it. But...' He laid both hands flat on the surface of his desk. 'I'm not sure I'll be able to. We've no idea who this arsonist is, and unless we stake out every building in town and catch him in the act, we're struggling. Plus, if there's anything suspicious about Scott Greaves's death...'

Catherine stared at him as Knight sat up straight.

'What do you mean?' she asked.

'Jo had a quick look at the body once the building was declared safe. You know how she is: she wouldn't say any more until she had him on the table.' He blew out a breath.

96

'No chance of that now. We've got Dr Kirby instead. He's completing the post-mortem on Andy Nugent, then he'll move onto Scott Greaves.'

'Who's Dr Kirby?' Knight looked puzzled. Kendrick smiled.

'He's new. Young bloke, not long qualified. Jo not mentioned him?' He winked at Catherine. 'Anyway, we'll see what he can tell us.' Checking his watch, he began to heave himself to his feet. 'I've got to get over to Lincoln. I'll leave it with you. See you back here at six.'

He tugged his coat from the back of his chair and clattered out of the room. Catherine turned to Knight.

'You're staying here?'

He shook his head. 'I'll come with you. We should both talk to Andy Nugent's parents. If you drive, I'll try to reach Jo, ask her to put a rush on the samples she took from Hollie's body.'

'Is she okay? Really, I mean?' Catherine asked as she got to her feet.

'I think so. The doctors at the hospital didn't seem concerned.'

Knight waited so Catherine could leave the room before him, and she caught the look on his face, which confirmed her suspicions. Something was wrong with Jo, something Jonathan Knight didn't want to talk about.

Knight's office was next to Kendrick's, two tiny cubicles built at the back of the CID room. Catherine watched him disappear inside. She sat at her desk, cast an eye around the main office. It was quiet, most of their team busy in the incident room or out of the building. Three deaths on their patch in less than twenty-four hours, and each was still a mystery. Often, when someone was murdered, the perpetrator was found standing over the body, covered in blood, the weapon still in their hand. They might even have called the police themselves, overcome with horror once the red mist had dispersed. Given that close to half of female murder victims are killed by partners or ex-partners, Catherine knew the likelihood someone other than Andy Nugent had wrapped their hands around Hollie Morton's throat and choked her to death were small. The statistic caused her pain each time she heard it, and Jamie Dobson's words echoed in her mind: '*If you coppers had done your jobs and arrested him…*' She hadn't needed the reminder, but she also knew the buck didn't always stop with the police. People had known, or suspected, Andy was violent towards his girlfriend, but they hadn't spoken up, hadn't reported him. Hadn't wanted to rock the boat. If it emerged Nugent had killed Hollie, Catherine knew there would be more than just herself feeling guilty. Hollie's parents and siblings could lash out all they wanted, but Catherine knew where the anger could be originating. They knew they might have been able to prevent Hollie's death, and it was easier to blame the police than accept that. Mr and Mrs Spence had also stuck their heads in the sand and ignored the problems next door. Would they too wake in the small hours and wonder whether Hollie might still be alive if they had made a single phone call? Catherine knew about guilt. It had been eating away at her own gut for long enough. In her job, there were always people you wanted to help, but couldn't. People who fell through the cracks. Those who turned away or refused to acknowledge there was a problem. Those addicted to substances that were killing them. Those who had fallen into crime in childhood and had never had the strength or opportunity to escape.

And Claire.

If Catherine was going to feel guilty about anything, it would always be Claire, but she knew she had a future now, both professionally and privately. Nothing was going to stop her making the most of both. Not her job, and certainly not her illness; it was still present, nudging her every now and then to remind her it was there and maybe always would be, but she was living with it. She had to.

Catherine grabbed her coat, phone and handbag as Knight reappeared wearing his jacket. He gave her a tired smile.

'Ready?' he said.

She nodded, following him across the grubby carpet tiles and out onto the landing. As they jogged down the stairs, she said, 'Have you heard from Caitlin recently?'

Knight hesitated, and for a second Catherine thought he was going to tell her to mind her own business. Caitlin was his ex-girlfriend. Knight had previously worked for the Metropolitan Police. He'd transferred to Lincolnshire after Caitlin had revealed she was pregnant, but since she had been sleeping with another man while still in a relationship with Knight, she didn't know whose baby she was carrying. Baby Olivia was now four months old, living with her mother and the new boyfriend in London, and, as far Catherine knew, the question of her paternity still hadn't been settled. How Jonathan Knight had been dealing with not knowing whether he was a father or not for so long, Catherine had no idea. He cleared his throat as he pushed open the outside door and held it for her.

'She sends the occasional email or text. The baby's fine.'

He said 'the baby', Catherine had noticed, seeming reluctant to use her name. Perhaps calling her 'Olivia' would make her too real. 'The baby' might be his way of keeping her at arm's length.

As she slid into the driver's seat of one of the unmarked cars, Catherine decided to pry a little further.

'What about the paternity test?'

'Caitlin hasn't mentioned it.'

Turning to look over her shoulder as she reversed out of the parking space, Catherine glanced at him. 'Maybe you could ask her?'

'Maybe.'

She decided to go for broke. 'Because I have to say, not knowing would be killing me.'

His expression darkened, and she wondered if she'd gone too far. Even mild-mannered Jonathan Knight must have his limit, but when he spoke again, his tone hadn't changed. 'And it's killing me, but Caitlin's her mother. The test won't be done until she says so.'

From what Catherine had surmised about the woman, Caitlin would never consider the effect the delay would be having on Knight or on Jed, her new boyfriend.

'You'd think Jed would have pushed for the test to happen though,' she said.

She waited for a bus to lumber past before pulling out onto the main road. On the opposite pavement, a gaggle of teenagers emerged from the grounds of the town's grammar school, pushing and jostling, heading for the corner shop across the street.

'Maybe he has, but Caitlin will be calling the shots.'

Catherine snorted. 'No doubt.'

Now he chuckled. 'Don't like her much, do you?'

She couldn't deny it. 'Well, I don't know her.'

'Still.'

'I don't like the way she's treated you.'

'Me neither.'

Catherine glanced at him. 'Will you talk to her?'

'Jo keeps asking me the same thing.' He paused. 'I think I'll have to.' He took out his phone. 'I'll text Caitlin now, ask when we can have a conversation. You're right, I need to know. I suppose I've been…' He cleared his throat. 'Well… afraid to know the truth. I've been fooling myself, allowing myself to hope… You know what I mean.' His phone began to ring and, startled, he fumbled, almost dropping it. 'Jo? Are you all right?'

Catherine slowed for a sharp corner as Knight began to splutter. She didn't want to listen in on what could be a private conversation, but she could hardly turn the radio on.

'But that's… They're sure?' He listened. 'Bloody hell, that puts a new spin on things.'

He listened again, for longer this time. 'What was her name?… When did it happen?'

Catherine tapped her fingers on the steering wheel, now desperate to know what the pathologist was saying. As she swung the car around the bend, Knight said his goodbyes and turned to her.

'Mick and Jo have already spoken about this, and she's just let Kendrick know. He asked her to tell us before we spoke to Andy Nugent's mum and dad.'

'What?' Catherine almost bellowed.

Knight exhaled. 'Andy Nugent's fingerprints.'

'What about them?'

'A couple of years ago, a woman reported a break-in and assault at her home. Someone broke in and she woke to find him on top of her. He didn't rape her, but he probably would have done if she hadn't fought so hard. He punched her, smashed her nose and gave her a black eye, but she managed to wrestle him off and started screaming. He ran. Scene of crimes managed to retrieve a couple of decent prints from the wooden headboard. He was wearing gloves, but he lost one in the struggle.'

She felt sick. 'And now Andy Nugent's are in the system, we have a match.'

Knight nodded. 'Yep, and there's more. The victim reported that when she woke, the assailant had his hands around her throat.'

Catherine remembered Hollie Morton's eyes, the tell-tale red petechiae blooming in them, indicating she had been strangled. The violence, the strength of her attacker.

'Shit. Then it could have been one of Nugent's trusted moves – he knew how to subdue someone quickly.'

'Yes. The woman was married, her husband working late when the attack happened, so she was alone in the house.' Jo must have given Knight the broad strokes during their brief call.

'You're thinking about who might have a motive for murdering Andy? But why would someone wait? You said this assault happened a couple of years ago?'

'It did, but the woman – her name's Rebecca Clough – the attack changed her,' Knight said, relaying Jo's words to him.

'It's understandable.'

'Of course.' Catherine heard Knight swallow. 'Rebecca took an overdose two weeks ago.'

Catherine felt the words like a blow to the stomach. 'Did she…?'

'She survived, just. This time her husband arrived home early and found her. They got her to the hospital on time. We never arrested anyone for the attack on her, never even had a suspect.'

'We'd failed her.'

He shook his head. 'Apart from the fingerprints, there was nothing to go on. No other physical evidence was recovered. She didn't see his face, and he didn't speak. There were no witnesses. There was nothing more we could have done.'

'Still. It makes me sick.'

'I know.' He paused. 'We need to speak to Rebecca Clough and her husband.'

She knew Knight wasn't unfeeling. He hated the thought of a man who would act in such a way roaming the streets they were supposed to keep safe as much as she did. He was closing off his emotions to focus on the task before them.

'You think Rebecca attempting to take her own life might have triggered her husband to want to take revenge now?' Catherine considered it. 'But how would he know who Andy Nugent was? How could he be sure Nugent was the man who'd attacked his wife? Why wouldn't he just come to us?'

Knight lifted his shoulders, let them fall. 'I don't know, but we need to consider the possibility that the two crimes are linked.'

Catherine was quiet, thinking it over. Then she said, 'If Nugent did break into the house and attack Rebecca Clough, chances are she wasn't his first victim.'

'No.' Knight sounded exhausted.

'Or his last.'

'Probably not. We need to check for similar crimes.'

'Meaning we could potentially be looking at an unknown number of women plus their families who won't have been crying into their cornflakes this morning when they heard Andy Nugent has been killed.'

She glanced at Knight and he met her eyes.

'Exactly.'

10

The house was on the outskirts of Northolme, part of a village that was gradually being swallowed by the town. It stood on the main road to Lincoln, a detached property with a well-maintained front garden and two cars, both less than two years old, parked in the driveway. Catherine pulled in behind them. The neighbouring gardens were equally immaculate, a man trimming the edge of his lawn in the house to the right of the Nugents' property. He turned to stare at them as Catherine turned off the engine.

'Neighbourhood Watch has spotted us,' she said.

Knight nodded. 'That's reassuring. Mr and Mrs Nugent are both teachers, aren't they?'

'She's the head of one of the primary schools in town, and he teaches at Lincoln College. Maths.' Catherine wrinkled her nose.

'Not your favourite subject?'

'Not even top five.'

Knight undid his seatbelt. 'I hated PE. Cross country on a freezing Monday afternoon.'

Catherine looked again at the Nugents' house. 'Unusual for someone from a background like this to end up on the Meadowflower.'

Knight nodded. 'People are usually working hard to move the other way.' He glanced at the house. 'The front door's opening.'

Catherine looked up to see a man barrelling towards them. He had a bald head and a full grey beard. He was scowling, but as he reached the car he seemed to run out of steam and stood with his arms folded, watching them climb out. Catherine braced herself, half expecting a torrent of abuse as Knight stepped towards him.

'Mr Nugent?' Knight introduced himself. 'I'm sorry for your loss.'

'Sorry, I thought you were...' Roy Nugent shook Knight's hand. 'Thank you. You're wanting to ask us some questions? My wife's in bed, I'm afraid. The news...' He pressed his lips together. 'Well, you can imagine. I'm sure in your line of work you have to make visits like this often.'

In turn, Catherine held out her hand. Now she was nearer, she could see the signs of grief on his face. Puffy red eyes, dark bags beneath them. His hand was cold, his grip firm without being overbearing. 'I'm Detective Sergeant Catherine Bishop. Thank you for seeing us, sir.'

Nugent stepped back. 'I don't mean to be rude, but I wasn't aware we had a choice.' He waved an arm. 'Let's go inside. No doubt all the neighbours know what's happened already, but we don't need to give them any more to talk about. We had a journalist here earlier, but your colleague made it clear we didn't want to talk. That's why I came running out of the house; I thought more had turned up.'

Catherine reached the front door and waited for Nugent to go in first. She wondered if the journalist had been Helen Bridges. It was possible, even probable. Though she'd be surprised if Helen had gone away without a fight, even if the people she was hoping to talk to were grieving parents.

'I believe a Family Liaison Officer visited you earlier today?' Knight said as they removed their shoes and followed Nugent into a homely kitchen. The cupboards were shabby, the floor tiled in grey slate. An old collie snoozed in a basket under a pine dining table. It opened its eyes but didn't bother to get up when it saw Catherine and Knight, its tail beating on the ground as it recognised its owner. Nugent bent to stroke the greying muzzle as he crossed the room to fill the kettle.

'Please, sit down.' Nugent pointed to the chairs around the dining table. 'Yes, an officer did call. He didn't stay long.' He flicked the kettle on to boil and leaned back against the worktop, his arms folded.

'Was there a problem?' Knight pulled out a chair and sat, his eyes never leaving Nugent. The other man shook his head.

'A problem? Apart from Andy being murdered and us not wanting strangers in the house, you mean?' He licked his lips, held up his hands. 'Sorry. I'm a little… Sorry. I know you're here to help.'

'Please, don't apologise. We understand this is an incredibly difficult time,' Catherine told him. More meaningless words. Nugent turned away silently, taking cups out of a cupboard, opening the fridge and a drawer. His shoulders were shaking, and they gave him a couple of minutes of silence to compose himself. When he placed mugs of black tea in front of them, setting down a sugar bowl and jug of milk, they thanked him and helped themselves. Nugent held his own mug in both hands, his head bowed, and Catherine realised he was drawing comfort from the warmth.

'You've questions you need to ask,' he said eventually. 'Please, let's get on with it. I want to help you find the person who did this to our son.'

'You're aware Andy's partner, Hollie, also died yesterday?' Knight said.

'Yes. We were horrified. She was a lovely girl.' He looked up at them, seeming unsure whether to continue. 'Do you think Andrew killed her?'

Catherine glanced at Knight. How were they supposed to respond? It was a telling remark, indicating Nugent was aware, or had at least guessed, about his son's violence towards his partner. She wondered whether he would still have asked had his son still been alive, and they were investigating the death of just Hollie. Knight put down his mug.

'We don't know,' he said.

'But it's a possibility.' It was a statement, not a question. Nugent tipped back his head, and Catherine knew he was trying to prevent tears from falling again.

'Why do you ask?' she said gently.

Nugent gave a strangled laugh. 'I loved my son, Sergeant, but he had a temper. He lashed out. His mother and I, we spoke to him about it more times than I can remember. He said he couldn't help it.'

'Was he always like that?'

He sipped his tea. 'No, I don't think so. The usual toddler tantrums, a few rows when he was a teenager, but no more than that. No problems at school. He was an only child, you see, so there was no one to fall out with at home. We wanted more children, but...' He pulled a tissue from his trouser pocket and wiped his eyes. 'Well, it never happened.'

'Were you a close family, the three of you?' Knight asked.

'We used to be.' Nugent sniffed, blew his nose. 'Excuse me. Yes, I'd say we were close when Andy was younger.'

'What about more recently?' asked Catherine.

Nugent took his time replying. 'We rarely saw him. They'd bring the children to visit sometimes, usually when we'd phoned Andy and begged him to. We've only met May a couple of times.'

Knight said, 'You never went to Andy and Hollie's house?'

'No. No, we were never invited, and we didn't want to just turn up.' He looked at them. 'I know it seems odd, but that was how it was. Andy was... not secretive, but private. I guessed he felt... It's going to make me sound like a snob, but I wondered if he was ashamed.'

'Ashamed?' Catherine thought about the house where Andy and Hollie had lived. It wasn't luxurious, but it was clean and tidy. 'Why might he have been ashamed?'

Roy Nugent was blushing. 'We... I mean, I'm afraid it might be our fault. You see, we always hoped Andy would follow in our footsteps. Not necessarily by going into teaching, but we hoped for a professional career of some sort. A solicitor maybe, or an accountant. Whatever he wanted.'

As long as it wasn't working at the local scrapyard, thought Catherine. 'I see. And what did Andy think?'

'He agreed. He always said he wanted to go to university, though he hadn't decided what to study. His GCSE results were good; he could have taken any path he chose to. But then...' Nugent paused, scrubbed at his eyes with his fingertips.

'Then?' Knight prompted.

'I don't know. The summer between sitting his GCSEs and when he should have started college or sixth form, Andy changed his mind. Said he'd had enough of studying, wanted to earn some money instead.'

'That must have been disappointing for you and Mrs Nugent?' As far as Catherine was concerned, it was up to Andy, but she could see why his parents might have protested.

Nugent nodded. 'But we told him we understood, that we'd be proud of him whatever he decided. And we would have been, if he'd trained as a plumber or mechanic, or… or *something*. But he didn't. He did nothing.'

Knight shifted position, crossed his legs. 'He didn't get a job?'

'No. He signed on the dole and was hardly at home. We were concerned, tried to ask where he was going, what he was doing. He was vague at first, said he was staying with friends, that we worried too much. He kept assuring us he was looking for work, though he never seemed to have any interviews.' Nugent took a breath. He looked haunted, as though remembering was causing him pain. 'We *were* worried.'

'What did you think was going on?' asked Knight.

Nugent groaned. 'We didn't know. We worried about drugs, crime… the usual things that give parents sleepless nights. We'd assumed we were over the most difficult age – shows what we knew.'

Knight nodded. 'Was there any evidence of drug taking?'

'Not that we saw, but we're hardly experts, even though we both work with young people. Anyway, Andy wouldn't tell us anything. We rarely saw him, and when we did, he was rude, aggressive. Not physically,' he said hastily, 'but verbally. Telling us to mind our own business, that he wasn't a kid any more. Basically, to leave him alone.'

'And all of this happened when Andy was, what? Sixteen, seventeen?' Catherine wanted to be sure. Roy Nugent's account was beginning to echo what they'd heard from Chloe Morton, and Ross Morton and Jamie Dobson had hinted at the same thing – Andy Nugent had changed once he left school. Why? Was it a straight-forward rebellion against the path his parents had been anxious for him to take? Or was there more to it, as Dave Lancaster had suggested? Catherine shot a glance at Knight. He was watching Nugent, who was rubbing his eyes again. Eventually he looked up.

'Yes, Andy would have been about sixteen. Why do you ask?'

'We like to get the facts right,' said Knight. 'And there was no specific event that could have triggered any of this?'

'You mean a death in the family, a divorce?' Nugent shook his head. 'No. Unfortunately, Andy never knew his grandparents. My wife and I both lost our parents before he was born. And we're happily married. We wondered at the time... I mean, we're both in education. We know young people; we've seen pretty much everything over the years. We were worried it was our fault somehow... Do either of you have children?'

'No,' Knight said quickly.

'Well, it sounds odd, but if something goes wrong in your child's life, your first instinct is often to blame yourself. We wondered if we'd put too much pressure on Andy, pushed him too hard. Wondered if he decided to not continue his education to spite us.'

'Do you still think that's what happened?' Catherine thought it probably was.

Nugent spread his hands. 'Who knows? Andrew moved out, shared a flat with some girl or other for a while. He kept in touch by text, but irregularly. I suppose he didn't need us any more.'

'Can you remember the name of the girl he lived with back then?' It probably wasn't important, but Catherine knew they should follow it up.

'No,' Nugent said immediately. He was being evasive.

'Could you check with your wife?' Catherine smiled to take the bite out of her words.

'I'm not sure it's worth disturbing her for, Sergeant.'

'You've told us your son changed around the age of sixteen. Other people have told us something similar. We'd like a clearer picture. It could be important.'

'You've spoken to people about Andy? Before talking to us, his bloody parents?' Nugent looked as though he was going to throw himself at them before he controlled his anger, taking a couple of deep, shuddering breaths. He fell back into his chair. 'Well?'

'We're investigating the murder of Hollie Morton alongside the enquiry into the death of your son.' Catherine spoke politely, but firmly. 'As they lived together, it's inevitable some of the witnesses we need to speak to will give information relevant to both cases.'

'And you need to dig into every area of their lives, do you?' Nugent was still furious, his hands clenched on his lap.

'As I said, it's sometimes difficult to know what's relevant to a case and what isn't, so we have to gather as much information as possible about the victim.'

Nugent stared at her. 'You mean you think Andy's decision not to continue studying could have some bearing on his... his death? Why should it have?'

'As we've said, at this stage, we need to find out all we can about your son and his life,' said Knight.

'You mean you've no idea who killed him?' Nugent glared at them. 'Isn't it obvious?'

Here we go, thought Catherine. 'Obvious?'

He sneered. 'Hollie's brother, Ross. He's known to be violent, and he'd told Andy he'd kill him before.'

'Ross Morton threatened to kill Andy?' Knight asked. 'Did you hear him say that?'

'Not exactly, but it was implied. Our granddaughter May was christened a month or so ago. Andy and Hollie rented a room at a local pub, and we went there after the church service. A buffet, a few drinks... you know how it is.' Nugent gulped his tea, shook his head. 'But some people can't enjoy a pint and leave it at that. Ross was drunk, Andy on his way to be. I don't know what happened, but they argued, and Ross stormed out. Anyone who was there will tell you he swore to Andy he'd kill him one day.'

'Those were his exact words?' Catherine asked.

Nugent blushed. 'More or less.'

Catherine assumed there had been also swearing, language Roy Nugent couldn't bring himself to repeat.

'Why did Ross threaten your son?' she couldn't help asking. Nugent shuffled in his chair.

'We've already discussed this. Andy had a temper, and I think when he and Hollie argued... Well, sometimes, it went too far.'

Catherine's tone didn't change. 'You mean he hit her?'

Nugent's eyes bulged. 'No, he… Look, I don't know.' His head dropped. 'I don't know what happened between them. I know my son wasn't perfect, but he's also a victim now.'

'And we're doing everything we can to find the person who killed him.' Catherine knew the words were inadequate, sounding almost trite. Nugent was nodding though, attempting to smile.

'I'm sure you are.'

'We will need to speak to your wife, sir.' Catherine glanced at the ceiling. 'Would you mind going to see if she's awake?'

'She's not,' Nugent said quickly. 'She couldn't sleep, and after a restless night she took a sleeping pill so she could have a nap. She won't wake for hours.'

It sounded like a speech he had prepared. Catherine waited, but he didn't say any more, just kept sipping his tea. The dog struggled to its feet and rested its chin on his knee. Nugent stroked its head, smoothing its ears. 'Good boy,' he said softly. 'Good boy.'

'Is it usual for your wife to need sleeping tablets, sir?' asked Knight. Nugent glanced at him.

'No, but then hearing your only son has been murdered would disrupt anyone's rest, I'd imagine.' Nugent spoke calmly, but his eyes blazed.

'But you had sleeping tablets in the house. Are they prescribed, or did your wife buy a version over the counter?'

Nugent shoved back his chair, the dog stumbling away. 'What the hell does it matter? If you must know, my wife went to pieces when we heard the news. I don't think you understand…' He covered his face with his hands, his voice breaking. 'Our son, our boy…' The dog whined, pressing himself against Nugent's legs. Nugent stooped, wrapping his arms around the animal and pressing his face into its fur. The dog looked up at Catherine, and she imagined she could see an accusation in his eyes. No one spoke, until a movement in the doorway made them all turn.

A woman stood there, watching them. She was tall; Catherine estimated around five feet ten or eleven. She had long grey hair, wore a red silk robe and matching slippers. Her face seemed frozen, her pale blue eyes studying them without interest. Catherine looked at Knight, and they both stood.

'Mrs Nugent?' Catherine took a step towards the woman, but she flinched, wrapping her arms around her body, and Catherine stopped in the middle of the room, waiting.

'Who are you? Why are you here?' Her voice was tiny, the words halting, as though speaking caused her pain. Catherine couldn't imagine her addressing an assembly hall full of children, but she knew the devastation grief could wreak. This woman was shrunken, wraithlike.

'Grace. I thought you were asleep.' Roy Nugent went to his wife, reached as if to hold her, then held back. Catherine could understand his hesitation. Grace Nugent looked as though she might shatter if she was touched. Catherine met Knight's eyes. This woman was in no state to be questioned, but she knew they had to try. Knight moved slowly, as if expecting her to bolt away like a startled deer. She watched him approach, her eyes half closed.

'We're police officers, Mrs Nugent.' Knight's voice was as gentle as Catherine had ever heard it. 'Could we ask you some questions?'

She laughed, the sound shocking in the quiet kitchen. It was a bitter, contemptuous sound which seemed to fill the room. She marched to the chair Catherine had vacated and threw herself down.

'Ask me whatever you like. What does it matter?'

'Grace—'

'Oh, shut up, Roy. Andy's gone, but we can't grieve for him yet. Not until…' She seemed to catch herself, realising who she was talking to. Her eyes fixed on Catherine. 'I assume you've arrested him?'

'Arrested…?' Catherine shot another glance at Knight. They needed to take control, otherwise they would never get any answers.

Grace Nugent clicked her tongue, rolling her eyes as though they were the stupidest people on the planet. 'Ross Morton, of course.'

'Mrs Nugent, we came to talk to you about Andy.' Knight took another step forward, hands loose by his sides, expression neutral. She glared at him.

'Andy? He's gone. None of us can help him now. Ross killed him, like he said he would.'

Knight held up his hands. 'We'd like to ask about Andy's life, his job. Could you help us with that, Grace?'

'His life? He had a wonderful life, until he decided to throw his future away and shack up with some slut from that housing estate.'

Roy Nugent winced, moving closer, laying a hand on his wife's arm. She shook him off and pushed him away, scowling. 'We did everything we could to give him the best chance in life, and he threw it all away. Mixing with all sorts of people, fighting, drinking, taking drugs… And where did it get him?' Tears were falling now, her face red and angry. 'It got him killed.' She scrubbed at her eyes with her fingertips. 'He wouldn't listen. He never did.' Her breath shuddered in her chest and she closed her eyes, falling back in the chair as though exhausted. The dog limped over, pushing his nose into her palm. She reached for him blindly, pulling him towards her.

'You believe Ross Morton killed your son.' Knight spoke softly.

'Of course he did.' Grace Nugent's eyes opened and she focused on Knight. 'Or Hollie did it, the poisonous little bitch.'

'Grace,' her husband said. It wasn't a warning or admonishment, more a plea.

'Come on, Roy, we've discussed it often enough. She dragged our son into the gutter and made sure he stayed there. Tying him down with children, not allowing him to see us, his own parents...' She pointed a trembling finger at Catherine. 'You let your boyfriend see his parents, don't you?'

'If I had one, I would, yes.' Catherine kept her tone neutral, but she doubted Grace Nugent would have noticed any edge. She was far beyond listening to reason, blinded by grief and pain.

'Well, Hollie didn't. She had to keep Andy for herself, spending all his money, nagging him constantly. No wonder he—'

'Grace,' Roy Nugent said again, firmer this time.

'No wonder Andy lost his temper sometimes, I was going to say.' She sneered at him. 'I'm not defending him, if that's what you think. There was no excuse for him hitting her, and he did, let's not pretend otherwise. He wasn't an angel. But he didn't deserve to be murdered either.'

Catherine ignored the remark. She doubted Mrs Nugent would be able to name a murder victim who *had* deserved their fate.

'The woman your son lived with before Hollie. Can you remember her name?' she asked.

Grace Nugent curled her lip. 'Not likely to forget, are we?'

'Your husband has.' Catherine smiled.

Roy coughed. 'Well, I...'

The look his wife gave him was difficult to read. 'Her name's Jade Walsh. I've no idea where she's living now. We only met her once.'

'Thank you. I'm sure we'll find her.'

The sneer again. 'I've no doubt. I gather she was well known on the Meadowflower Estate. She seemed determined to have a child with most of the men who live up there, anyway.'

Again, Catherine didn't respond. 'We were also asking your husband about Andy's earlier life – around the time he left school?'

'When he turned into a layabout, you mean?' Grace Nugent snorted. 'He broke our hearts that summer, didn't he, Roy?'

Her husband mumbled an indistinct reply as he went back to his own chair. Catherine knew how much Grace Nugent was fighting to remain in control. Her anger, her snappishness, her hostility to her husband – she was trying to avoid the pain the questions Catherine and Knight had to ask would cause her. As she had with Hollie's parents earlier, Catherine sympathised, knowing the Nugents' world had been blown apart. But if they were going to find the person who killed Andy, they needed answers.

'What happened?' Knight asked gently. 'Why do you think Andy changed his mind about further study?'

Grace Nugent's mouth tightened, and for a moment Catherine thought she would refuse to answer. Then she said, 'He said he was sick of exams and wanted to earn some money.'

'Did you try to change his mind?' Knight spoke quietly, but she turned on him nevertheless.

'Of course we did,' she spat. 'He could have been anything he chose to be – a doctor, or… He could have studied the law. But no, he wanted to go and play happy families with that…' Her voice trailed away, and she shook her head, tears glinting in her eyes. 'He wouldn't listen. Such a waste.'

Catherine found it interesting she had used the phrase when talking about her son's change of heart about his career rather than about his death.

'You don't think there was any other reason?' she asked.

'What do you mean?'

'Nothing else happened?'

'What are you implying? Nothing happened, or at least nothing we ever heard about.'

'And so you blamed Jade for Andy deciding to turn his back on his education?' Catherine said.

'Why not? It was her fault. She introduced him to that lifestyle, those layabouts – signing on, thinking the world owes you a living. Have a few kids, claim every benefit known to man and live the high life while other people work to pay for your house and your bills.' Grace Nugent took a breath, her chest heaving. 'Yes, we blamed her. Why wouldn't we?'

Because Andy had a mind of his own, Catherine wanted to say. Because he decided against the life you'd planned for him, and you didn't like it. Because your own prejudices are blinding you to that fact. 'Did Andy have children with Jade?'

'No. Thankfully he wasn't quite that stupid. I'm sure she's made up for it since. She had two before she was twenty-one.'

Roy Nugent shifted in his seat. 'So did your mother.'

The glare he received was pure venom. 'She was married at eighteen, Roy, as you know, and remained that way until my father's death. It's hardly the same thing.'

Catherine and Knight exchanged a glance. He gave a tiny shrug, and Catherine nodded. Listening to Grace Nugent's vitriol was getting them nowhere. She was blaming everyone but her son for what she saw as his failures in life. It was understandable, perhaps, but they didn't need to listen to it. Catherine looked at Knight, and they stood.

'Thank you for your time.' Catherine held out her hand, but no one took it. Mr and Mrs Nugent stared at her.

'That's it?' Grace Nugent demanded. 'You've no more questions?'

'The investigation is at an early stage,' Knight said. 'We're trying to find out as much as we can about Andy, about who he spent time with and his movements yesterday. You've told us you rarely saw him, and so we won't intrude any longer. We understand how devastating the news of Andy's death has been.'

Mechanically, Roy Nugent hauled himself to his feet. 'I'll show you out.'

His wife closed her eyes as the detectives passed her. As she went through the door, Catherine turned her head and saw Grace Nugent's expression had changed when she thought no one was watching. Bemusement, shock, and raw pain. Catherine hurried away, feeling as though she had witnessed an extremely private moment. Grace Nugent might be full of bitterness and bluster, but underneath, she was in agony. Her world had been shattered once by what she viewed as her son's betrayal, and again by his murder. Whatever Catherine thought of the woman, she recognised acute distress when she saw it. She hurried after Knight as Roy Nugent opened the door.

'I'm sorry about… well, the way we spoke to you,' he said, not looking at them. 'I understand you've a job to do, and of course we want the person who… who hurt our son found. But…' He made a vague gesture with his hand, as though unable to find the words to explain how he was feeling.

The dog had followed Catherine, and she bent to stroke his head and rub his ears. She wanted to hug him close, to bury her face in the thick fur around his neck as Roy Nugent had done. She missed having a dog around. There had always been at least one in the house when she had been growing up. Her job made it impossible for her to have one now, but one day… She straightened, telling herself to focus.

'No need to apologise, sir,' Knight was saying. 'You're devastated, and it's completely understandable. We can organise for the Family Liaison Officer to come back and support you, if you think it would help?'

Nugent glanced over his shoulder, as though bracing himself for a bellow of complaint. Catherine half expected one too.

'Thank you, but I think we'll manage.' He attempted a smile, but Catherine knew he was desperate for them to leave.

In the car, Knight took out his phone.

'What do you reckon?'

Catherine glanced over her shoulder and began to reverse. 'Other than we need to speak to Jade Walsh?'

'Definitely. I think Mr Nugent knew more than he was prepared to say about Andy's decision too.'

'Maybe.' Catherine waited for a lorry to trundle by before edging out onto the road. 'After speaking to Andy's parents, I can understand him wanting to earn some money and leave home though.'

'You don't think you'd have been disappointed with his decision in their position?' Knight was scrolling on his phone.

'Of course, but I've always though the point of having a child is watching them grow up into the person they want to be, not to create a perfect copy of their parents.'

'They wanted the best for him.'

'I know, and I understand the news of his death has knocked them for six, but...' Catherine braked as a van pulled out in front of them without indicating. 'She was furious, Jonathan. I know grief affects people in different ways, but it didn't seem to be his death she was angry about.'

'We asked about something that's obviously still a sore subject. She was clearly devastated.'

'I'm not saying she wasn't.' Catherine glanced at him, surprised by his reaction. Was it because he was beginning to dare to see himself as a parent? Wondering how he would react if the child that might be his daughter turned her back on the path he had expected her to take? Catherine had thought about the possibility of children

122

herself, but she hadn't wanted to do it alone. When her only previous long-term relationship had ended because of the pressures of her career, she had wondered if the chance had gone. It was far too early to be even considering such a commitment with Isla, but she had to admit the idea had crossed her mind again. The realisation was startling, and she pushed it away immediately, knowing she wouldn't broach the subject with her new girlfriend. Even a casual remark in passing would seem like she was coming on too strong, and the last thing Catherine wanted to do, knowing how difficult Isla had found it to come to terms with her sexuality, was to frighten her away.

'I did think it was interesting that Mrs Nugent acknowledged Andy's violence towards Hollie.'

'Even though she hinted that Hollie provoked him?'

Knight lifted his shoulders. 'At least she was willing to believe he'd done it. His dad didn't seem to want to admit there was a problem.'

'I suppose it's not an easy thing to accept your son to be capable of.'

'Especially when he's just been murdered.' Knight's phone beeped and he read the screen. 'Jade Walsh's address. She still lives on the Meadowflower.'

'With her fifteen kids, if Mrs Nugent is to be believed.' Catherine tried to keep the scorn out of her voice, but it wasn't easy. People making assumptions generally got her back up.

'Mrs Nugent didn't like her husband mentioning her own mother. I know it's not the best time to judge their relationship, but…'

Catherine said nothing as she flicked on the indicator, waiting to turn right towards the Meadowflower Estate. Knight glanced at her.

'What are you thinking?' he asked. 'That maybe one of them could have killed their son and his girlfriend? That Andy learnt about violence from one of his parents?'

'Or both of them.' Catherine made the turn. 'They're trying so hard to be respectable – call me a cynic, but you have to wonder.'

Knight paused, then said, 'And we'll need to check where they were yesterday, when we have time of deaths.'

'Probably at work, at least when Hollie was killed.'

'I'm struggling to see Mrs Nugent as a headteacher,' Knight said.

'As you said, we're seeing her at her worst. She's probably sweetness and light in school.'

Knight pursed his lips. 'You think?'

11

'You're here about Andy?' Jade Walsh asked when Catherine had introduced herself and Knight. Jade hadn't seemed surprised to find two police officers at her door, offering coffee and waving them towards the living room. It was small and cosy, with a box of toys in the corner and framed school photographs on top of the fireplace. Catherine sat at one end of the sofa, leaving Knight to settle in the only armchair.

'You have two children?' Catherine asked as Jade returned to the room. Her movements as she handed out the drinks were quick, almost clumsy, and Catherine wondered whether she was nervous. Finding the police at your door was enough to ruffle most people's feathers, even if you were half expecting them. Jade nodded as she lifted a textbook and pile of notes from the sofa and set them on the carpet.

'That's right. Bet Andy's mum told you I'd have enough kids for a football team, didn't she?'

Catherine had to smile. 'Something like that.'

'She would. No wonder Andy couldn't wait to get away. I'm glad my children don't go to her school – talk about Miss Trunchbull.' She tucked her legs underneath her. 'I'm halfway through a history degree now the kids are at school, planning to become a teacher myself eventually. Tell Andy's mum that when you see her next. She won't believe it. She thinks I'm a waste of space. Thinks everyone who lives on the estate is. Fair enough, some of them are, but not everyone.' Jade took a mouthful of coffee and gave them a shaky smile. 'Is it true Andy was murdered?'

Catherine hesitated, but couldn't see the harm in being honest. It wasn't as though it was a secret. 'I'm afraid so.'

Jade nodded, frowning. She took a sip of her coffee, screwing up her face as she swallowed it. Catherine watched, knowing it was too hot to drink, wondering again if their arrival had sent Jade's nerves on edge. She might be upset about Andy's death, but this didn't feel like grief to Catherine. It was more like apprehension. Jade's shoulders were hunched, and she was curled into the other corner of the sofa, angling her body as far away from Catherine as possible. If Catherine had been asked to name the emotion Jade was trying to conceal, she would have said the other woman was feeling guilty.

Why?

Jade's eyes flicked from Catherine to Knight. She was smiling again, but her eyes remained watchful. She cleared her throat, bringing the mug up to chin height as though she were hoping to hide behind it.

'What do you want to know?' she asked.

Knight leaned forward in his seat, and Catherine knew he too had noted Jade's unease. 'How long were you and Andy together?' he asked. An easy one to start.

'Not long, less than a year. He didn't live with me all the time. He shared a flat with some of his dodgy mates and went back to them once I kicked him out.'

'Dodgy? How do you mean?'

Jade waved a hand. 'I know we were young, but they were more like kids. Drinking all day, staying up all night, driving like idiots. I had the children, responsibilities. When he was with them Andy acted differently, and I didn't like it. When I told him so, he took offence. Told me he was too young to settle down. I agreed, said he knew where the door was.'

'Was he ever violent towards you?' Catherine asked.

'Never. He shouted at me a few times, but I wouldn't have stood for anything more. Saw my dad batter my mum when I was a kid and promised myself I wouldn't end up like her.' Jade sipped her coffee, her expression bleak. 'He threw her down the stairs in the end. She died, and he's still inside.'

'I'm sorry,' said Knight.

Jade blinked, then beamed at him. 'Not your fault, was it? Bet you don't thump your missus. Bet you've never hit anyone in your life.'

It was Knight's turn to smile. 'Not since I was at school,' he said.

'Not even then, I reckon.' Jade focused on him, ignoring Catherine completely. Was this going to be her tactic to avoid their questions? Try to flirt with Knight, hoping to charm him? Catherine knew it wouldn't work, but Jade didn't.

'Did Andy ever get involved in violence?' Catherine asked.

Jade glanced at her. 'I've just said, he never touched me, not like that.'

'I don't mean towards you. I mean in general. Did he get into any fights?'

'Fights? Not that he told me about.' Jade looked puzzled.

'No brawling, no arguments when he was out drinking? You know how lads can be when they've had a few.' Catherine was trying to be matey, but Jade wasn't having any of it, her face now blank.

'No. At least, he never said so. Is this about him being murdered? You're trying to find out if he had enemies?'

'Did he?' Knight asked.

'No.' Jade set her cup on the carpet by her feet and sat with her knees together, her hands folded in her lap. 'Listen, I lived with him for a few months about four years ago, and I've no idea what he's been up to since. You're talking the wrong person.'

Catherine said nothing, allowing the silence to stretch while Knight eased himself back and focused on his mug of tea.

Jade looked at him. 'Is that it?'

Finishing her coffee, Catherine took a coaster from the pile on the side table beside her and set the empty cup down.

'Did Andy work when he lived here?' she asked.

Jade flushed. 'I didn't claim anything I wasn't entitled to if that's what you're implying.'

'I don't care about your benefits, Jade. Did Andy have a job?'

Jade wound a strand of hair around her forefinger. 'He did a few hours at a scrapyard sometimes. Casual, cash in hand. Did some removal work too, when they needed an extra man.'

'Do you remember the name of the removal company?' Catherine asked.

'Sorry.'

'What was the scrapyard called?' As yet none of the local scrapyards had confirmed that Andy was working for them recently, and it might be the same place.

Jade stared. 'No idea. I don't even know where it was. There was a bloke called Vic involved.'

'Vic...?'

'Andy never told me his surname, and I didn't ask. I didn't want to know.' Jade glared at her feet, chewing her bottom lip as though regretting her words. Catherine decided to let her stew.

'Vic. Okay, thanks. We'll find him,' she said.

Another pause, this one even longer than the last. Eventually, Knight cleared his throat.

'Jade? Why didn't you want to know?'

Reddening again, Jade folded her arms. 'What do you mean?'

'You said you didn't want to know Vic's last name.' Knight lifted his shoulders, tipped his head to one side, deliberately casual. 'I wondered why.'

'I don't...' She didn't complete the sentence, shooting a look at Catherine that was hard to read. Was it a plea? Jade didn't want to discuss what she had said, and they all knew it.

Knight's smile was friendly, his tone not changing. 'Because you could have just left it at "I never asked", but you didn't.'

Jade's mouth worked. 'Yeah, well, I didn't mean anything by it.'

'Didn't you like Vic?' Knight spoke gently, as though Jade would be doing them both a favour if she confided in him. She shook her head like a stubborn toddler.

'I never met the bloke.'

'Then what was your problem with him?'

Jade stood abruptly, as though she was going to storm out. Her hands went to her hips as she glared down at Knight.

'I've already told you, Andy hasn't been part of my life for years. Why should it matter if I liked or disliked his boss back then?'

Unruffled, Knight looked up at her. 'It probably doesn't, but this is a murder investigation. Knowing as much as we can about Andy will help us find the person who killed him.'

'Really?' Jade sneered. 'Has anyone told you what he was like?'

Knight shrugged. 'Why don't you tell us?'

Her head dropped, all the fight leaving her. She trudged back to the sofa and curled up again. 'We had a good time at first. Andy had loads of money, or at least more than anyone else I knew. We'd take the kids to the seaside, have fish and chips and ice cream. It was... It probably doesn't sound like much to you, but to me, to my children...'

'He was good to you all. Generous.' Catherine spoke softly.

'Yeah.' Jade's voice was choked now, tears beginning to fall. She scrubbed at her eyes. 'I didn't ask where the money was coming from. We were happy, and I didn't want to rock the boat.'

'How old was Andy when you met him?'

'What do you mean? I knew him at school.'

Bingo, thought Catherine. 'And when you got together?'

'Seventeen, eighteen?'

Catherine told herself to tread carefully. 'Are you older than Andy?'

Jade scowled. 'Eighteen months or so. Does it matter?'

'You say you knew him at school. What was he like back then?'

'Like? He was… just Andy. A mate, a laugh. I don't know what you mean.'

'He was a mate. Would you say you knew him well at school?' Knight asked.

Jade's eyes flicked between him and Catherine. 'Not especially. I knew his name. You don't tend to bother with younger kids when you're a teenager, do you?'

'How did you get together?' Catherine asked.

Jade smiled a little at the memory. 'He asked to be my friend on Facebook. I accepted him, he sent me a direct message and it went from there. Before I knew it, he was moving in.'

'Was he the person you remembered?'

'What do you mean?' Jade looked bemused.

'Andy's parents say he changed around that age. Said he had wanted to go to university, but he decided not to.' Knight shook his head. 'I wondered whether you had any thoughts? You lived with him, and who talks to their parents at that age?'

Jade snorted. 'Not Andy, not to his mum at least. His dad was okay, from what he said.' She rubbed her eyes again. 'I don't think it was complicated. Andy had earned some money after his exams, working at the scrapyard. He knew if he carried on studying, he'd go back to having no cash, so he changed his mind. His parents didn't like it, and so he left home. There's no mystery.'

'And we're back to the scrapyard. Back to Vic,' Knight said.

'Like I said, I didn't ask Andy about his work.'

'Did he work nights?' Catherine asked.

'Sometimes.' Jade sniffed. 'Usually, I suppose.'

'And you didn't think that was strange?'

'Why?'

'A scrapyard that was open all night?' Catherine raised her eyebrows.

Jade stared. 'Open all... I'm sorry, you've misunderstood. Andy sat in a shed, walked the perimeter once an hour and kept an eye on the place. He was security, that's all.'

'A teenaged lad doing security work?' Knight's tone made it clear how unlikely it sounded.

Jade bristled. 'Why not? All you need is a pair of eyes and a phone. It's not like there was ever any trouble.'

'As far as you know,' Catherine said.

'Andy never mentioned any. Like I said, we weren't together long.'

'Come on, Jade, you have to admit it sounds unlikely. Why would a scrapyard need security?' Knight asked.

'I've no idea. Ask Vic, or...' Jade stopped, blinked. 'I was going to say ask Andy.'

Catherine gave her a second. 'When DI Knight asked if you thought Andy changed once he'd left school, you didn't really answer the question. Can I ask again?'

'Look, I don't know what you want me to say. Andy's parents, his mum especially, had big plans for him. University, a career, no doubt a suitable marriage eventually. The only thing was, they forget to ask Andy what he wanted. Turns out he had different ideas.'

'You never heard about any trouble Andy might have been in at that age? Anything that might have happened to him?' Catherine was beginning to feel they were heading nowhere with this line of questioning, but she had to ask.

'No. Nothing.' Jade rubbed her cheek, moving restlessly. 'Is this going to take much longer? I've an assignment to finish.'

Knight stood, and Catherine followed his lead.

'If you think of anything that might help us…'

'I'll get in touch. Northolme police station?'

Knight nodded, made his way to the door, Catherine on his heels. Jade trailed behind them, her arms wrapped around her body. She looked stricken now, her smile tremulous as she watched them walk down her path and over to the car. She lifted a hand, stepped back and closed her front door.

Knight said he would drive and as she reached for her seatbelt, Catherine imagined Jade going back to her books and notes, maybe remembering the young man who had once made her and her children smile as she picked up her pen.

'She didn't tell us much,' Knight said as he took off the handbrake.

'No.' Catherine touched a finger to her bottom lip. 'Maybe she's right, and Andy just changed his mind about uni.'

'Security at a scrapyard though?' Knight said. 'Something dodgy there, I think. We need to find this place.'

'Jade might have been lying, or maybe Andy lied to her about where he was spending his evenings.' Catherine frowned. 'Did you get the feeling Jade wasn't being honest with us?' She wasn't sure, remembering the impression of Jade she'd had at first – that she was nervous, apprehensive. It could mean nothing; most people would feel the same if the police turned up at their door.

'Evasive, maybe. We should keep it in mind,' Knight said.

'True. Okay, I'll get someone onto tracking down Vic and the mysterious scrapyard, as well as finding out if any assaults similar to the one on Rebecca Clough have been reported.'

Catherine reached for her phone.

—

Rebecca Clough, the woman they now believed had been attacked in her home by Andy Nugent, lived five miles away from Northolme itself. The road to the village ran alongside the River Trent, and the Cloughs' house overlooked the water. It was a stone cottage, in the centre of a block of three. In the small front garden, the grass needed cutting while the hedge was threatening to take over. Catherine could understand gardening hadn't been a priority for a while.

As Knight bumped the car up the kerb, Catherine saw a movement in the window beside the front door. It was already opening as they walked up the cracked concrete path. The woman who stood watching them was around five foot three, and slight. Her blonde hair hung around her face and she pushed a hand through it as they reached her. Knight hung back, allowing Catherine to take the lead and she understood why. After her experience, there was a possibility Rebecca Clough would be uneasy of a man she didn't know entering her home. Knight was making himself as unobtrusive as possible.

'You're the police?' Rebecca Clough's voice was quiet, tinged with anxiety. She spoke slowly, her eyes passing over Catherine's face, then skittering away. Was it shyness, reluctance, or fear?

'That's right, Mrs Clough.' Catherine introduced them, held out her identification. 'Thank you for agreeing to see us.'

The woman nodded, stepping away from the door, allowing them into a narrow hallway. She waved towards the nearest door, the movement jerky, almost hesitant, as though now they were here she had changed her mind about speaking to them.

'They said on the phone it was important,' she said.

They were in the living room. A log burner blazed in the brick fireplace that took up most of one wall, the room hot and stuffy. Bookcases covered two of the walls, while the largest keyboard Catherine had even seen stood against the third. A brown leather sofa was in the centre of the floor, as though providing somewhere to sit had been an afterthought. The book Rebecca Clough had been reading when she'd seen them arrive rested on the arm of the sofa, bookmark sticking out, marking her place. *Wolf Hall*. Catherine had read it and tried to think of something to say about it to break the ice. Rebecca Clough stood staring around as though she had never been in the room before, and it was disconcerting. It crossed Catherine's mind she could be on some kind of medication. After her ordeal and subsequent suicide attempt, it would be no surprise. Catherine thought about the boxes of tablets in her own bathroom cupboard. She had been reluctant to take them at first, but she had come to realise they had calmed her mind, allowed her some space to begin to recover. She recognised now she had been fragile before going undercover, and that taking on the role had been a mistake. Now though, she was learning to manage her illness, and she had Isla to help her. Without that case, they wouldn't have met, but watching Rebecca Clough now brought back the sense of dread and despair, the physical sensations she could never had imagined a mental illness would cause – snakes curling and writhing beneath her skin, the clenched stomach and dry mouth. The panic, the urge to run. Feeling her heartbeat quicken, Catherine took a couple of deep breaths. She saw Knight glance at her but she didn't meet his eyes as she steadied herself.

'Mrs Clough?'

Catherine spoke as gently as she could, but the woman still jumped as though she'd been slapped.

'Sorry, I was miles away,' she said immediately. 'I'll make some tea.'

Catherine moved a step closer, ready to move away if Rebecca seemed obviously uncomfortable.

'We've just had a cup, thank you, so we won't trouble you. Would it be okay if we sat down?'

'Yes, I...' Rebecca looked flustered. 'Please do.' She drifted over to the sofa, and hesitated, realising there wouldn't be room for the three of them unless they sat in each other's laps. Pretending not to see her blushing, Catherine sat at one end of the settee, while Knight moved over to the keyboard and pointed at the stool that was pushed under the stand.

'You sit with DS Bishop, Mrs Clough. I'll be over here, if that's okay? Do you play, or is this your husband's?'

Rebecca sat, twisting her neck to look at him, her cheeks still pink. 'It's mine. Dale has a guitar, but he's never really learnt to play it.'

There was no judgement in her tone, just affection. Mentioning her husband had strengthened her voice, focused her thoughts. She turned back to Catherine and said, 'How can I help you?'

Catherine saw the resolve in her face. Rebecca Clough knew she was going have to talk about her ordeal, and she was determined to get through it. Catherine respected that and warmed to her.

'It's just a chat really,' she said. 'We've read your state-ment, and we'd like to go through what happened again if we may. I know it's difficult…'

Rebecca kept her gaze fixed on the fireplace. 'You've been told about the overdose.'

'Yes,' Catherine said gently. Rebecca gave a slow nod, her jaw tightening.

'You're probably wondering why I waited so long? The… It happened two years ago, after all.'

'That's none of our business. We wanted to ask about the man who attacked you,' said Knight. 'What you can remember about him, if he spoke to you.'

Rebecca turned to look at him. 'I told them everything I could remember at the time. They took the bedding away. I saw a doctor – she was kind, but I didn't want her to touch me…' A tear escaped, slid slowly down her cheek. She didn't seem to feel it, did nothing to prevent it falling onto the collar of her shirt. Another followed, darkening the pale blue material to navy as they landed.

'As I said, we've read the reports, but there are some questions we'd like to ask you,' Catherine said. 'There's no hurry, and we don't want to cause you any more pain.'

Rebecca fumbled in her pocket now, bringing out a folded tissue and wiping her eyes. 'All right.'

'Thank you,' Catherine said. 'You said in your state-ment you didn't see your attacker's face. You couldn't describe his build, his height, or anything about him. I know it's difficult, but is there anything you can add now?'

'Now? After two years?' Rebecca stared at her. 'Why would there be?'

'Sometimes things come back to people that they didn't remember at the time. When you gave your statement, you were physically hurt, understandably traumatised…' Catherine allowed her voice to trail away. What was she talking about? Why should Rebecca remember any more now?

The other woman's lip curled slightly. 'Why didn't someone come back to take another statement then? What, when I'd calmed down? Is that what you mean?'

'Not at all,' Catherine said hastily. 'We're aware how difficult it can be to remember exactly what happened immediately after an incident, that's all.'

Rebecca's laugh was scornful. 'You think so? Except I relive it whenever I try to sleep, when I'm trying to relax in my own bed. Every time I hear an unfamiliar sound, every time my husband tries to touch me…' Her voice disappeared. She closed her eyes, her arms tight around her body. When she spoke again, it was in a completely different tone, her voice now harsh and unflinching. 'I remember every detail. That's the problem.'

'You fought the man who attacked you,' Knight said. 'Did he speak?'

'No. At least, he made a few noises as I tried to push him off me. Grunts and groans, nothing I could recognise, if that's what you mean.'

Knight nodded. 'And nothing was stolen?'

'No. We assumed he… We think he only came into the house with one thought in mind, and it wasn't burglary.' Rebecca's eyes were bright with tears, but she was in control again. Catherine sat silently, content to let Knight do the talking, especially since Rebecca seemed to be responding better to him.

'Okay, thank you. As you know, a glove was found in your bedroom after the attack. Can you tell us about that?' Knight asked.

Catherine knew DNA had been recovered from the glove, but it would take time for it to be matched to Andy Nugent's profile. She heard Rebecca swallow, saw her take a shuddering breath. Her hands clenched around each other in her lap.

'I... Do I have to?'

'I realise it's extremely painful, but we wouldn't ask if we didn't have a good reason,' Knight told her.

Rebecca sat up a little. 'You mean you might know who he is?'

Knight paused. 'We have lines of enquiry to follow.'

'Meaning you've still no idea,' Rebecca said softly. 'When I woke, he was on top of me, his knees digging into my thighs. I could smell him – cigarettes on his breath, and wet clothing. Wet wool, something like that. Maybe it was his jumper – I know he was wearing one, it was rough against my skin. His hands... They were around my throat. I was terrified. I grabbed his fingers, but he was wearing gloves – they felt like leather. It was too dark to see anything. I tried to pull him away, but he was so strong. I began to scream, knew I had to defend myself, tried to sit up and throw him off. He hit me then, punched me in the face – twice. Then he... It was as though he fell back. It was dark, I couldn't see, and the pain... By the time I'd managed to sit up, he was gone. He ran.'

Knight was nodding, encouraging her to keep going. 'You fought back, and he gave up.'

Rebecca glared. 'You mean people who don't fight deserve what they get?'

'Not at all.' Knight spoke calmly.

'It was instinctive. I didn't think about what I was doing, I just... I wasn't going to lie there and let him do whatever he wanted.'

Catherine took out her phone, found the photograph they had of Andy Nugent. She held it out to Rebecca.

'Have you ever seen this man?' She watched Rebecca's face, waiting to see if there was any recognition there. She saw nothing. Rebecca leaned closer to the screen, her eyes widening now, though Catherine thought she was curious, not shocked. She didn't believe Rebecca recognised Andy Nugent.

'Is he the one you think attacked me?' she demanded.

'We just want to know if you've seen him before,' Catherine said.

Rebecca stared at the image. 'I don't know. Can I hear his voice?'

Catherine thought quickly, not wanting to tell Rebecca Andy Nugent was dead. If the journalist, Helen Bridges, had her way, his face would be all over the news soon enough. 'There may be a chance we could find a recording.' Maybe there would be video footage of Andy on his or Hollie's phone. It was a long shot, but they could hope.

'But not now?' Rebecca asked.

'I'm afraid not.'

Rebecca stuck out her chin. 'Then I don't know. He seems familiar, but...'

'If your attacker didn't speak...?' Knight said.

'He didn't, but like I said, he groaned, he made sounds... I thought I might recognise something.' Rebecca flushed. 'I just want to help.'

Knight smiled. 'We know. Thank you.'

'What has he done?' Rebecca demanded. She folded her arms across her chest, looking at Catherine and then at Knight. 'The man in the photograph, I mean.'

'Why do you think he's done anything?' Knight asked mildly.

'It stands to reason, doesn't it? He must have done something similar, or why else would you be asking me? Has he hurt someone? Has he...' She gulped.

'He's dead,' Knight told her gently. She stared at him, mouth open, then began to cry – sobbing uncontrollably, as though Andy Nugent had been a relative.

'Thank you for telling me,' she managed to say eventually. As Rebecca wept into her hands, Catherine frowned at Knight, wondering why he'd told her. He gave a tiny shrug, and she guessed what he meant – Rebecca would soon know anyway, as soon as she switched on the TV, looked at the news online or picked up a newspaper. Better they break it to her now. But she hadn't recognised Andy Nugent's face, Catherine would swear it, even though she had said he looked familiar. She could have seen him around town, in a shop or supermarket. He had been in her bedroom though – they had proof. Rebecca Clough admitted she had never seen the face of her attacker. Nugent's fingerprints placed him at the scene; it was probable that analysis of the DNA from the glove would too.

Rebecca wiped her face and gave them a shaky smile. 'I'm sorry. It's all... such a relief.'

'A relief?' Knight made it a question.

'Knowing he's gone, that he can't come back. I might be able to... start to put it behind me now.'

'Mrs Clough, we're not confirming this is the man who attacked you,' Knight said gently.

'I know you won't tell me, you can't, but why else would you be asking me if I recognise him?' Rebecca was pulling her phone from her pocket. 'I'll have to phone Dale, he'll be so—'

'No,' Catherine said, more sharply than she had intended. Rebecca Clough's tears had brought back more memories. She had been in Lincoln's city centre, exhausted, tears she couldn't control leaking from her eyes, her body heavy, the snakes writhing. Rebecca stared, her face crumpling.

'Why? What's the problem?'

'This is an ongoing investigation, Mrs Clough. We'll need to speak to your husband ourselves,' Catherine told her.

Rebecca's mouth closed, her lips trembling. 'But why? Why is this anything to do with us?'

Knight stood, fastening his jacket. 'Does your husband still work at the same place as he did at the time of the attack, Mrs Clough?'

'Yes, but… I don't understand.' She sounded plaintive, like a child whose day out had been cancelled for reasons they didn't understand.

'Thank you for your help today,' Catherine said, getting to her feet. Rebecca reached out as though she was going to grab Catherine's arm, stopping herself as she remembered who they were.

'Was this man murdered? Is that what this is all about?'

'We can't say any more, I'm afraid.' Knight was polite but firm. She followed them to the front door, opening it automatically. It had begun to rain, the path already damp, the overgrown garden shimmering.

'Do you know why I took the overdose?' she said as Catherine followed Knight out into the drizzle. Catherine paused, turned back as Knight kept walking.

'You don't need to—'

'Because I couldn't stand it any longer,' Rebecca whispered. 'Remembering his breath on my mouth, his fingers on my skin. His *filth* in my house, and in our bed. We were going to try for a baby this year. Now I can't stand my husband being close to me.'

'I'm—'

'Dale sleeps in the spare room, or I stay down here. I won't say I sleep on the sofa, because I don't. I lie awake, thinking, or I take enough pills to knock me out so I can forget for a while. Either way, we're not together. Dale and I… We're trying, but some days it feels like our relationship is ruined.' She took a breath. 'Ruined by *him*, because he thought he had the right to come into our house and do whatever he wanted. Take what he wanted. And he took – us. Me.'

'Mrs Clough—'

She smiled, her face cold and empty. 'If this is the man who attacked me, and he's dead, even if he was murdered, I can't say I'm sorry to hear it. Maybe now we'll find some peace.'

12

Knight was behind the wheel again. That day in Lincoln, he had found her, taken her back to their headquarters and begged her to go home, to walk away from her undercover assignment. She hadn't listened, wanting to stay until the operation was over. Perhaps that had been a mistake.

'Do you think she'll call her husband, warn him we're on our way?' Knight asked.

Catherine took out her phone, checked her emails. Nothing of note. 'Even though we asked her not to? Probably. I would, in her shoes.'

'What did you think of her?'

'She's... brittle. There's strength there, but I don't think it would take much more to destroy her completely.'

Knight nodded. 'It's understandable after what she's been through. What did she say to you as we left? I didn't like to wait, I thought she might talk more freely to you.'

'Really? I thought she responded better to you.' Catherine relayed Rebecca Clough's comments about Andy Nugent stealing her relationship and future. 'She also said if he was the man who attacked her, she wasn't sorry he was dead, and maybe she and her husband would be able to find some peace now.'

As they approached a roundabout, Knight braked. 'We have to consider them as suspects for now.'

Catherine screwed up her face. 'I'd swear she didn't recognise Andy Nugent when I showed her the photograph of him. Like we said before, how would they have found out who he was?'

'Maybe she bumped into him somewhere, recognised his voice or something else about him.'

'It's possible, I suppose. Wait a second, she mentioned his smell, didn't she? Cigarettes and wet clothes. What if she was behind him in a queue or something, caught the scent of his clothes? You know how smells can trigger memories. I know it's far-fetched, but...'

Knight changed gear and they moved off again. 'Even if she did, it's a huge leap from recognising him to going to his house and killing him.'

'Maybe she followed him, made sure he was the right person.' Catherine heard the doubt in her own voice. 'Oh, I don't know. Nothing makes sense about this case.'

'From what we've discovered so far, Andy Nugent could have hurt a lot of people, not just his girlfriend. Someone could have been trying to work out who he was, to track him down for months, even years. We don't know if Rebecca Clough was his first victim, but I doubt it.'

'Then we're back to the idea he was killed by someone he's attacked, or a relative of a victim.' She pulled her phone from her pocket. The call was answered quickly, the noise of the incident room almost drowning out DC Anna Varcoe's greeting. Catherine fought the urge to ask how Anna was feeling. Being constantly reminded of the stabbing she'd suffered three months before wouldn't help her on her return to work, as Catherine understood. Instead, Catherine explained what she wanted to know, and waited as Anna found the information.

'Okay, there are two other possibilities,' Anna said.

'Really?' Catherine was shocked. 'Three occasions where someone in our area's woken to find an intruder in their bedroom?'

'You were expecting more?' Anna sounded surprised.

'No, I was hoping there weren't any at all. They can't have all been in town, we'd have remembered.'

'One in Northolme itself, one in Lincoln, then the incident involving Rebecca Clough a few miles away.'

'When were they reported?'

Anna paused then said, 'All within the last five years.'

'None before then? You're sure?' Catherine knew Anna would have checked but remembering what people had said about Andy Nugent changing around his sixteenth birthday, she wanted to be sure. Perhaps he had carried out his first burglary and assault then.

'The first one in Lincoln was early 2013, the victim a forty-five-year old nurse. The next was 2016 – that was the attack on Rebecca Clough. The third was in December last year. That was a woman in her late fifties. She lived on the outskirts of Northolme – Osborne Road.'

Catherine shook her head, imaging the terror and confusion she would feel herself if woken by an intruder. She remembered Rebecca Clough's haunted eyes, her jittery movements.

'And all these incidents had similarities with the one reported by Rebecca Clough?'

'Yeah, except there were no fingerprints found in the other cases. The intruder didn't speak, and they didn't see his face. Barely saw more than a shadow. No descriptions at all to speak of.'

'Did the other two women live alone?'

'Yep.'

Catherine nodded to herself. 'How old is Rebecca Clough? Late twenties?'

There was another brief pause as Anna checked. 'She would have been at the time of the attack. She's thirty-one now.'

'Quite a range in the ages of the victims then.'

'Do you think that's important?'

'Not sure. What about sexual assault?' Catherine hoped not. 'Rebecca Clough seems to believe Nugent broke in intending to rape her. He was on top of her when she woke up.'

'According to the other victims, he never got anywhere near them. He fled as soon as he realised they were awake.'

Catherine mulled it over. 'Maybe he realised Rebecca was still asleep and decided to take his chance.' She shuddered. 'Was anything taken from the other houses?'

'Yes and no,' said Anna. 'He managed to grab the older woman's purse on his way out of her bedroom. A bunch of keys were found in the hallway in the nurse's house in Lincoln even though they'd been left on a hook. Either he snatched them and dropped them, or he knocked them off the hook as he ran.'

'She kept her keys on a hook by the front door?' Catherine blinked.

'Apparently so: house and car keys, even the one that unlocked her shed. Good thing he didn't actually nick anything, the insurance company would have laughed at her.'

'How did he get into the properties?'

'The place in Lincoln, he smashed a panel in the back door – it was locked, but the key had been left in the lock on the inside. The older lady had forgotten to lock her back door.'

Catherine felt a tug of sympathy. 'I bet she remembers now.'

'You'd hope so, though it's easily done. At Rebecca Clough's house, he stuck his arm through a small window they'd left open and opened the larger window.'

'Opportunistic then. I can't imagine he knew their habits unless he watched them for a while first.'

'Nothing to suggest that from what I've seen,' Anna said. 'Although he might have known Rebecca Clough's husband was at work when he broke in there. Maybe he was just lucky, but...'

But they both knew better than to assume.

'Okay, thank you.' Catherine chewed on her bottom lip. 'Three incidents over five years... That's – thankfully – quite a gap between each one.'

There was a pause. 'You think other incidents might have gone unreported?'

Catherine shrugged, even though Anna couldn't see her. 'Maybe, or maybe this was nothing to do with Andy Nugent but it's a burglar who attacks women if he finds them alone. Can you find out if there have been similar incidents reported elsewhere, please?'

'No problem,' Anna said. 'I'll email you what I've got so far. Do you want someone to go and speak to the other victims involved?'

'Maybe, but not yet. Keep digging around though, please. We're going to see Dale Clough now. Maybe he'll be able to help us. I'll see you at the briefing later. Cheers, Anna.' She ended the call.

'Three,' Knight said. He too sounded appalled. 'We need to follow up on them, however unlikely it is they're involved.'

'Agreed.' Catherine knew they had no choice, but the argument was the same – if any of these women had recognised Andy Nugent as the man who had been in their home, why would they confront him instead of contacting the police? 'I think it's a dead end though – Rebecca Clough was almost destroyed by what happened to her. I can't imagine either of the other women marching up to Andy Nugent's front door to attack him, can you?'

'No, but they'll have family, friends. Some people still live by an eye for an eye. Let's see what Dale Clough has to say for himself.'

Clough owned a company that restored and maintained classic cars. His premises were over on the same industrial estate where Catherine had kept watch with Nat Roberts for the arsonist. As Catherine and Knight crossed the car park, a huge shuttered door screeched open. Inside they could see a workshop, crowded with vehicles in various states of repair. A man strode towards them. He was dressed in dark green overalls, around six feet tall and solidly built with blond hair cut close to his scalp. He had a huge beard, and he ran a hand over it as he moved towards them.

'I think you're here to see me?' He spoke politely but didn't smile.

'Mr Clough?' Knight held out his identification as he introduced them. 'Did your wife inform you we were on our way?'

Clough had the grace to blush. 'She sent me a text, yeah. Wouldn't you have done?' He looked at Catherine as he spoke, and she stared back at him.

'Definitely,' she said.

Clough smiled. 'We understand each other then. What happened that night...' He tugged at his beard. 'I blame myself. If I'd been there...'

'You were working on the night of the break-in?' Knight said.

Clough's eyes narrowed. 'The "break-in"? You mean the night that bastard came into our house to rape Rebecca?'

'Mr Clough—'

'Because that's what he wanted.' Clough's face was red, his fists clenched by his side. 'That's what he was there for. To hurt her, terrorise her. And he did, even if she fought him off.' He stared at his boots. 'And yes, I was working late, really late. I had a customer, more money than sense, and he wanted a rebuild doing as quickly as we could, willing to pay way over the odds if we could do it. I was doing eighteen-hour days, planned to have a fortnight's holiday once it was done.'

'We realise it was a terrible ordeal for your wife,' Catherine said gently. In the workshop behind Clough, three mechanics were pretending they weren't listening. 'Is there somewhere we can talk privately?'

Clough turned, and the men averted their eyes, bent their heads closer to the car they were supposed to be working on.

'We can use my office,' Clough said, scowling. Catherine and Knight followed him into the building. 'Watch yourselves,' he warned as they passed a rack of tyres. A corner of the workshop had been bricked off, and Clough beckoned them inside. There was a battered wooden desk and office chair with a laptop on it at one end, a scruffy sofa and coffee table at the other. Behind the door were a couple of cupboards and a length of work surface providing a small kitchen area. There was a sink, a tiny fridge, a kettle and a microwave, with an assortment of crockery and cutlery waiting to be washed in a bowl. Clough washed his hands then grabbed the kettle and filled it at the tap.

'Bloody Ollie, I've told him to stop leaving his dirty pots in the sink.' He took three clean mugs from one of the cupboards. 'Tea or coffee?'

Knight went for coffee, while Catherine asked for tea. Dale Clough appeared tense and she hoped the familiar ritual of making the drinks would calm him. Clough nodded, squatting to retrieve tea bags and a jar of coffee from a cupboard.

'Is this your own business?' Catherine asked, raising her voice over the hiss and rumble of the kettle. They already knew it was, but she wanted to keep him talking.

Clough pushed his hands into his overall pockets. 'That's right. My dad started it thirty years ago.'

'Looks as though you're busy. What exactly do you do here?' Catherine wanted to keep him talking.

'We specialise in classic cars, anything from a full rebuild to a service. We've made a name for ourselves over the years; we ship parts all over the world.' He nodded towards the workshop. 'I employ three people and give myself and Rebecca a decent life.' His voice was flat, as though he took no pride in his achievements.

'Your wife no longer works?' Knight asked. Clough swallowed.

'She's more or less housebound, so no. She's on antidepressants that do nothing, and knowing the man responsible has never been caught doesn't help.' The kettle was still gurgling, and in the end, he snatched it up and poured water into the cups though it hadn't quite boiled. He slopped milk into their drinks and handed them over. 'Are you going to tell me what's going on? Rebecca said in the text that you showed her a photo.'

Catherine blew across the surface of her tea, waiting for Knight to take the lead, but he was silent.

'A man was found dead last night,' she said. 'You may have seen the story in the news?'

'No.' There was no curiosity in Dale Clough's voice. 'The lads were going on about some bloke on the Meadowflower dying, but I didn't take any notice. Load of smackheads up there, it's not surprising.'

Catherine took out her phone, showed him the picture of Andy Nugent. Clough gave it a careless glance then stared, his mouth working.

'Is this the bastard that hurt my wife?' He made as though to snatch the phone from Catherine's hand, but she pulled it away.

'We just want to know if you recognise him,' she said. Clough took a step towards her, his face thunderous.

'What's his name?'

'Do you recognise him, Mr Clough?' Catherine was sure Clough didn't. Like his wife, he'd shown no reaction to the photograph, not until he'd guessed why they were asking about Nugent.

'What does it matter? If he's the one who broke into my house, I want to know his name. Wait a minute… is he the bloke who's been found dead?'

'Yes.' Again, Catherine watched Clough's face.

'Couldn't happen to a nicer person then, could it?' He smirked at Catherine. 'One less for us taxpayers to keep in prison.'

'It can't have been easy for you since your wife was attacked.' Knight moved away from the wall where he'd been standing. He set his mug on the worktop. 'We saw how much she's been struggling.'

Clough looked bullish. 'What do you expect?'

'Has she seen a doctor, a counsellor?'

'Yeah, like I said, she's on medication but...' Clough shuffled his feet. 'Nothing seems to help. I've fitted bolts on the doors; we had new locks on the windows. If I'm working late, I go home to eat with Rebecca, then bring her back here to stay with me. She's bad enough during the day, but at night...' He shook his head. 'She's terrified.'

'Do you think not knowing who was responsible caused her more distress?' Knight asked.

'Pretty obvious, isn't it? If he was in prison, he couldn't come back. If he's still out there...' Clough gulped. 'I wish I'd been there when you talked to her. Think I'll close up early today, make sure she's okay.'

Catherine realised the cause of his belligerence hadn't been unwillingness to speak to them, but the fear of what he might find when he got home.

'Did you find your wife when she overdosed, Mr Clough?' she asked.

He stared at her. 'Why are you asking?'

'It must have been a terrible shock.'

He ran a hand over his mouth. 'You think? Realising my wife would rather have been dead than carry on living with her pain? Yeah, it was horrible, almost as bad as when it first happened. I realised I needed to take better care of Rebecca.' He pointed over his shoulder with his thumb. 'I was spending too long here, trying to put what had happened out of my mind. I'd forgotten Rebecca needed me, was thinking too much about myself.' He pressed his lips together.

'And you're concerned us speaking to her will upset her even more?' Catherine asked.

'Wouldn't you be?'

She nodded. 'If there was any way to have avoided it, we wouldn't have troubled her. But a man's dead, and we need to find out what happened.'

'Am I a suspect?' Clough demanded.

'Why would you assume—' Knight began.

'Two detectives turn up asking questions about the attack on my wife, then show me photo of a murdered man? Doesn't take much working out, does it?'

'We didn't say he'd been murdered,' Knight said. There was no accusation in his tone, but Clough bridled again anyway.

'Trying to trip me up, are you? Catch me out? It won't work. I've never seen that man before, and anyone who says I have is lying. When did he die?' Clough's hands were on his hips, his chin thrust forward, mouth screwed tight.

'Yesterday evening,' Catherine told him.

'Really?' Clough smiled. 'Well, I was here until six with the lads, went home, had a shower, changed my clothes and then took Rebecca out for a meal. It's taken me weeks to persuade her – we've only been out in the evening a few times since the attack. There are twenty or so people who'll confirm we were sitting in the bar of our local between seven thirty and closing time.'

'Which pub?' Catherine asked.

'The Ship, in our village.' He looked almost smug. 'Hopefully that puts us both out of it?'

Catherine raised her chin. 'Thank you, Mr Clough.'

He nodded. 'Have the pair of you heard enough? Because I've work to do.'

'We'll be in touch if we need to speak to you again,' Knight said. Clough wrenched open the door and marched them out, not bothering to wait for them to follow him.

'Yeah? I'll look forward to it.'

13

When Catherine and Knight arrived back at the station, DCI Kendrick's office door was closed. Knight disappeared into his own office as Catherine dropped into her chair and rubbed her eyes. She picked up her desk phone and dialled Mick's number. When she explained that the DCI wanted him to obtain Hollie Morton and Andy Nugent's children's DNA, Mick sounded unenthusiastic.

'Is it necessary?' he asked.

'Kendrick thinks so. If the baby, or either of the kids, aren't Andy's, we need to know about it. It could provide a motive for killing Hollie, Andy too.'

'Taking samples from such young children doesn't often happen in criminal cases, especially when they're not victims.' Mick was quiet for a few seconds. 'I'll need to look into how, or if, we can do this. Shall I come back to you, or direct to Kendrick?'

Catherine twirled a strand of hair around her finger. 'Probably best to speak to the DCI. If we can go ahead with it, he'll be able to approve it all straight away.'

'Will do.'

'Cheers, Mick.'

She replaced the receiver, worried by Mick's lack of conviction, but knowing it was out of her hands. There was plenty more going on that they needed to focus on.

'Anything on our mysterious scrapyard owner?' she called to Anna, who was at her desk.

'Not yet. The nearest scrap yard is ten miles away, and there only a few in the county. No mention of anyone called Vic owning any of them so far, but we've not finished going through the list yet. We're checking neighbouring counties too. Vic could have been a nickname, even an alias. Maybe he never existed. We checked with Andy's dad, and neither he nor his wife had heard anything about Andy working at a scrapyard.'

'His mum wouldn't have been happy.'

'I'll keep working on it.'

Catherine grinned. 'In other words, leave me alone so I can get on with it.'

Anna smiled back. 'You said it, I didn't.'

'Is the DCI in?'

'Just.' Anna grimaced. 'He didn't look happy.'

Kendrick's door flung open and he stomped out. 'Happy? I've long forgotten what that feels like.'

Anna disappeared behind her monitor. Catherine stood.

'How did the post-mortem go?' she asked Kendrick.

He lifted his eyebrows. 'About as fun-filled as they usually are. Where's Jonathan?'

'Here.' Knight hurried into the room, his mobile in his hand.

Kendrick raised his eyebrows again, nodded at the phone. 'Something urgent you need to tell us about?'

'It was personal. Sorry.' Knight met Kendrick's eyes, though his cheeks had reddened. Catherine felt a flash of anger. What did it matter if Knight took a couple of minutes to make a call? Kendrick was aware Jo had collapsed earlier. Why shouldn't Knight check on her? He hadn't even gone home last night. It wasn't as though he'd been skiving.

Kendrick crooked a finger. 'Come into my parlour. I need a quick word with you both.'

He held his office door wide, waited until Catherine and Knight were inside. 'Thank you.' He thumped the door closed, shouldered his way past them and sat, his chair creaking and groaning beneath him. 'Sit down, then,' he ordered. 'What have you found out?'

They updated him quickly, though Catherine was aware there wasn't much to tell. Kendrick shuffled in his seat.

'What did you find out during the post-mortem?' Catherine asked.

Kendrick picked up a glass of water from his desk and drank. 'It's a bloody nightmare.'

Catherine felt Knight shift in the seat beside hers. 'Meaning?'

'Meaning, Scott Greaves, the man who we found dead at the scene of the latest so-called arson attack, was already dead when his office was set alight. Meaning, the pathologist – our new friend Dr Kirby – tells me Greaves was killed between six and midnight last night. I'll spare you the details of a post-mortem conducted on a man who looked like a Sunday joint halfway through roasting – you can read the full report. Suffice to say, Greaves didn't have a chance to die of smoke inhalation.'

Catherine gawped at him. 'He was already dead? Then the fire was set to cover up the murder?'

'Possibly.' Kendrick checked his watch. 'But there's a chance this particular blaze wasn't the work of our arsonist after all. Maybe whoever killed Greaves just borrowed the idea.'

'What did Dr Kirby say about Andy Nugent?' Catherine asked.

'Nugent also died between the hours of six and midnight. As Jo suspected, the blow to the back of his head killed him. Kirby couldn't find anything in the wound to suggest what caused it, as you might if he'd been hit by a wooden baseball bat or something that might leave traces behind, so it's possible he did crack his head on the toilet. There was blood on it, after all, but we need to know whose it was.'

'What about the belt around his neck?' Knight said.

Kendrick shrugged. 'We don't know. All Kirby could say was that it didn't contribute to Nugent's death in any way. It hadn't been tightened; it was just hanging there. It's a weird one. Hopefully Mick will be able to get some fingerprints from it.'

'And if Andy's are on it, it must have been his,' Catherine said.

'Unless he was fighting his attacker as they put it around his throat,' Knight said. 'That could have been what caused him to fall and hit his head.'

'If it was Andy's there'll be loads of fingerprints, especially around the buckle. That wouldn't happen if he just grabbed it once.'

'Fair point.' Kendrick pinched his lower lip. 'Like we said before – best guess at the moment is Andy nips upstairs for a pee, one of the Dobson brothers goes into the kitchen and finds Hollie's body. He, or his brother, storm upstairs, whip off their belt and it's around Andy's throat before he has a chance to undo his fly. Andy tries to turn, they struggle, Andy falls and smacks his head. Whichever Dobson it was panics and runs, leaving his belt behind.'

'But if it had been looped it around Andy's neck intending to strangle him, wouldn't it have left a mark?'

Kendrick stared at her. 'Depends how quickly Andy turned around I suppose. We need answers from Mick.'

'We could also show the belt to Jamie and Cal Dobson, see what their reaction is?' Catherine suggested.

'Worth trying. We need to get them in anyway, for fingerprinting,' Kendrick said. 'Can you get that set up for tomorrow? Get Mick to send over some images of the belt.'

Catherine nodded. 'No problem.'

'What—' Knight coughed, cleared his throat, tried again. 'How did Greaves die?'

'According to Nathan Kirby, he was strangled.' Kendrick shrugged his massive shoulders. 'You can imagine the scene was too much of a mess to try to figure out what happened to him, much less what was used to do the deed, but Kirby says he was definitely dead before the fire started. It looks like he was strangled with rope or possibly some kind of cable. Whatever it was sliced through his windpipe.'

Catherine frowned. 'The killer didn't use his hands?' Not like Hollie Morton then.

'No, but Greaves was a different proposition altogether. Kirby says he was six feet tall, allowing for the effects of the fire on his body.' Kendrick grimaced.

Catherine frowned, shaking her head, finding it hard to take in. 'Cal and Jamie Dobson say Andy was still alive at eight when they left. So Scott Greaves probably died before Andy Nugent, but after Hollie Morton, who was also strangled.' She looked at Knight, then focused on Kendrick. 'You don't think...?'

Kendrick pushed back his chair and hauled himself to his feet. 'That Nugent killed him, or the person who killed Nugent also killed Greaves? Who knows? Though with the times of death we've been given, Greaves could also have killed Nugent. We have to consider the possibility there's a link, but as to what it could be, your guess is as good as mine.'

Knight groaned. 'We need to speak to almost everyone we've interviewed so far, again.'

'And I think we should start with Scott Greaves's wife, Ashley. We need to talk to her anyway, and if she tells us her husband knew Andy Nugent, we can consider focusing our enquiries in that direction,' Kendrick said. 'But it's always possible it's unrelated. We don't know anything about Greaves yet. There could be people queuing up to kill him for all we know.'

Catherine held a hand to her aching forehead. Their case was already complicated and confusing, and adding another murder to the mix wasn't going to make matters any easier, related or not.

'Maybe Andy, Hollie and Scott were at school together,' Catherine suggested. 'They're all the same age.'

'Let's find out.'

'Jade Walsh should be able to tell us,' Knight said. 'We need to dig into what she said about Andy Nugent doing some removal work too. Maybe there's an innocent explanation for his fingerprints being on the Cloughs' headboard.'

Kendrick's eyebrows bounced. 'Or a not so innocent one. Nugent could have met Rebecca when he moved them into their house, then been invited back to test the bed he'd lifted up the stairs. What do you reckon? You've met Rebecca Clough.'

'I think it's unlikely,' Catherine said. She didn't buy it at all.

Kendrick scowled. 'No? Better ask the Cloughs who helped them move then, and when. Who employed Andy Nugent to do this removal work?'

'Jade Walsh couldn't remember. It's on the list of stuff to follow up,' Catherine told him. 'We'll get Anna onto it tomorrow.' She eyed her boss, gauging his mood, which didn't seem as bad as Anna had suggested. 'You still think we're going to be able to run both enquiries alongside each other?' she asked Kendrick. He had his tissues out again, blowing his nose.

'Why? Don't you? I don't want to have to ask for help. We've already had a load of officers from Lincoln foisted on us that I didn't want. If I'd used them, got them to help us out, it would have proved we can't deal with this alone. Yes, at the moment we're stretched, as is every force in the country, every hospital, GP's surgery, school and ambulance service. You know how it is. We've a lot on, but we have to be seen to be coping, to prove we're needed here. Otherwise...' Kendrick didn't finish his sentence. He didn't have to. Otherwise, their station would be closed. A town the size of Northolme having its own team of detectives was unusual anyway. Resources were being shared, amalgamated; teams like the one Isla was part of, being created. It wasn't the first time they had spoken about the possibility of Northolme police station closing. Catherine had considered her options on more than one occasion, but she would prefer the decision to transfer to be one she made by choice, not through necessity.

'Does the Superintendent know Greaves was murdered?' Knight asked,

Kendrick snorted. 'She knew almost as soon as I did. She wanted to be briefed the second I left the mortuary. I assured her everything was in hand, but she might decide to pay us a visit in the morning to see for herself.' Kendrick took a deep breath. 'Seems as though we might be making space in our incident room for your pals from EMSOU after all, Catherine.' He glanced at his watch again. 'We're late for the briefing. Let's go and tell the troops the latest – our double murder, if that's what it is, is old news.'

-

The incident room was stuffy, the smells of coffee and food grabbed on the run lingering. Catherine spotted three different people yawning before she found a chair. Her colleagues were already beginning to feel the demands they knew the case would make on them. Eighteen-hour days, the case haunting the time you did manage to get home for some rest. No time to see your partner, your kids, or anyone not working on the investigation. Kendrick strode to the front of the room. Jonathan Knight joined him as Kendrick rocked back on his heels, waiting for quiet.

'Now I know it's been a long day, so let's get on with it,' he said. 'Firstly, I need to tell you about what came to light during the post-mortem of Scott Greaves.' He updated them quickly. 'This development will obviously mean we'll all have even more to do, but I know we can cope.' Surveying the faces in front of him, he managed a smile. 'I'm confident of putting the Hollie Morton and Andy Nugent case to bed over the next couple of days.'

'What about the arsonist? Is our surveillance going to continue?' Nat Roberts, seated on the front row, asked. Kendrick shook his head.

'No. We won't have the manpower, or the room in our budget. It's possible the fires will stop now, after the death of Scott Greaves. Whether the blaze at his premises was started to try to disguise his murder, or whether our arsonist set fire to the place not realising Greaves's body was already inside, we don't know.'

'Then we just wait and see if anywhere else goes up in smoke?' Nat wasn't going to let it go.

Kendrick grimaced. 'Do you have any better ideas? What else can we do?'

'I don't know, but it seems wrong to me to give him the opportunity to do whatever he likes.' Nat folded her arms, and Catherine waited for a withering comeback from Kendrick. He surprised her.

'I don't like it any more than you do, Constable, but I've no choice. We have to concentrate on the murders.' The DCI began to pace. 'DS Bishop, can you tell us about your conversations with Hollie Morton's family and the Dobson brothers, please? It's all on the briefing notes, but let's hear it from the horse's mouth.' He raised his eyebrows at Catherine. 'As it were.'

She moved to stand beside him and began to talk. Running through the main points of the interviews she and Knight had conducted, she was reminded again how little they had to go on. Everything they discovered or were told seemed to raise more questions. Kendrick listened, his eyes on the officers gathered in front of him, searching every face as Catherine finished speaking and took a seat in the front row. As Knight stepped in to update the team on the interviews they had conducted with Andy Nugent's parents, Jade Walsh, and Rebecca and Dale Clough, Catherine remembered the reserved, awkward man he had seemed when he had first arrived in

Northolme. He had seemed the most unlikely detective inspector she had ever met. Other officers had joked about him, doubting his suitability for the job. And yet, he had proved himself as well as supporting her through situations that might have had some officers turning their backs, more concerned for their own careers than being there for a colleague. She wouldn't forget that, whatever happened. If Northolme police station did close, as seemed likely sooner or later, she knew she could do much worse than follow Detective Inspector Jonathan Knight wherever he decided to go next.

'Next: Forensics. This won't take long, because as expected, we've had nothing back yet. Mick Caffery's doing everything he can, but we know it all takes time. The pathologists did remove some fibres, hairs and other potential evidence from both Hollie and Andy's bodies, but again we'll have to wait to see if anything they found can help us. We have Hollie and Andy's phones which are being examined and we've contacted the network for any information they can give us. As you're all only too aware, house-to-house enquiries have been ongoing all day, but so far, we haven't uncovered anything new. Thank you all for all the traipsing around and knocking on doors you've done. Hope you're looking forward to doing it all again tomorrow.' There were some good-natured groans.

Knight ended his update with a few words of encouragement to the team, and Kendrick took centre stage again.

'To summarise, we now have three victims. Hollie Morton and Scott Greaves were definitely murdered, Andy Nugent's death could have been accidental, but either way we need answers.'

'But Nugent could have killed them both?' Chris Rogers, one of the DCs, said. Kendrick blew out his cheeks.

'It's complicated, and we need to figure out the timings. That's work for tomorrow. It's obvious we have a lot to do, but I know you'll give everything you have.' He clapped his hands. 'Go and get some food and rest. I'll see you in the morning.'

As people began to file out of the room, Kendrick blocked Catherine's path.

'I suppose you were thinking about working late?'

She nodded. 'I'm sure you're going to?'

'But you're not. You were up all last night. Make the calls asking the Dobson brothers to come in tomorrow, then go home.' He nodded at Knight. 'You too. Neither of you will be any use to me if you're knackered.'

'But—' Knight began.

Kendrick shook his head. 'Get out of here, the pair of you. I don't want to see either of you before seven tomorrow morning.'

Knowing it was pointless to argue, Catherine went back upstairs. She called Jamie Dobson, who confirmed he and his brother would come into the station the following day, though he didn't sound happy about it.

'Coming to the pub?' Anna Varcoe asked as Catherine pulled her jacket on. 'Thomas is meeting us there, and Nat's bringing her fireman.'

Catherine smiled as she grabbed her bag. 'Can't say no then, can I? I'm not staying long though. I need to sleep.'

'Just one drink.' Anna checked her phone. 'Thomas is there already.'

'Ask him to get the beers in then.'

Catherine's brother, Thomas, was leaning on the bar when they arrived. He turned with a smile, his eyes immediately seeking out Anna. As she approached, he held out a glass of wine. She smiled as she took it from him, kissed his cheek.

'That's what I call service,' Nat Roberts said.

Thomas nodded at the line of drinks waiting for them. 'Pint of stout and packet of pork scratchings are yours, aren't they, Nat?'

She pulled a face at him. 'Very funny.'

He handed Catherine a bottle of alcohol-free lager, then held one out for Nat, knowing they would both be driving. 'Where's this new bloke of yours then?' he asked Nat.

She drank, set her bottle back on the bar. 'Thanks, Thomas. Jimmy's on his way.' She gave Thomas a shove. 'And you're a worse gossip than anyone at the station.'

Thomas met Catherine's eyes. 'You okay?'

She nodded. She hadn't thought about it on the drive through town, but this must be the same pub Dale Clough had mentioned he and his wife had spent the evening in. This was the village she and Knight had visited earlier, and as far as she was aware, there were no more pubs nearby. She smiled at her brother. Time to switch off. When she and Knight had been talking to Rebecca Clough earlier, her reaction to the other woman's distress had unsettled her. Knight had noticed, of course he had, but he had said nothing. Both things worried her. If there was any hint she was struggling, Knight would have to tell Kendrick, who would probably pick up on it anyway, even if Knight kept quiet. She was confused about her career, it was true, but she didn't want to be pushed out of the door and back onto sick leave either. It had been necessary before. She had been barely functioning, and in their job, that couldn't continue. Those feelings, the ones she had felt stirring when they had been at the Cloughs' house, couldn't be allowed to resurface. 'Just tired,' she told Thomas. 'How's the new job?'

He hesitated, and Catherine thought he was going to press her about how she was feeling, but in the end he didn't. 'Good, though I don't think my Year Elevens like me,' he said.

'Why? You've only been at the school a fortnight.'

He laughed. 'Had them playing hockey today when it started raining. You should have heard them moaning – worried about their hair, their trainers, their make-up.'

'You're enjoying it though?' Catherine looked at the bar as he nodded. 'I could fancy some crisps.'

'Why don't we stay, have some food? They do a decent meal here.' Thomas looked at Anna and Nat. 'What do you reckon?'

Anna slid her arm around his waist. 'Sounds good to me.'

'Here's Jimmy.' Nat ran a hand over her hair and smoothed her shirt as the door opened again and a man stepped into the room. He hesitated, glancing around. As he recognised Nat, he smiled and held up a hand. She hurried towards him, kissed his cheek.

'Wow. Where'd she find him?' Anna whispered to Catherine. Jimmy was a shade over six feet tall, a black fitted T-shirt and skinny jeans emphasising a lean physique.

'He fell off the back of a fire engine,' Catherine whispered.

Nat led him towards her friends and introduced them. Jimmy shook hands, his eyes never quite meeting anyone else's. Catherine hid a smile. No wonder Nat had asked for his phone number and not the other way around.

Thomas stepped forward. 'Can I get you a drink, Jimmy?'

The other man smiled. 'Cheers – just a Coke, thank you, I'm driving. I'll get the next round.'

Nat asked Jimmy about his day, and after a few sips of his drink, he seemed to relax, soon allowing Nat to lead him over to a table in the corner. She shuffled her chair close to his as they talked.

Thomas rolled his eyes. 'Do you reckon there's a chance she fancies him?'

Anna grinned. 'Can't blame her really.'

'Cheeky,' he said. 'Shall we sit down?'

Catherine hesitated, took out her phone. No messages. Seeing the closeness between Anna and Thomas, the chemistry between Nat and Jimmy, she missed Isla more than ever. Sitting around a table with two couples wasn't her idea of a good time, and she made her way over to them intending to make her excuses.

Nat had clearly guessed her intention and she pulled out a chair, handed Catherine a menu. 'Come on, Sarge, have a seat. I know you're knackered, but you have to eat.'

Catherine smiled as she sat down. 'Go on then.' What was waiting for her at home? An empty house and a microwave meal? She sat back, content to sip her drink and listen to them chatting. Her head ached, her eyes were scratchy. She needed to sleep.

'How long have you been a firefighter, Jimmy?' Anna asked.

'Almost ten years now. I joined as soon as I was old enough.'

Thomas set his empty bottle down on the table. 'Was it something you always wanted to do?'

He nodded. 'Following in my dad's footsteps. You could say it's the family trade.'

'Is he still in the service?' Nat asked.

Jimmy blinked. 'No, he... he died. Cancer.'

Nat looked stricken. 'I'm so sorry, I didn't—'

He turned to her, shaking his head. 'Don't worry about it. How could you have known? It's okay, honestly.' He reached for his glass, his eyes bleak for a second, but when he lifted his head again, he smiled at her. 'Shall I get some more drinks?'

Anna pushed back her chair. 'I'll come with you. May as well order the food while we're at the bar, if everyone's ready?'

When Jimmy and Anna were out of earshot, Nat whispered: 'What do you think?'

'Why don't you just sit on his lap and have done with it?' Thomas teased her.

Catherine gave him a playful push. 'Just because he's taller than you.'

Thomas laughed. 'So are most people. I'm used to it.'

'I think he's shy.' Nat watched Jimmy as he pulled his wallet from his jeans pocket.

'When you've brought three of your mates along on your first date?' Catherine said. 'I can't think why.'

'And two of them are police officers,' Thomas pointed out. 'Hardly going to make him relax, is it?'

Nat screwed up her face. 'Come on, he's used to coppers.'

'At work, yeah. Not watching his every move when he's with a woman he's trying to impress. Got to feel sorry for the bloke really.'

'He doesn't need to impress me.' Nat was still watching Jimmy as he and Anna ordered their drinks and food.

Thomas waited for Anna and Jimmy to sit back down and the drinks to be handed round before saying, 'The kids at school were talking about the arson attacks. One of them said her dad might lose his job because his lorry went up in flames.'

Catherine exchanged glances with Anna and Nat. 'We can't really—'

'Talk about it.' Thomas nodded. 'I know.' He looked at Jimmy. 'It must piss you and your colleagues off though? Risking your lives because a fire's been started deliberately?'

Jimmy nodded. 'But it's part of the job. We just deal with the blaze and ask questions later.'

'It's something that doesn't need to happen though. It's bad enough when a fire starts accidentally, but when it's because some arsehole decides to throw matches around...' Thomas shook his head.

'Yeah, especially if we've been called out because of arson and then there's another incident. It could mean a delay in response, units having to travel from further away.' Jimmy sipped his drink. 'That's when lives could be lost.'

'Like the bloke who was in the garage,' Thomas said.

Jimmy glanced at Nat, then at Anna and Catherine. 'Is there any progress? I'm not asking you to give me details, but we were talking about it back at the station and we're worried. Whoever's setting these fires knows what he or she's doing. They're intending to cause maximum damage.'

Catherine leaned forward. 'We'll get him.' She spoke with a confidence she didn't feel, but she wasn't going to tell Jimmy and everyone in the pub they'd no leads. 'I don't know how you do it, going into burning buildings when everyone else is running in the opposite direction.'

He smiled. 'Well, I wouldn't want to attend post-mortems or murder scenes either.'

'You have to attend RTAs too. I don't think your job is any easier than ours,' Nat said with a smile.

'Maybe not, but at least we don't have to deal with teenagers all day.' Jimmy wrinkled his nose at Thomas. 'Nat said you're a teacher? I wouldn't wish that on anyone.'

'Here's the food.' Anna had been keeping an eye on the kitchen door. 'I'm starving.'

Catherine ate quickly, her steak pie, chips and peas delicious. The others were still chatting and eating, Jimmy now with his arm across the back of Nat's chair, and she decided it was time to call it a night.

'Lovely to meet you, Jimmy.' She gave Anna and Nat a mock stern look. 'I'll see you two tomorrow. Talk to you soon, Thomas.'

Thomas lifted his hand. 'Make sure you ring Mum. She was complaining they haven't heard from you.'

With a wave, Catherine turned away from their good-byes, heading for the bar. There were two people behind it, a man who barely looked out of his teens polishing glasses on a white cloth, and an older woman who was concentrating on her phone. The man looked up and smiled at Catherine as she approached.

'What can I get you?'

Catherine smiled. 'I'm leaving, so I'd like to pay for my food please, but I wonder if I could ask you some questions first?'

He looked suspicious. 'Questions? What do you mean?'

The woman put her phone on the bar and turned her head. 'What's going on, Josh?'

'I'm a police officer.' Catherine took out her warrant card and held it up. 'Do you know a couple called Rebecca and Dale Clough? I'm told they come in here sometimes.'

Josh frowned, shook his head. 'I've not been working here long.'

The woman was by Josh's side now, hands on hips. 'Why are you asking?'

'Just some routine enquiries.'

The woman stuck out her chin. 'Tells me nothing.'

That's the idea, Catherine thought. 'Is this your pub, Mrs...?'

She nodded. 'Williamson. Dawn Williamson. Myself and my husband own the place. He's the chef.'

'The food's lovely.'

'Thank you. I'll tell him you said so.' She didn't smile, but her expression had thawed a little. 'Why are you asking about Rebecca and Dale?'

Catherine noted the use of their first names. 'We were told they were in here eating from around seven thirty last night. Is that right?'

Dawn Williamson didn't look at Catherine. 'I don't know. I wasn't working last night.'

'Is there anyone here who was?'

'I'll go and speak to my husband.'

'But if he was in the kitchen, how will he—' Catherine closed her mouth as Williamson hurried away. Catherine looked at Josh, who kept his eyes fixed on the glass in his hand. She pulled a bar stool nearer and climbed onto it, reasoning she may as well be comfortable while she waited. She knew Anna in particular would be wondering what she was up to, would probably have figured out this was the same pub the Cloughs had mentioned. If it was genuine, as alibis went, it was a good one. Sitting in a public place for the evening in question was about as watertight as it got.

A thought struck Catherine, and she looked around, then leaned forward, resting her forearms on the bar. 'Do you have CCTV in here, Josh? I can't see any cameras.'

He looked up. 'I'm not sure. I told you, I've not worked here long. You'd have to check with Mrs Williamson.'

'Can I help you?'

The voice came from behind her. Catherine turned to see a man standing there, arms folded. He wore black and white checked trousers and a black jacket. He was completely bald, clean shaven, stocky.

'Mr Williamson?'

He nodded, held out his hand. Catherine shook it.

'Thank you for coming out to talk to me,' she said. He shrugged, climbing onto the bar stool beside hers.

'No problem. We've almost finished serving anyway.'

'Your steak pie's the best I've ever tasted.'

That raised a smile. 'We try our best. Dawn says you were asking about Dale Clough and his wife?'

'That's right. Were they here last night?'

Williamson looked at Josh and said, 'Pour me a lemonade, would you, please?' He turned to look at Catherine. 'Bet you've never heard of a man who runs a pub not drinking, have you?'

'It's none of my business.'

He nodded his thanks as Josh placed the lemonade in front of him. 'I'm an alcoholic, but I haven't had a drink in almost ten years.'

Catherine waited, not knowing what to say. Why was he telling her this? Williamson took a sip, smacked his lips. 'If you look me up when you get back to your station, you'll see I made some mistakes when I was younger. Driving under the influence, shoplifting to pay for the booze. In the end, I cut out the middle man and just stole vodka by the bottle.'

'Mr Williamson—'

He held up a hand. 'Call me Pete. I know, you're here to talk about the Cloughs, not a daft old drunk. Yes, they were here last night.'

'If you were working in the kitchen, how do you know?'

'Because their name was on the order slip – we still use a pad and pencil, you see. We start serving food at seven, and theirs was almost the first order – must have been seven thirtyish by then. It was their anniversary. Dale mentioned it to the waitress, and so when we sent out their puddings, we wrote "Congratulations" in chocolate sauce on one plate, "Happy Anniversary" on the other.' He took another mouthful of lemonade. 'I know it's not much, but… We might not be a fancy restaurant, but we try to make people feel welcome.'

'Do you know Dale and Rebecca well?'

'Not really. We know what happened to them, of course. To Rebecca. Everyone in the village knows. That can't be easy, knowing everyone around you is aware of what you've been through.'

'Do you know what time they left here last night?'

Pete Williamson took his time replying. 'Not exactly. We weren't busy early on, at least not for food. I came out here for a drink and chat around eight and they were here then, sitting at the table by the fireplace. I left the kitchen again soon after nine when we'd finished serving, and I don't remember seeing them again but they could easily have still been around. It was quiz night – the place was pretty full by then.'

Catherine remembered what Kendrick had said – Andy Nugent had died between six and twelve the previous evening. If Rebecca and Dale Clough hadn't arrived at the pub until seven thirty as Dale had told them, and as Pete Williamson seemed to be confirming, but there were no witnesses to confirm they had stayed until closing time, were both still in the frame for Nugent's murder. 'Is there anyone else I could ask? Other customers? Who was behind the bar?'

'My daughter Alexandra was here – she covers a shift for us now and again if we're stuck. Ask Dawn to give you her phone number. Alex isn't here tonight and my mobile's upstairs.'

'Someone will come in tomorrow, take a statement from you and get your daughter's contact details, if that's okay.'

'No problem.'

'Did you recognise any regular customers last night? Anyone else we can talk to?'

He ran a hand over the top of his head. 'A couple of people.' He gave some names. 'I don't have numbers for them.'

'That's okay, we'll find them.' Catherine made a note of the names on her phone. 'What about CCTV?'

'We don't have any. We've never had any trouble, and we live on the premises – it seemed an unnecessary expense.'

Catherine wasn't sure she agreed. 'You mentioned your daughter – were any of your other members of staff working?'

'Josh was around, and Kelsey.' He shook his head. 'If you want to talk to her, you'll have to go to her house. We sacked her last night.'

'Sacked her? Why?' It was irrelevant, but Catherine wanted to keep him talking.

'We caught her with her hand in the tips jar. I know she's just a kid, but we pay fair wages, and the tips are shared equally between the staff. We don't encourage people helping themselves.'

'Fair enough.'

He drained his glass. 'Listen, I don't know why you're asking about Dale and Rebecca Clough, but can I say something?'

'Of course. It's a free country.'

'So they say. Well, like I told you, we're all aware of what happened to Rebecca. We also heard no one was caught for it. All I'm saying is...' He exhaled. 'I know what it's like to face your demons.'

Catherine stared at him. 'I don't understand.'

'Why do you think I run a pub? I'm an alcoholic. Every day, I force myself to get up and walk past the beer pumps, all those bottles of spirits. I work in the kitchen six days a week – it's twenty feet away from the bar.'

'You mean you're punishing yourself?' She still didn't see what he was getting at.

'That's part of it, but I'm proving to myself that I'm winning. I can work near alcohol, even live in the same building, but I'm in charge – it doesn't rule my life any more. Every time Rebecca Clough comes in here – and it isn't often – it looks to me as though she's doing something similar – not so much punishing herself, why should she – but facing her fears. Her demons.'

'That makes two of you.'

He smiled. 'Reckon so, but Rebecca still looks haunted by them. She almost jumps if you speak to her, flits around like a butterfly, and every time the door opens and someone new comes in, she's terrified. But she's here. Her experience hasn't destroyed her. She hasn't let that bastard win.'

Catherine nodded. 'You sound as though you admire her.'

'Of course I do. She's fighting, giving herself a chance. I know how difficult that is.' He slid off the stool. 'Now, I need to get back in the kitchen.'

'Thanks for talking to me.'

He nodded, and Catherine watched him walk away. Had he been trying to ask her to leave Rebecca Clough alone? He'd been vague about the time the Cloughs had left, but positive they had been in the pub until at least eight o'clock. They'd have to get a formal statement, and speak to the other members of staff he'd mentioned, but for now Catherine needed to get home and try to sleep.

As the kitchen door swung closed behind Pete Williamson, Catherine took out a twenty-pound note and handed it to Josh.

'For my meal. Put the change in your tips jar.'

–

It was a cool night, the town centre quiet as Catherine drove through it. She lived on an anonymous estate, up

178

by the town's golf course. She turned onto her street and saw a car parked outside her house. It was small, silver, and she recognised it immediately. She swung onto her driveway, grabbed her bag and almost fell out of the car.

Isla Rafferty stood waiting, sports bag in one hand, bottle of wine in the other. 'Trick or treat?' she said.

Delighted, Catherine beamed at her. 'What are you doing here?'

Isla set the bottle and bag on the ground and rushed forward. Catherine closed her eyes, savouring the moment as Isla kissed her.

'I've missed you,' Isla said against her cheek.

'Not as much as I've missed you,' Catherine said, smiling at the cliché.

Isla laughed, pulling away from Catherine and taking her hand. 'Can you grab the wine? I was going to bring a takeaway, but I wasn't sure if you'd eaten. I wasn't even sure if you'd be home yet but I thought I'd take the chance. I'll have to leave before six tomorrow, but I wanted to see you, even if only for a few hours.'

14

Soon, they were on the sofa, glasses of wine on the coffee table in front of them. Catherine slid her arm around Isla and pulled her closer.

'I'm so glad you're here,' she said. 'On a school night too.'

'Don't tell the boss.' Isla picked up Catherine's hand and kissed it. 'There's something I need to talk to you about.'

Unease gripped Catherine's stomach. 'Oh. That sounds—'

'Ominous?' Isla raised her eyebrows. 'Don't worry. If I was going to dump you, I'd do it by text.'

Catherine sat up straight, giving her a mock filthy look. 'Not funny.'

Isla pulled her down and kissed her. 'Believe me, that'll never… It's not going to happen.' She blushed, and Catherine felt the tension in her belly melt into warmth.

'So what's up?' she said lightly, not wanting to make too big a deal of what Isla had said.

'It's Mary.'

DCI Mary Dolan was Isla's boss. 'Is she okay?' Catherine asked, concerned. She'd worked with Dolan before, liked and respected her.

'She's fine, but she took me and Adil into her office this evening just before we left, said she had some news.'

'And?'

Isla turned her body, tucked her legs beneath her and snuggled into Catherine's side. 'She's been offered a Super's job.'

'Well, that's good isn't it?'

'Yeah, she's been after promotion for a while.' Isla glanced up at Catherine. 'They also want her to put together a new team, and guess who she wants to be part of it?'

The warm feeling turned to apprehension again. 'Oh, I don't know. You?'

Isla nodded, grim faced. 'And Adil. It'd be what we do now, on a larger scale. Serious crime, major incidents. Promotions for us too – me to DI, Adil to DS.'

Catherine kissed her. 'But that's great news. Why don't you sound happy about it?'

Isla sighed. 'Because the jobs are in London. We'd be joining the Met.'

'Oh.' Now Catherine's stomach did a backflip. She swallowed. 'Even so, you have to do it. You might never get another chance to—'

'I've already refused,' Isla said softly.

'You've turned it down? Why?'

'Why do you think?' Isla sat up. 'A few months ago I'd have said yes before Mary had finished explaining, but now? I hardly see you as it is. What would it be like if I was living in London?'

It was what Catherine had been waiting to hear, that Isla was as committed to their relationship as she was. She had known, of course, or at least believed, but some doubt had remained. She didn't want Isla to go to London, couldn't think of anything worse, but she also knew she couldn't be the reason why Isla didn't grab this opportunity.

'I'll still be here,' she said. 'Less than two hours away by train, that's all.' She didn't even sound convincing to herself.

'That's all? You're only an hour's drive away now and it's still too far.' Isla ran a hand through her hair, loosening the messy bun she always pinned it into for work. 'We'd be sent all over London, have to be available at a few minutes' notice.'

'You'd get time off. They couldn't expect you to be around twenty-four-seven.'

'You know how it is. Look at today. I bet you were out of the door by seven, home fourteen hours later. An hour to eat and relax, a few hours' sleep and out of the door again before you've barely closed your eyes.'

'It's the case we're on; it's not like that all the time.'

Isla shook her head. 'Most of the time.'

Catherine knew she was right. Policing was a way of life, not just a job. You didn't arrive at the office at ten to nine and walk out again at five past five. 'What did Adil say?'

'He's going to talk to his wife about it, but I think he feels the same as me – if we were going to be based here, then yes, he'd bite Mary's hand off. Promotion, a pay rise... But having to move down there, it's a huge thing. There's their daughter to think about, his wife has a job she loves, they've just bought a house...' Isla picked up her wine and frowned at it. 'It's a big decision.'

'Of course it is, and maybe you should give it some more thought,' Catherine said gently. 'This is a massive chance for you.'

Their eyes met and Catherine was surprised to see tears in Isla's. 'So's this,' she said softly. Catherine pulled her close again.

'We'd make it work, I promise,' she said.

'You don't know that.'

'I know we'd give it a bloody good go.' She also knew that if Isla didn't take the job there was a chance that, as time passed, she would grow to resent Catherine for the opportunity she had refused. That Isla turning the job down could damage their relationship more than her moving to London would. 'Just think about it. I don't want you to go, of course I don't, but I know how hard you've worked. Dolan doesn't impress easily, and she wants you for her right-hand woman.'

Isla put down her glass, stood, and reached out a hand to Catherine with a tired smile.

'Shall we go to bed?' she said.

15

Catherine forced her eyes open as a phone began to ring, fumbling for the handset on her bedside table. Beside her, Isla rolled onto her back.

'Is it mine or yours?' she mumbled.

'Mine. It's Jonathan.' Rubbing her eyes, Catherine answered the call, anticipating bad news. Five a.m. phone calls usually meant death or disaster, and in their line of work, potentially both. 'Hello?'

'He's torched a pub,' Knight said.

Catherine sat up, swung her feet onto the floor. 'Shit. Where?'

'The outskirts of town. The Plough on Armitage Street?'

She knew it. 'I've not been in there for years but the licensee and his family used to live above it. Were there—'

'People asleep inside? Yes,' Knight said. 'The son managed to get out of the window. His parents and sisters were brought out by firefighters.'

Catherine swallowed. Behind her Isla moved close, pulling the duvet up around Catherine's shoulders. 'Brought out as in they're alive, or…?' She hardly dared ask the question.

'They're all in hospital. The young lad who jumped broke his leg, and they all have varying degrees of smoke inhalation. The two girls are okay: the parents managed to carry them to the windows and they were taken out first. The parents will survive, but their condition is more serious than the kids'.'

Catherine was horrified. Torching vehicles and property was bad enough, but now the arsonist had targeted a family home? She gave Isla a quick kiss as she got to her feet and opened her wardrobe door.

'The fire's under control, but the building's gutted. We've not had confirmation it's arson but I think we can assume proof will be found sooner or later,' Knight went on. 'I'll pick you up in half an hour.'

'How's Jo?' Catherine asked as she grabbed a shirt and a pair of trousers from the wardrobe.

Knight was silent, then said, 'She's okay, thank you. She's fine. See you soon.' He ended the call.

'This is a nightmare.' Catherine told Isla what Knight had said. 'I need to have a shower, get moving.'

Isla checked the time and got out of bed. 'Me too.'

They stood for a second, smiling at each other. Catherine felt almost shy. She reached for Isla's hand. 'Thank you for coming over. It means a lot.' They weren't the right words, but she couldn't find the ones that would explain what she felt.

'Hopefully next time we'll have longer than seven hours together,' Isla said.

—

Once again, they were standing outside a fire-damaged building, the stench of smoke overwhelming. There were two fire engines still at the scene, a cordon preventing Catherine, Knight and their uniformed colleagues getting too close, but the fire crews were preparing to leave. It was only just light and, this early, there wasn't an interested crowd of onlookers, but no doubt there would be as the morning went on. Catherine sent Kendrick a text, reminding him they should have someone watching the scene to see if anyone suspicious came back to it. He'd no doubt already thought of it, but it didn't hurt to check. The air was damp and thick and Catherine was already coughing. She gazed at the building, hands on hips.

It was hard to believe anyone had escaped. The white bricks of the pub's upper floor were blackened and the roof had all but collapsed, but the main entrance still stood, the double doors splintered, either by the blaze or the firefighters. There were puddles on the concrete at the front of the building where the red firehoses still lay coiled, water running down towards the road.

Catherine saw one of the firefighters over by the engines raise a hand and she realised it was Jimmy, Nat Roberts's date who she'd met the evening before. He came over, offering a smile.

'Here we are again,' he said.

'Worse this time, with people involved,' Knight said.

Jimmy nodded, his lipped pressed tightly together. 'And a dog.'

Catherine looked at him. 'A dog?' She turned back to the building, taking in the devastation again. The human members of the family were safe, but if the dog had died, she'd have to work hard not to cry. 'Did it…?'

Jimmy pointed at the building. 'She was in the bedroom, the mum and dad's bedroom. Once they'd handed the kids to us and we'd got the parents out too, they were all crying, screaming the dog's name. Bonnie, Bonnie, over and over. We could hear her howling, like she was screaming too.' He shook his head as though he could still hear it.

Catherine put a hand on his arm, tears in her eyes now. 'You don't need to—'

'I went back in for her. I shouldn't have done, was told not to, but I couldn't just listen to her...' He gave a tremulous smile. 'A neighbour's taken her to the vet to be checked over, but she seemed fine to me. The neighbour will take care of her until the family can take her again.'

'You saved her.' Knight smiled at him.

Jimmy blushed. 'All part of the service.'

Catherine nudged him. 'Wait until Nat hears.'

He laughed. 'Hopefully I'll be seeing her later.'

'But I'm guessing you wouldn't tell her yourself, so I'll make sure I do,' Catherine teased.

'What can you tell us about the fire?' Knight asked.

'Looks like it started downstairs, around the front doors, but don't quote me on that.' Jimmy nodded towards the building. 'If I were a betting man, from what I've seen and smelt, I'd say arson.' He glanced over at his colleagues. A few of them had noticed him talking to them. 'Sorry, I need to go and give them a hand. See you later.'

Catherine and Knight moved further from the cordon.

'Two fires in two night,' Knight said. 'Either we've got a copycat, or he's escalating.'

'Yeah, and there were people in there, not vehicles.' Catherine chewed on her thumbnail. 'We're lucky no one died.'

Knight blew out his cheeks. 'Next time, they might.'

'What if...' Catherine said slowly, a horrible idea coming to her. 'What if our arsonist did start the fire at Greaves's premises? Maybe turned up just wanting to torch the cars but then looked inside the building, wondering why there was still a light on late at night, saw Greaves in there, and decided to set the fire anyway?' She paused, imagining the scene. 'He or she might not have realised Greaves was already dead, maybe thought he was just asleep, and that excited him.'

'And out came the matches.' Knight rubbed his cheeks with his palms. 'And then last night, he went for the big one. A pub where he'd know people were definitely asleep inside.'

Catherine shuddered. 'I bet he was here somewhere, watching. Waiting for the flames to take hold, the fire engines arriving, the ambulances. Waiting to see if anyone walked away.'

'It's likely,' Knight said.

Catherine wrapped her arms around her body, feeling a chill. She thought of her house, her warm bed, Isla lying beside her, and the job that had brought them together: standing outside a smouldering pub first thing in the morning, anticipating another day of trying to piece together why three people who should still be alive were dead, when in another life she could be just waking up and wondering what to have for breakfast before heading off to a warm office. There were other jobs she could do, other careers. She loved her work, always had, but lately it hadn't felt the same. Whether it was because of her own state of mind, Catherine couldn't say, but if Isla was to go to London, maybe Catherine could follow – and not necessarily as a police officer.

She turned away from Knight and the fire-damaged pub to stare down the street, wondering why they bothered. For every criminal the police removed from the street, there were ten, twenty, a hundred more they would never catch. Catherine had known this to be true since before she joined the force, but she had never felt it as keenly as she did now. She had worked on cases she never wanted to think about again, seen ruined bodies, faced heartbroken victims and relatives, spoken to people destroyed by violence and cruelty. Many of them still visited her in quiet moments, or at crime scenes that mirrored their own. She guessed they always would. Some days she had gone home and cried until she fell asleep, but she had always got up the next morning, gone to work and started again. She'd returned to work after her time off not exactly raring to go, but not hating the thought either. Now though… Now she didn't know whether she still wanted this life, and that was the hardest challenge of all.

'Where would you have waited, if you'd started the fire?' Knight said from behind her.

Catherine turned. 'Around here? I don't know.'

He moved so he was standing beside her, and Catherine knew he had picked up on her mood. In his quiet way, Knight noticed everything. 'What about over there?'

There was a bus shelter, made of brick, the inside still shadowy. Knight walked towards it, and Catherine followed. He shone the torch on his phone into the corners, picking out a couple of lumps of chewing gum, some cigarette ends, a plastic bottle and a crisp packet.

'I reckon it's a possibility. It's got a good view of the pub, it's sheltered, and no one could see you from outside. You could probably even make a video from here, relive it all again and again.' Knight turned off the torch. 'We should check around Scott Greaves's property too. I've not worked on many arsons, but like you said, why start a fire and not be there to watch what happens?'

'Mick will check the whole area out.' Catherine believed Caffery was the best in the business.

Knight's phone began to ring. He took it from his pocket, his eyebrows raising as he checked the screen. 'It's the Super.' He answered the call. 'Good morning, ma'am.'

It wasn't a surprise that Jane Stringer wanted an update on this most recent fire, but why was she phoning Knight at this hour? Knight was listening, frowning now. 'Yes, ma'am, we're at the scene… Well, we attended the blaze at the second-hand car dealership, the property where the body of Scott Greaves was found… The fire's out but forensic investigation hasn't started yet…'

As Catherine waited, scuffing her feet outside the bus shelter, she saw a movement in the corner of her eye and turned. Over by the cordon, just a flash of a figure in dark clothes as they moved quickly out of sight. Catherine stared. Was it the kid on the bike again? She ran across the road, Knight turning, confused, as she raced past him.

When she reached the cordon she stood, hands on hips, looking around. No sign of him, but there were tyre prints on the road, where he'd pedalled through the water that was running down from the puddles outside the pub. She took out her radio again. This couldn't be coincidence – what the hell would a teenage kid be doing out here at this time in the morning if he wasn't involved? They had to find him.

Knight arrived beside her, phone still to his ear, eyebrows raised. 'Yes, ma'am. Understood. We'll be there in ten minutes.' He put the phone back in his pocket and turned to Catherine. 'We're in trouble.'

'Why?'

'The Super's at the station, waiting for an update. She doesn't understand why we're out here when we should be over there eager to speak to her. We better get moving.'

'We've just missed that kid again. Let's go after him. The Super can wait.'

'I don't think she'd like that.' He began to walk and Catherine fell into step beside him.

'She won't like half the town going up in flames either.'

'Can't they send someone else?' Knight asked.

'They are doing, but we're already here.'

Knight shook his head. 'We need to get back.'

'He can't have gone far.'

'He could have gone in any direction. The Super's waiting.'

Inclining her head, Catherine said, 'And that's an order, is it?'

He smiled. 'Yeah. Get in the car.'

'Would have helped if she'd told us to expect her.' Catherine respected the Superintendent as a police officer, but as person Stringer was a mystery. 'And she knows why we're here, why everyone else' – she jerked a thumb at the group of uniformed officers over by the pub who were receiving instructions from their sergeant – 'is here.'

'Keith did warn us she might turn up this morning.'

'So why can't he update her? He's the SIO.'

'Who knows.' They were back at Knight's car now. Catherine cast a last look at the burnt-down pub, imagining the flames, the smoke, the desperate parents, screaming children, the howling dog.

The terror.

If the arsonist had started to target people's homes, they had to catch him, and fast.

16

Kendrick was waiting for them in the main office. It was almost empty, just Anna Varcoe and Chris Rogers already at their computers. Kendrick stood by Anna's desk, reading over her shoulder. As Catherine and Knight approached, Kendrick nodded towards his own office door.

'She's waiting inside.' He pushed his hands into his trouser pockets. 'Ready?'

'As we'll ever be,' Knight said.

As he spoke, Kendrick's office door opened and Jane Stringer strode into the room. The Superintendent was tall and slender with shoulder-length blonde hair and understated make-up. She could easily play the role of the headteacher of an exclusive public school or lady of the manor. With one hand on the doorframe, she surveyed the scene.

'DI Knight, DS Bishop. I realise it's early but the Assistant Chief Constable has requested a nine a.m. meeting with me and I need to be able to give him an update.' She looked at each of them in turn. 'A positive update.' She managed a smile, gesturing inside Kendrick's office. 'Shall we all sit down?'

The three exchanged a glance as Stringer disappeared back inside the office.

'Going to be cosy in there,' Kendrick muttered.

It was. Stringer sat behind Kendrick's desk and Kendrick dragged the spare chair from the corner to sit beside her. Catherine chose to remain standing and so did Knight, not that there was really room to do otherwise. Stringer eyed them.

'Why did you both feel the need to attend the scene of the fire earlier?' she asked. 'As far as I'm aware, we've had no confirmation it's linked to our arson case. I realise it's a strong possibility, but I'd have rather you'd both got some rest, since you already have two murders and one suspicious death to solve. There were uniformed officers already on the scene this morning, and Inspector Dhirwan was also in attendance.'

Catherine glanced at Knight. They hadn't spoken to their colleague, hadn't even realised he was there.

'You didn't sign the scene log.' Stringer leaned back in her chair. 'Didn't talk to anyone other than a firefighter who seemed to know you.'

Catherine stared at her. What was she implying? That she and Knight hadn't followed procedure, had done something wrong? And who told Stringer she and Knight had been there, what they'd done? One of the uniforms? Did Stringer have spies around Northolme police station? Catherine wouldn't be surprised.

'We weren't there long enough to sign the log, and we didn't go near the cordon,' she said. 'We'd only just arrived when you called to ask us to come here.'

Stringer bent to retrieve a leather handbag from the floor beside her chair. She removed a bottle of water, unscrewed the top and set the bag back on the floor. 'You didn't need to be there at all. Your priority should be finding answers for the families of Hollie Morton, Andrew Nugent and Scott Greaves.'

Hoping Kendrick or Knight would speak up, Catherine hesitated before responding, but neither jumped in. 'We will. It seems likely this fire is the work of our arsonist, and we thought it wise to see the scene for ourselves.'

Even as she said the words, she knew she was giving Stringer more ammunition.

'"Seems", Sergeant? Meaning you have no idea if there's a link with the previous fires, much less a link to the deaths you're already investigating.'

Catherine ignored that. 'There could have been more victims in this morning's fire, ma'am,' she said. Stringer had always seemed to her like someone who would appreciate deference to her rank. 'We wanted to get some idea of what we'd be dealing with.'

'Then you could have waited for the fire investigator's report. *Should* have waited.' Stringer set her bottle of water on the desk and frowned at it. 'Could someone make us some coffee, Keith?'

Kendrick got to his feet, his expression sour. 'Have you eaten? We've lost our canteen now, of course, but there's a café up the road that does a decent bacon sandwich.' He squeezed past Catherine and Knight, turning when he reached the door. 'It's just a caravan in a lay-by, but the food's decent if you get there early. Fancy a butty?'

Stringer just looked at him, and Kendrick gave her a knowing smile. 'Coffee it is then.'

Catherine kept her gaze on a spot on the wall just above Stringer's head. If the Super wanted to show Kendrick who was boss, to treat him like a tea boy, let her. She was impressing no one. Beside her, Knight stood with his hands behind his back as though he were on the parade ground. Stringer eyed them but didn't speak. The silence

194

was uncomfortable, at least for Catherine. They should be discussing the investigation, the Super listening to their progress, offering guidance, encouragement. Instead, she and Knight were lined up here like schoolkids in the headteacher's office.

'How's your partner, DI Knight?' Stringer said abruptly. 'Jo Webber?'

Knight shifted. 'She's fine, thank you, ma'am.'

Stringer nodded, her expression not changing, and Catherine knew this was another attempt at proving she had her eye on them. 'Good.'

The door opened and Kendrick thumped back into the room and sat heavily in his chair. 'Coffee's on its way. No biscuits though.' He raised his eyebrows at Stringer. 'Budget cuts, you know.'

Stringer ignored him. 'Tell me about your progress,' she said.

She wasn't being fair, and no doubt she knew it. Kendrick would have reported to her the previous evening, updated her on what they'd done so far and what they'd learnt. To arrive at the station this early in the morning, before the actions they would share out between the team were agreed, before any briefing had taken place, and demand a progress report was unacceptable, and yet here Stringer was. Kendrick sat back in his chair and crossed his legs.

'Today, we want to talk to a man about a scrapyard,' he said. Stringer looked down her nose at him.

'The one where you've been told Andrew Nugent worked? Is it a priority?'

'It needs following up, as do several other lines of investigation.'

Stringer glared. 'Such as?'

'We need to speak to the victim's families again about the removal work we've been told Andy Nugent did. If there's an innocent reason for his fingerprints being found on Rebecca Clough's headboard, we need to know about it.'

'But if he'd helped the Cloughs move into their house, surely she would have recognised him when she woke to find him in her bedroom?' Stringer said.

Kendrick spread his hands. 'Not necessarily. She's already said she saw nothing of the man who attacked her. She didn't even hear his voice.'

'What else?'

Kendrick's eyes flicked to Catherine and Knight.

'We need to verify some alibis,' Knight said. 'We have the names of some of the people who were in the pub where Dale Clough says he and his wife were eating around the time Andy Nugent died.'

Catherine said, 'We're also checking with neighbours of Hollie Morton's family. They say they were at home together when Andy died—'

'I'm aware of that, Sergeant.' Stringer interrupted. 'Why haven't we checked their alibis already?'

Forcing herself not to react to the other woman's rudeness, Catherine bit the inside of her cheek. 'We've had a lot to work through, and not much time to do it.'

Stringer looked down her nose. 'Yet you had time to go out for a meal with your colleagues last night?'

Again, Catherine tried not to react. 'You said yourself we need time to rest, ma'am.'

Did Stringer have people following them, or what? What was she trying to prove here? Stringer met Catherine's gaze and held it. 'Time to relax, a good night's sleep? Of course.' The Super's lips twitched, then thinned. 'And now you're rested, I want to see progress.'

Catherine realised Stringer knew about her relationship with Isla too. Had she guessed that they'd spent the previous night together? It was none of her business, no one's business, but if Stringer could twist it to make it look as though it was having an effect on Catherine's work, no doubt she would. As she listened to the Super demanding to know which tasks each officer in their team was going to be assigned, Catherine guessed what the point of Stringer's early morning visit had been.

'Sounds as though you're going to be extremely busy,' Stringer said. First they weren't doing enough, now they were going to be overworked? Kendrick sat up straight and Catherine guessed his suspicions had also been raised.

'We'll cope.' He tried for a smile. There was knock on the door, and Knight went to open it, and one of the support staff squeezed into the room. As he set a tray of cups, a jug of milk and an insulated coffee mug on the desk, Kendrick stood and thanked him.

'Shall I be mother?' he said to Stringer. She ignored him.

'Do you need extra officers?' she asked Kendrick.

Kendrick picked up a cup and set it on a saucer in front of her. 'Not at the moment.'

He poured the coffee and handed her the cup. Stringer accepted it, poured in a drop of milk. 'Thank you. I think when the new Assistant Chief Constable hears about your lack of progress, he'll have some recommendations,' she said. She looked at Catherine, no doubt remembering her involvement in the downfall of the previous ACC. Kendrick leaned towards Stringer.

'Lack of progress?' His face was red. 'We've had no time to make progress, and there aren't as many of us around as there used to be.'

'I've just offered you more officers, and you were sent extra personnel as soon as we heard about the first two deaths.' Stringer's voice was cold. 'How did you use them?'

Kendrick smiled. 'I didn't, at least not for long.'

'Exactly. Why?'

'I didn't need to. Once the scene was secure, my officers could get on with the investigation.'

'Maybe if you had, I'd be drinking coffee in my own kitchen this morning.' Stringer sipped her drink. She glanced at Catherine and Knight. 'Help yourselves.'

Kendrick's eyes bulged. Knight moved to the desk and poured three cups. As he handed one to Kendrick and one to Catherine, he said, 'We have a good team here. We'll work together to manage both investigations.'

Stringer set her coffee cup down. 'I have every confidence you will.' She checked her watch. 'You've not given me enough to take back to Headquarters. Why haven't you spoken to Scott Greaves's widow yet?'

'We have,' Catherine told her calmly.

'She was informed her of her husband's death, yes. Do we know the reason for their separation? Has she been asked about her movements on the day her husband died? Do we have a timeline for Scott Greaves's own movements on the day of his death? What about those of Hollie Morton and Andrew Nugent?'

Kendrick finished his coffee before replying. 'We're still collating that information.'

Stringer's eyes narrowed. 'That's the sort of meaningless sentence you'd try to send a journalist away with.' Her eyes went to Catherine again and she blinked. 'In other words, DCI Kendrick, you have none of the information you could reasonably be expected to have at this stage.'

'I disagree,' Kendrick said. His voice was quiet, a warning to anyone who had worked with him. Usually he could be heard for miles around. Stringer picked up her bag again and pushed back her chair, leaving her bottle of water on the desk.

'I'm sure you do. Unfortunately, I doubt the ACC will.' She stood. 'Well, thank you all for your time. I'll look forward to a progress report later today.'

Catherine stepped back as she opened the door, and Stringer swept through it. Kendrick followed her out of the office, and they disappeared.

Catherine turned to Knight. 'She's going to tell the ACC that we're useless.'

Knight was nodding. 'She already thought that before she drove over here. Maybe they decided it between them.'

'She made a point of mentioning Jo, even that we spoke to Jimmy just now. Like she's keeping tabs on us.'

Knight went over to the window that overlooked the staff car park, and Catherine followed him. '*Did* you go out for a meal last night?' he asked.

'It was supposed to be a quick drink, but we were hungry. It's not like we were out getting pissed. It's nothing to with her.'

'But how did she know about it? Who was there?'

Catherine told him, and he frowned. 'Anna and Nat Roberts? I can't imagine Stringer even knowing their names. A DC and a uniformed constable? Far beneath her notice.'

Who else had been in the briefing room when Anna had asked if she fancied a drink? Catherine thought back. Too many people to remember. She'd have a word with

Anna about it. Maybe she would remember someone had been standing close to them but really, why would Stringer bother? She would have access to information about the progress of the investigation, updates from Kendrick, anything she wanted, so why have someone spying? It seemed juvenile, beneath the image Stringer liked to project of herself. It didn't fit.

In the car park below them, they watched Stringer open the driver's door of a dark grey Mercedes. Kendrick was beside her, waving a hand as she pulled away. He turned as the car disappeared from view, looking up at them. Catherine made her way back to her own desk and switched on her computer. The office was quiet, everyone tapping away at their keyboards, Knight heading for his own office.

'Why did she bother to come over here?' Catherine said as he reached her desk. 'She'd made up her mind before she left Lincoln.'

'Something's brewing,' Knight said.

Kendrick stomped back into the room. 'Yeah, a vat of shit, and I reckon they're going to drown us in it.'

17

Kendrick ordered the team down to the incident room. Catherine hadn't spent much time in here during the investigation so far, but she could see that even this early in the morning there were the beginnings of the usual buzz of activity. Uniformed officers and civilian support staff were arriving, removing coats and setting cups of coffee on desks. Kendrick stood in a corner watching the room come to life, rocking on his heels, hands in his trouser pockets. He wasn't often silent, and Catherine wondered what he was thinking. They were already under pressure from above and, looking around the room, she saw evidence of what she already knew to be true – there just weren't that many officers based at Northolme any more. They'd lost one of their detectives, DC Simon Sullivan, when he'd transferred out of the county, and he hadn't been replaced. Their CID team now consisted of six, and how much longer would they be working together? They'd been colleagues for a while now, and the idea that any of them would shirk their responsibilities, not give the job their all, was an insult. Stringer had been subtler than that though – she'd hinted that they simply didn't have the staff to cope, and looking at the scene in here, who could argue? Kendrick hadn't helped matters by refusing Stringer's offer of more officers, but Catherine could understand his reasoning. They had to be seen to be coping with the officers they already had, and Stringer would be aware of that when she offered more.

The incident room manager was DS Robin Cuthbert, who had also been based at Northolme in the past but had recently been transferred to the force's Headquarters on the outskirts of Lincoln. He had brought officers with him to cover some of the most important positions in the incident room, roles that in the past would have been filled by officers known to everyone else in the station, familiar with each other and used to working as a team. Now though, Catherine looked at the receiver, who would assess all the material coming into the incident room, prioritise it and identify developments and opportunities, and didn't know that officer's name. As soon as Catherine had entered the incident room, she'd felt the urge to leave again. As a sergeant, Catherine could go out and ask questions, talk to witnesses, interview suspects. The higher you climbed up the career ladder, the further away you seemed to be from actual policing, and Catherine had no desire to be the next Detective Superintendent Jane Stringer. The incident room could be seen as the hub, the administrative centre, but to Catherine, it wasn't really where cases were solved. That was out on the street, in witnesses' homes, in the station's grubby interview rooms. Occasionally, and not just on the TV or in the movies, a flash of instinct, a chat between colleagues, or a gut feeling led to the truth.

The incident room manager, DS Cuthbert, had always been known throughout the station as Monk. Once glance explained why – the top of his head was bald but he had thick black hair around the back and sides, and with his serene expression, he just needed a habit to complete the look. Monk stood by a whiteboard displaying photographs of Hollie Morton and Andy

Nugent, studying the notes written below the pictures. Catherine sidled up to him.

'Fancy seeing you here,' she whispered into his ear. Monk jumped.

'Bloody hell, why do you always have to creep up on me?' He held his palm to his chest.

'Because you make it so easy. Didn't you hear all of us walking through the door?'

He pulled a face at her, jabbed his thumb at the whiteboards. 'I'm concentrating on my work, not who's wandering around.'

There was a smart board on the wall opposite and Catherine nodded towards the blank screen. 'Have you broken it?'

As he rolled his eyes, Catherine looked over his shoulder at the photographs of the dead couple. They stared back at her, and she felt chastised.

Kendrick was sitting at an empty desk, and the others were pulling chairs over to gather around him. Catherine headed over to join Anna, Knight, DC Chris Rogers and DC Dave Lancaster, who'd just arrived. She found a chair and sat next to Anna as Kendrick rubbed his hands over his face.

'Before the briefing, I wanted a quick word with you all. As you'll no doubt all know by now, Superintendent Stringer has been here, interrupting her busy schedule to tell us to get our arses in gear. Never mind that we're just starting day two of the investigation, never mind that we've got half the officers we used to have.' He scanned the room. 'I've got people in here I don't know, and who don't know me. I'm happy to work with them, not that it's going to be easy. We've got two cases on the go now and need to prove we're needed and relevant. We might have to rely on extra people from outside the station, but I want you lot out there talking to people, following up leads, asking questions. I know you, know how hard you work, the commitment you have to getting answers for the victims and for their families.' He made eye contact with each of his officers in turn. 'As you know, I'm not usually one for pep talks, because here, I've never seen the need for them. But I'll be honest with you – the Super and everyone above her are breathing down our necks, and as I'm sure you'll agree, that's not a pleasant position to be in. We need to clear these cases up, and quickly.'

'Boss, not to take the piss, but isn't that what we always aim for?' Chris Rogers said.

'Of course it is, but this time it's different. We're always under scrutiny, but I'm not giving away any secrets when I say that this station, this team, is costing money that some people don't think is justified.'

'So if we don't prove our worth, we're to be closed?' Rogers shook his head. 'That's bollocks, surely? It's totally unfair.'

'It won't be that simple, no, but it won't help our cause,' Kendrick said.

'Is there a cause?' Catherine asked. There had been rumours for months, if not years. Over the last decade, many other stations had closed and Catherine had never quite understood how their own had survived. She thought again about what would happen if her job at Northolme disappeared.

'Resources and personnel are being pooled,' Kendrick reminded her. 'Teams can be parachuted into any station to take over an investigation or work with the existing team – you know that better than most. It's the future, or so I'm told. I think I've even got the lingo right.' He rested a hand on his belly, and Catherine saw him take a deep breath. 'And if that *is* the future, it would make teams like ours obsolete. None of this should be news to you.'

Dave Lancaster forced a laugh. 'It's not, but when you put it like that...'

'Should we be considering our options?' Rogers asked.

Kendrick gave a grim smile. 'Your options? Who knows. It can't hurt.'

Rogers exchanged a glance with Catherine. 'That's shit.'

'It's a decision other people will make, not us. Let's concentrate on what we can control.' Kendrick glanced over at Monk, who now had a crowd of officers around him. 'Priorities for today – we need to focus on whether there's a connection between Scott Greaves, Hollie Morton and Andy Nugent. We know Greaves was strangled, but whether the fire was started by the person who killed him, or whether our arsonist somehow picked a building that already contained a dead body, we need to find out. We've no CCTV footage to go through and I don't anticipate getting any. There just aren't any cameras near Hollie and Andy's property, either council-owned or private.'

'Maybe we'll get lucky and the garage across the road from Scott Greaves's place will have cameras we can check,' Chris said.

'It's possible. We already know there were no cameras around Greaves's own premises.' Kendrick clicked his tongue a few times. 'We'll work on the assumption that the fire at Greaves's place was arson. We've not had the official report yet, but the crew commander has already said it's all but certain. What else?'

'As the Super helpfully pointed out, we need to talk to Scott Greaves's wife – widow – and find out if he knew Hollie or Andy,' Catherine said. Kendrick raised his eyebrows at her.

'Well volunteered,' he said. 'We can also check their phone records when the information comes in, Facebook pages, all the usual stuff. I'll get someone onto it. Hopefully we'll have some preliminary stuff back from forensics today, at least on the Hollie Morton and Andy Nugent case. I'll be giving Mick Caffery a call later if not. We need to know what they found in Hollie and Andy's house. He says he's been able to get DNA samples from the kids after the grandparents gave their permission, so that's sorted. Now we just need the results.' He took a breath. 'I'm going to ask a few uniforms to help us out today – our own uniforms.' Another glance at the group from Headquarters. 'Who do we reckon?'

'Nat Roberts,' Anna said immediately.

'Emily Lawrence,' Catherine added. 'Tim Riley.'

Kendrick nodded. 'We need all the help we can get. I'll ask Control to locate them, get them back here. Other priorities?'

'We still haven't tracked down any of the people who disappeared from the church near the Greaves scene, or the kid on the bike that did a runner,' Chris said.

'And I doubt we will. Don't worry about it,' Kendrick told him.

'You don't think it's a priority?' Chris was surprised, but Catherine could understand Kendrick's reluctance to spend time on it. Time would tell whether he was making a mistake, and she knew if he was, that it would be noticed.

'I'm not saying we won't follow it up, I'm saying it's not something this team needs to be concentrating on,' Kendrick said. 'What else?'

Knight cleared his throat. 'As you've mentioned, we need to know whether Andy Nugent was the father of both the children.' Catherine glanced at him, but Knight kept his eyes on Kendrick. 'And we should speak to Hollie and Andy's families again about their movements the day they were killed. We don't have enough information.'

'There's also the question of the Cloughs' alibis,' Catherine said. She told them quickly about the conversation she'd had the previous evening with Pete Williamson, and the names he'd given her.

'So that's what you were up to,' Anna said.

Catherine grinned at her. 'What did you think I was doing, chatting him up?'

'Anna, can you and PC Lawrence speak to these people from the pub, and the Cloughs?' Kendrick said. He then looked to DC Dave Lancaster. 'Dave, take PC Roberts and talk to Eric and Michelle Morton again. I want to know whether they knew Scott Greaves, or if Hollie did, and ask them again about where they were when Andy and Hollie died. That'll cover the time period for Scott Greaves's death too. Family members giving each other airy-fairy alibis isn't good enough.'

'Right, boss.' Dave spoke uncertainly, and Catherine wondered if he was more concerned about facing the Mortons again, or about spending the day with Nat Roberts.

Kendrick pinched his lower lip between his thumb and forefinger, then nodded at Chris Rogers. 'Chris, you and PC Riley need to speak to Andy Nugent's parents again. Same questions – their movements on the day our three victims died. We also need to know if Andy mentioned working at a scrapyard and anything else they can tell us that might help. Your guess is as good as mine about what that might be.'

'Okay. We're treating the cases as linked then?' Chris asked.

'Not necessarily, not yet at least. We're utilising our resources – you lot – in the most effective way possible,' Kendrick said. 'That's the kind of bollocks I have to listen to in meetings at HQ, so I may as well inflict it on you too.' He checked his watch. 'Catherine, Jonathan – talk to Scott Greaves's wife. I want you to talk to Hollie and Andy's next-door neighbours again too – what are they called?'

'Mr and Mrs Spence,' Catherine told him.

'Thank you. I'm going to chase Mick about the kids' DNA tests. I want you all back here at two and we'll see where we are.' Kendrick stepped away from the desk and glared at them. 'Off you go then.'

'What about the briefing?' Catherine said. She was surprised Kendrick didn't want Knight, as deputy SIO, beside him. Then again, Kendrick didn't need his hand held.

'I'll do it myself. I'm going to get some more house-to-house sorted, ask around the Meadowflower again. Someone killed Andy Nugent, even if he'd already killed Hollie himself. Consider this your briefing, and now I want you all out there asking questions.' Kendrick turned away.

Catherine pushed back her chair, following Anna and the others as they headed for the door. She was conscious of the eyes of Monk and his team as they crossed the room and wondered if Kendrick had made the right decision.

By sending them out before the briefing had even started, he was separating them from the team from Lincoln, singling them out. Making the point that they were his team, his officers. What would Jane Stringer make of that?

Back upstairs, Knight disappeared into his office while the others gathered around Anna's desk.

'That was weird, wasn't it?' Chris Rogers said. 'Sending us out before the briefing?'

'Is the boss trying to wind the Super up, or what?' Anna said. Catherine shrugged.

'Rather him than me,' she said.

18

Catherine drove out of the station's car park, Knight sitting beside her, eyes on his phone.

'What did you make of that?' Catherine asked.

'Kendrick showing the lot from Lincoln who's in charge?' Knight smiled. 'Can't blame him.'

'Do you think Stringer has asked someone here to keep an eye on us?'

'Not sure why she'd bother. Why should she care if you and a few of the others went out last night? You worked late, you wanted to relax, you were hungry. So what?'

'It's like she wants to justify shutting us down,' Catherine said. 'Gathering evidence that there's no point in us being here.' She braked as they approached the pedestrian crossing outside the local grammar school. Kids in navy blazers and grey skirts or trousers streamed across, talking and laughing, jostling each other. Some didn't look old enough to have left primary school, others were almost adults. Catherine reached for the gearstick as the last few reached the pavement on the other side, then noticed a young lad approach, hesitating as he saw everyone else had crossed. He glanced at their car, and Catherine smiled, waving him across. Lifting a hand in thanks, he scurried over the crossing. On the other side of the road, the driver waiting opposite them glared, shaking his head at Catherine. She resisted the temptation to raise a couple of fingers at him as she accelerated away.

'Have you given any thought to what you'd do if they did close our station?' she said.

'Not really. I wouldn't re-join the Met, that's for sure.'

'You wouldn't be tempted?' Catherine thought about Olivia, the child who might be Knight's daughter, living in London with her mother.

'No way.' Knight was definite. 'And Jo would never want to live down there.'

'Isla stayed over last night, and guess what she told me?' Catherine wondered whether she should confide in Knight, but Isla hadn't asked her to keep the news to herself and she knew she could trust him. She explained and Knight whistled.

'It's a great opportunity,' he said.

'As I told her.'

'But I can understand her saying no. She loves you.' Knight turned to look at Catherine with one of his shy smiles. She gave a tiny nod, then concentrated on the road. Isla had never said the words, not that she was going to tell Knight that, and she had never said them to Isla. Even after their conversation the previous evening, she was afraid of scaring her away, and if that happened, the job in London would give Isla the perfect bolthole.

There was silence for a couple of minutes, Knight gazing out of the window and Catherine trying to forget Isla, closing her mind to everything but the job in hand. Ashley Greaves deserved her full attention.

'She's going to do the test,' Knight said softly.

Catherine glanced at him. 'What?'

'The paternity test. Caitlin's agreed, says we all need to know.' He paused, licked his lips. 'She should have the results by tomorrow evening.'

Catherine hesitated, not sure what to say. 'Well, that's... good, isn't it?'

He smiled. 'They're going to use Jed's DNA, and obviously Olivia's. And if it's not him...'

'Then it must be you.'

Knight gave a strangled laugh. 'Hopefully.'

'What do you mean? Caitlin wasn't...?'

'Not as far as I know, but she was already seeing Jed when she and I were still together, and I just... Well, what if there was someone else as well? Even if this test proves Jed's not Olivia's dad, I want to do another one myself.'

'I can understand that. You need to know for sure.' He was using Olivia's name now, not just calling her 'the baby', Catherine realised. Maybe now he was being promised an answer, Knight was allowing himself to hope. Catherine's grip on the steering wheel tightened for a second; she just hoped he wouldn't get hurt.

'Exactly,' Knight said. 'Problem is, Caitlin's being awkward.'

She snorted. 'Surely not.' In Catherine's eyes, Knight's ex was a selfish, thoughtless nightmare, but at least she was finally doing the right thing.

'I've told her I need to be a hundred per cent certain, for Olivia's sake as well as mine. And Jo's.'

'Of course you do, and Caitlin should understand that,' Catherine told him. Caitlin should, but probably wouldn't.

'If Jed's test is negative, I've said I'll go down to London, pay for another test myself. If it turns out I *am* Olivia's dad, I want everything done properly, legally. But Caitlin doesn't see why I can't just take her word for it.'

'Because you can't. It's too important, for you, Jo and above everything, for Olivia. Caitlin's lied to you before.'

Knight nodded. 'She swears there was only me and Jed, but her trying to avoid another test makes me wonder.' He rubbed his face with both hands. 'Of course, it's more likely Jed's Olivia's dad, so it won't matter.'

He turned back to the window, and Catherine took the hint, driving the rest of the way in silence.

—

The house Ashley Greaves had shared with her husband was on a new housing estate, close to the edge of town. The Greaveses' house was semi-detached, built over three storeys and the houses further into the estate were larger, detached, the kind places that were few and far between in Northolme. Knight glanced around as Catherine nudged the car close to the kerb.

'Nice area,' he said.

'I looked at one of these houses with my ex,' Catherine said. 'They might have three floors, but all the rooms are tiny.'

Knight opened his door. 'That's why I bought my old cottage.'

'You made the right decision.' Catherine glanced at the house, saw a figure move behind the glass in the front door. As she got out and locked the car, she saw the door open. Knight waited for Catherine and they approached the house together. A woman waited in the doorway, her arms wrapped around her body. She wore jeans, a baggy T-shirt, and her feet were bare. Her long blonde hair hadn't been brushed, and she looked exhausted. Two small boys stood beside her, one with his thumb in his mouth, the other hiding behind his mother's leg. Catherine's throat tightened at the sight of Scott Greaves's tiny sons.

Ashley Greaves watched them. As they reached the house another woman appeared behind her, older than Ashley, probably her mother, and led the children away.

'You're here to talk about Scott,' Ashley said. Her voice caught on his name, and she took a deep, shuddering breath.

'That's right,' Knight said. 'We're sorry for—'

'My loss?' Ashley gave a shaky smile. 'Thank you. You'd better come in.' She stepped back.

Catherine followed Knight, almost bumping into his back as he stopped to slip off his shoes.

'No need for that,' Ashley said. 'You should see the mess the kids make.'

Knight smiled. 'But we're old enough to know better.'

Catherine stepped out of her boots and debated taking her jacket off too. It was another mild April day but the temperature inside the house was stifling. Someone must have turned the central heating up to its maximum temperature.

'Are we okay to talk in the conservatory?' Ashley asked. 'The boys are in the living room with my mum and I don't want them to overhear any of this. I haven't… They don't know about Scott yet.'

'Of course,' Knight said.

Ashley turned away and they followed her down a carpeted hallway. As they passed the open living room door, Catherine could hear a TV, cartoon voices, but no laughter.

Ashley led them into the kitchen, the black floor tiles and granite work surfaces gleaming. Beyond the kitchen was a small dining area, and then Catherine saw what Ashley had undersold as 'the conservatory'.

It was a huge space, as wide as the house and just as long, the walls and doors full-length glass panels, the framework black metal and a roof made of more glass. The tiles beneath Catherine's feet were warm, and she saw discreet spotlights ready to illuminate the room as night drew in. There was a huge TV and games consoles on a cabinet with two large leather sofas arranged around it, a coffee table, and a couple of crammed bookcases. Looking around, Catherine made a note to find out if Ashley had a job and if not, how much money Scott Greaves had been making on his second-hand motors. The house itself might be fairly modest, but this space would have cost a fortune to build.

Ashley waved a hand towards one of the sofas. 'Sit down,' she said. 'Can I get you some tea? Coffee?'

'No, thank you,' Knight said. 'We just have a few questions; it shouldn't take long.'

Ashley nodded, hugging herself again, her eyes never still. Catherine moved towards her.

'Shall we all sit here?' She settled herself in the nearest seat and smiled up at Ashley. 'This is an amazing room.'

Ashley gazed around as though she'd never seen the place before. 'Room? That's what Scott calls it, the garden room. He loves sitting in here.' She huddled in the corner of the same sofa Catherine sat on. 'Well, he did. Before he left, before... before all this.'

Knight sat on a different sofa, his legs uncrossed, and his hands resting on his thighs. Relaxed, unthreatening. Ready to listen. Catherine adjusted her position so she could see Ashley without having to turn her head. Ashley drew her legs up beneath her and wrapped her arms around them, almost curling into a ball.

'They told me there was a fire at Scott's dealership.' She smiled, her eyes filling with tears. 'He always said that, "dealership", like he had a posh showroom instead of a bit of concrete and a shed.' She sniffed, took a tissue from her jeans pocket. 'He shouldn't have even been there. He should have been here, at home with his family. Then he'd still be alive.' She scrubbed at her eyes with the tissue. 'Was the fire started deliberately? There've been loads around here recently... Well, you'll know that.'

'Mrs Greaves, your husband didn't die because of the fire,' Catherine said gently. 'I'm afraid he was strangled.'

Ashley's eyes widened and she clapped a hand over her mouth. She seemed to shudder, and it looked to Catherine as if she was trying to hold in a surge of emotion, physically preventing it from bursting out. 'But I thought... I assumed...'

'I'm sorry,' Knight said. 'We've only just received the confirmation ourselves.'

'You mean Scott was murdered?'

'Yes, he was,' Catherine said, hating what they were doing to this woman. What someone else had done to her. 'I'm so sorry.'

Ashley shook her head, her eyes unfocused, staring at nothing. 'Murdered. But why?'

'We don't know yet, but we're going to find out. Can you help us, Ashley?' Knight spoke quietly, as he would to a child. Some people would be angered by this, lash out either verbally or physically, but Knight had read Ashley well. She screwed up her face as though speaking caused her pain.

'How?' she said, her voice stronger now. 'What do you want to know?'

'We were told that Scott had been sleeping in his office,' Knight said. 'Is that correct?'

Now Ashley snorted. 'It was his decision. I didn't force him to leave.'

'What was the problem?' Catherine asked.

'Scott had the problem,' Ashley said. 'He'd been different for a while, and I'd had enough. I asked him what was going on. He didn't like that, said nothing was wrong, that I was paranoid, seeing things that weren't there.' She stopped, took a deep breath. 'Even after I'd asked him about it, nothing changed. He was weird about his phone, started keeping it in his pocket all the time when he just used to chuck it down on the table with his wallet and keys when he got in. He was late home a few times and wouldn't tell me where he'd been. And he took money from our joint account, not loads but enough that I noticed. I mean, we don't keep tabs on each other, we can both spend whatever we like within reason, once the bills are paid and the boys have everything they need. But Scott never told me where the money had gone.'

'How much are we talking about?' Catherine asked. Did Scott Greaves have a gambling, drug or alcohol addiction? She thought Ashley would have suspected if he'd developed a habit, though some people were good at hiding them.

'Fifty quid here, fifty quid there,' Ashley said. 'Couple of hundred quid a month. Like I said, not a massive amount but you know – we're not rich, and you notice.' She closed her eyes for a second. 'Then one night, about a month ago, he was late home again. I asked him where he'd been and he just mumbled something about someone wanting to go on a late test drive. It really pissed me off, him thinking I was stupid enough to believe his lies. I asked what her name was.'

'You assumed he was having an affair?' Knight said.

Ashley stared at him. 'Wouldn't you?'

He looked back at her. 'What did Scott say?'

Ashley made a sound that was half laugh, half sob. 'He denied it, so I showed him our bank statement, asked him where the money had gone. He was angry, told me they were business expenses. I knew he was lying because he's never used our account for business stuff. He doesn't work like that. Our personal finances are kept completely separate. In the end he walked out.'

'Did you believe Scott?' Catherine asked. Ashley had said she and Scott weren't rich, and Catherine had to wonder who she was comparing them to. If their house was anything to go by, they were doing okay.

'I wanted to, but...' Ashley shook her head, wiped her eyes again. 'Why wouldn't he tell me what he was using the money for if nothing was going on? He was lying about it being for expenses; I could see he was.'

'Did he come back to house that night?'

Ashley nodded. 'Eventually. I tried calling him a couple of times, but he didn't answer, and I thought... well, I thought maybe he'd gone to her, whoever she was. But when he came home, a couple of hours later, he said he'd just been driving around and I believed him. He was tired, upset...' She sniffed. 'Then a couple of weeks ago, more money had gone from the account, and I... I just lost it. I found a suitcase, packed a load of his clothes and left it outside the front door. I sent him a text, told him he could come to collect it and that I didn't want to see him until he was willing to tell me the truth about what was going on.' She gulped. 'But he didn't come back. He sent me a couple of messages asking how I was, if the kids were okay, asking for photographs of them or videos. But he never came to the house, never mentioned coming home.' Her arms tightened around her legs, tears starting again.

'Can I get you a glass of water?' Knight asked gently.

Sitting up straight, Ashley scrubbed at her eyes with the tissue. 'No, thank you. Can we just…?' She waved a hand, and Catherine knew what she meant – just get this over with. Knight nodded.

'If you believed Scott was having an affair, did you have a suspicion who he might have been seeing?' he asked.

Ashley shook her head. 'No, not a clue, and believe me, I've thought about it a lot. We've always done everything together, had the same friends – we started going out when we were seventeen. Whoever she is, he must have met her through the business, maybe sold her a car. He went out with his mates once a month and I thought maybe he'd met someone then, but I sent texts to the ones I have numbers for asking if they knew anything or if they'd noticed anything weird about the way Scott was acting. No one had, or if they knew anything, they weren't going to tell me.'

'We'll need their names and numbers, please,' Knight said. Ashley pulled her phone from her pocket.

'Yeah, they'll have to tell you the truth, won't they? Even if they wouldn't tell me.'

Knight smiled. 'You'd be surprised.'

Catherine tapped the two names and mobile numbers that Ashley read out into her phone. Neither of the names were familiar and she sent Kendrick a text with the details, knowing he would get someone onto looking into the backgrounds of the men as soon as he could. At this stage, it was impossible to know what information would prove relevant to the enquiry, and what was a waste of time. Best to play it safe and check everything they could. She thought back to her conversation with Hollie Morton's sister, Chloe. She'd said there had been rumours about her sister, that her youngest child wasn't fathered by her partner, Andy Nugent. Could Hollie have been Scott Greaves's new girlfriend?

Catherine scrolled to photographs of Andy Nugent and Hollie Morton. She decided to show Ashley the picture of Andy first, reasoning that if Ashley saw Hollie, she might guess what Catherine was thinking.

'Would you have a look at some photographs for us please, Ashley?'

The other woman looked apprehensive. 'It's not... They're not of Scott, are they? Not of... of his body?'

'No, no,' Catherine reassured her.

'I wondered... I didn't know.' Ashley gulped again. 'Will I have to see him? Identify him?'

'No,' Knight said. 'As you'll know, in some cases we do have to ask people to identify a loved one, but in other situations, we have different ways of getting the answers we need.'

Ashley tipped her head back, blinking tears away. 'You mean if a body's been in a fire.'

Knight nodded. 'Sometimes.'

'You're talking about dental records? You'll need the details of our dentist?' Now Ashley spoke calmly, her eyes on Knight's face.

'Yes please,' Knight said. 'I'm sorry to have to ask, but we need to be certain—'

'That it was his body you found. I know. Scott used a different dentist to me and the kids. He's been going there for years. I've got an appointment letter somewhere. I'll find it.'

She stood, left the room. Knight mouthed, 'Hollie and Scott?'

Catherine raised her eyebrows, spread her hands. 'Maybe. The money?' she mouthed back.

'Business problems? Don't know.' Knight was already stabbing at his phone, and Catherine guessed it would be another request for one of the team to obtain the Greaveses' bank records, if it hadn't already been done.

As Ashley came back into the room, they both smiled at her. She held a letter out to Knight, and he took it from her. 'Thank you.'

As she sat back down, Ashley's hands covered her mouth for a second. 'Is there any possibility it isn't him?'

It was a question Catherine had been expecting, one the families of victims often asked, a grain of hope they could latch onto.

'All the evidence we have so far tells us that the body we found was Scott's,' she said, trying to make her tone as gentle as Knight's.

Ashley gave a slow nod, as though resigning herself. 'The officers who came to tell me that the dealership had burnt down, that they'd found a body... they showed me photographs of a watch and a wedding ring. They wanted to know if they were Scott's. The watch, I couldn't tell – it was damaged so badly – but I knew the ring was Scott's. It's engraved, we had them both engraved.' Tears were falling freely again now, and Ashley rubbed them away with impatient movements of her hands. 'I'd like them back. I know it won't be for a while, but I want them. I'm still his wife, after all.'

'They'll be returned to you as soon as possible,' Knight said.

'They asked about his tattoo.' Ashley's chin trembled. 'The one on his arm. The boys' names and dates of birth, and my name, inside a heart. I told him it was tacky, but he loved it. The officers knew about it; they described it to me.'

Catherine knew that the tattoo had been noticed when Scott Greaves's body had been removed from his office building. His skin had been damaged enough that there was no possibility of his family seeing his body or of an open casket, but they had been able to find some clues about his identity from the remains.

'That's right,' Knight said.

Ashley took a deep breath and blew it out slowly. Catherine could almost see her steadying herself, drawing on a strength she'd seen so many times before from victims, from the relatives of victims. Even if they were a long way from accepting what happened to them or to the person they loved, they were often somehow able to help the police find answers. In some cases, Catherine wondered if maybe it helped them too.

'Okay,' Ashley said. She took another breath and managed a shaky smile. 'Okay. You said you had some photographs to show me?'

Catherine held up her phone. 'If you're sure?'

'Please, I just want to—' Ashley made another gesture of impatience.

'Okay.' Catherine showed the picture of Andy Nugent. 'Do you recognise him?'

Ashley studied the image, her expression bleak. 'They showed this photo on the news this morning. He's dead, isn't he, him and his girlfriend? More death.'

'I'm afraid so.' Catherine found the photo of Hollie and showed it Ashley. 'This is his partner. Have you seen either of them before?'

Ashley studied the image. 'She was on the news too, but no. No, I'm sure I haven't seen them before then. I might have passed them in town, in the supermarket or whatever, but I don't remember their faces. I've never spoken to them.'

'Their names were Hollie Morton and Andrew, or Andy, Nugent. Can you remember hearing Scott mention either of them?' Knight asked. Ashley frowned, thinking about it.

'I don't think so.' She lifted her head, looked at Knight then at Catherine. 'I thought you were here to talk about Scott? This town is tiny. How can three people have died like this in one night? Are you saying there's some link between his death and theirs?'

'Not at the moment, but we need to—' Catherine began.

Ashley's eyes widened. 'Wait a minute. Was it her?' She stabbed a finger towards Catherine's phone. 'Hollie whatever her name was. Is she the one Scott was seeing?'

'We're just trying to establish whether your husband knew either of these people,' Knight said. 'As DS Bishop said, we don't know whether his death is linked to theirs, but at this stage we've no reason to believe they'd even met each other.'

Ashley sneered. 'Find out if she had a new car, that might give you a clue.'

Catherine knew work would already be underway to discover whether that was the link between their three victims, but she wasn't going to tell Ashley that.

Knight ignored the comment too. 'When did you last hear from Scott?'

'I'd have to check.' Ashley picked up her phone from her lap. 'I hadn't spoken to him on the phone since he left, it was just texts, and I sent him a few photos and videos.'

'And what about the evening your husband died?' Knight said. 'Were you at home?'

Ashley's eyes narrowed. 'I'm effectively a single parent, and I've got four-year-old twins. I'm not going to be out clubbing every night, am I?'

Catherine watched her expression change as she realised what she'd said. She was definitely a single parent now.

'What about earlier in the day?' Knight asked. 'Do you have a job?'

She seemed shell-shocked again now, her voice quiet, uncertain. 'Yes, but I've had a couple of weeks off. As you'll understand, since Scott left I've needed some time.'

'Of course. Where do you work?'

'At Robertson's, in town.' She saw Knight frown. 'It's a law firm. I manage the reception, do some admin.'

'Full time?'

'Until the kids were born, now I do five hours a day. My mum has the boys.'

Reception and admin work wouldn't pay for this house, Catherine knew. They weren't expecting to recover any of Scott Greaves's financial records from his ruined office building, but there might be something in this house. A search team would be arriving within hours to go through the place.

'The kids and I were at home all day,' Ashley said. 'We went to the playground after lunch, about one thirty maybe, but not for long because it started raining. We

224

didn't see anyone we knew. Then back here. The kids went to bed about seven, I had a couple of glasses of wine and watched TV until eleven, then went to bed myself.' She spread her hands. 'That's it.'

Knight nodded. 'Thank you.'

Ashley's head turned quickly as they heard one of the twins begin to cry in the living room. The sound quickly became full-on screaming, and Ashley scrambled to her feet.

'I need to go and—'

'That's fine,' Knight said. 'We'll see ourselves out.'

Ashley hurried out of the room, not looking back at them.

19

'That was interesting,' Knight said as he started the car's engine.

Catherine knew what he meant. 'Her going from devastated to furious, to devastated again?' She checked her phone. Nothing from Isla. 'I think she was genuine though.'

'Genuinely shocked and grieving? Yeah, agreed.' Knight performed a neat turn in the road. 'She seems determined he was having an affair though.'

'I don't understand why he would be secretive about his phone but then take money from their joint account. He must have dealt with cash in his business – why not use that, and his wife would have been none the wiser?'

Knight turned back onto the main road. 'She might be wrong and the money was for business expenses.'

'We need his phone records.'

'What else could he have needed the cash for? Could be drugs or drink, but there's no point chasing Jo for toxicology results yet.'

'You never know.' Catherine nodded at the car's dash-board. 'Why don't we give her a call?'

Knight flicked the indicator on as a car abruptly stopped in at the side of the road in front of them and pulled around it. 'I don't want to disturb her. She'll still be catching up from yesterday. She'd have let us know if there was anything to say.'

Catherine didn't push it, but again she wondered about Jo's health. Knight didn't want to talk to her when Catherine could hear, that much was clear, and it was unusual because she knew neither Jo nor Knight would have said anything embarrassing or unprofessional. Lovey-dovey conversations during working hours were not their style. 'If Hollie Morton was the woman Greaves was having an affair with and Andy found out, maybe he killed Hollie then went out later to find Scott Greaves?'

'We don't know where Andy was between Hollie's death and Jamie and Cal Dobson arriving just after six o'clock, but—'

'But Scott wasn't killed until later.' Catherine ran her hands through her hair.

'Maybe Scott killed Hollie, and Andy killed Scott.'

'Then who killed Andy?'

'Maybe Ashley Greaves killed all three of them.'

Catherine whistled. 'Bloody nightmare.'

'Like you said, we need Scott Greaves's phone records. There might be no link between his death and Hollie and Andy's at all.'

'It's possible.'

Knight smiled at her. 'But not likely.'

'Who knows. Our original arsonist has to be a suspect in Greaves's death too. Greaves could have come back to his office and found the fire being set, the arsonist panicked, grabbed the nearest bit of cable and strangled Greaves then left the fire to destroy the evidence.'

They were approaching the Meadowflower Estate now. Knight slowed for the first of the speed bumps as Catherine saw a group of kids standing in a garden further down the road. One of the lads was on a bike, a bright green bike. Catherine squinted at him. Could this be the kid they'd been looking for, the one she and Knight had seen in the group watching Scott Greaves's property burn while he lay dead inside? He was the right age, the right build and he had the bike that had been mentioned, but the description also probably fitted half the lads in town. As she watched, he pointed at the car and said something. The others laughed, and the boy broke away from the group, pedalled towards the car and knocked on Catherine's window as they crawled over the speedbump. Knight braked and they stared out at the boy. His mates were strolling towards them now. He should have been at school, they all should have, but Catherine knew better than to ask why they weren't.

'What do you want?' she mouthed at him.

'You the police?' he shouted.

Knight turned off the engine, opened his door. He stood, leaning on the roof of the car.

'What's the problem?' he said. The boy stepped back, smirking up at him. Catherine wound down her window. They needed to speak to him, but she didn't want to scare him off either. The estate was like a warren, and plenty of people on the police's radar had disappeared there before.

'No problem, just wanted to know what's happening,' he said. 'We're getting a bit worried, all these people being killed in town. Bit scared.' Behind him, the other kids laughed. 'Shitting ourselves. Fires and murders, and you lot riding around town doing nothing.' The boy glanced back at his friends, then leaned closer to Catherine's door. He lowered his voice. 'How much do you pay for information?'

He was too close, and Catherine leaned as far back in her seat as she could. It wasn't enough. He was big enough to be intimidating, skinny though he was.

'Information about what?' she said.

'Wouldn't you like to know?'

Knight tried a smile. 'What's your name? If you know something, why don't you get in the back of the car? We can talk about it at the station.'

The boy's face changed. 'Fuck you.' He turned the bike around and started pedalling. His friends were jeering, shouting abuse as they ran. Catherine wound the window up as Knight got back into the car and accelerated away.

'All right, that was a stupid thing to say,' he said. 'Which way did they go?'

Catherine couldn't disagree as she grabbed her radio. 'Into one of the gardens. If they get into the back, they can cut through, go further into the estate and they'll be streets away in no time. I'll get onto Control, there might be another car around, and if not they can send someone. He could be the kid we've been looking for, the one we saw at the Greaves scene. Did you recognise him?'

'The bike's the right colour.' Knight grimaced. 'I'm an idiot, I should have gone to him, spoken to him properly. If he lives here on the estate, he might have known Andy or Hollie. He could have heard a rumour, even seen something, even if he knows nothing about the arsons.'

'Or he was just showing off in front of his mates. He wouldn't have talked to us when they were around anyway.'

Knight checked the rear-view mirror and pulled away as Catherine spoke to their control room. They were told there was a car a couple of minutes away that could try to pick the boy up, but Catherine thought it was hopeless.

He wouldn't speak to them now, even if they found him. The best they could hope for was he would come to them.

They were almost around the corner before the stone hit the car.

Knight stood, hands on hips, looking at the chip in the car's back window. The stone had left a gouge in the paintwork by the car's rear number plate. 'Great,' he said. 'I didn't even see where it came from. Thought the kids had run away?'

'I don't think it was the kids.' The stone could have been thrown by anyone; the kid on the bike had shouted that they were police loudly enough for most of the estate to hear. Catherine was watching the net curtain in the front window of Irene and Des Spence's house.

'The front door's already opening,' she said.

Knight turned away from the car, still shaking his head. 'Better than a CCTV camera, these two.'

They approached the house, Irene Spence watching from the doorway, her arms folded.

'I'd have thought you'd have phoned if you wanted to speak to us again.' She inclined her head at Catherine. 'I'm afraid I can't remember your name.'

Catherine told her. 'And this is Detective Inspector Jonathan Knight.' She tried a smile. 'We just need to ask you a couple more questions.'

'An inspector?' Irene Spence looked impressed, despite herself. She huffed. 'I suppose you better come in then. You're lucky we're at home.'

'Thank you.' Catherine stepped inside the house in her socks, her boots already in her hand. Mrs Spence gave an approving nod as Catherine placed them on the mat just inside the door. She looked expectantly at Knight and Catherine widened her eyes at him. He smiled at Mrs Spence, gave Catherine a mock glare as Mrs Spence turned away.

In the living room, Mr Spence was dozing in his chair by the unlit fire. There was a blanket tucked over his lower body and legs, a newspaper open on his lap. An untouched cup of tea stood on a small table by his side. Catherine and Knight stood awkwardly in the doorway while Irene Spence went over to her husband.

'Des,' she said, her as voice soft as a parent talking to a newborn baby. She reached out, cupped a hand around his cheek. 'Des?'

Catherine looked at the carpet, embarrassed, feeling as though she and Knight were intruding. Irene Spence's voice, the gentle touch of her hand on her husband's face, it all spoke of the severity of Des Spence's illness and the reality the couple were facing. Catherine guessed he had just months to live.

As her husband's eyes opened, Irene moved away and reverted to the tone Catherine had heard on her last visit. 'The police are here again.'

He sat up, blinking, the newspaper falling to the floor. Irene tutted and bent to pick it up as her husband started to cough.

'Where's your hanky?'

Des shook his head, one hand covering his mouth, the other reaching for the pocket of his cardigan. Irene took a tissue from her own sleeve and gave it to him. She turned to Catherine and Knight. 'Tea?'

'Please.' Knight smiled.

'Milk and sugar?'

'Just milk in both. Thank you,' Catherine said.

She nodded and abruptly turned away. Des gave a last cough and cleared his throat a couple of times.

'I'm sorry, excuse me,' he managed to say. Knight approached him and introduced himself. Des laughed. 'I won't shake your hand,' he said. 'Mind you, it's not catching.' He winked at Catherine. 'Sit down, the pair of you.'

Catherine took the seat on the sofa nearest him, and Knight sat at the other end, leaving the remaining armchair for Mrs Spence.

Des smoothed the blanket over his thighs. 'You want to ask more questions, is that it?'

'That's right.' Catherine replied. 'Are you okay to—'

'Don't worry about me. Ask away.'

'Okay. Thank you.' Catherine found her phone and showed Des Spence a photo of Scott Greaves. 'Do you recognise him?'

Des said, 'Hang on a minute.' He began to pat himself down, then reached under the blanket and brought out a pair of glasses. Putting them on, he leaned forward, squinting at the screen. 'I don't think... Does he live in town?'

'Have you seen him before?' Knight wasn't going to give anything away.

'I'm not sure.' Des took the glasses off, polished them on the blanket and pushed them back onto his nose. 'Maybe I have, but he's... well, he's just a bloke, isn't he? Nothing about him you'd remember. Nothing distinctive.'

Irene bustled back into the room with four cups on a tray. She set it on the table, handed one each to Catherine and Knight, who thanked her, and replaced her husband's cold tea with the fresh one. Sitting down with her own drink, she said, 'Who is it, Des?'

'Show it to Irene.' Des nodded at his wife. 'She's got a better memory for faces than I have.'

Catherine handed the phone to Knight, and he held it out to Irene. She pursed her lips.

'I don't think he lives on the estate, or if he does, we don't know him.' Sitting back in her chair, she sipped her tea. 'I don't think I've ever seen him before.'

'He lived nearby. He had a business in town,' Knight said.

Des just nodded, more focused on his tea, but Irene was sharper. 'Lived?'

Knight nodded. 'I'm afraid this man died the night before last.'

Des and Irene both gaped at him.

'Died where? In town?' Irene had her hand on her chest. 'That's the same day the people next door died. He wasn't in the house as well, was he?'

'Would you have been surprised if he'd been found next door?' Knight asked. 'Did Andy and Hollie often have visitors?'

'Not often. I mean the Dobson lads were here the other night, and they had deliveries sometimes, but visitors, no. They were noisy, like we told you, but it wasn't as though they were having parties every night. It was just them,' Irene said.

'Have you seen Jamie or Cal Dobson visiting Andy and Hollie before, or was the night before last the first time?' Catherine met Des's eyes as she asked the question, but it was Irene who answered.

'I'd never seen them here before. I looked out when I heard the car because I knew we weren't expecting anyone

233

and I like to know who's wandering around. When I saw Jamie Dobson and his brother get out, I knew it was okay.'

'They were in a car?' Catherine glanced at Knight. Jamie Dobson had said he'd been asked to come and look at Andy and Hollie's faulty boiler. If he was a plumber, surely he had a van for his work? And if so, wouldn't he have been driving it if he believed he was coming to the house to do some work? They needed to check. Knight gave her the phone back and she tapped out another text to Kendrick. 'Can you describe it?'

'The car? Small, a dark colour.'

It wasn't much, but it was better than nothing. Catherine added the information to the text, then turned back to Irene.

'Thank you. When we talked last time, you said that the Dobsons arrived next door at about six and left about eight o'clock,' Catherine said. 'Is that correct?'

Irene raised her eyebrows. 'Well, we weren't making it up.'

Catherine leaned forward, meeting the other woman's eyes. 'I'm not suggesting you were. Did you hear anything from next door, other than the video game, in that two-hour period? You mentioned before that they were "Laughing and joking, making a row" when they arrived.' Catherine held Irene's gaze. 'Those were your exact words, Mrs Spence.'

Irene snorted. 'You did write something down then.'

Catherine smiled. 'My colleague did. I just borrowed her notes.'

Des laughed. 'Notes? Isn't it all high tech these days? Computers telling you what to do, finding criminals because they dropped one hair at the crime scene?'

'We wish.' Catherine focused on him. 'How long did the noise go on for?'

'Not long.' Irene butted back in. 'As soon as the game started up, we couldn't hear a thing above it.'

And no doubt you were trying to, Catherine thought.

'Did Andy sound happy to see Jamie and Cal Dobson?' Knight asked.

'Yes, he was laughing with them, like I said.' Irene was frowning again.

'You saw them arrive; they came up to the door; you heard a conversation; then the video game started?'

'Yes, a few minutes after they arrived.' Scowling now, Irene crossed her arms.

'Did you hear Hollie's voice when the brothers got here? Did she greet them?' Hollie was already dead by that time, but Catherine knew what Knight was doing – keeping the Spences focused on what they'd heard, keep them thinking.

'No,' Irene said. 'Just him – Andy.'

'But he was talking loudly,' Des said anxiously. 'Hollie might have been there and we just didn't hear her. You'd hear men's voices above a woman's, wouldn't you? You know what lads are like when they get together, they—'

'We didn't hear Hollie.' Irene looked at her husband. 'We didn't, Des. Maybe she was there, maybe she wasn't, but if we didn't hear, we don't know either way.'

Des nodded, blinking behind his glasses. Catherine noticed the hand holding his tea shook a little. Knight wasn't exactly interrogating Irene Spence, but his quick-fire questions were beginning to get her back up. Catherine decided to keep her mouth shut as Knight smiled at Des, then turned back to Irene.

'But you're certain it was Andy who let them into the house?'

'Yes. I heard his voice,' she said.

'And what about when the Dobsons left? You said previously that you didn't see them go?'

'No, but we heard them. The door slammed and we heard an engine start.'

Knight nodded. 'And no one went outside with them, no one shouted goodbye from the house?'

'Not that we heard.'

'Was there any sound from next door at all as they left?'

'Like we told this young lady last time' – Irene jerked her head at Catherine – 'the game went off and apart from the slam of the front door, there was silence until the baby started crying a while later.'

'You didn't hear or see anyone else enter the house?'

'No.'

'And there was no noise from the house, even though you didn't hear Andy or Hollie leave?'

'No!' Irene almost shouted. 'But if you're thinking of accusing those Dobson lads of murder, you're wrong. I've known them since they were little boys, we know their parents. Their mum… she's not well, and the last thing those lads need is you lot making accusations.'

'We're not accusing them of anything,' Knight said quietly. Catherine knew he'd got the answers he wanted, but it was unlike him to be so direct.

Now Irene Spence's hand was also shaking.

Des glared at Knight. 'We've told you the truth, told you as much as we can.'

'And we appreciate it.' Knight spoke gently. 'But you have to understand that we have to find out what happened to your neighbours.'

'Of course.' Des drank some tea. 'We just want to help, don't we, Irene?'

She nodded, all the fight leaving her. 'It's been a shock, all this. What with our Matthew suddenly being taken ill, all this next door, and Des...' She swallowed. Her husband smiled at her, and again Catherine saw the bond between them. She finished her own tea, replaced the cup on the tray. Knight glanced at her and followed suit.

'Is that it? That's all you wanted to ask?' Irene looked from Knight to Catherine. 'But we've told you nothing new.'

'You've told us what you know,' Knight said as he got to his feet.

Des reached for his walking stick, started to shuffle forward in his chair.

'Please don't get up, sir,' Catherine said quickly. She stood and moved towards the door.

'Thank you both for the tea and for your time,' Knight said.

Des nodded. 'I hope you find them, whoever did this. Next door were noisy, inconsiderate, and the things we've said about them in the past, I bet their ears were on fire ten times a day.' He sniffed, wiped a hand over his eyes. 'But this... Those kids left without their parents.' He grabbed Knight's wrist. 'You'll find them, won't you?'

—

'Jamie Dobson has a Ford Transit van, and his mum owns a black Vauxhall Corsa,' Catherine told Knight as she tucked her phone back into her pocket. Again, Knight was driving slowly through the streets of the Meadowflower Estate. Catherine was looking out for the boy who had stopped them earlier, but the area was quiet.

'Sounds like a small, dark coloured car to me. Where's Jade Walsh's house from here?'

Catherine looked around, trying to get her bearings again. In Meadowflower, most of the streets looked the same. Catherine had once known the area well during her time in uniform but these days the place seemed like a maze. 'Left here,' she said.

When they arrived at the house, Jade took a while to answer to the door. When it finally opened, she was in a dressing gown, looking harassed, her face red.

'Look, both my kids have a sickness bug.' She frowned at Catherine. 'I really don't have time to talk, and believe me, you wouldn't want to come inside. Anyway, I've already told you everything I know.'

'We just need a few minutes of your time,' Knight said.

Jade scowled. 'Like I said, I'm looking after my children. What do you want?'

Catherine was shocked at her tone. Jade had been friendly before, if a little nervous, now she was abrupt and hostile. Why? She found the photo of Scott Greaves again on her phone. It was already feeling like a long day. 'Do you know him?'

Jade looked back into the house as they heard one of the children begin to cry. She scanned the photograph. 'No.'

'Could you have another look, please?' Knight asked. Jade glared at him but focused on the phone again.

'No, sorry.'

'He wasn't a mate of Andy's?'

Jade made a sound of impatience. 'Like I've already said, I don't know who Andy's friends were, not now. I've never seen that man before, I can tell you that.'

'His name's Scott Greaves,' Catherine told her. 'He owned the second-hand car place near the Trent bridge.'

'I don't have a car,' Jade said quickly. Both children were crying now, and she turned her head towards the sound.

'Did you ever hear Andy mention Scott Greaves's name?' Knight asked as more wailing came from the kitchen. Jade shook her head.

'No, but like I told you my relationship with Andy was years ago. How would I remember who he talked about back then? I'm sorry I can't help you, but I really need to get back to my kids.'

She stepped back and closed the door in their faces.

20

Rebecca Clough sat on a pile of tyres in her husband's workshop. Beside her, Dale rocked back on his heels, clearly not happy to have another two police officers on his premises again.

'We thought this was over,' he said. 'Why do you need to talk to us again?'

'There are a couple of things we need to ask you about,' Anna Varcoe said. She wasn't intimidated by his size, or his attitude. She and PC Emily Lawrence stood in front of the couple. It was an interesting location for an interview, and she'd been surprised to find Rebecca here as well as her husband.

Dale clicked his tongue. 'Like what? We've nothing more to tell you.'

Rebecca reached out, took her husband's hand. The gesture seemed to calm him, and his expression changed as he moved closer and squatted beside her.

'All right. Ask whatever you like,' he said.

Catherine had said Rebecca Clough was frail but determined, and, meeting her, Anna could see what Catherine meant. Dale had been belligerent since he'd seen them getting out of the car, hostile to the point of rudeness, but one touch from his wife had defused his anger. It was an interesting dynamic, and Anna knew that if Catherine and Jonathan Knight had seen husband

and wife together, they would have noticed it too. Dale was physically imposing, Rebecca petite and slight. Dale was desperate to protect his wife from outside threats and harm, and Rebecca was ready to protect her husband from his own fear, anger and guilt. Anger was often rooted in fear, as Anna knew only too well, both from her time as a police officer and her life before it, and she guessed Dale Clough had a lot of fear as a result of the attack on his wife. Beside her, Emily Lawrence shuffled her feet and Anna told herself to stop the amateur psychology and get on with asking some questions.

'Thank you,' she said. 'We've spoken to several people who were in the pub two nights ago, when you were there for your anniversary meal.'

'And?'

'We have several witnesses who saw you arrive at the pub at around seven thirty and can confirm you were there until at least ten o'clock.'

'Ten? We were there until almost eleven.'

Anna spread her hands. 'None of the people we spoke to saw you after ten.'

Dale looked at his wife and then up at Anna. 'That's bullshit. We were there for another hour.'

Seeing he was about to explode, Anna kept talking. 'Can you think of anyone you spoke to, anyone else we can ask to confirm what you've said?'

'You mean anyone who can give us an alibi?' Dale shook his head, amazed. 'Are you still banging on about this bloke who's been killed? I told you, I don't know him. Rebecca doesn't either.'

Rebecca let go of Dale's hand and stood. 'The first officers who came to talk to me – they wouldn't tell me if this man who's been killed was the one who attacked me, but the fact you're back again seems to confirm he was.'

Anna hesitated, and Emily Roberts said, 'We can't—'

'Can't tell me, I know. But your colleagues asked me if I knew this man, then they asked me about the attack, and finally they tell me he's dead. You want to know where we were the night he died, so we must be suspects, or at least people you need to speak to.' Rebecca paced a few steps away, then turned and came back. 'We understand, but all we can tell you is the truth. We left the pub just before eleven o'clock. It was still quite busy, they'd been doing a quiz, so I'm not surprised if no one saw us.'

Dale was nodding. 'We just wanted a quiet meal together. We weren't there to talk to people. Didn't expect to be interrogated later about our every move.'

'Okay. And you spoke to no one as you left the pub around eleven o'clock?'

'No one.' Dale spoke calmly, but Anna could see he was making an effort to stay polite. She couldn't say she blamed him. It didn't matter anyway – whether they'd left the pub at ten, eleven, or even a little later, they'd have had time to get to Andy Nugent's home and kill him before midnight, plus drop in on Scott Greaves on the way home. Anna chewed on the inside of her cheek, choosing her words carefully.

'What happened when you left the pub?'

Dale stared at her. 'We went home.' He watched as Rebecca pushed her hands through her hair, agitated.

'We went home, went to bed,' she said. 'Separately, even though we want to have a child, because even now we struggle to be close to each other.' She took a deep breath. 'Are you married?'

Unconsciously, Anna glanced down at her left hand. 'Engaged.'

'Can you imagine how it would feel if something happened, something completely out of your control, that had such a massive effect on your relationship?'

'I—'

Rebecca kept talking. 'No, you can't, not until you've been there. I wouldn't have been able to. People split up because of things like what that man did to me. I wouldn't wish death on anyone, not even him. We didn't kill him, but now someone has, maybe we can start living our lives again.'

Anna said nothing, and beside her, Emily Lawrence tucked her hands behind her back.

Dale got up, watching Anna. 'I thought I'd seen you before.'

Rebecca looked at him. 'What do you mean?'

'She was in the news a while ago.' He furrowed his brow, thinking about it. 'You were stabbed, weren't you? You almost died.'

Anna swallowed, the memories hitting her. The sudden intensity of the pain, then the absence of it as she started drifting, floating. Waking up confused, not knowing how many days she'd lost, to concerned faces and beeping machines. Her parents, worry and fear tightening their faces making them look much older, and Thomas sitting by her bed for as many hours as they would let him. 'So I'm told,' she said.

Rebecca moved closer, touched her arm. 'Then maybe you do understand. I'm sorry.'

Anna did. Jumping at shadows, checking over your shoulder. Even when you survived, your attacker still dogged your every step. Determined to get the conversation back on track, Anna asked, 'Did you walk home from the pub?'

'Yes.' Even Dale was subdued now.

Emily said, 'Did you see anyone on your way, call anyone, send any texts?'

'At that time? No.'

'All right.' Anna managed a smile. 'How long have you lived in the village?'

Dale squinted at her as though expecting a trap. 'Three years.' He glanced at his wife. 'After the attack I suggested moving, a new start, but Becca wouldn't hear of it.'

'Why should we move? Why should he drive us out of a house we love?' Rebecca said. Her voice was higher, the words running into each other.

'When you moved in, did you use a removal company?' Emily asked.

'What does that have to do with anything?' Dale demanded.

'Just answer the question, please.' Emily was stern.

Anna hid a smile as Dale's cheeks flushed. 'We used my work van, did most of the move ourselves, but we did hire a company for one day, just to bring the heavier stuff in. Wardrobes, the fridge freezer, stuff like that.'

'Can you remember which company you used?' Anna asked.

Dale's expression said he wasn't happy, had no idea where they were going with this, but he took his phone from his pocket. 'Can't remember the name, but I might still have their number.' He scrolled on the phone. 'Here you go. Neil's Wheels.' He glanced up. 'That's a shit name, isn't it?'

Emily took a note of the number as Anna took out her own phone and held it out to Rebecca.

'Can you tell me if you recognise this man?'

Rebecca took the phone, and Dale moved so he could look over her shoulder.

'No,' Rebecca said. 'I don't know him.'

'Never seen him before,' said Dale. 'Who is he?'

'He's dead.' Anna waited. 'His name was Scott Greaves.'

There was no reaction.

'And why are you asking us about him?' Dale said. 'Are you just going to come to us every time someone dies and show us a photograph? We've told you we were in the pub until eleven the other night, whatever the significance of that is, and we don't recognise them men in either of the photos you've shown us.' He screwed up his face. 'You're investigating the deaths of both the blokes you've asked us about?'

'We don't know who they are,' Rebecca said, sounding close to tears. 'I don't understand why you keep asking us about them.'

--

They saw the blue van just where Neil Wilcox had told them he'd be parked, on a side street not far from the centre of town. Wilcox had the driver's seat pushed back, a Styrofoam tray overflowing with chips on his lap. His mouth was crammed but he waved as they approached. He held out the chips and, with a smile, Anna took one.

'Knew you wouldn't be able to resist.' Wilcox looked at Emily. 'Go on.'

She grabbed a couple and he grinned. 'Now we're all friends, how can I help you?'

Anna nodded at his name on the side of the van. 'You own the company?'

'Yeah, though I'm trying to take a back seat. My two lads are ready to run the show themselves.'

'You're retiring?' Anna was surprised, having guessed Wilcox was in his late fifties.

He ate a few more chips. 'Got a camper van, want to make the most of it. I'll do some hours here and there, but why work when you don't need to?'

Anna couldn't argue. 'Do you employ other people, apart from your sons?'

Wilcox reached for the open can of Coke that sat on the passenger seat. 'Not at the moment. It's hard work if you're not used to it, and a lot of the lads out there these days want the money without putting the graft in. If that's the case, they don't last long.'

'What about in the past?'

'The past?' He squinted at her. 'How long ago are we talking? And why do you want to know?'

'Have you employed anyone called Andy Nugent?'

'No.' The answer came instantly. Wilcox didn't break eye contact, but his expression had changed.

'You've a good memory,' Anna said.

He forced a laugh. 'For names, yeah. Not for faces.'

Emily had the photograph ready. 'Funny you should say that. Do you know him?'

Wilcox made a point of studying the image. 'I've seen him in the news.'

'Then you'll be aware he died recently.'

'His girlfriend too, if I remember rightly? Very sad, but I didn't recognise either of them.' Wilcox licked his lips, dropped his empty can in the door pocket.

'You're sure?'

He raised his eyebrows. 'Would I lie to you?'

'Do you remember a removal job you did three years ago, a couple called Clough?' Anna gave him the address, but was Wilcox was laughing.

'Are you kidding? Have you any idea how many people we've moved since then? How am I supposed to remember a single job?'

'You could check your records,' Emily said.

Wilcox set his jaw. 'As you can see, I'm in the middle of a move.'

Anna held up her hands, adopted a reasonable tone. 'All we want to know is if you've ever employed a bloke called Andy Nugent. Then we'll get out of your hair.'

'I've already said no, I haven't. Not now, not three years ago, not ever.' He shifted in his seat, licked his lips again.

Anna guessed what the problem was. 'Mr Wilcox, we're not interested in how you run your business. If you've taken someone extra on for a big job now and again, paid them cash in hand to help out, we're not going to make trouble for you.'

'That's what they all say.' He turned to stare at the house he was parked outside. 'Is this going to take much longer? It doesn't look good for me, you questioning me like this. People will think we've been nicking from properties or something.'

'We have to be sure about this, Mr Wilcox. If Andy Nugent was part of your team when you moved the Cloughs into their house, you need to be honest with us.' Anna smiled. 'I assume you do keep proper records?'

Now he glared at her. 'Of course I do. I'm not some cowboy.'

Anna inclined her head. 'Then we could check, if we needed to?'

'Yes.' Wilcox didn't look at her. 'My accountants deal with all the payroll stuff. I just do the grafting.'

'And you're sure Andy Nugent has never worked for you, legitimately or otherwise.'

'Positive.'

'Okay.' Anna nodded. 'Do you know Scott Greaves? He—'

'Flogs second-hand cars?' Wilcox nodded. 'Yeah, I know of him.'

'Then you'll also know he's dead.'

Now Wilcox turned his head. 'Scott is? You're sure?'

Anna remembered the grim photographs in the incident room. 'Certain.'

'Bloody hell.' Wilcox glanced at the house. 'He must have only been my eldest lad's age. Car accident, was it?'

'Why would you think that?'

Wilcox shrugged. 'He's in the motor business – was, I should say. Makes sense.'

'His office building burnt down with him inside it.' Anna wouldn't usually have been so blunt but sometimes the direct approach was best.

Wilcox's mouth opened, but he didn't speak.

Emily gave him a second, then said, 'Sir?'

'Sorry, I… That's terrible.'

'As you've probably heard, an arsonist has been targeting business properties in town recently,' Anna said. 'Do you have an office yourself?'

They already knew Wilcox operated from his home address.

'No, the wife runs the admin side of things from the spare bedroom,' he said.

'What about your vans?'

'I rent part of a warehouse building to park them in.'

'You employ your wife and sons? A real family business.' Anna smiled.

'Something wrong with that?' Wilcox looked from her to Emily. 'I don't know what you want me to say.'

'If you can't help us, we'll leave you to it.'

Anna turned and walked away, Emily close behind her. When they were out of earshot, Emily said, 'You could almost see his nose growing.'

'But what was he lying about?' Anna checked her phone. Nothing from Thomas; her sharp words about him texting every chance he got to ask how she was feeling must have finally got through to him. She hadn't pretended to feel that moment's connection with Rebecca Clough – the understanding had been there. One event, one minute, even a few seconds could change your life, and Anna was only too aware how lucky she was to have recovered from her injuries. She had been determined to come back to work as soon as she was cleared to, because what was the good of sitting at home thinking about it all? She'd been stabbed, hovered near death, recovered. Time to move on. There were scars on the inside, the nightmares, the panic and anxiety, but Anna had chosen to conceal them the way she might have pulled a sleeve over a visible one. Amongst her colleagues, she knew she wasn't the only one.

'So what do we do?' Emily asked. 'You reckon he's had a few cash in hand workers and that's as far as it goes?'

Anna nodded. 'Probably, but he knows Scott Greaves and from his reaction, at least recognised Andy Nugent's name.'

'He did say he'd seen Hollie and Andy's deaths on the news. Maybe it was a shock to see Andy in the photo.'

'It's possible, but I think we'll be speaking to him again.'

21

Ross Morton stood with another man, both of them pointing at various areas of the building site as they talked. When he saw Nat Roberts and Dave Lancaster picking their way through pallets of bricks and piles of scaffolding, he said something to his friend and marched over to them.

'You're the police? What now?'

Dave lifted his chin, emphasising the fact that as big as the other man was, he was taller still.

'Ross Morton?'

Ross sneered. 'What do you want?'

'I'm DC Lancaster and this—'

'I don't care who you are. I'm trying to earn a living here.' Ross's hands were on his hips, shoulders back.

Nat Roberts looked him up and down. 'We need to talk to you about the day your sister died.'

They saw him swallow. 'When she was murdered, you mean.'

Nat nodded. 'I'm sorry.'

Ross lifted his hard hat to rub his forehead, staring at the floor. 'Why are you still asking questions? Andy killed her, anyone who'd met them would tell you that. No one else would want to hurt her.'

'But Andy's dead too—' Ross began to shout over Nat, but she kept talking.

'And we need to find out why. I understand if he was hurting your sister, you feel you don't much care who killed him, but our job is to find some answers. Andy had a family too.'

Ross said nothing, his face red, his mouth working.

'Is there somewhere we can talk privately?' Dave asked quietly.

Ross shrugged. 'Not unless you want to sit in the van.'

'That's fine,' Dave told him.

Ross turned away and started walking. There were several vehicles parked together at one side of the site and Ross made for a blue Transit, pulling a set of keys from his pocket. He took the driver's seat, leaving Nat and Dave to squeeze together in the passenger side. Nat nearest Ross, Dave by the door.

'Do you enjoy your job?' Nat asked.

Ross reached for the steering wheel, let his hands rest on it. 'Yeah. I wanted to work outside. Being in an office all day would drive me crazy.'

Lancaster said, 'Me too. It was either the police or the army for me.'

There was a pause and then Ross said, 'That's the bonding done then, is it?'

Nat smiled. 'As I said, we need you to tell us about—'

'The day my sister was murdered? Fine. You want to know what I did?'

'Please. We know it's not easy,' Dave told him.

Ross drummed his fingers on the steering wheel. 'I started work at eight thirty, had an hour for dinner at twelve, left at five thirty, same as always. Apart from my sister being murdered across town, it was just an average day.'

'Did you leave the premises on your lunch break?' Nat asked.

'Yeah, I went to Tesco. Bought a couple of sandwiches, pizza for my tea, and a few beers.'

'Do you have a receipt?'

Ross turned to look at her. 'I didn't bother picking up the receipt. I used my card, contactless.'

'And then?' Dave said.

'What do you mean?'

'What did you do then? Did you come back here? Did you go somewhere else?'

Ross had answered the question with a question of his own, and now Nat and Dave were both expecting him to lie to them. Instead, he surprised them. He tipped his head back to look at the van's roof, blinking hard.

'I'm going to tell you this because I think you need to know. I still think Andy killed my sister, but if there's a chance he didn't…' He gulped and rubbed his eyes. 'I don't know who killed Andy, and to be honest I don't give a shit, but his parents… snotty bastards that they are, they still should get some answers.' His voice was flat, devoid of emotion.

'I didn't come back here once I'd left Tesco. I went to my sister's.'

Nat raised her eyebrows. 'To Hollie's? Why?'

'I'd sent her a couple of texts and she hadn't replied. I tried to call her – no answer.' Ross swallowed a couple of times. 'I was worried, I thought maybe he'd hurt her, so I went up there.'

'What time was this?' Dave asked.

'Must have been just before half twelve when I got there. I tried to phone again, got her voicemail. I knocked on the back door, but no one answered.'

Dave frowned. 'The back door? How did you get to the back of the house if Hollie didn't come to the door? There's a padlocked six-foot gate between the side of the house and the garage, so you couldn't have gone around there.'

Ross was blushing. 'No. Like you said, you can't get into the back garden from the front, not without a key, and only Andy has that. If you got to the road behind Hollie's though, there's a fence running all the way down that part of the street that the council put up years ago.' He paused. 'Can't believe I'm telling you this, but one of the panels is loose and you can get through. Some people have planted hedges or put their own fences on their side so it's not just the council one, but in Hollie's garden there's only this massive old shed that backs right up to the council's fence.'

'So how do you get into the garden?' Nat asked.

'I cut a door in the back wall of the shed when Andy was out one day,' Ross said.

'What? Why?' Dave asked.

'Andy didn't know about it. The shed's been there forever, it's falling down and it's full of crap people have left behind. Andy never goes in there, and if he did, he'd have to look hard to find anything, especially since he wouldn't be expecting it to be there. I did a pretty good job, did my best to hide it. There's some old wooden shelving in there and I screwed that to the door, then nailed a load of plant pots and crap to the shelves. The whole things swings out when you open the door. You'd never realise it was there. You use the shed as a passageway between the street behind the house and the garden. It was an escape route for Hollie if she ever needed it, and I knew I could always get in to see her.'

'Clever. Who else knew?' Nat said.

'Just me, Chloe and Hollie. We didn't tell Mum and Dad, or anyone else.'

Which didn't mean no one else knew about it. 'You don't think people living in the next street would have noticed you disappearing through the hedge?' Dave asked.

Ross shook his head. 'No. There's a concrete bus stop in front of the loose panel. It's not that close, there's plenty of room to open the panel, but it gives you some cover. People walking up the road might see you, but it's a quiet street and if you're careful I don't see why anyone would notice, plus I only used it a couple of times. Chloe didn't go through, she waited at the bus stop. It was all about protecting Hollie.'

'Why go to all the trouble, just so you could get to the back door?'

Ross leaned forward so he could look past Nat. 'What?'

'Why the back door?' Dave repeated. 'Why didn't you just walk up to the front?'

'Because the old couple next door to Hollie are as nosy as shit. If I'd gone to the front door, they'd have seen me and they might have told Andy. It's safer to go around the back, plus you can park there. Hollie's street's a nightmare for parking.' Ross closed his eyes. 'Hollie's neighbours wouldn't know who I was. If I went to the front door and they told Andy that some bloke had been to the house... well, you can imagine. He wouldn't stop to think it might have been me, he'd just batter her.'

'You weren't worried the neighbours would see you in the garden?'

'Not really. They've a six-foot fence and loads of tall plants in the way. I suppose they might have seen me from upstairs, but the bathroom window's on the side of the

254

house and Hollie said they sleep in the front bedroom, so unless they were looking out of their spare room window, I'd be okay.'

Dave nodded. 'How often did you visit Hollie?'

Opening his eyes, Ross sat up straight. 'Just a couple of times, when she's not answered her phone. It was more for peace of mind than anything. One time Hollie came to the back door and waved, and I could see she was okay. Another time, Chloe hadn't been able to reach her and we went up there together.' He pressed his palms against his cheeks. 'Hollie came to the window, said she was okay, but we could she was in pain. I don't know what he'd done to her; I couldn't see any bruises. Chloe said maybe it was her ribs.'

'Was Chloe with you when you went to the house this time?' Nat asked.

'No. I was on my own. Chloe was at work, and I didn't tell her I couldn't reach Hollie. No point worrying her.'

That needed checking.

'You said you knocked on Hollie's door but no one answered. What next?'

'I tried to look through the windows but there was no one around, so I gave up, came back here.' Ross sniffed, rubbed at his eyes with his sleeve. 'I walked away and left her. She was probably already dead by then.' Nat and Dave kept quiet, and Ross made a sound, half laugh, half sob. 'I was too late.'

'Did you see Andy while you were there?' Nat asked.

Ross's hands clenched around the steering wheel. 'No. If I had, I'd have killed him, the bastard.' He froze, realising what he'd said. 'No, I didn't mean that, I'd never... I didn't kill him.' He gave a strangled laugh. 'If I had, I'd hardly be telling you about the secret way into the garden that only me and my sisters knew about, would I?'

Nat ignored that. 'Were you worried Andy had hurt your sister so badly she couldn't get to the door, couldn't even use her phone?'

Ross's head went down. 'It crossed my mind. Or that she was avoiding me. She did that sometimes. It was like she was ashamed, like it was her fault Andy beat her up. We tried to talk to her about it – me, Chloe, our mum and dad. We all wanted her to leave him, and come home, bring the kids, but she wouldn't.'

'Do you know why that was?' Dave asked.

'Pride, maybe? Though that's a stupid reason to stay in a house where you're not safe. I don't know. She said she loved him.' Ross was scornful. 'How she could, I don't know.'

Nat said, 'Did you hear any noise inside the house? The children crying, maybe?'

'No. If I had, I'd have broken a window, made sure I got inside.'

'Did you try the back door?'

He looked shocked. 'Of course not.'

'Why?'

'I wouldn't have just walked in, not unless I heard something.' He blushed. 'Anyway, I didn't think about trying the handle. Stupid bastard.'

'And you didn't break a window either.'

She sounded faintly accusing, and Ross turned on her. 'Yeah, Hollie would've been so pleased to see me if I'd gone smashing in there and she was fine, but her phone battery was flat. I was protecting her.'

Nat frowned. 'How?'

'If I'd broken in, made a fuss, Andy would have taken it out on Hollie. I told you, it's what he does. What he did, I mean. And he would be asking questions about how I'd got into the back garden. Either way, I'd be dropping Hollie in the shit.'

'You know a lot about how Andy treated Hollie,' Nat said.

Ross glared. 'Strange that, me wanting to know what was happening to my sister.'

'How did you know?'

'What do you mean, how?'

'Did Hollie have bruises when you saw her? Injuries she couldn't explain, wouldn't talk about? Did she tell you what Andy had done when you spoke to her on the phone?'

Ross's eyes blazed. 'She didn't need to. I could tell when he'd had a go at her. She sounded different, depressed. Even the kids couldn't cheer her up.'

'Maybe she *was* depressed,' Nat said. Dave wondered what she was up to. She was winding Ross up, deliberately, it seemed.

'Of course she was. She wasn't safe in her own house!' Ross paused. 'Wait a minute – what are you saying? That Hollie made it up, or we imagined it? Fuck me, you've got a cheek.'

Nat was far calmer than Dave would have been had he been sitting so close to Ross. 'Why didn't you come to us?'

Ross took a deep, noisy breath in through his nose. 'You? What are you talking about?'

'You suspected your sister was a victim of domestic abuse. Why didn't you contact us – the police?'

He turned away, muttered something they couldn't make out.

'Pardon?' Nat said softly.

'Because you wouldn't have fucking listened!' Ross turned back, his face wet with tears. 'We've all heard the stories – rape victims too scared to go to the police because they're treated like shit, blokes given a few months inside for smacking their partners around, then they come straight back out and start on them again. We didn't know what to do. We just kept hoping Hollie would see sense and come home.'

Nat wasn't going to comment on his accusations. 'Which rooms are at the back of Hollie and Andy's house?'

Ross wiped his face with his sleeve. 'What?'

'You said you looked in the windows. Which rooms were you looking into?'

He looked confused. 'The kitchen and – well, my mum calls it a utility room. Just the downstairs toilet, the back door and a bit of room for a freezer or whatever.'

The kitchen. If Nat had guessed that there was a chance Ross had seen his sister's body through the kitchen window, Dave was impressed. They knew where Hollie's body had been found but Jo Webber had also confirmed that it had been moved and they were none the wiser about where she had actually died. Unless forensics came up with the answer, they'd probably never know.

'So you could look into the kitchen and the utility room. What did you see?' Nat asked.

'Nothing,' Ross said. 'Empty rooms.'

'How much could you see of the kitchen? Most of the room, or…?'

Ross shook his head. 'Enough to know Hollie wasn't in there. The table, some of the floor.'

'And it looked… well, normal? Nothing out of place?'

'I didn't see anything, but I've hardly been inside Hollie's house. We think Andy used to lock her in, but she never said so.'

Dave knew they'd have to check the house, see how much of the room could be seen from outside, but depending on how much of the floor was visible, what Ross was saying could help them. If his sister's body hadn't been on the kitchen floor around half past twelve when he peered through the window, it must have been moved there later, as Jo Webber believed Hollie had been killed that morning. According to Irene and Des Spence, Hollie had been alive and arguing with Andy at ten a.m., so if Andy had killed her during the argument her body hadn't been moved until after twelve thirty. Dave's head was beginning to spin trying to work the timings out. Of course, Ross could be lying. He could easily have seen Hollie lying there, gone into the house and killed Andy… but no, that didn't work. Andy hadn't been killed until after eight o'clock in the evening, and there was no way Ross would have gone tamely back to work if he'd seen Hollie's body. But if he'd gone back to the house after work…

'Have we finished?' Ross said. 'Only I'm not on an official break here. If my boss comes in…'

'Just a couple more questions,' Dave said.

Ross blew out his cheeks. 'Fine.'

'You said you finished work at five thirty. Did you go straight home?'

Ross snorted. 'Tried to. I was halfway there when I got a call from Mum. Said she couldn't be arsed to cook, and would I pick up some chips on my way.'

'What time was that?'

Ross made a show of pulling his phone from his pocket. 'Five thirty-eight.' He turned the screen so they could look at it. 'All right?'

'And after you collected the food you went home, ate with your family and watched TV with them until you went to bed,' Dave said.

'Yep.'

Dave didn't say anything and he hoped Nat wouldn't either. After a few seconds, Ross shifted in his seat. 'Can I go, or what?'

'You told us you were worried about your sister because she wasn't answering her phone, you even went to her house on your lunch break because you were so concerned,' Dave said.

'After you'd been to Tesco for food and beer, of course,' Nat put in. 'Did you eat the pizza as well as the fish and chips?'

Ross forced a laugh. 'No, it's still in the fridge.'

'Okay. So you rushed across town at twelve thirty when you had less than an hour to spare, but at five thirty, even though you still hadn't been able to reach your sister and you'd finished work for the day, you got fish and chips and went home for a quiet night in?' Dave shook his head. 'You didn't go back to Hollie's house?'

'No, I decided to leave it.' Ross turned away, staring out of the window beside him. Nat and Dave exchanged a glance.

'Why?' Nat asked.

'Because I thought Andy would be there and Hollie wouldn't want any trouble.' Ross spoke quietly, as though ashamed. Still, Dave couldn't see it.

'You just went home and forgot about your sister?'

Ross's voice was tight now, as if he was struggling to keep his temper. 'No, I went home and worried myself shitless.'

Dave remembered Ross's arrests. 'You've been in fights before, and from what you've told us, you knew Andy was capable of hurting your sister. You expect us to believe you just went home and didn't go back to the house?'

'It's the truth. Believe what you like.'

'You have to admit, it sounds strange,' Dave said. 'You're desperate to know if your sister's okay; you've a secret way into the garden; you've already admitted to looking in through the windows – are you sure you didn't go back?'

'You're asking if I killed Andy,' Ross said, his voice flat.

'I didn't say that.'

'No, but it's what you're implying.'

'We've been told you've threatened to kill him before,' Nat said.

Ross laughed. 'Threatened to kill him? I mouthed off at him when I was pissed, yeah. Doesn't mean I'd ever do it, does it?'

Dave shrugged. 'You've been picked up by our colleagues in Lincoln a few times when you've been involved in fights.'

'Fights? It's happened twice. Once, a mate of mine was jumped by two blokes. What was I supposed to do, leave him to it? Second time, some twat had his girlfriend by the hair, and I wasn't just going to walk past without stepping in, was I?' He sneered. 'If that's your idea of being violent, then yeah, I hold my hands up.'

Again, Dave let the silence stretch, then half opened the van door. 'All right, Mr Morton. Thank you for your time.'

'That's it?'

Nat followed Dave out of the door then stuck her head back inside. 'Unless there's anything else you'd like to tell us?'

Ross didn't reply, just got out and slammed the door.

Nat looked at Dave. 'Take it that's a no.'

Walking quickly, hands in his pockets, head down, Ross strode away from them.

In the car, Nat seemed almost gleeful, like a kid on Christmas morning.

'So Ross was at the house around the time his sister died.' She put her seatbelt on and started the engine. 'What if he killed Hollie himself?'

Dave knew they had to consider it, especially now. 'But why would he?'

Nat waved a hand as she drove away from the kerb. 'I don't know. Because she wouldn't listen to him about coming home where she'd be safe? Because she stole a colouring book from him when they were kids and he's hated her ever since? It's possible, isn't it?'

'Most things are. Why would he tell us he'd been there though?'

'Because he knew we'd find out about the door eventually, and thought it would look better if he told us?'

Dave frowned. 'When we spoke to him before, the Sarge and me, he told us not to expect any help from him or his family in finding the person who killed Andy.'

'You can understand that. But maybe he killed Hollie *and* Andy.'

'I still don't see why he would tell us about this secret door if he did.'

Nat shrugged. 'The door thing is weird anyway. I can understand it, having a way of getting to his sister, giving her an escape route, but it seems over the top. Anyway, I don't understand how he wasn't seen using it.'

'It seems unlikely, but as far as I know, no one's mentioned noticing him, and uniforms have talked to everyone in that area at least once.'

Nat snorted. '"Uniforms" have? I know, I was one of the uniforms that was knocking on their doors.'

Dave blushed. 'I didn't mean—'

'I know you didn't, I'm messing with you.' Nat threw him a quick glance. 'What I'm saying is, how far did the house-to-house go? Did we speak to the people living on this street behind Hollie and Andy's house? I know I wasn't sent there. From what Ross has just told us, half of Northolme could have been sneaking down this short cut.'

'Forensics will have examined the garden, but if we didn't know about this hole in the fence, why would they? I don't know if the people on that street have been spoken to yet.'

Nat put her foot down. 'Then maybe we should find out.'

22

Nat's call came in as Catherine and Knight were on their way back to the station.

'What's up?' Catherine said. Nat explained about the short cut and queried the house-to-house, and Catherine realised she didn't have a clue where they were going door knocking today.

'Honestly, Nat, I've no idea. Let me speak to the DCI, and I'll come back to you.' She ended the call.

'What's the problem?' Knight asked.

Catherine told him what Nat had said. 'I'll call Kendrick now, ask him if he's sent anyone over there.' She gritted her teeth. 'We should already know. What was he thinking, not telling us anything this morning? You're deputy SIO.'

'He wanted us out and asking questions as soon as possible. What difference an hour would have made so we were aware of what else was going on, I don't know.'

'Like he said, he's trying to prove we can cope, that we can handle both cases. But if half of us don't know what's happening, it's hardly going to help the investigation.' Catherine tapped the DCI's name on her phone and waited for him to answer.

'We also need to check with Mick,' Knight said. 'If we didn't know about this short cut, he wouldn't have done either, not that I'd expect them to find anything after this amount of time.' He grimaced. 'We should have been told about this before.'

Kendrick wasn't answering his phone. 'None of Hollie and Andy's neighbours mentioned it and the Spences can't have known about it either, because I've no doubt they'd have mentioned it.'

'Ross knew,' Knight said.

Was there criticism in his tone? Catherine didn't think so, but she felt it all the same, if only from herself. 'When Dave and I first spoke to him he told us he'd been at work all day and I didn't press him. I should have asked about his breaks.'

'You should have?' Knight said mildly. 'Dave was there too.'

'I did most of the talking.'

'He probably won't get a word in today either, being paired with Nat Roberts.'

Catherine smiled. 'What do you think Jade's problem was?'

'Why she slammed the door in our faces? No idea.'

'When we first spoke to her, I said I thought she seemed nervous, though we both agreed she seemed to have been telling us the truth. Now though…' Catherine thought about it. 'Maybe she does have something to hide.'

'Such as?'

'Do you think she recognised Scott Greaves?'

Knight screwed up his face. 'Not sure. She turned away as you tried to show her the photograph, but that might have been a coincidence. She was determined she wasn't going to listen as soon as she saw who we were.'

'But why?'

'Well, we're still looking for Scott Greaves's new girl-friend,' he reminded her.

'If he even had one.'

Knight nodded. 'We need those phone records.'

'Ashley Greaves did say Scott had been weird about his phone. I thought the idea was you bought another handset, a pay-as-you-go, if you're having an affair?'

'Fairly sure that's not the voice of experience.'

'Not personal experience, no.'

'He might have had another phone, dodgy business records and who knows what else in his office. Since it all went up in flames, we'll never know.'

Catherine's phone rang, and she saw Kendrick's name on the screen. As usual, she didn't manage a greeting before he started talking.

'I need you both back here,' he said. She heard him sneeze, then cough. 'Bloody hell, my throat.'

'We wanted to call at Hollie Morton and Andy Nugent's house on the way back to the station,' Catherine told him.

'Why?'

Catherine explained about the short cut.

'And Ross Morton didn't think to mention that there was another way his sister's murderer could have entered and exited the property?' He gave another cough. 'All right, call at the house, check he's telling the truth about the fence and I'll get Mick to have a look on his way home – he's on his way over here now. I doubt it'll be worth his while, but you never know. He may as well make himself useful.'

'He's got information for us?' Catherine was glad Kendrick hadn't mentioned her failure to find out about the short cut in her initial interview with Ross Morton.

He wouldn't have missed it, she knew, and he might raise it again later, but for now it seemed she was off the hook.

'He says so, and whatever he's found it's enough to make him scurry over here from Nottingham, so let's hope it's worth hearing.'

'Is the house-to-house continuing today?'

'Yes, Sergeant.' Kendrick sniffed. 'If you're asking whether we've covered the street Ross Morton's talking about, not yet, but I'll send someone over there now. If they see you and DI Knight skulking around the area, tell them I sent you. Don't want you getting arrested.'

He ended the call.

'Did you hear all that?'

Knight laughed, but to Catherine it sounded forced. 'Jo probably heard him in Lincoln.'

Catherine wanted to ask him again about his partner's health but she held back. If Knight wanted to confide in her it would be in his own time, but he didn't speak again until they'd retraced their route, passed the end of the cul-de-sac where Hollie and Andy had lived, and turned into the road behind it.

'Willow Avenue,' Knight said as they passed a sign and he found a parking space at the side of the road under a tree. 'Except it's full of horse chestnuts.'

Catherine nodded towards the gates of the primary school at the bottom of the road. 'Pity no one plays conkers any more.'

'My grandad used to do drainage work, out in the middle of nowhere most of the time. He used to bring bags of conkers home for us.' Knight smiled at the memory.

They stood on the pavement, getting their bearings.

'That must be the bus stop Nat said Ross Morton mentioned.' Knight pointed.

'And the fence.'

They walked over. There was graffiti on the fence, a mural of abstract shapes in vivid colours. Catherine squinted at the panels.

'They look sound to me.'

Knight had his hands on his hips. 'We're behind the right house.' He pulled a pair of nitrile gloves from his pocket and slipped them on as Catherine did the same. She prodded at the nearest panel, but it was solid.

'Not this one.'

Knight pushed the next one along. 'Here we go. The whole thing moves back.' He squatted, stuck his head and shoulders into the gap, twisting his body to look around. 'There are hinges on this side. Looks as though Ross Morton's a bit of a DIY expert.' There was a pause then he called back to her. 'Yeah, there's another door here in the shed wall. It would be easy enough to get through.'

After a few seconds he was back, brushing down his trousers. 'I took a couple of photos, but it's just like Morton said. Very neat job – I doubt you'd notice it unless you knew about it.'

'And Ross told Nat and Dave that only he and his sisters knew it was here.'

'But someone could have seen them coming and going. Hollie might have told someone. Andy might have even known about it.'

'If he knew, wouldn't he have boarded it up, or smashed it to pieces?' Catherine said.

'From what we've been told about him controlling Hollie's life, you'd think so, unless he used it too.' Knight shrugged. 'Could have been busier than the M25 down here.'

'When we spoke to Andy's parents, his mum said Hollie didn't want Andy to see his parents. Do you think that's true, or was it her grief talking?'

'Andy had the knife wound, not Hollie, but there was the bruising on Hollie's arms and the wound inside her cheek where it looked like she'd been hit,' Knight said. 'At this stage, we can only assume Andy was responsible for that, but…'

'But it's a safe bet, I agree. I don't doubt Andy was violent, but his knife wound was fresh, he was injured the day he died.'

Knight frowned. 'The post-mortem report said the wound was hours old, so it didn't happen at the time Andy died. I'm not sure what you're getting at.'

Catherine blew out her cheeks, frustrated. 'Neither am I, not really, but I keep coming back to it. Does it back up the possibility that Andy did kill Hollie, and she tried to fight back? It's unlikely Andy cut himself accidentally because the wound was on his right arm and we know he was right-handed. Surely if he'd been using a knife and it slipped, the cut would be on his left arm?'

'You'd think so, but…' Knight shook his head. 'The whole case is too complicated to get your head around. The injuries, the timings, who knew who. If Mick's got something for us, hopefully we can start making some progress.'

'We've still got nothing on the arsons.'

'We can only focus on what we've been asked to do. Kendrick's not going to let either case go without a fight.'

Catherine looked at the graffiti. 'This is actually really good. I wonder if Ross did it, or asked someone to spray this on here to disguise what he'd done.'

'We should ask him,'. Knight said. 'If he did, it would mean at least one more person knew about it.'

23

Back at the station, Catherine grabbed some crisps from the vending machine and made herself a cup of tea. She didn't want to disturb Knight, who'd disappeared into his office and closed the door, and there was no one else around yet. Checking her emails, she saw nothing of note other than a report from Mick, and she knew there was no point opening that yet if he was coming to see them. She leaned back and closed her eyes, slowly spinning the desk chair around. There were often lulls in investigations, periods of time where initial interviews had been completed, evidence found but not yet processed, families of victims waiting for explanations and for justice. Sometimes they lasted for days, even weeks, but now she knew she only had a few minutes to catch her breath. Catherine sipped her tea, hoping Kendrick and Mick wouldn't be long. She could go down to the incident room but she knew Kendrick would want to hear what Mick had to say in his office before sharing it with the rest of the team. She was glad to have a few moments to sit quietly, to still her thoughts.

Catherine opened her eyes as the door crashed open, and DCI Kendrick appeared. She almost fell out of the chair as she planted her feet on the floor and brought it to a stop, then quickly shuffled it closer to her desk. Kendrick raised his eyebrows. 'That was impressive. You're doing tricks now?'

'Is Mick here yet?'

'No, but he shouldn't be long. When are the Dobson brothers due?'

'Not for an hour.'

'Good, then you've plenty of time to stick the kettle on.' He bared his teeth at her, which was as close to a smile as he ever managed.

'Since you asked so nicely.'

Kendrick sniffed. 'You mean you want another cup yourself.'

As she stood and went over to the length of kitchen worktop that had been fixed to the wall to serve as a mini kitchen, he said, 'Did you find this short cut?'

'Yep, it's there, just as Ross said.' She filled the kettle from the wonky tap and set it to boil. Grabbing her own cup from her desk, she took two more from the cupboard under the worktop and dropped tea bags into them. 'There are hinges on the panel; the gap has been made deliberately.'

'By Ross Morton?'

'He said so. I tried to call him on our way back here, but he didn't answer. I left a voicemail.'

Kendrick nodded. 'If he doesn't ring back, get Dave to keep chasing him. We need a clearer idea of who knew it was there, though from what you've said anyone in the area might have seen Ross using it. I'm surprised the neighbours weren't aware of it.'

'Mr and Mrs Spence?'

'Thought you said a fly couldn't fart without them knowing?'

'I don't think they were my exact words. Anyway, it might not be important.'

'Maybe not, but it needs looking at.' Kendrick checked his watch. 'Where the hell's Mick?'

Catherine ignored her boss's rhetorical question. 'How's it going downstairs?'

Kendrick bounced on his toes. 'Like a dream. Monk's in his element, showing off to his new Lincoln colleagues, playing with his smartboard every five minutes. It's a bloody circus. I've already had the Super asking for an update. She must have made the call in as soon as she got back to Headquarters. Pain in the arse.'

'Her or Monk?' Catherine raised her voice over the noise of the kettle, but Kendrick didn't need to.

'The whole bloody investigation. The only new bit of information I had for her was that I've had the initial report from the fire scene investigator. They found petrol at the scene and a few matches, and he's confident it was arson, though he's still going over the place.'

'Not exactly news.'

'But another "tick in the box", as the Super helpfully put it. Little Miss Jargon.' He peered at her as the kettle came to the boil. 'Come on, I'm gagging for a drink.'

'Should have asked one of your new team downstairs to make you one then.' Catherine turned to look at him, leaning back against the worktop. He eyed her.

'Don't do that; it's only fixed to the wall with chewing gum.' He pinched his bottom lip, a sure sign he was mulling something over. Catherine swirled the tea bags around with a teaspoon and hoped for the best. She poured a dribble of milk in each and handed one to Kendrick, who peered inside the mug.

'It'll do.' He blew on the tea and took a sip. 'Right, Sergeant. Who killed Hollie Morton?'

Catherine picked up her own mug and the third one. 'No idea.' She knocked on Knight's office door and went in. He was at his desk, head in his hands.

'Sorry, Jonathan.' Flustered, wondering what was wrong, Catherine made to back out quickly. Knight lifted his head.

'No, don't worry.' He rubbed his eyes. 'Is Mick here yet?'

She gave him the tea. 'No. Are you okay?'

Knight blinked a few times. 'Headache. Knackered, to be honest.'

Kendrick loomed in the doorway. 'Mick's just pulled into the car park. Let's get some work done, shall we?'

'I'll make another tea,' said Catherine as she turned and Kendrick moved out of her way.

'All right, Jonathan?' she heard him say as she reached for another mug. He could be gruff, occasionally intimidating, but beneath his bluster, he cared about his team. Knight mumbled a reply and Kendrick stepped further into his office. Catherine couldn't hear what was said over the noise of the kettle, but Kendrick soon reappeared.

'Obviously our next steps depend on what Mick's got to say, but we also need some people on the arson case,' he said. 'I was thinking of asking DC Varcoe to take the lead on that. What do you reckon?'

'Good idea,' Catherine called.

'Nat Roberts can help her. I hear she's got a close contact in the fire service.' Kendrick smirked behind his mug of tea.

'Listening to gossip now?' Catherine said. 'You're as bad as the Super.'

'She was making a point – they're watching us, and I don't like it.' Kendrick rubbed his stomach. 'It feels as though there's a target on our backs.'

'If they want to close us down, nothing we say or do will make any difference.'

Kendrick raised his mug as though toasting her. 'That's the attitude. Go out fighting.' He turned as Mick Caffery pushed the door open. 'Here's the man with the answers.'

Mick's smile was rueful. 'I wouldn't go that far.'

Kendrick scowled. 'Don't give him that tea, Catherine.'

–

Kendrick had decided he didn't fancy squeezing into his office with three other people again, and he led them down to one of the interview rooms. It was only slightly bigger, but with the incident room crowded and noisy it was the best they could do. He'd found a jug and they each had a glass of water, Mick still nursing his mug of tea. Catherine wished she'd bought a chocolate bar as well as the crisps. It was a long time since her steak pie and chips, and she'd had no time for breakfast.

'I'll start with what we found in Hollie and Andy's house,' Mick said. 'As you saw when we were at the house, there was a knife on the kitchen and a smashed mobile phone. The phone was covered in Hollie's fingerprints, plus a few of Andy's, as well as skin cells, Hollie's saliva, grease – the usual muck. As for the knife – just Hollie's fingerprints on the handle, and Andy's blood on the blade.'

'Andy wasn't much of a chef then,' Kendrick said.

'We found nothing else in the kitchen of note – no blood on the floor or other surfaces. Andy's cut was superficial and if he'd put a plaster on it straight away, there'd have been no mess. There were fingerprints on the cupboard doors, the fridge, everywhere you'd expect, but they all belonged to the people who lived in the house.'

'We've been told Hollie and Andy didn't have many visitors,' Catherine said.

'On to the living room then, and it seems there had been visitors in there – unidentified prints on both sides of the door handle, and a couple of beer bottles we found on the coffee table.'

'It's a fair bet the prints belong to Jamie and Cal Dobson,' Knight said.

Mick nodded. 'And we'll be able to confirm that once their prints are in the system. We had a look at the controllers for the video game system, but we couldn't lift anything – it was just a smeared mess.'

'Cal told me he left the room to go to the toilet,' Catherine said. 'I'm guessing the prints on the door handle were his.'

Kendrick was frowning. 'Mick, you've just said you couldn't get prints from the controller, I'm assuming because it had been handled so many times, but the people who live in the house touch door handles tens of times a day. How could you distinguish these unidentified prints from all the rest? I've never heard you say you've managed that before.'

Mick smiled. 'Because at some point before this mystery person grabbed the handle, it had been wiped clean.'

Knight and Kendrick's mouths opened, and Catherine realised she was gawping at Mick too.

Mick laughed. 'That's the reaction I was expecting,' he said.

'Wiped clean? You're saying there were no other prints on it, other than the ones we're assuming belong to Cal Dobson?' Kendrick demanded.

'None whatsoever. Whoever did it was thorough. There was nothing else there.'

Catherine said, 'Then it's possible Hollie was killed in the living room, and the person who did it wiped the handle knowing they'd touched it, before Cal and Jamie arrived at the house.'

Kendrick was pinching his lip again. 'Then the living room door must have been closed and they had to open it to get the body out, but the kitchen door was already standing open.'

'Or Hollie let them into the house, they went into the living room and closed the door, but the person left the room at some point, maybe to go to the toilet like Cal, and left prints then. After killing Hollie, they realised they'd done so and gave the handle a wipe,' Knight suggested.

'Or the killer knew Hollie and – or – Andy well enough to walk into the house without being invited and opened the living room door then,' Mick put in.

'Unlikely,' Kendrick said. 'It seems people didn't just walk into the house without being asked – they weren't even invited to visit.'

'As far as we know,' said Knight. 'Remember the rumour Hollie had had an affair. We can't be sure other people weren't at the house when Andy wasn't around.'

'Except the neighbours didn't see them,' said Kendrick.

'They couldn't have been looking out of the window constantly.'

Catherine raised an eyebrow. 'From what we've seen, it must be a good ninety per cent of the time though. And don't forget the short cut.'

Mick looked confused, and Catherine explained.

'Last possibility then,' Kendrick said, 'otherwise we'll be here all afternoon. Jamie Dobson killed Andy and wiped the living room door handle, aware he'd touched it even though he hadn't been near any of the others. Then he got his brother to open and close the door and leave his prints on the clean surface, knowing he'd touched it before, when he went to the toilet. Jamie didn't bother wiping the kitchen one because he knew he hadn't touched it, but he couldn't be sure about the living room.'

'Then why bother with Cal's new set of prints?' Catherine asked. 'Why not just leave the door handle clean?'

Kendrick pursed his lips. 'Because then he could say, if we asked, that whoever killed Hollie must have wiped the door handle and Cal touched it later. Or he was giving himself a chance to frame Cal if the need arose. Or...' He stopped.

'But if Jamie hadn't gone into the kitchen, he couldn't have seen Hollie's body and so wouldn't have a reason to kill Andy,' Catherine said. 'Unless Cal opened the door, saw Hollie and started screaming.'

Kendrick looked at Mick. 'Did you get any usable prints from the kitchen door?'

'No, and the handle hadn't been wiped.'

'All right, enough guessing,' Kendrick said. 'Carry on, please, Mick.'

'We collected plenty of hair and other bits and pieces from the living room, but we're still working through them. As you know, we've not had much time and I wanted to process what we had from the bodies and the rooms the victims were found in first.'

'Even though you knew Hollie had been moved?' Kendrick said.

Mick's eyes narrowed. 'I'm not a miracle worker. This all takes time, as you know.'

'All right, point taken.'

'Thank you.' Mick checked his notes. 'As we all know, Andy Nugent's body was found in the bathroom. I can confirm that the blood we saw on the toilet seat and on the floor did belong to Andy. Again, we found no other fingerprints on any of the surfaces other than those we'd expect. The same unidentified prints that we found in the living room were also found on the toilet seat, the flush mechanism and the sink tap. We don't have the results from the hand towel yet, but I'm guessing we'll find traces of Cal Dobson there too, if we have a DNA sample to confirm it.'

'What about the door handle?' Catherine asked. She was relieved that again, the evidence was proving Cal had told the truth about going to the bathroom. That didn't mean he'd told the truth about everything else though.

Mick shook his head. 'Lots of prints, nothing we could use.'

'And the belt?' Knight said.

'The belt's interesting. I've no idea why it was placed there, it's not my job to work that out.' He glanced at Kendrick. 'Obviously, we were hoping to find traces of someone other than Andy on it, to help establish whether that someone was there when he died or afterwards.'

Kendrick raised his eyebrows. 'But?'

'But the only fingerprints on it are Andy's, and they're on the leather and around the buckle, where you'd touch it as you fastened it.'

'It was his then,' Catherine said.

Mick nodded. 'It looks like it. We've found nothing else on his clothes, skin or hair to help answer the question of whether anyone did push Andy. but I still think the fact he'd hit the back of his head and not the front suggests he'd turned away from the toilet and then he was shoved, but I can't give you any evidence to back that up.'

'All right, let's go back to the belt. If there are only Andy's prints on it, whoever left it around his neck probably wore gloves, or at least covered their hands.'

'But where did it come from?' Knight asked. 'Did they remove it from his body, then put it around his neck or…?'

'Andy was wearing jeans without a belt,' Mick said. 'But that doesn't mean he'd had one on and it was taken off him. It wouldn't have been easy to do, even if he was lying down. Whoever left it could have gone into the bedroom and found it, or maybe it was in the bathroom already. There is one thing that might help though: we found a tiny thread caught in the buckle.'

Kendrick leaned forward. 'What sort of thread?'

'Well, it's eighty-five per cent cotton, fifteen per cent polyamide. Dark blue, probably from a jumper or cardigan. It could have come from something Andy had worn of course, and we're going to go through his clothes and see if anything matches. He was wearing a red T-shirt when he died. It's possible, though, that thread came from the clothing of the person who left the belt there.'

'Or from Hollie's clothing, or something belonging to one of the kids…' Kendrick shifted in his chair.

'Or anyone Andy's ever met, yes, agreed,' Mick said calmly. 'I can only tell you what we found.'

Kendrick nodded. 'All right, I'll shut my face.'

Catherine raised an eyebrow and Mick said, 'I doubt it.'

'I'm hurt,' Kendrick said.

Mick checked his notes. 'On the right leg of Andy's jeans, we found a hair that didn't belong to him, a short, blond hair from someone's head, not their body. It was on the back of the thigh, possibly transferred when he sat on a chair or sofa, or a car seat, but he could just as easily have picked it up anywhere. There was no match to any of our records.'

'It could belong to Jamie or Cal Dobson,' Catherine said. 'They're both blond.'

Kendrick looked at Catherine. 'We'll need DNA samples as well as their fingerprints.'

She nodded as Mick continued.

'We found saliva on Andy's face, lots of tiny traces.'

Kendrick wrinkled his nose. 'You mean someone spat at him?'

'More like shouted in his face.' Mick paused to take a mouthful of tea and Kendrick couldn't help himself.

'No doubt it was Hollie's. We've been told they had several screaming matches a day,' he said.

Slowly, Mick should his head. 'No, it wasn't Hollie's. It belongs to a man, but again, we don't have a match.'

'And it can't belong to any of Hollie's family, because they'd share enough DNA with her to link what you found on Andy to Hollie anyway,' Knight said.

Mick nodded. 'And if it belonged to either of Andy's parents, we'd have a match with Andy's own DNA.'

'Unless Roy Nugent isn't actually Andy's father.' Kendrick pulled a face at his own suggestion. 'That was a joke, but we need samples from the lot of them anyway.'

Catherine was more confused than ever. 'We have witnesses who say when Jamie and Cal Dobson greeted Andy as they arrived at his house, they were joking and laughing, making a lot of noise. Could that explain the saliva?'

Mick screwed up his face. 'Possibly, but the saliva and the blond hair belong to different people. If it turns out the blond hair belongs to one of the Dobson brothers, the saliva can't do. Their DNA would be similar enough for me to tell you that now.'

Kendrick chewed on his bottom lip. 'You're saying that there's someone's spit all over Andy Nugent's face, and a rogue blond hair stuck to his arse that may or not be relevant, but if it is, it definitely doesn't belong to the person who owns the saliva?'

'The hair was stuck to his leg, but yes.'

Linking his hands behind his head, the DCI sighed. 'More questions, no answers.'

Mick didn't smile. 'All I can report on is what we find.'

'We're assuming someone pushed Andy, causing him to fall back and smack his head. If they were arguing, and the other person stepped in close enough to shove him, chances are it's their saliva,' Catherine said. She knew they shouldn't assume anything at all, but how else could Andy's death have happened?

'Or they were shouting in his face when they bent over him to drape the belt around his throat.' Kendrick drummed his fingers on the table.

'Would they scream at someone who was already dead?' Knight asked.

'Because he was still breathing at that point? Dr Kirby said death would have been almost immediate, but that's not the same as instantaneous. There could have been anything from a few seconds to a couple of minutes during which our mystery person realised Andy was out of it but not yet dead and decided they'd help him along.' Kendrick spread his hands. 'Or because it was an accident and they were shocked, terrified? Angry with him for dying? Who knows.'

Mick said, 'Before I forget, remember the glove that was found in Rebecca and Dale Clough's bedroom after the attack on her?' They all nodded. 'Well, we got a hit. It was worn by Andy Nugent.'

Kendrick tipped his head against the back of his chair, staring at the ceiling. 'Then we need DNA samples from Rebecca and Dale Clough as well. They can deny knowing who Andy was all they like, but if one of them is a match, it's game over. Even if Andy did work for the firm that moved them into the house, he wouldn't have been wearing leather gloves while he did it. He could have left the fingerprints then, but the glove places him at the scene at the time when Rebecca was attacked.'

Catherine drained her glass of water and poured herself another. She'd had three months away from all this. Three months without looking at the wreckage of a body, of a life, without having to pore over the details of the horrors one human being could inflict on another. But listening to Mick's findings, she remembered the thrill of trying to fit the pieces together, the excitement that felt almost indecent because this wasn't a simulation or exam question, it was the premature end of someone's life. She would never admit it out loud, not even to Isla, but if she was looking for reasons to stay in the job, one would be this feeling. The thrill of the chase, the satisfaction of the capture and the knowledge that you'd done your part in making sure the streets were that bit safer.

It was bullshit, of course. There would always been more criminals, more family rows boiling over, more domestic violence, abuse, exploitation, more drugs, guns, and knives. She was a tiny part of a huge machine that would never achieve its purpose, but if she accepted that she'd never get out of bed again. Holding onto this feeling was vital, because without it there was no point in wading through the mess of their world.

'Let's talk about Hollie Morton,' Mick was saying.

Kendrick got to his feet. 'Give me a minute to get us all a brew, Mick. I don't know about anyone else, but I could do with some coffee.'

Catherine looked at Knight. 'Is all this helping your headache?'

'Not exactly. Do you have any paracetamol handy?'

'In my bag.' Catherine pushed back her chair.

She took her phone from her pocket as she jogged upstairs. Nothing from Isla. She scrolled to her number and dialled. By the time she'd reached her desk, she was listening to an automated voice asking her to leave a message.

'It's me,' she said. 'I just wanted to... well, I'll talk to you later.' Feeling stupid, she set the phone on her desk and reached for her bag. What would she have said if Isla had answered? I'm worried you'll leave me? I'm afraid I'll lose you to our careers? She was alone most of the time anyway, though the days she and Isla had spent together during her three months' leave of absence had made her certain the relationship was worth fighting for. Their two-week holiday had brought them even closer, especially since by then, Catherine was feeling more like herself. Where they went from here was another story.

Leaving the phone behind, she grabbed the packet of pills and made her way back downstairs. Kendrick had acquired four cups of coffee. After pushing a mug towards each of them, he opened a packet of shortbread. Setting the pack in the middle of the table, he grabbed two biscuits.

'Look what I found.' He winked. 'Don't tell the Super.'

Catherine handed Knight the tablets and took a biscuit, wrinkling her nose as Knight swallowed the pills with a mouthful of coffee.

'Where were we?' Mick frowned at his notes again.

Kendrick looked at him over the rim of his mug. 'You were confusing the arses off us.'

Mick ignored him. 'Hollie Morton. As we know, as well as the damage to her throat there were bruises on her upper arms, and a cut inside her cheek. The bruising on her arms was a few days old, the throat injuries were obviously new, but here's the interesting part – the cut on her cheek was inflicted a few hours before Hollie died.'

'Jo said that?' Knight demanded. 'She didn't mention it at the PM.'

'It'll be in her full report. She'll be sending it over any time now,' Mick said.

Kendrick scowled. 'She didn't think it would have been helpful to have phoned and told us?'

Mick looked at him. 'Would it have made a difference?'

'Probably not,' Kendrick had to admit.

'As I said, the cut was a few hours old when Hollie died, and any kind of impact could have caused it – a blow to her cheek, something accidental like one of the kids throwing their head back or hitting her with a toy.'

Kendrick pulled a face. 'More than likely it was caused by a slap from Andy.'

'Maybe,' Mick said. 'But the bruises on her arms couldn't have been caused by Andy Nugent.'

Catherine looked at Knight. Again, Mick had stunned them.

'Why do you say that?' Kendrick demanded.

'The marks left by the fingers of whoever held her prove it – they're spread too far apart. Someone with bigger hands than Andy grabbed Hollie.'

Kendrick groaned. 'You're sure?'

'Positive. I talked to Nathan Kirby about it and double checked with Jo – they both agree it would have been impossible for Andy to have held her in the way the bruising indicates.'

'Could it still have been Andy who strangled her then?' Catherine wanted to know.

'Yes. You wouldn't need particularly big hands to kill someone in the way Hollie was murdered,' Mick said. 'You'd just need strength and a lot of anger.'

There was a silence.

'Did you get any fingerprints?' Catherine asked.

'From Hollie's skin? No.'

'Bollocks,' Kendrick said.

'What about the samples from beneath Hollie's finger-nails?' Catherine asked. 'Were there any skin cells or anything else that could help us identify this person?'

'The one with the shovel hands,' Kendrick said through a mouthful of shortbread.

'Jo didn't find much, but we're working on what we have. Don't hold your breath though.' Mick drank some coffee. 'To be honest, there wasn't much in the way of trace evidence on Hollie's body or clothes.'

Kendrick grabbed another biscuit. 'It's looking to me as though Mr and Mrs Spence were mistaken when they said Hollie was arguing with Andy at ten o'clock on the day she died. Sounds possible that she was yelling at the person who grabbed her by the arms. Whether that's the same person who killed her, we're none the wiser.'

286

'There could have been three different people,' Knight said. 'The one who grabbed her, the person she was arguing with, and the person who killed her.'

Kendrick shook his head. 'Either way, it's looking more likely that Andy's not the dead cert we thought he was for her murder.'

'And whoever screamed into Andy's face, it wasn't Hollie,' Catherine said.

'Or Scott Greaves,' Mick reminded them. 'We have his DNA in the system; he would have shown up as a match.'

Kendrick checked his watch. 'Jamie and Cal Dobson should have arrived by now and been fingerprinted. Catherine, will you ask them if they'll provide DNA samples?'

Catherine got to her feet, coffee cup in hand. 'And if they say no?'

'Well, that would look suspicious, wouldn't it?' Kendrick raised his eyebrows. 'Wouldn't be in their interests at all.'

Jamie Dobson was standing by the window in one of the rooms downstairs. He turned as Catherine pushed the door open.

'Not much of a view,' she said with a smile.

Dobson scowled. 'It's not much of a room.'

Catherine couldn't argue. These were places for witness interviews or for solicitors to speak to their clients. They were functional, with scruffy carpet tiles, bland furniture and a glugging water cooler. They weren't going to win any design awards. She went over to the table that stood in the middle of the room and pulled out one of the chairs.

'Why don't you have a seat?'

He looked like he might refuse, then sat opposite her.

'Why are we still here?' he demanded. 'I assume you're holding Cal somewhere as well?'

'We're not "holding" him. He's fine.'

Jamie didn't look convinced. 'Is his social worker still with him?'

'Yes, and she will be until Cal leaves.'

'Good. He was upset that we were coming here. He needs his routine.'

'I understand that.' Catherine waited a beat, then said, 'What car do you drive?'

'What? What's that got to do with anything?'

'I assume you have a van for your work?'

He sneered. 'Wouldn't be much of a plumber with all my gear in a shopping trolley, would I?'

'Does the van have your name on the side?'

'Yeah, and my phone number.'

'You told us Andy Nugent called you and asked if you could come to his house because they were having a problem with the hot water.'

'And?'

Catherine leaned back and crossed her legs. 'If you were expecting to do some work on the boiler, why weren't you driving your van?'

Jamie opened his mouth, then closed it again. He blushed. 'Who says I wasn't?'

'What were you driving?'

'What difference does it make?'

'If you weren't driving your van, it suggests you were going to the house for a reason other than the one you told us about.'

'Does it f—' Jamie stopped himself. 'I've already told you, when Andy rang, we'd been to see our mum in the hospital. I'd decided to give my mum's car a run out – it's been sitting on the drive for months and it needed it, that's why we weren't in the van.'

'So when Andy called…?'

'When people ring about their boilers, it's sometimes a simple problem. I was planning to call in at Andy's, have a look, and go back for the van if I needed to.'

'Okay.' It was a reasonable explanation, and Catherine decided to let it go. It was probably irrelevant anyway.

He folded his arms. 'Can we go home now?'

'Not yet. There's something else I need to talk to you about.'

He placed both hands flat on the table as though he was readying himself to leap over it. 'What now? You asked us to come here to be fingerprinted, and we've done that, as promised.'

'And we appreciate it. This won't take long.' Catherine looked at his hands. Were they bigger than Andy Nugent's had been? It was impossible to tell.

'We need to get over to the hospital. I'm not going to miss visiting time with our mum. We don't know how long—' He choked. 'Look, just let us go. Please?'

'This is about Hollie's death, about us finding the person who killed her. We need your help.'

'My help? I've already told you who killed her, no doubt her family have too: Andy fucking Nugent. End of story.' He looked at the door and Catherine wondered if he was thinking of making a run for it. She couldn't stop him if he did; he wasn't under arrest.

'We haven't been able to prove that,' she said quietly. She couldn't tell him much, but she wanted to keep him talking.

He stared at her. 'What?'

'If Andy didn't kill Hollie, do you have any idea who else might have done?'

'No, because Andy did it.' Jamie blinked. 'He must have done.'

'As I said, we don't know that.'

'I don't understand this.' He rubbed his eyes. 'Why would anyone else hurt her?'

'Anyone else?' Catherine frowned.

'I'm assuming Andy did it because she was there, because he blamed her for his shitty life, because it was easier than taking a hard look at himself – all the usual reasons men smack women around. But if he didn't do it, I can't help you.'

'That's what I want to talk to you about.'

Catherine leaned over to the cooler for two cups of water and pushed them across the table. Jamie drank them both down.

'Cheers,' he said.

'As you know, we asked for your fingerprints because we know you were in Hollie and Andy's house on the day they died, and we need to match yours in any prints we can't identify in the house. Would you also give us a DNA sample?'

His frown deepened. 'Why?'

'The same reason. You were on the premises. If we find DNA we can't identify, we need to know if it's yours or Cal's, or if it belongs to someone we don't know about who was also in the house.'

He looked suspicious, as though expecting a trap. 'I didn't kill Hollie. I didn't kill Andy either.'

'I'm not saying you did. You'd be giving the sample on a voluntary basis.' And if you refuse, you'll be given no choice, she thought.

'And this would help you find the person who killed her?'

'It could help.' Maybe, possibly, one day. Again, Catherine found herself studying Jamie's hands. Perhaps she should ask if she could measure them. It wouldn't be the weirdest request she'd made in her career.

'How would you do it? It's not a blood test, is it? Only I'm not a fan of needles.'

'No, we just swab the inside of your cheek.'

He pursed his lips. 'Okay. What about Cal?'

'We need his too, if he's willing.'

'I think he'll do it, when it's explained to him.' Jamie managed a grin. 'He likes you.'

24

At two o'clock, the team was back in the CID office as requested. Kendrick stood in his office door, watching his officers as they checked emails, made tea or coffee, ate sandwiches, pasties or salads as quickly as possible. There was already a buzz in the room, the team eager to share what they'd learned with their boss. Catherine sat at her desk, mulling over what Mick had told them. Kendrick had already authorised the extra funding needed to speed up the processing of the samples the Dobson brothers had given, because at the moment, the unknown DNA was their best lead.

Kendrick clapped his hands. 'Gather round then.' He moved further into the room and perched on a spare desk. Knight emerged from his office and Catherine caught his eye. He smiled, letting her know he was okay.

The rest of the team sat behind the desks nearest Kendrick, looking expectantly at him, like a class of kids on their first day at school. Catherine grabbed a chair next to Anna, and Knight sat beside her.

'Firstly: forensics.' Kendrick explained what Mick had told them. Chris Rogers looked bemused, and he wasn't the only one.

'The saliva's got to be Jamie or Cal's then. No one else was in the house,' he said.

'There's no "has to be" about it,' Kendrick said. 'Either Andy was the man Hollie argued with at ten o'clock, and he killed her then left the house, or he'd gone before the person who Hollie was yelling at arrived.'

'And the second person was the one who'd grabbed Hollie before, and maybe the one who killed her?' Emily Lawrence asked.

Dave Lancaster said, 'Yeah, and then Andy came home to find her dead body, panicked, and called the Dobson brothers to try to provide himself with an alibi.'

'That makes no sense. Hollie had been dead for hours by then,' Nat Roberts said.

'He wouldn't have known that though,' Catherine pointed out. 'For all he knew, she could have been killed minutes before. Her body wouldn't have been completely cold, even if he'd found her just before he phoned Jamie Dobson. Not enough time had passed.'

'What about rigor mortis?' Emily wanted to know.

'Depends when he found her,' Kendrick said. 'It usually starts between two and six hours after death, but it begins in the jaws and neck, so even if you move the body it might not be noticeable. And anyway, Andy was hardly going to be an expert in what happens once someone's died. He probably wouldn't have even wanted to touch her. He'd have been in shock, most likely.'

'Why not put a 999 call in as soon as he found her though?' Nat asked.

'He hadn't killed her, but he was guilty of domestic violence. He'd probably have panicked, knowing he'd be the first person we'd suspect,' Kendrick said.

'And hiding a dead body in the kitchen while you play Call of Duty with your mates is a great way to prove your innocence.' Nat rolled her eyes. 'What a bastard.'

Kendrick threw her a glance and Nat shut up.

'It must have been Andy that moved her though,' Dave said. 'We know she wasn't on the kitchen floor at twelve thirty.'

Chris stared at him. 'How?'

Kendrick held up his hands. 'Let's stop there and you can give us your reports. Nat and Dave, tell them about Ross's visit to his sister.'

Nat took the lead, as Catherine guessed she might, though she was concise, giving her colleagues the facts.

'Did you believe Ross when he said only he and Chloe knew about the short cut? It seems unlikely their parents wouldn't have been in on it too, especially when they were all so worried about Hollie's safety,' Anna Varcoe asked.

Nat shrugged. 'Not sure, but that doesn't mean Chloe didn't tell anyone. And Hollie knew about it too. She could have mentioned it to her parents, a friend, anyone.'

'We need to speak to Chloe Morton and Mrs and Mrs Spence again,' Kendrick said. He raised his eyebrows at Catherine. 'Your next two interviews, DS Bishop. Weren't you meant to have seen Chloe again before now?'

Catherine held in a sigh. 'Mrs Spence will be delighted to see us again.'

'Tough luck.' Kendrick turned back to Nat and Dave. 'What about Hollie's parents? Did you get the confirmation we needed about their alibis?'

'Yeah, we did. Both of them were telling the truth. Michelle Morton works at a hairdressers' in town. According to her boss, she arrived about eight forty-five as usual, had a cup of coffee and a cigarette before her first appointment at nine a.m.,' Dave said.

Nat took over. 'She had clients all day, didn't leave the salon until just after five. Had a sandwich in the back room at lunchtime, a couple of smokes out the back. We spoke to another of her colleagues, got phone numbers for a couple of women whose hair she'd done and they all said the same thing. Safe to say Michelle was telling the truth.'

'Good work,' Kendrick said. Nat beamed. 'I mean, she still could have gone and given Andy a shove in the chest after tea, but at least we can be sure she didn't kill Hollie. What about Hollie's dad?'

'Eric Morton works at the pet supplies place down by the river. He's in the warehouse, shifting stuff around by forklift, picking and packing orders, loading and unloading trailers. He's part of a team of seven blokes and three women and isn't alone for a minute of the day unless he's in the toilet. He's in the clear too,' Dave told them.

'But they can't offer anything than "we ate fish and chips with our kids then watched TV until bedtime" for the evening?' Kendrick folded his arms. 'They might have solid alibis for when their daughter died, but they're still in the frame for Andy's death.'

'But the saliva on Andy's face—' Nat started to say.

'Like I said before, we don't know what Andy was doing for most of the day, and the saliva could still belong to Jamie or Cal Dobson, or half the town. We can't make assumptions.'

Nat blushed. 'Okay. Sorry.'

Kendrick bared his teeth at her. 'Don't start apologising, Constable, or you'll never stop. You're here to learn, because I think you might be worth teaching.' He eyed Emily and Tim. 'That goes for you two as well.' He unfolded his arms. 'DC Varcoe and PC Lawrence. Amaze us.'

Anna snorted. 'We spoke to the Cloughs again, who don't recognise Scott Greaves and can't help us. Then we talked to Neil Wilcox, the bloke who helped them move into their house. He admitted to knowing Scott Greaves and he reacted to Andy Nugent's name but denied knowing him.'

She glanced at Emily, who nodded. 'It could be as simple as he paid Andy cash in hand and is worried he'll get into trouble because of that, but...'

'But we need to get him in an interview and put the thumbscrews on.' Kendrick looked around the group. 'Anyone fancy telling Dale Clough he needs to let us have a sample of his DNA? No?' He explained about the glove and the proof they now had that Andy Nugent had been wearing it. 'After we've had the DNA result, we'll bring Mr Clough for a chat.' He rubbed his hands together. 'I might even sit in on that one. Right. Chris and Tim: Andy Nugent's parents?'

Chris shrugged. 'Nothing much to say, boss. Mrs Nugent was in school all day; arrived just before eight, left at six thirty after a staff meeting. The reception desk is just outside her office so she couldn't have left the premises without being seen. As you'd expect, the perimeter fence is completely secure and the gate is locked. You have to use an intercom to get inside.'

'As the headteacher, surely Mrs Nugent has a key?' Kendrick said.

Tim Riley cleared his throat. 'She does, sir, but again, she'd have to pass reception to get in and out of the building. There's no way.'

'Okay. What about her husband?'

Chris shrugged. 'Mr Nugent checks out too. He works at Lincoln College, as we know. He signed in at eight thirty, and one of the admin team confirms that as she had a chat with him about some photocopying he wanted doing. Then he had a class from nine until twelve, and after that he went for a wander.'

Kendrick's eyebrows raised. 'A what?'

'Wander,' Chris repeated. 'His words. He walked down into the city centre, browsed in a bookshop, bought socks and underpants in Marks and Sparks, and had a coffee and a panini in a café.'

'Lovely,' Kendrick said.

'He got back to college about one thirty, then had classes from two until half past four. He drove home, cooked a spaghetti bolognaise. When his wife got home, they ate together, he took the dog out for a walk and then they watched TV until bedtime.'

'I wonder if they watched the same programme as the Mortons.' Kendrick sniffed. 'Must have been a good one. I'm assuming you were able to find people who could back up Mr Nugent's statement?'

Tim nodded. 'Yes, sir. The admin lady we've already mentioned, a couple of students, a bloke who served him in the coffee shop. Roy Nugent's a regular, so they remembered him.'

'No chance he could have nipped home between classes and strangled Hollie then?'

Chris shook his head. 'No way. The timings don't work.'

'But he's another person without an alibi for the evening.' Kendrick pinched his lower lip. He looked at Chris. 'Anything else?'

'We spoke to the blokes whose contact details you sent us – the friends of Scott Greaves, the ones his wife mentioned to you, Sarge?'

Catherine nodded. 'What did they say?'

'Nothing helpful. Scott was the same person he'd always been, his wife was making a fuss about nothing, they'd know if there was a new woman on the scene, and there wasn't. Two of them work in Lincoln and one was in London for the day, so we didn't have time to see them face to face and so we thought a few questions on the phone would be better than nothing. I didn't get the feeling any of them were lying, but I think follow-ups might be in order.'

'We'll put it on the list,' Kendrick said. 'DI Knight, DS Bishop?'

Catherine updated the group on their conversations with Ashley Greaves and Irene and Des Spence, and also about the short cut they'd investigated. She also mentioned their encounter with the boy and his gang of friends on the Meadowflower Estate.

'Is it worth following up?' Kendrick demanded. 'Some of our colleagues in uniform have probably dealt with this lot before.' He shuffled forward and slid off the desk he'd been sitting on. 'Any ideas, you three?'

Tim, Nat and Emily exchanged glances. 'Lot of possibilities, sir,' Tim said.

'Lots of kids who'd throw stones at a police car?' Kendrick's eyebrows bounced. 'Good to see the Meadowflower going down in the world.'

'I thought the kids ran away?' Nat asked.

Kendrick just looked at her.

'We'll ask around,' she said.

'That can be your task this afternoon.' Kendrick nodded at Emily and Tim, then pointed at Catherine and Knight. 'Get these two to give you a description of this kid – not sure how good their observational skills will have been though.' Nat frowned, and Catherine waited for her to ask what she was going to be doing, but she stayed quiet.

'Dave, Chris – I want you to join the house-to-house team.' Kendrick held up a hand. 'And before you start moaning, this is important. Now we know about this oh-so-secret way into Hollie and Andy's back garden, I want to know who used it. Take photographs of everyone linked to this case with you and ask around the cul-de-sac where Andy and Hollie lived.'

Chris was looking like he might protest, but Dave was resigned. 'Are we including Ashley Greaves, the Cloughs, Jade Walsh?'

'Everyone,' Kendrick repeated. 'You never know. I've had officers out there already today, so find out how far they got.' He bared his teeth. 'Don't go to the Spences' house though; DS Bishop and DI Knight are going to pay them another visit.' He narrowed his eyes at Catherine and Knight. 'If they can manage to get to the house without losing their way in the Meadowflower.' He paused for effect. 'Right, there's more to come from forensics – or we hope there is, though it won't be until tomorrow,' Kendrick told them. 'Now Mick can compare the Dobsons' DNA with what was found at the scene, and if it is Jamie or Cal's saliva that's on Andy's face, we'll need to talk to them again. For now, you've got your jobs.' He checked his watch. 'DC Varcoe, PC Roberts, follow me.'

Anna and Nat looked apprehensive but trailed after the DCI as he strode towards his office.

Chris Rogers took Catherine aside. 'Are they in shit?'

'No. He wants them to focus on the arsons.'

'Really?' Chris winced as Kendrick's office door thumped closed. 'Last throw of the dice then, I reckon. Rumour is, the Super's got another team on standby, ready to take over tomorrow morning. An EMSOU team.'

Did he mean Isla's team? 'Who told you that?' Catherine demanded.

Chris tapped the side of his nose. 'Someone who knows these things.'

'Monk?'

'I can't reveal my sources. I'll tell you one thing though.' He leaned closer. 'If I were you, I'd go home, shave my legs and change the sheets. Rumour has it one of this new team needs somewhere to stay.' He winked, and then raised his voice. 'Come on then, Dave, let's go and knock on some doors.'

Before Catherine could react, Chris and Dave were on their way out of the office.

'They haven't found him yet, our boy on the bike. I feel like a bloody idiot, I should have kept my mouth shut.' Knight held up a car key. 'Hopefully we won't have stuff thrown at us this time.'

25

As they reached the Spences' house, Catherine's phone rang. When she saw the number on the screen, she considered ignoring it.

'Who is it?' Knight asked.

Catherine pulled a face. 'Helen Bridges.'

'The journalist?' He held out his hand. 'Let me speak to her.'

Surprised, Catherine gave him the phone.

'Detective Inspector Knight speaking,' he barked. Catherine raised an eyebrow, wondering what he was up to. 'Yes, I know who you are, Ms Bridges. DS Bishop isn't available at the moment.'

She could hear Bridges' voice but couldn't make out what she was saying.

'The body at the car dealership?' Knight was nodding. 'Murder. Yeah, definitely.' He paused. 'Print whatever you like, post, publish, whatever. Tell the world. If you could make an appeal for information at the same time, we'd appreciate it. Usual contact numbers.' He listened. 'I wouldn't say we're desperate, no, just keen to explore every avenue. We've got reinforcements from Lincoln and we're putting everything we can into finding the people responsible for the recent deaths and the arsons.' Another pause. 'We're still trying to discover whether the cases are linked. Yeah, quote me if you like… In return for your help? You mean you won't just do it from the goodness of your heart?'

Catherine heard Bridges laughing.

'Okay, how about an exclusive once we have our culprits?' Knight raised his eyebrows at Catherine as she made a 'what the hell' face at him. 'Deal. Yes, the second we close the cell door. Thanks, Helen.'

He ended the call and held the phone out to Catherine with a smile.

'Quite assertive, I thought,' he said.

'I didn't recognise you. Why did you say all that?'

'The DCI had a word while you were making Mick's tea. He said one of us should call Bridges, tell her about Greaves and see what happened, but Bridges just saved us the trouble. Maybe he tipped her off.'

'What's he playing at? The Super will go spare – you know how she likes a press conference.'

Knight smiled. 'I think Keith's beyond caring. He wants the arsonist found before the Super brings another team in.'

'Chris mentioned that. It's true then?'

'Who knows. The way things are going, it'd probably be a good thing.'

'Don't let the boss hear you say that.'

'Times are changing, and he knows that.' Knight tipped his head towards the Spences' front door. 'Ready?'

'As I'll ever be. Better take your shoes off now.'

–

'A what?' Irene Spence demanded.

'A door cut into the fence at the back of the property,' Catherine said.

'Meaning people could come and go without us seeing them?' Irene was outraged.

'It's unlikely, unless you noticed them go into the shed and not come back out again.' Catherine didn't mean the words sarcastically, but Irene gave her a sharp glance.

'We'd no idea,' she said. 'None. And if we had, we'd have done something about it.' She looked at her husband. 'I'm glad we didn't know. I wouldn't have felt safe.'

'At least when people come to the front door, we know who's around,' Des agreed.

'They shouldn't have been allowed to go cutting holes in council property,' Irene went on. 'Who do you think's been sneaking through this thing then?'

Catherine smiled. 'We were hoping you could tell us.'

'If we'd seen anyone, we'd have phoned the police straight away.' Des Spence began to cough. He lifted his hand to his mouth, his eyes watering. Irene stood and went through to the kitchen.

'Are you okay, sir?' Knight asked gently. Des nodded, still coughing.

'Some days are worse than others.' He glanced towards the kitchen. 'Irene doesn't like to talk about it. I think she's hoping for a miracle cure, but I've told her, the doctors don't say six months unless they mean it.' His smile was sad, and Catherine's throat caught. 'I worry about her, you see. She's never lived alone.'

Irene bustled back in and shoved a glass of water under his nose. 'Drink this, and stop being maudlin.'

Des took the glass with a wink at Catherine and Knight.

Irene sat back down. 'Will the council replace this fence panel then? We don't want every Tom, Dick and

Harry to know they can come wandering through the gardens.'

Catherine's phone began to ring, and when she saw Kendrick's name appear, she excused herself to take the call in the hallway.

'Jade Walsh is here asking to speak to you,' he said. 'Though why it's up to me to phone and tell you that, I don't know.'

'She made it clear she didn't want to talk to us earlier, slammed the door in our faces.'

'Don't shoot the messenger.' He ended the call.

Catherine went back to the living room. 'We're needed back at the station, DI Knight.'

Knight was too professional to leap out of the chair, but Catherine was sure he wanted to.

'Thank you for your help,' he said.

Irene looked aggrieved. 'Is that all you came for?'

'We're grateful for your time,' Catherine said. She smiled at Des. 'Take care of yourself, Mr Spence.'

'I'll do my best.' He turned away and for a second, Catherine saw desolation in his expression. Guessing he wouldn't have wanted her to say any more, she turned away and kept walking.

—

Jade waited for them in the same interview room where Catherine had spoken to Jamie Dobson, while sipping water from a paper cup. She looked up as Catherine and Knight entered the room, clearly apprehensive. Catherine smiled at her.

'Can I get you another drink?'

Jade forced a smile. 'A vodka would be good if you're offering. No, thanks, I'm okay.'

Knight pushed a chair towards Catherine and sat down himself. 'How are the children?'

'They're okay, thank you. They seem to have stopped throwing up, at last. My neighbour's sitting with them.'

Knight nodded. 'How can we help?'

'It's more how I can help you.' She looked away then forced herself to meet Catherine's eyes. 'I was rude earlier, and I'm sorry. I was panicking, didn't know what to do. I hadn't expected you to come back, and I thought...' Her eyes flicked between them. 'It wasn't that I lied to you, but I didn't... I didn't tell you everything.'

'Okay,' Knight said. 'Will you tell us now?'

'It's about Andy. I know his girlfriend was killed the same day he did – what time did she die? Are you allowed to tell me?'

'Why do you want to know?' Catherine asked.

Jade took a shaky breath. 'Do you think Andy killed her?'

'We're not going to comment on that,' Knight said.

'Well, he can't have done. He was with me for most of the day.'

Catherine hadn't known what to expect, but it wasn't this. She leaned back in the chair, not taking her eyes off Jade, not letting her surprise show. 'Why didn't you mention this before?'

'I'm sorry. I didn't think it mattered.' Jade took a tissue from her jeans pocket and wiped her eyes.

'Didn't matter? Didn't you think we'd be chasing all over town, trying to find out where Andy had been on the day he died, whether he'd been at home when his girlfriend was killed? Whether he'd killed her himself?' Catherine forced herself to speak calmly, but it wasn't easy.

'Yes, of course I did, but Andy's dead and I thought…
I'm sorry, I should have told you.' Jade's head went down.

'Yes, you should have. You would have saved us a lot
of time.'

'Am I going to get in trouble over this?' Jade's voice
was little more than a whisper. 'I've got my kids to think
about, my studies…'

'You need to tell us what happened,' Knight said.

Jade nodded, wiped her eyes again. 'Okay.' She took
a deep breath and blew it out slowly. 'I'd taken the kids
to school and was doing some of my uni work. Someone
knocked on the door, and when I opened it, Andy was
standing there.'

'He just turned up?' Catherine said. 'He didn't text or
phone you?'

'No. He could have done; my number hasn't changed.
But I hadn't heard from him since he walked out, so maybe
he'd deleted it. I was surprised, shocked really – I asked
what he was doing, what he wanted, and he seemed so…
I don't know, sad. Not like himself at all, or at least not as
I remembered him.'

'This was definitely the first time you'd seen him since
you split up?' Catherine asked.

'Yes. I'm telling you the truth.'

About time, Catherine thought. 'Can you give me
your phone number, please?'

Jade did so, and Catherine noted it down.

'Thank you,' she said. 'Go on.'

'He asked if he could come in, said he wanted to talk
to me. I was hesitant, because I hadn't seen him for so
long, and him just turning up… I'd heard rumours about
the way he treated his girlfriend, and to be honest, I didn't
want him in my house.'

306

'But then you spent the day with him?' Catherine raised an eyebrow.

Jade blushed. 'Nothing happened, not like that. He told me he'd heard I was at uni, a mature student, whatever you want to call it. He asked if he could talk to me about it.'

'He wanted to talk about your degree course?' Knight looked bemused, and Catherine couldn't blame him.

'It sounds weird, I know. I asked if he was having a laugh, but he said he was serious. Eventually I asked him in, said he could stay for a coffee but after that I needed to get on. And… I don't know, we just kept talking. He told me about his kids, showed me photos, asked how mine were getting on. He mentioned his girlfriend, said things weren't always easy at home.' Jade snorted. 'I told him maybe he should stop beating her up then. That upset him. He showed me a plaster on his arm, said Hollie had cut him.'

Poor thing, Catherine thought. 'What did you say?'

She curled her lip. 'That he was lucky she hadn't chopped his balls off. I've heard it all before: the woman being as bad as the bloke who's knocking her around, it's not his fault, she provokes him, and all that shite. My dad used to spout all the same crap. Andy shut up about it then, just drank his coffee.'

'Why did he want to know about your studies?' Catherine asked.

'This was the bit I really found hard to believe. Andy reckoned he wanted to start again – get some training, get himself a decent job. Earn some money to support his family, take some of the pressure off himself and Hollie.' She shook her head. 'He wanted to learn about brick-laying, then maybe do a plumbing or electrical course.

Obviously, he was too old for an apprenticeship, so he was looking at college courses.'

'So he came to you for career advice?' Catherine's tone made it clear she found this unlikely, and Jade glared at her.

'Why is that so hard to believe? Yes, I got pregnant while I was still at school, and then again at seventeen. Doesn't make me thick, you know. Doesn't mean I have to give up on life.'

'I wasn't talking about you. I meant that from what we've been told, Andy didn't want to consider college or university after school,' Catherine said. 'For what it's worth, I admire what you're doing.'

Mollified, Jade nodded. 'I said the same thing to Andy, but he seemed serious so I said I'd help him. No time like the present and all that, so we got the train to Lincoln.' She opened her bag, removed two train tickets from her purse and put them on the table. 'I brought these to show you. We went up to the college, he got some information and we had a walk around. Had another coffee, came back to Northolme. We picked my kids up from school and took them to the park and had ice cream. We got soaked because it started chucking it down with rain, but it didn't matter. We had a good time. It was like it used to be.'

Catherine had a suspicion she knew what Andy might have been up to – having killed Hollie, he was attempting to provide himself with an alibi. Then, when he'd returned home, he'd phoned the Dobson brothers and invited them over, hoping to make them believe Hollie was still alive. When Knight shot her a glance, she knew he was thinking the same way.

'Why didn't Andy just look up the information he needed online?' she asked.

'He said he wanted to have a look at the area, see if there was any housing nearby. He was talking about them moving over there, having a completely new start. I know, he could have looked that up online as well, but… I don't know, he was excited.' She met Catherine's eyes. 'I just wanted to help him.'

'What time did Andy get to your house?' Knight asked.

'Nine thirty, and he left at about four.' Jade looked from Knight to Catherine. 'Does that mean he was with me when Hollie died?'

Knight rubbed his eyes. 'Are you telling us the truth about all this?' Jade made to speak, but he kept talking. 'Because you have to admit, it sounds unlikely.'

'Andy's dead now,' Jade said softly. 'Why would I lie?'

'I don't know. To protect someone?'

'To protect yourself?' Catherine suggested.

Jade laughed. 'Yeah, you've got me. I killed Hollie, and Andy too.' She pushed back her chair. 'I'm sorry for wasting your time.'

'Sit down please, Jade,' Catherine said. 'You'll need to give a statement.'

Jade looked down at her. 'You mean you believe me now?'

Catherine watched her until, reluctantly, Jade dropped back into the chair. 'Like I said, we'll need a statement.'

-

The incident room was quiet, most of the team from Lincoln having left for the day. Kendrick sat at a desk in the corner, delving into a bag of crisps and squinting at a laptop screen.

'I don't know whose idea it was to give me this to work on. Can't see a bloody thing.' He closed the laptop. 'What did Jade Walsh want?'

'To give us an alibi for Andy Nugent.' Catherine reached for a crisp.

'Why bother?' Kendrick snatched the bag away as Knight began to tell him what Jade had told them.

'It would explain where Andy was all day,' Knight said. 'And if Jade was telling the truth about when he arrived at her house, it confirms Hollie was arguing with someone else at ten a.m.'

'She said he arrived before that?' Kendrick chewed, staring into space. 'Makes sense. Can anyone confirm what she said?'

'Her neighbours might have seen him,' Catherine said.

'And we can ask at the college. Someone might remember them,' Knight suggested. Catherine mentioned the train tickets too, though they could be anyone's.

Kendrick clicked his tongue a few times. 'We could send someone over, but the way our house-to-house is going, no one will have seen a thing, and we could have Mick look at the tickets for fingerprints but I'm not sure if it's worth the time or expense. Anyway, Mick's got enough to do. He sent one of his minions over, and the DNA samples from Rebecca and Dale Clough should be arriving with him soon. He won't be going to bed tonight.'

'Did you say we've got nothing from the house-to-house?' Catherine asked.

'Nothing at all.' Kendrick grabbed another fistful of crisps. 'And our intrepid constables have had no luck in tracking your runaway delinquent down.' He opened the laptop again and Catherine followed Knight to the door, both of them turning back when Kendrick bellowed:

'And you might want to go up and see Anna. We've finally got some stuff from the victims' phones.'

26

'Kendrick called it stuff?' Anna said. 'This is gold. I was just about to call you.'

'Gold?' Catherine leaned over Anna's shoulder, peering at the sheets of paper on her desk. 'That's a new one.'

Anna blushed. 'It's something Thomas says.'

'That doesn't surprise me.' Catherine rolled her eyes. 'Tell us what you've got.'

Knight stood at Anna's other shoulder as she tapped a finger on the top sheet. 'These are the records from Andy's phone, but there's nothing that can help us. He makes the call to Jamie Dobson at five twenty-three, just as Dobson said, but he didn't use his phone at all for the rest of the day. In fact, he doesn't seem to use it much at all. They couldn't find any social media accounts for him and other than a couple of betting sites, a music app, and loads of photos of his kids, there's nothing to see.'

'Are there any calls or texts to this number?' Catherine read out the mobile number Jade Walsh had just given her, but Anna shook her head.

'No contact with that number at all.'

'There's no messages between him and Jade Walsh?' Knight asked.

Anna shook her head again. 'Nothing. It's like he was a recluse or something.'

'Weird,' Catherine said. But then with a distant relationship with his parents, no work colleagues and no friends they'd been able to find, who would Andy Nugent have been in touch with?

'So what's this "gold" information you've got for us?' Catherine demanded. 'I hope it's as good as you're building it up to be.'

Anna grinned. 'It is.' She found a different page. 'Here. These are the records from Hollie's phone. You see the lines I've highlighted?'

'The bright pink ones?' Catherine narrowed her eyes. 'Yeah, I can just about make them out. They're texts?'

'They are. And look who's she's sending them to.'

'Ross Work Phone,' Knight read. 'They're to her brother?'

Anna smiled. 'No.' She held up another sheet of paper. 'I've matched the texts sent on Hollie's phone with the same texts being received on this phone.'

The relevant lines had been highlighted in orange this time.

'Have you got a new pack of pens or what?' Catherine grumbled. 'Tell us what you mean.'

'Okay.' Anna flourished the page with the orange highlighting. 'These records come from Scott Greaves's phone.'

Catherine's eyes met Knight's over the top of Anna's head, both of them stunned. Anna turned to laugh at them.

'Your faces. That was—'

'Gold?' Catherine bent closer to look at the text, Knight doing the same. 'You're saying that Hollie had Scott Greaves's number hidden on her phone?'

'Yep. Why would Andy be interested in her brother's work phone? If he went through her contacts, and he probably did, he'd just pass over it. If Hollie deleted the texts as she received them, she'd probably get away with it.'

Catherine's mind was scrambling over the possibilities – if Hollie was the person Scott was having an affair with, what did that mean for their investigation? 'What do the messages say?'

'Hollie sent the first one six weeks ago,' Anna said. She laid the sheets next to each other on the desk and pointed.

'"Need to talk"',' Knight read. 'Might be innocent.'

'Scott replies, "Why?"'

'But how did they meet?' Catherine wondered. 'How did they get each other's numbers?'

'And then Hollie writes, "you know why".' Knight lifted his shoulders. 'Could still be innocent.'

'Could be.' Anna pointed at Hollie's sheet again. 'Until you read this one.'

'"Need you round here now".' Catherine looked at Scott's sheet. 'And he doesn't reply. Probably just rushed around to the house.'

'It goes on like that. "Need to see you", "want more", "I'm waiting". I don't know, it's not exactly explicit, but…' Anna tipped her head to the side, eyebrows raised. 'At half past nine on the day Hollie died, she sent Scott a message saying "need you here now".'

'And at ten o'clock, she was arguing with a man who wasn't Andy Nugent,' said Catherine. Anna was right. This *was* gold.

'Have you shown Keith this yet?' Knight frowned. 'Weren't you and Nat supposed to be working on the arsons?'

'We were, but she's gone off duty and when all this' – Anna nodded at the records – 'came in, the boss asked me to have a look at it. It's not as though we were making any progress anyway. The full reports aren't back from the fire scene investigator; there were no witnesses and, as far as we've been able to tell, no one acting weirdly in the crowd at each scene, except for the lad you saw on the bike, and we haven't found him yet.'

'Maybe we'll get more information once Helen Bridges' story breaks,' Catherine said. 'Did the DCI mention that?'

Anna snorted. 'Yeah, he thinks he's onto a winner there. I told him it depends what Bridges writes, that she's just as likely to tear us to bits because we haven't arrested anyone as she is to ask people to help us, but he wasn't listening.'

Catherine nodded at the highlighted sheets on the desk. 'He will when you show him those.'

Anna's phone beeped and she checked the screen.

'Nat's seeing Jimmy again,' she said. 'They're going to be in the pub until closing if anyone fancies a drink.'

'They want us to join them again? Is he scared to be alone with her, do you think?'

Anna laughed. 'Wouldn't you be?'

'I am.' Catherine checked the time. 'Let's go and see the DCI now.'

'You never know, he might let us go for last orders,' Knight said.

Kendrick was on the phone when they reached the incident room. He mimed drinking as they approached him, then propped the phone between his neck and his shoulder and made a T shape with his hands.

'Think he wants a coffee,' Catherine said.

'I'll go,' Anna said. 'Will you take these?' She handed Catherine her highlighted sheets.

'You're sure about this?' Kendrick was saying. He paused. 'And how soon can you do that?… I'll authorise anything you like as long as you get us some answers. Speak to you soon.' He put the phone on the desk and stretched. 'That was Mick. He had some interesting news.'

'Anna has information too,' Catherine said.

'From the phone records?' Kendrick rubbed his hands together. 'We're blessed tonight.' He looked at Catherine. 'Have you heard from that missus of yours?'

Catherine remembered what Chris Rogers had said about the team Stringer had ready to take over their case, and the hints he dropped about Isla being involved. Kendrick was clearly thinking the same way.

'If you mean has she told me she's turning up here tomorrow to steal our case from under our noses, no.'

Kendrick closed his eyes and covered his face with his hands. Alarmed, Catherine and Knight looked at each other.

'Sir?' Catherine took a step forward. 'Are you okay?'

Kendrick lifted his head. 'Can't seem to shake this cold. Ready for my bed, that's all.' Rubbing his belly, he picked up his phone again and started stabbing at the screen. 'Quick text to the Super, telling her we're making good progress.' He held the phone up to show them. 'And she'll ring me in ten, nine, eight, seven, six, five…' Sure enough, the phone rang and Stringer's name appeared. 'Good evening, ma'am.'

Knight whispered, 'Do you think he's all right?'

'Who knows. He wouldn't admit it if he wasn't.'

Anna returned with a mug as Kendrick told the Super he was waiting for an urgent call from forensics and promised to call her as soon as he knew more. He beamed at Anna as she placed the tea in front of him.

'Thank you. I'm told you have news.'

Anna showed him the highlighted sheets and explained what she'd found. Kendrick looked gleeful.

'I knew these cases were linked. This fits in with what Mick's just told me.' He sat back, watching them, making them wait. 'You remember the rumours that Hollie and Andy's youngest child, May, wasn't Andy's at all?' The three of them nodded. 'Well, as it turns out, the rumours were right. Andy's definitely the father of the older child, but he's not May's. That raises some interesting questions, doesn't it?'

'You're thinking that Scott Greaves is May's father?' Anna said.

'But Mick would know by now, wouldn't he? Like we said before, Scott's DNA is in the system,' Knight said.

'They've compared May's DNA to Andy's and found no match but haven't compared the child's to anyone else yet. It's his next job. There's no reason he would have linked May to Scott anyway, since we didn't know he and Hollie even knew each other existed until now.' He grabbed his phone again. 'Mick? Change of plan. Scott Greaves could be May's father. Can you have a look?... Just now. Blame DC Varcoe for sitting on information. Cheers.' He saw Anna looking at him. 'What?'

'I think we should speak to Neil Wilcox again,' Anna said.

Kendrick picked up his tea. 'The removals man? Why?'

'Because I'm sure he recognised Andy Nugent's name, and he admitted to knowing Scott Greaves. Now we know there was a link between Scott and Hollie, it might be worth going back to him.'

'Agreed. Go now, take Chris or Dave with you.' Kendrick drank some tea.

'They've gone home,' Catherine pointed out. Kendrick shrugged.

'Sorry, Anna. You'll have to slum it and take DS Bishop.'

27

Neil Wilcox lived at the end of a long row of terraced properties on the outskirts of town, not far from Andy Nugent's parents' house. He answered his front door with a can of lager in his hand and a belligerent expression on his face. Recognising Anna, he took a step forward to look up and down the street.

'What are you doing here?' he demanded.

'Just some follow-up questions,' Anna said.

He looked at Catherine. 'Who are you?'

She held up her ID and Wilcox scanned it.

'I can't help you.'

'You don't know what we're going to ask you yet.' Catherine looked over his shoulder. 'Can we come inside? I can already see your neighbours' curtains twitching.'

'No bloody wonder, when you've turned up at the door.'

'They can tell we're police by looking?'

'Plain clothes don't fool anyone. We like the quiet life around here.'

'We talk here or at the station,' Catherine told him. 'Your choice.'

Wilcox scowled at her. 'Where'd you find this one?' he said to Anna. She said nothing and Wilcox moved away from the door. 'All right, let's get it over with.'

Inside, the smell of fried food and cigarettes hung in the air. The stairs were to their left and Wilcox nodded towards a door on their right.

'Through here.'

The living room was long and narrow, cluttered with furniture. A woman sat on a flowery sofa, a glass of red wine on the coffee table in front of her. She was concentrating on her phone, but she looked up as Catherine and Anna followed Wilcox into the room.

'What's going on?'

'Mrs Wilcox?' When the woman nodded, Anna smiled at her. 'I'm DC Varcoe, Lincolnshire Police. I spoke to your husband earlier—'

'What?' She stared at her husband and Wilcox squirmed.

'I haven't had a chance to tell you about it, Janine.'

'You've been home for nearly four hours.' She turned back to Anna. 'What's this about?'

Anna explained about Scott and Andy's deaths.

'Mr Wilcox, you told us you knew Scott Greaves, but said that you didn't recognise Andy Nugent by name or his face when we showed you his photograph, just that you'd seen him on the news.' Anna found the picture of Andy. 'Do you know him, Mrs Wilcox?'

Janine Wilcox frowned at the image. She glanced at her husband, then back at Anna. 'Yes. That is, I've seen him before.'

Neil Wilcox let out a long breath. 'All right, I'll come clean. I'm not going to ask my wife to lie for me. Yes, we employed Andy Nugent a couple of times when we needed an extra pair of hands. Cash in hand, no questions asked.'

Anna nodded. 'Why didn't you tell us earlier?'

'You knew anyway, didn't you? That's why you're here.'

'You never were any good at lying,' his wife said. 'Why did you bother?'

Wilcox blushed. 'It was cash in hand. Why do you think?'

'As I said before, we've no interest in your business activities,' Anna said.

'When did Andy work for you?' Catherine asked.

'Like I said, it was just a casual thing. Someone I knew mentioned him, said he was reliable.' Wilcox looked at his wife. 'You'll have a record somewhere, won't you?'

She sighed. 'I'll see what I can find.'

As she left the room, Catherine said, 'This person who told you about Andy. Who was it?'

Wilcox swigged from his can. 'Doesn't matter. He's dead now.'

Catherine glanced at Anna. 'Do you mean Scott Greaves?'

Wilcox shook his head. 'Bloke called Vic Henshaw.'

That name again. Vic Henshaw hadn't come up in their enquiries so far, but Catherine doubted it was a coincidence. Jade Walsh had told them the owner of the scrapyard Andy worked at was called Vic, and it wasn't the most common name in the world. She felt her heartbeat quicken. 'What line of business was Vic in?'

'I never knew for sure. He was one of those blokes, you know. Bit dodgy. Better not to ask. Better not to know.'

'What does that mean?'

'Just a feeling I had. I knew him years ago, bought a van off him once. It was a decent runner, cheap. He had the paperwork, and there was no need for me to ask any questions. It was only later, once I'd scrapped it, that he told me it was nicked.' Wilcox took another gulp of lager and put the can on the coffee table. 'Dodgy bastard, like I said.'

Anna was sceptical. 'He sold you a stolen van, and you knew nothing about it?'

'I run a legitimate business. Do you think I'd get involved in crap like that? Yeah, okay, I've paid the odd person cash in hand over the years, but that's as far as it's gone.'

'When Vic recommended Andy to you, did he say Andy had done some work for him?' Catherine was thinking of the break-in at the Cloughs' house and the other two women who had woken to find an intruder in their home. Anna had said one of them found their keys abandoned on the floor, hadn't she? So if the intruder was Andy Nugent, as they knew to be the case in the Cloughs' house because of the evidence of the fingerprints and the glove, had he broken in intending to grab their keys and steal their car?

'Yeah, Vic asked how business was and I mentioned we had a couple of big jobs on. I've used agency workers in the past, but it's expensive and the people they send aren't always reliable. Vic mentioned this bloke, Andy, gave me a phone number. Said I could trust him.'

Catherine nodded. 'And you've no idea how Vic made his living?'

'He was a businessman. As you no doubt know, that could mean anything. I never asked.'

'But he dealt in stolen cars?'

Wilcox spread his hands. 'All I can tell you is that he sold one to me. Whatever else he did, I know nothing about it.'

'And you said Vic's dead?' Anna asked.

'Died last year. Heart attack.'

They'd need to check, but Catherine doubted Wilcox was lying this time. There would be no point.

Janine Wilcox came back into the room with a blue cardboard folder in her hand. She sat back down and opened the folder. Drawing out a couple of sheets of paper, she handed them to Catherine. Anna moved closer so they could both read. The first sheet gave Andy's name and address, which was the house he'd lived in with Jade. A phone number was listed, which Catherine thought was the same as his current number, but they'd have to check to be sure. On the second sheet was a list of jobs, five in all.

'And these are the only times Andy worked for you?' Catherine asked.

'Yep. Five days at a hundred quid each time.'

'We'll need to take this information with us,' said Anna.

Janine nodded. 'Fine. I don't know why I kept it, to be honest.'

'Is that everything?' Neil Wilcox asked. 'I'm sorry I didn't tell you the truth before, but… You know how it is. There won't be any… any comeback from this? Nothing about the stolen van or cash in hand stuff or anything?'

Catherine folded the sheets of paper in half. 'Thank for your time.'

She turned and made for the door, and Anna followed with Neil Wilcox scurrying along behind them.

'You didn't answer me,' he said as Catherine opened the front door. She allowed Anna to pass first and then smiled at him.

'I didn't, did I?'

—

'Was Andy Nugent nicking cars then?' Anna said as they pulled away from Wilcox's house.

Catherine stretched out her legs, glad Anna had taken the wheel. She yawned, rubbing her eyes, the late night with Isla and five a.m. start beginning to catch up. 'It would explain why he was in the Cloughs' house, and why he was wearing gloves.'

'Dale Clough has his restoration business too – maybe Andy was hoping to find keys that would get him into the building. Some of those old cars must be worth a decent amount of money.'

'You'd think so.' Catherine didn't have a clue, but it made sense.

'And if this Vic Henshaw did have a scrapyard, albeit one we haven't found yet, they could all be in it together.'

Catherine closed her eyes. 'Or Andy could just be a burglar, not interested in the cars at all.'

Her phone rang and she saw Knight's name on the screen. 'Jonathan, we're on our way back. Wilcox told us—'

'Hang on, Catherine. Mick just phoned – we know who the father of Hollie's daughter, May, is.'

28

As she sat opposite Jamie Dobson in the interview room, Catherine thought that he looked as exhausted as she felt. His blond hair was greasy, his eyes dull, his skin sallow under the fluorescent light.

'You've got my fingerprints, my DNA and now for some reason, you're obsessed with my hands. I've been cautioned and you're recording this conversation. What's going on?' He didn't sound angry, just resigned.

'You've said you don't want a solicitor present,' Knight said.

'I don't need one. I've done nothing wrong.'

'Mr Dobson, we need to speak to you about some new information which has come to light now we have your DNA sample,' Catherine told him. She had a sheet of paper face down on the table in front of her, and for the moment she linked her fingers and kept her hands on top of it.

Jamie looked bemused. 'What have you found? You already know I was in Hollie and Andy's house.'

'Can you tell us about your relationship with Hollie Morton?' Catherine asked.

He stared. 'Hollie? Well, I knew her.'

'From school?'

'Yeah.'

Catherine nodded. 'Were you friends?'

'I mean, we hadn't really kept in touch, just on Facebook or whatever, but then Andy deleted her account. He didn't like her having friends.'

'Why not?'

'Because he wanted to control her. He kept her a prisoner, more or less.' Jamie shifted in his chair. 'I've told you already, he hurt her, beat her up.'

'How do you know that?'

'What?'

Catherine repeated the question. 'If you only kept in touch on Facebook, but her partner had deleted her account, how did you know what Hollie's life was like?'

He was scowling now, his face red. 'Doesn't take a genius, does it?'

'Do you know Hollie's brother? Her sister?' Knight asked.

'I know the whole family. Why?'

Knight nodded. 'Did they tell you Andy was hurting Hollie?'

Jamie ran a hand through his hair. 'It was mentioned.'

'Did you ever go to see Hollie, to check if she was okay?'

He looked away. 'I might have done, a couple of times. I didn't go up to the house or anything, I just…'

'Watched?' Now Catherine folded her arms.

'No, it wasn't like that. You're making it sound like I'm some kind of stalker. I was just looking out for her, that's all.'

'Okay.' Catherine waited, but Jamie stayed silent. 'Where were you, when you watched the house?'

He scowled. 'I didn't *watch*.'

'Did Hollie know you were there?'

'Well, no, but—'

'Did you tell anyone else you'd been there?'

'No. I'd have looked like a weirdo.'

'How close did you get to the house?' Catherine asked. 'Did you look through the windows?'

He shook his head. 'Of course I didn't. What do you think I am?'

'Then where were you?' Knight's voice was quiet, but firm.

Jamie glared at him. 'Why does it matter?'

'In case you've forgotten, Mr Dobson, Hollie Morton and Andy Nugent are both dead, and it's our job to find out who killed them,' Catherine said.

'All I can tell you is that it wasn't me.'

'You say you went to the house. Did you ever go inside?'

Jamie licked his lips. 'I've told you, I just went to check on Hollie.'

'That doesn't answer the question,' Catherine told him. 'When you went to the house, did you use your mum's car?'

'Would have been daft to have been driving a van with your name on it when you were sneaking around like that, wouldn't it?' Knight added.

Jamie looked down at the table. 'I've done nothing wrong.'

'Have you ever seen Hollie's children, Mr Dobson?' Catherine asked.

His head jerked up. 'What's that supposed to mean?'

'It's a simple question.'

'You making me out to be some sort of pervert now? Saying I watch kids?'

Catherine smiled, her voice gentle. 'Maybe one in particular?'

'I don't know what you mean.' But he did, Catherine could see it in his face. She picked up the piece of paper, turned it over and pushed it across the table to him.

Jamie glanced down at it. 'What's this?'

'The results of a DNA comparison proving you are the father of Hollie Morton's youngest child, May Nugent.'

Jamie's lips trembled as he studied the paper. When he looked up, there were tears in his eyes. 'I'd hoped, but…'

'Didn't Hollie tell you?' Knight asked.

'How could she? We only met that one time, when we…' He blushed. 'And she was terrified of Andy. If he'd found out May wasn't his…'

'We've been told there were rumours as soon as people heard Hollie was pregnant,' Catherine said.

Jamie snorted. 'There were, but Andy wouldn't have believed them. I don't know where they came from; no one could have known about what happened. Hollie wouldn't have told anyone, and Andy knew Hollie wouldn't have dared cheat on him.'

Catherine gestured towards the sheet of paper. 'But…'

'But there's the proof.' Jamie bit his lip. 'It happened once. I was doing some contract work for the council and was sent to the house. That time, there really was a problem with the boiler.' He blinked a few times. 'Andy wasn't there, and obviously Hollie and I recognised each other, but she was strange, distant, like she didn't want to talk… She had a mark on her face, a red mark, and she kept turning away, holding herself strangely, like she didn't want me to see it.' He swallowed. 'Anyway, I sorted the boiler, and needed to show Hollie how the new room thermostat worked. Her son was having his nap upstairs and we were standing there together, I'm showing her how to program it, and she turned to me, just looked

328

at me, and then… Well, I'm sure I don't need to spell it out. It just… just happened. I suppose she was lonely, and hurt. She needed someone, and I was there. I was familiar.' There were tears on his cheeks now, and he scrubbed at them. 'That was it.'

Knight gave him a moment, then said, 'You never tried to contact her, never went back to the house?'

Jamie looked shamefaced. 'A couple of times, yeah, since May was born. I'd wondered, you see, knowing the date when Hollie and I had been together, and that May was born nine months later. I wanted to see her, I thought…'

'That she might look like you,' Knight said softly.

'Yeah, exactly. I thought Hollie might bring them out into the garden to play, but she never did, or at least not while I was there.' Jamie's eyes widened as he realised what he'd said.

'You went through the door in the fence and hid in the shed,' Knight said, making it a statement, not a question.

Jamie looked shamefaced. 'And watched the house through the keyhole in the shed door. Yeah. I know it sounds terrible. Ross told me about the door. He didn't know what had happened between Hollie and me, but he knew I had the van and asked me if I'd help move Hollie's stuff if they ever persuaded her to leave Andy. Ross has access to a van but it belongs to the company he works for, and if Hollie needed to get out in a hurry, he knew I'd be able to sort something since I own mine. He wanted me to know where to go.'

'But he doesn't know you went there to try to see May?' Knight said.

Jamie shook his head.

'Didn't you want to ask Hollie if May was your daughter?' Catherine knew it was a stupid question, but they knew now that Jamie had the motive to confront Hollie.

'Of course, but I also wanted to protect her from Andy.' Jamie's mouth twisted. 'I've been saving some money. I was going to try to help her, get her away from him. Even if she didn't want to be with me, I didn't care. I just wanted her out of there, and the kids too.'

'You never talked to Hollie about May, never contacted her in any way?' Catherine asked.

'No, never. I didn't have her phone number, and I never went any nearer the house than the shed, not until the day Andy phoned and invited us there.'

'How did you feel about going to the house, knowing Andy would be at home?' Knight asked.

Jamie shrugged. 'I wasn't worried. I just wanted to see May. I knew Andy hadn't taken any notice of the rumours about the pregnancy, because he'd have done something about it. Thrown Hollie and May out, at least.'

'But you didn't see May, or Hollie?' Knight said.

'No, not once.' He looked wretched.

'We need to talk about the day Hollie and Andy died,' Catherine said.

Jamie flinched. 'Okay.' He managed a smile. 'Suppose I'm the prime suspect now.'

'Where were you at ten o'clock that morning?' Catherine knew it was still possible that it hadn't been Scott Greaves in the house with Hollie at that time, and they had to cover every base.

'At home. I'd taken the day off so we could go to the hospital. We're trying to spend as much time with our mum as we can, because...' He swallowed.

Catherine nodded. 'And after that?'

'We were on the ward most of the day with Mum. I can't remember exactly what time we left home to go to Lincoln though. About eleven, I think, to be there when visiting started.'

'Was Cal with you?'

'Yeah, but he wouldn't know what time it was. It's not like he can back me up.'

'Can you remember what time you arrived at the hospital? Do you have a car park ticket, anything like that?' Knight asked.

Jamie's eyes lit up. 'No, because they have this new system. There's a camera as you drive into the car park, and it takes a picture of your car and a note of the time. Then when you're leaving, you go to a machine in the hospital entrance, type in your registration number and it tells you how much you need to pay. I used my bank card, contactless. Could you check all that?'

Catherine made a note. They'd be able to check his phone records too, see which masts his phone had pinged as he'd travelled. 'Possibly. What time did you leave?'

'Like I said, we stayed most of the day. We were still on our way home when Andy called just before five thirty, so I'd say we left just before five. It'll be on the camera again.'

'Let's talk about when you got to Andy and Hollie's house again,' Knight said. 'Did you knock on the door?'

'No, Andy had already opened it. It was like he'd been looking out, waiting for us to get there.'

'Were you worried he'd guessed about May, that he'd made up the boiler problem to get you to the house because he wanted to confront you about the baby?'

'No. If that was why he wanted to see me, he'd have turned up at my house, not invited me to theirs. Anyway,

I wasn't scared of him. I'd have liked an excuse to punch him, to be honest.'

'How did Andy seem when you arrived?'

'He was… I don't know, it was like he was excited, maybe? Sort of giddy. He more or less dragged us into the house. Pleased to see us, which was a bit weird, I suppose, since we weren't exactly close, but I didn't think anything of it. He told us he'd fixed the boiler himself and he was sorry to have wasted our time, so why didn't we come in for a beer? I didn't really want to spend any time with him, but I thought I might see Hollie and May, so…'

'And did you? Did you go upstairs?'

Jamie bit his lip. 'No. I chickened out. Andy said Hollie had a migraine, that she was in bed, and I thought shit, I bet he's hurt her. How could I go up there, sneak into the kids' room to see May, knowing I was putting Hollie at risk? It was one of the hardest things I've ever done, but I stayed downstairs.'

'Cal went up there though,' Catherine said.

'Oh yeah, he went to the toilet. Andy told him to be as quiet as he could, straight upstairs and back down again. Cal didn't know about Hollie and me, not that it would have crossed his mind to have a look at May even if he had. Not to be cruel, but he just doesn't think like that.'

'And neither of you went into the kitchen?' Knight asked.

'No, Andy had some cans in the living room, a couple of bags of crisps. Hollie was lying in there dead, wasn't she? He wouldn't have wanted us opening the door.'

Jamie closed his eyes, and Knight gave him a moment before saying, 'What time did you leave the house?'

'I told you before. Just before eight.'

Catherine nodded. 'And Andy was alive and well when you did?'

Jamie glared at her. 'Of course he was. What are you trying to say, that I killed him?'

'Or maybe Cal did.'

Fury took over his face, and in that second she could see it – Jamie or his brother going into the kitchen before Andy could stop them and stumbling over Hollie's body – perhaps even physically. Maybe Andy was upstairs, maybe he ran up there to get away, but either way, he'd ended up dead.

'How fucking dare you?' Jamie snarled. 'My brother's like a kid; he's not capable of hurting anyone, and you say that about him?'

'Calm down, Mr Dobson,' Knight said.

Jamie's eyes bulged. 'Calm down? Calm fucking down?'

A couple of uniformed officers came into the room and stood either side of the door.

Jamie sneered. 'Back-up now, is it? Scared I'm going to hurt you?'

Catherine met his eyes, watching as the fight went out of him. It wasn't them he was angry with.

'We'll need to talk to you again,' Knight told him. Jamie scrubbed at his eyes with his fingertips, and Catherine saw he was crying again.

'I'm not going home,' he told them. 'I'm not leaving here until you've checked everything I've said and proved to yourselves that I'm telling the truth.'

'Go and get some rest,' Catherine told him gently. 'What about Cal?'

Jamie hesitated, tears running down his cheeks. Catherine stood and handed him the piece of paper, the proof that he had a daughter.

'Go home,' she said.

-

Back in their office upstairs, they discovered Anna had been out for pizza and soft drinks. Catherine grabbed a slice and between mouthfuls said, 'Do you think Jamie did it?'

Knight wrinkled his nose. 'I didn't have time to mention it before – the blond hair that Mick found on Andy's jeans belongs to Jamie, but as we already know he was in the house, I don't see that it's relevant. Thing is, I've used one of those hospital car park cameras myself and you can't see who's actually in the car. All that we might be able to prove is that Jamie's mum's car entered and left the car park at whatever times. We'd need more – witness statements from nursing staff, footage from inside the hospital or whatever.'

'I could give the hospital a call, see if there's anyone who could help us.' Anna checked the time. 'Though at this hour, I doubt it.'

'Worth a try.' Knight took another slice of pizza and bit into it.

'We've got a squad car outside his house tonight,' Catherine said. 'If we need him back here, it won't be a problem.'

Kendrick strode through the door. 'Do I smell pizza?' He sniffed the air. 'I knew it. Caught a whiff of it all the way down in the incident room. Amazing sense of smell – it's a talent I have.'

'Or I sent you a text telling you it was up here,' Anna said.

Kendrick ignored her. 'The interview with Jamie Dobson was pointless then.' He bit off a chunk of pizza and kept talking. 'Though you did manage to tell him he had a child and make him shout and cry. Not bad going.'

Catherine reached for a bottle of fruit juice. 'Why was it pointless?'

'We already knew he was the baby's father even if he didn't, which meant he'd been quite close to Hollie at least once. He had a motive to kill Hollie because she kept the fact that he had a child from him, and we've only his word for it that the man she was arguing with that morning wasn't him. He could have killed her.'

'But Hollie's brother, Ross, says she wasn't on the kitchen floor at twelve thirty,' Anna reminded him. 'If Jamie killed her, someone else moved her.'

Kendrick flapped a hand. 'Or Jamie left the back door open and went back later to move her. Risky, because Andy could have found the body first, but who knows. Or Ross is lying, or he couldn't see Hollie on the floor from where he was standing. We had one of our constables go and look through the window and he was the same height as Ross Morton – it's not clear whether he would have seen her or not. And that's assuming he was telling truth about what he did and that he didn't kill her himself.' Kendrick took another slice of pizza.

'Jamie knew about the door in the fence. That was new information,' Catherine said. Kendrick pulled a face.

'If he killed Andy Nugent, he walked in and out of the front door when he did it.' Kendrick's mobile began to ring and he pulled it out of his pocket. 'It's the Super.' He set the phone on the desk next to the pizza box. 'She can wait, I'm eating.' He looked at Catherine, then Knight. 'Next move?'

'We need to find out more about Hollie's relationship with Scott Greaves,' Catherine said. As far as she could see, there was only one person who was likely to be able to help them understand it. 'I think we should bring Chloe Morton in.'

29

In the women's toilets, Catherine brushed her hair and washed her face. She needed twelve hours' sleep, a shower and a change of clothes, but a quick spray of deodorant was as good as it was going to get for now. Leaning against the wall by the sinks, she dialled Isla's number, closing her eyes when she answered.

'Are you at home?' Isla asked.

'No, I'm still at work, hiding in the toilets.'

'Oh. How romantic.'

'As it gets.'

Isla laughed. 'I'd say I wish I was there with you, but...'

'We're waiting to do an interview, so I'm in here throwing cold water on my face and trying to wake up.' Catherine wanted to ask if their arson case had been mentioned to Isla's team, but knew she shouldn't. If Isla was going to arrive in Northolme tomorrow morning she'd mention it... wouldn't she?

'Going to be a late one then,' Isla said.

'It's one step forward, two steps back.'

'One of those.' Isla paused. 'I keep thinking about our holiday.'

Catherine smiled. 'I'm ready for another one.'

'Listen, Catherine—'

The door was flung open and Anna stuck her head into the room. 'Sarge? They're waiting for you.' She realised

Catherine was on the phone. 'Oh, sorry.' She backed out quickly.

'Sounds like you need to go, DS Bishop,' Isla said. 'Call me when you can.'

'Okay.'

There was a pause, where many couples would have said, 'I love you.'

Neither of them did.

–

Chloe Morton looked fearfully around the interview room. Catherine had to admit: it wasn't the best. The last occupant had left a terrible mix of smells: sweat, kebab meat and vomit, and further down the corridor, someone in the cells was rotating between screaming abuse, crying and singing. As Catherine sat down, Chloe leaned forward as though she wanted to grab her hand. Catherine kept her expression blank as Knight ran through the caution and formalities for the recording. She had warmed to Chloe at their first meeting, and she knew she had to harden her heart now.

'Can we get you a drink, Chloe?' Knight asked. 'Water, tea, coffee?'

Chloe shook her head. Huddled into an oversized sweatshirt, she pulled the sleeves over her hands and hugged herself.

'Okay. We'd like to talk to you about your sister, Hollie,' Knight said.

'All right.' Chloe's voice was little more than a whisper.

'When we spoke the day after your sister's death, you told me and my colleague that as far as you were aware, your sister had not been unfaithful to her partner, Andrew Nugent. Is that correct?'

'Yes.'

'You said she had denied rumours that her partner wasn't the father of her youngest child.'

'That's right.' Chloe looked puzzled.

This was a conversation Catherine knew she should have made time for before now. Kendrick had said as much, but he hadn't needed to.

'So if we told you we have conclusive proof that it's impossible for Andy to be May's father, that would come as a surprise to you?' Catherine watched Chloe's face as she spoke, knowing Knight was doing the same. Chloe's mouth opened and she blinked, over and over.

'No, that's...' Chloe frowned, her mouth forming words that never came out. 'No, Hollie wouldn't have done that. Even if she had, she'd have told me. She'd have said.' Chloe looked shell-shocked, almost dazed. Unless she was the best liar Catherine had ever seen, and she'd met a few, she genuinely had no idea that the rumours about her sister had been true.

'You're saying you were unaware of this?' Knight asked.

'Completely unaware.' Chloe sat up straighter, frowning as though she was trying to work something out. 'Who was it?'

Catherine ignored the question. 'It surprises you?'

'Yeah, I'm amazed. I can't... I thought Hollie would have told me. I thought she trusted me.'

She was angry now, Catherine realised, angry with her dead sister.

'How did you and Hollie communicate?' she asked. 'We have Hollie's phone records, and apart from a few short calls, you don't seem to have spoken much.'

Chloe looked away. 'We had our ways.'

'You mean the door in the fence that led into Hollie's garden?' Catherine deliberately sounded bored.

Chloe stared. 'You know about that?'

'Most of Lincolnshire knows about it.' Catherine folded her arms. 'You should have told us, Chloe.'

She bowed her head. 'I know. I'm sorry.'

'So you'd go to Hollie's house when you guessed Andy would be out so you could talk?'

'Yes. If Andy was around, Hollie would leave one of the kids' teddies on the back bedroom windowsill, so I could see it and know she wouldn't be coming out.' Chloe chewed on her bottom lip. 'I didn't go there often, because Hollie worried her neighbours would notice. Sometimes I'd meet her in town and walk around Tesco with her, or we'd catch the same bus and just ride around for a while, talking. We met in the park sometimes. Anywhere we could.'

'But Hollie didn't tell you about May's father?'

'No. When I asked her about it, she said it was lies, people making stuff up to cause trouble. I told you, when Andy heard he really hurt her, even though he knew it was crap.' She glanced at Catherine, registered her stern expression and focused on Knight instead. 'So who is May's dad?'

Catherine ignored the question. 'Do you know Scott Greaves?' The reaction was immediate – Chloe recoiled as though a snake had reared up in front of her. Catherine saw disgust in her expression, disgust and fear. There were tears in her eyes, her arms tightening around her body.

'Chloe?' Knight spoke gently. 'Are you okay?'

'Not him,' Chloe whispered. 'Not him. She wouldn't, not unless he...' She stared at them. 'Did he rape her?'

340

Catherine forced herself not to look at Knight, but it wasn't easy. What was this?

'Why would you think that?' she said.

Chloe snorted. 'Because that's what he did, or tried to. That's what he liked.'

'I'm sorry, Chloe,' Knight said. 'Can you explain that to us?'

'Okay, I...' Chloe wiped her cheeks with her palms.

'Would you like some water now?' Catherine asked.

'Yes, please.'

Catherine nodded and went to the door. Anna was already at the water cooler in the corridor outside, and Catherine made a 'what the fuck?' face at her. Anna widened her eyes as Catherine took the cup of water, then spread her hands.

After a few sips of water, Chloe tucked her hair behind her ears, took a deep breath and let it out slowly. 'When I spoke to you before, you asked about Andy, about why he changed, and you asked about drugs, stuff like that.'

'And you said Andy wasn't into drugs,' Catherine said.

'He wasn't. He was a thief.'

They'd been right then. 'What did he steal?'

'At first, when he was a younger, it was stuff like mobiles, PlayStations and games, things like that. Cash. He knew loads of people who drank a lot, smoked all sorts of stuff, and it was easy enough to go to parties and take things he could sell. Kids whose parents were away, students who were out of it. Then, he met someone who got him into nicking cars.' She drank some more water. 'That's when things changed.'

'How do you mean?' Knight asked.

'I think to Andy it had always been a bit of a laugh, a bit of danger – like people who jump out of planes or race motorbikes. He was nicking a few things from people who were so off their faces they didn't even notice. I'm not making excuses for him,' she said quickly, 'but stealing cars seems a lot more serious somehow. And he got in over his head.'

Catherine remembered what Jade had said about Andy having loads of silly mates, about him having loads of money, what they'd been told about Andy changing, and Dave Lancaster's idea that they should be paying more attention to that. She'd tell him he'd been right.

'What happened?' she asked.

'There was a bloke in charge, and he told them what to nick. The idea was to break into houses, get the car keys and then get the cars away before anyone realised. They took them to some industrial estate somewhere where they were broken down or shipped out, I don't know the details. Whatever. Andy wasn't involved in that side of it.' Chloe picked up her water again.

'Did Hollie tell you all this?' Knight asked. 'When?'

Chloe nodded. 'Is it okay if I just tell you everything I know, so you can see how it all fits together? I don't want to miss anything out.' She gave him a tremulous smile.

'That's fine.' He gave her a stern look. 'We'll be asking questions though.'

She nodded. 'So Andy was told he had to work with someone else – Scott Greaves.'

This time Catherine did turn to Knight, just as he looked at her. That was one possibility they hadn't considered. 'They were stealing cars together?'

'Yes, to order. They'd be given an address and they had to get in, grab the keys, and take the car before anyone noticed. Andy was told if he was caught, he was on his own, and if he grassed, his kids would be hurt.' Chloe sipped her water. 'But the stealing wasn't the worst of it.'

Catherine thought of Andy Nugent's fingerprints on the Cloughs' headboard, his glove on their bedroom floor, Rebecca waking to find a man on top of her.

Her stomach seemed to freeze as a thought came to her. Two men. One fingerprint. One lost glove.

Did he rape her?, Chloe had asked.

'What happened?' Catherine demanded. She knew Knight would pick up on her tone and wondered if he'd had the same idea as she had. Kendrick would be watching on the video feed, Anna too.

Chloe took a deep breath. 'Andy only told Hollie all this a few weeks ago. The bloke he was working with, Scott, he... well, a couple of times when they were in a house, Andy would be looking for the keys and Scott would disappear. Andy would find him in the bedroom. Andy hated it, told him it was wrong, that stealing was one thing but this was something else and he wouldn't work with Scott any more. But like I said, he was in too deep. He was told again that his kids would be hurt or taken and sold if he didn't do as he was told.' Chloe gulped, tears in her eyes again. 'Andy told Hollie he'd been scared for years, scared of being caught but also of what would happen if he tried to walk away. He was anxious, stressed, angry – and took it all out on Hollie. I'm not making excuses for him, there's no excuse for what he did to her, and he was only stuck in that situation because of his own stupid decisions. But I want to tell you everything I know.'

'Take your time,' Knight said.

'Like I said, he only told Hollie this recently, and she only told me last week. All the stuff about controlling her, he reckoned it was to protect her, keep her safe – well, I have my own ideas about that. He said he wanted to get out of that life, but he didn't know how to do it.'

'One quick question,' Catherine said. 'The bloke who was in charge – do you know his name?'

'It was Vic,' Chloe said, 'but he died. Scott gave the orders then – he'd made contacts, Andy said.'

The car dealership, the big house – it made sense.

'Is it possible… Do you think Hollie could have been having an affair with Scott?' Knight said.

'No!' Chloe almost shouted the word. She glanced at the floor, around the room, anywhere but at the two police officers sitting across the table from her. 'This is going to sound bad, but… Hollie was blackmailing him.'

'She was…' Those texts: 'Need more', 'I'm waiting' – Hollie was talking about money, the missing money Ashley Greaves had told them about. She had told Scott to come to the house and he had – and then strangled her. Catherine realised it was the only explanation that made sense. Scott Greaves had killed Hollie after arguing with her, and Andy Nugent had arrived home later that to find his partner dead. She had probably been killed in the living room, since Ross hadn't seen her body and the door handle had been wiped prior to Jamie and Cal Dobson's visit. Catherine imagined Andy's panic as he remembered attacking Hollie that morning, and the wound on his arm. He knew he would be blamed, or at least suspected, and in panic had phoned the first people he could think of to try to provide himself with an alibi. But why hadn't he called Jade? She would be able to tell anyone who asked where Andy had been all day, but then she'd also said Andy hadn't contacted her, and they knew from Andy's phone records that he definitely hadn't done so by phone. Maybe he had deleted her number, as Jade had suggested.

Chloe was still talking. 'I know it sounds terrible; it really doesn't show Hollie in a good light, but she was desperate. She didn't believe Andy would ever break away from Scott and so she'd made the decision to leave him, but she needed cash. Andy told her what Scott had done – there was a woman in town who Scott had ended up on top of while they were in the house. The other times Scott hadn't gone that far, but this time, Scott already had his trousers down, had punched this poor woman because she woke up and he panicked. Andy grabbed him, dragged him off her and out of the house, and I think that was when it really hit him how much trouble he was in. This was a couple of years ago, but as I said, Andy only told Hollie about it recently.'

'And Hollie saw an opportunity?' Knight asked.

Chloe's head went down. 'It wasn't like that. She was desperate.'

'But she could have moved back to your parents' house, brought the children there. Why blackmail Scott?'

'She wanted to leave the area, not come back home,' Chloe said. 'Get away from Andy completely.'

'And Scott just paid up? He didn't argue?' Catherine was sceptical.

Chloe chewed her bottom lip. 'I don't want to... It makes Hollie look...'

'Hollie's gone,' Knight said gently.

'I know.' Chloe took a shuddering breath. 'Scott did argue. He told Hollie that she'd be hurt, me and Ross would be hurt, the kids would be taken, all the same threats that were made to Andy, but Hollie just turned them around on Scott. Told him she'd go to the police herself, that she didn't give a shit if Andy was arrested as well. If he went to prison, she'd have no reason to move anyway, and when Scott's wife found out what he'd been doing, he'd lose access to his kids as well. They'd already separated, and Scott didn't want that. He started paying. Hollie wasn't going to do it forever, just until she had enough cash to get away.'

Catherine's mind was running through things she'd heard, things they'd been told, a conversation she'd had with Knight, just after they'd first spoken to Rebecca Clough. Andy Nugent hadn't attacked Rebecca – Scott Greaves had. And that meant…

'Did Andy smoke?' she demanded.

Chloe looked bemused. 'Andy? No, never.'

It was the final piece in the jigsaw. Catherine got up again and went to the door. Again, Anna stood waiting.

'Get a couple of cars to Rebecca and Dale Clough's house, please, one arriving before the other.' Catherine told her. 'The first car needs to bring Dale in alone quick as they can, and don't give him a choice. Then the second car needs to collect Rebecca.'

Anna frowned. 'Okay, but—'

'I'll explain after we're done with Chloe.' Catherine was already turning back into the interview room when a uniformed constable appeared.

'Can I have a word, Sarge? I know you're interviewing, but it's about the same case,' he said.

'Can you make it quick?'

'Very. I've just taken a call from a woman who says she looked after Hollie Morton and Andy Nugent's kids on the day the parents died. Reckons Hollie dropped them first thing in the morning and Andy picked them up about four thirty. She didn't like the bloke, didn't really like him taking the kids, and she said he was acting weird – agitated, impatient. She was worried because she'd seen Hollie had a mark on her face when she dropped the kids off.'

Catherine closed her eyes for a second. 'And she's just telling us this now? She was so worried that even though she knew Hollie had been murdered she didn't come forward?'

'You know how it is. She didn't think it was important, didn't want to get involved, blah blah blah.'

'All right, thank you. We'll need a formal statement.'

He nodded. 'I'll sort it.'

Catherine smiled at him, and turned away. The same old story – head in the sand and hope for the best.

'How did Hollie make the initial contact with Scott?' Knight was asking as Catherine sat back down. He gave Catherine a quick look and she knew he'd reached the same conclusion that she had.

'She asked me to take him a note.' Chloe was blushing. 'At the time I didn't know what it said – she said something about enquiring about a car – but I should have known that was bullshit. I suppose I didn't want to think too hard about it. I was just desperate for Hollie to get away from Andy, and I thought if she was thinking about cars, well, maybe she'd come to a decision.' She bowed her head. 'Do you think Scott killed her? I thought Andy had guessed she wanted to leave him and flipped.'

'You've given us a lot to think about, and there's a lot of work we need to do to establish just what happened,' Knight told her.

Chloe looked distraught. 'I should have told you all this before, phoned you or come here to see you. But my mum and dad didn't know what Hollie had done. They'd never imagine she would blackmail someone, and she was gone anyway, and I just… I didn't know what to do.' She rubbed her eyes again. 'My niece, May – are you allowed to tell me who her father is?'

Catherine pushed back her chair. She guessed that Jamie would want custody of his daughter. 'I think you'll soon find out.'

30

An hour later, Dale Clough sat in the interview room next to the one where they'd spoken to Chloe Morton. Looking at him on one of the video feed monitors, Catherine wondered how they should play it. He had his arms folded, his chin up, a blank expression on his face. Already defying them, though he was alone in the room.

'Are you sure about this?' Kendrick was pacing, a cup of coffee in one hand and a chocolate muffin in the other.

'There's only one way to find out,' Catherine told him. She was on her feet, exhaustion giving way to excitement because she could finally see themselves making progress.

Knight had been in the corner, his phone to his ear, but now he came to stand beside Catherine.

'Ready?' he said.

She nodded. 'How's the headache?'

Knight smiled. 'Forgotten all about it. Must be all this action.'

'Go on then,' Kendrick told them. 'Let's see what he says. His wife's just arrived as well.'

Clough watched them enter the room. Knight sat down first, Catherine taking her time, making herself comfortable, placing a folder on the table. Clough watched them silently, the hint of a smirk on his face.

'Let me guess,' he said. 'You've got a photograph to show me.'

'How did you know?' Catherine picked up the folder. She removed a photograph of Scott Greaves and put it down on the table in front of Clough. 'When did your wife first realise this was the man who attacked her?'

She hadn't been expecting a reaction quite as dramatic as Chloe Morton's had been a short while earlier, but Clough's face barely changed.

'A few hours before I strangled him,' he said.

Catherine said nothing, and Knight was silent too.

Eventually, Clough said, 'So what happens now?'

'Now you've confessed to murder?' Catherine raised an eyebrow. 'Why don't tell us what happened?'

Clough sighed. 'Why? I've already told you I did it.'

'And now you've got that off your chest, we'll need some details.'

'All right.' Clough stretched his arms, hands above his head and yawned. 'Sorry. Haven't been sleeping well.' He cleared his throat. 'Okay. I've already told you that Rebecca struggles to leave the house these days, but recently we've been working hard – *she's* been working hard – to start trying to overcome that. I suggested getting her a car, just a runabout so she could go out, but she'd be protected, if you know what I mean. She could lock the doors, even just drive somewhere and sit in the car if she wanted to.' He paused. 'She doesn't like driving mine, says it's too big, and so we thought we'd go for something small, cheap – boring. I have a bit of cash tucked away, and since Rebecca seemed keen on the idea, I thought we'd go out and buy something there and then, not give her a chance to change her mind.'

Catherine felt like she was holding her breath as Clough went on with his story.

'We went to the second-hand place down near the river – the one that piece of shit owned.' He jerked his head at the photo of Scott Greaves. 'He had a few decent runabouts, and it wasn't like he could rip us off – I know a crap car when I see one. So we get there and we're looking around the lot in the fucking rain when the man himself comes over, all smiles. We're all getting soaked; he's talking bollocks about the cars; I'm asking him questions.' His face changed, the fury coming off him in waves, as though Scott Greaves is in the room with them. 'And then I saw Rebecca's face. People talk about someone going pale, white as a sheet, looking like they've seen a ghost, all that crap. And she does all of that. She just turns and walks away. So I, thick bastard that I am, I apologise to him, actually apologise to this fucker for wasting his time, thinking Rebecca's just frozen up, decided she can't go through with it. I go back to the car, and I admit it, I was angry. But before I can say a word, she tells me. Just two words. "That's him." And we sit there and watch him, and he just goes back inside his shitty little office, as though nothing's happened. I want to go back in there and beat the shit out of him, but Rebecca tells me we need to do it properly, that we have to go to the police. And I like my idea better, but I know she's right, so we go home, and we have a cup of tea, like civilised fucking humans, and all the time all I'm thinking is: "I want to kill him. I want to smash this fucker to pieces."'

'How did she know?' Catherine can't help asking. *Wet wool and cigarettes.*

Clough stares at her. 'The smell. He was wearing a jumper over his shirt and tie, and from the stink of him, he must have been on forty a day. Like I said, it was raining.

351

We were all wet through… Rebecca said it was the same smell.'

Catherine managed not to cheer as her theory was confirmed.

'Seems a bit flimsy,' Knight commented. 'That was all it took?'

Clough glared at him. 'As soon as she smelt him, she knew,' he said. 'And I believed her.'

'What did you do then?' Knight asked.

Clough smiled. 'Went home and talked. Had an early night, really early, actually went to bed together and had sex. Amazing. It was a relief, I suppose, a release, something like that. Get a psychologist or whatever to tell you. Rebecca was more relaxed than I'd seen her in what felt like forever. Then she fell asleep, and I lay there next to her, fucking seething. We'd agreed to come to talk to you useless bastards, tell you what we knew, but Rebecca had said she wanted a few days to sort herself out, come to terms with seeing him, she said. I wasn't happy about it, but we agreed to wait. She was the one who'd be going through it all again when she spoke to you, questions, a court case, all of that. But then…' For the first time Clough looked discomfited. He ran a hand over his mouth. 'I must have fallen asleep myself in the end. When I woke up, she wasn't there. I found her in the kitchen, bottle of vodka in her hand and boxes of tablets all over the table. When I saw her, crying, completely destroyed again when she'd just seemed to have turned a corner, I knew it wasn't going to be enough for me. I was worried we'd come to you, you'd fob us off with some bullshit, and that prick would get away with what he did. Rebecca was scared, frightened you wouldn't believe her, that there was no evidence and you'd laugh at her if she said she knew it was him from the smell. She said she couldn't go through with coming to speak to you, and I decided to sort him out myself. I couldn't live with knowing he was walking around like nothing had happened after he'd wrecked my wife's life, both of us knowing he lived in town, that she might bump into him anytime. The fucker didn't even recognise her. He'd no idea she was the woman he'd attacked. One of many, I suppose.' He gave a bitter laugh. 'Imagine if we'd bought a car, sat down to fill in the paperwork. Seeing our address might have given him a shock.'

'And that would have been helpful when we'd questioned him,' Knight said.

Clough scowled. 'If you bothered to speak to him. Anyway, he'd made some shit joke about living at work, told us his wife had kicked him out and he was sleeping in the office. We'd laughed, but I started to wonder, what if it was true? I had no idea where he lived, but if he was there, well, I'd pay him a visit.' He swallowed. 'So I did. I had no intention of killing him. I just wanted him to feel some fear, some pain, like Rebecca had every day since he hurt her. But when I saw him sitting there fucking smirking, I lost it. There was a cable of some sort on the floor, and I grabbed it, looped it around his throat. It only seemed to take a second, though it can't have been. He was dead.'

'What about the fire?' Catherine said.

Clough shrugged. 'Nothing to do with me. I just left him lying there.'

'You didn't set the building on fire to cover up the murder?'

'No, I've just told you I didn't. I thought it was just luck that the arsonist covered my tracks for me.'

'Okay.' Catherine nodded. Knight looked at her, and he nodded too. Catherine picked up the photograph and tucked it back inside the folder then leaned back, studying Dale Clough.

'Are you going to charge me now?' he demanded.

'We might,' Catherine said, 'if we believed a word you've just said.'

'What?' Clough slammed his hands down on the table. 'What the fuck? I confess to murder and you don't believe me?'

'You said you used a cable to strangle Scott Greaves,' Catherine said. 'What sort of cable was it?'

'What?'

'What sort of cable? Was it an electrical cable, like an extension lead? Or a car part?'

'I don't...' His eyes flicked from side to side. 'Clutch cable. It was a clutch cable.'

Catherine nodded. 'Okay, a clutch cable. So why didn't you say that to start with?'

Clough was rattled now. 'What do you mean?'

'You deal with car parts every day. If you'd used a clutch cable to strangle Greaves, you would have said so without even thinking about it. You would have recognised it instantly. You said "cable" because you've no idea what was actually used, because you didn't kill Scott Greaves. You weren't even there. You wife killed him, but she had no idea what she grabbed to strangle him with. To her, it was just a cable.'

Clough opened his mouth as though gasping for air. 'You can't arrest her, you can't. Prison would kill her. I did it, I'm telling you. Even an hour in your cells...'

'She's already here,' Knight told him.

31

'Go home, the lot of you,' Kendrick told them. 'I want you in early tomorrow – we still don't know who killed Andy Nugent, though it looks like we won't have to worry about the arsons.' He gave Catherine a sideways glance. 'An EMSOU team will be arriving first thing to take over the case.'

Catherine's stomach somersaulted. She'd spoken to Isla only a couple of hours ago, and she hadn't said a word. Okay, they hadn't had much of a chance to talk, but Isla could have sent a text at any time.

'Which team?' Catherine demanded. If he was talking about Isla and her colleagues, she wanted to know.

Kendrick picked up the last slice of cold, congealed pizza and sank his teeth into it. 'No idea. They didn't say. I'm only in charge of this dump.' He waved the pizza at them, shepherding them in front of him and out of the office. They all clattered down the stairs together, and out into the car park at the back of the building. Kendrick gave them a wave as he clambered into his car, and Catherine, Anna and Knight headed for their own vehicles. Anna was checking her phone.

'Nat sent a text, asking if we were still here. She's just sent another saying she's bought chips, and she's on her way up to the office now.' They both looked up at the building. 'She must have gone in through the front door. I'll—'

The force of the explosion hit Catherine like a punch to the chest, the searing heat coming a second later as windows shattered, alarms began to shriek and the building in front of them seemed to shimmer, flames already visible in the room nearest to the them on the ground floor – the incident room.

Frozen for a second, Knight, Anna and Catherine stared at each other before starting to run. Anna had her radio out requesting every service she could think of as they raced towards the front door of their station, the fire already beginning to take hold on the lower floor.

'What the fuck was that?' Catherine shouted as they ran.

Knight was alongside her. 'Our arsonist showing us what he can do?'

'Fire engines are on their way,' Anna told them. The fire station was just a few streets away. They reached the front door, flames already lighting up a third of the ground floor.

'They still won't get here in time. Nat's in there some-where.' Catherine could see officers stumbling out of the side door, leading out prisoners and moving them away from the burning building. The alarms inside continued to scream as Catherine pushed the door open, Knight close behind her. Anna tried to follow, but Catherine yelled at her to stay back. She'd been through enough recently.

'You need to tell the firefighters what's happening,' she shouted over her shoulder.

Anna didn't look happy but she backed away.

The heat hit them again like a tidal wave, making them stagger. They were coughing already, Catherine's chest tight, her throat burning. They reached the bottom of the stairs, bellowing Nat's name, waiting for a second for an answering shout before stumbling forward.

Nothing.

The heat was intensifying, though that didn't seem possible. They were on the first floor now, and at the far end of the corridor Catherine saw part of the floor collapse as flames forced their way through from below.

'We can't go down there,' Knight shouted.

'Nat's in here somewhere,' Catherine yelled back. 'I'm not leaving her.'

Then there was someone else beside them now, tall and slim. Jimmy. He was in casual clothes, not his fire-fighter gear, his forearm over his nose and mouth, his eyes streaming.

'Where is she? Nat!' He pushed past them. 'Nat!'

There was a creak and a groan as another part of the floor collapsed and disappeared into the flames below. Jimmy stared as though mesmerised by the horror of what he was seeing.

'Nat!' he screamed.

Knight grabbed his shoulder. 'Your colleagues are on their way. They'll find her. We need to get out of here.'

Catherine's lungs felt like they might explode, her eyes streaming so much she could hardly make out Knight's face. Jimmy shook his head.

'There's no time. Look at the way this thing's spreading. She'll be dead before the engines arrive.'

Knight kept hold of him. 'This is crazy. The floor's half gone. You'll never reach her.' His voice cracked. 'We need to go, now.'

'Nat!' Catherine heard herself scream. 'Nat, where are you?'

There was another crack, another roar as the flames surged again. Jimmy turned, seeming to at last take in what Knight was saying.

'We can't just leave her,' he said, so quietly Catherine almost missed the words over the roar of the fire and her own coughing.

'We have no choice.' Knight pulled on his arm, and this time Jimmy didn't resist. He was crying now, sobbing, and Catherine knew she was too as they half fell down the stairs. They could hear sirens nearby as they stumbled through the door and collapsed onto the tarmac outside. As Catherine lay there coughing and choking, she heard a familiar voice behind them.

'What the fuck?'

Nat Roberts stood there, clutching a stack of polystyrene cartons to her chest with one hand, gaping at the blaze. Anna spun around and threw her arms around Nat.

'We thought you were inside! Your text said you were on your way upstairs!'

'I was, then I had to go back to the car.' Nat held up a sachet of ketchup. 'Forgot the sauce.'

Catherine groaned. 'We could have died because of you and your bloody chips.' She coughed and retched as she started to laugh.

'Steady on, Sarge.' Nat put the cartons on the floor and stood over Jimmy, hands on hips. He looked up at her, his eyes red and swollen.

'You said you were going home,' she said. Catherine was surprised at her tone, and Jimmy seemed to cower in front of her.

'I thought you were inside. I went in—'

Nat curled her lip. 'You went in there? Very brave. I appreciate the gesture. But then, you know all about fire, don't you?'

He stared at her. 'Of course I do. It's my job to know.'

Nat just glared at him.

Knight realised first. 'You don't mean—'

'That's exactly what I mean,' Nat told him. 'This is our arsonist. Ask him why he was here tonight. Why would an off-duty firefighter be hanging around a police station just when, incredibly, it's set on fire? And not only is it set on fire, it goes up like an oil field. Almost like the fire was set by someone who knew exactly what they were doing. I checked back, realised every time there's been a fire, you've been sent to the scene afterwards.' She sneered at Jimmy. 'What a joy, hey? What a fucking thrill. You must have shat your pants when you realised Scott Greaves's body was inside his office that you'd set a fuse in.' Jimmy's head dropped and Nat's mouth twisted. She looked at Catherine and Anna. 'You remember he said his dad died of cancer? That was bollocks. He was killed in a fire. I was nosing around online, looking for the social media profiles of the person I hoped would be my new boyfriend, as you do, when I saw the story. "Local firefighter dies a hero, proud son hopes to follow in his footsteps."' She glared at Jimmy. 'Only you chose a very different way to make your mark, didn't you?' She half turned away. 'One of you better arrest him. I don't think I can.'

32

The next morning, Catherine curled on the sofa in her pyjamas with her third mug of tea of the day. Her chest ached a little, her eyes stung, but otherwise she was fine and although she and Knight had been taken to the hospital along with Jimmy, they'd both been allowed home soon afterwards. Kendrick had got the message to Isla via her boss, and she'd phoned constantly until Catherine was able to speak to her. No one had been hurt in the fire, everyone else having managed to escape before it spread throughout the building.

An hour later, Catherine stood with Knight, Kendrick, Anna, Nat, Chris Rogers, Dave Lancaster, and most of the other officers based at Northolme outside the smouldering wreck of their station. Catherine was surprised at the tug of emotion she felt.

'It was an ugly old place, but it was home,' Chris said.

Catherine heard the catch in his throat as he spoke.

Kendrick clapped his hands. 'Superintendent Stringer sends her congratulations. We managed to catch our arsonist – or PC Roberts did – and the fact that we destroyed our police station while doing it will probably be considered as killing two birds with one stone by the folk at HQ.' He gathered his team around him, including Nat. 'Right, you lot. Just because half of you nearly died last night doesn't mean we're slacking. I think we all agreed that it's certain Scott Greaves killed Hollie Morton, despite our lack of physical evidence. Nothing else fits. We'll need to go through everything we have again, talk with Mick, but since Greaves is dead anyway, it's not exactly justice for Hollie's family.' He looked at each of them in turn. 'And we still don't know who killed Andy Nugent.'

Catherine smiled at him. 'I was thinking about this last night while I was coughing my guts up.'

Kendrick pulled a face. 'Charming. And what were your conclusions?'

'That there's only one person the saliva found on Andy's face could belong to.'

—

Irene Spence was already in the doorway as Catherine and Knight approached.

'You'd better come inside. No point taking your shoes off. I don't suppose you'll be staying long.'

'We need to have a word with your husband, Mrs Spence,' Catherine said gently.

She bowed her head. 'He's waiting for you.'

When they reached the living room, Des Spence was on his feet, leaning on his walking frame.

'You know then,' he said. Catherine nodded. He sighed. 'It's a relief, if I'm honest.' He eased himself into his chair. 'How much have you worked out?'

'Why don't you tell us what happened?'

He nodded, wiped his lips with his handkerchief. 'It was all as we told you before. We heard the arguing around ten in the morning, listened to their computer games until eight o'clock, but then… well, that's when it happened.'

Irene came in with a tray of tea and handed them around. She sat on the arm of her husband's chair, her arm around his frail shoulders. 'We should have come to you, we know that, or told you the truth when you came here. But we were frightened, we didn't know what would happen, and Des is...'

'Dying,' he said. 'I'm dying anyway. I suppose that'll happen in prison now.' His eyes filled with tears but he blinked them away. 'Where was I? Yes, eight o'clock. The two lads left, but the noise got worse. The video game turned on, the music turned on and played even louder. We were beside ourselves. I got up, said I was going around there. Irene didn't want me to, but I couldn't stand it any more. I went and knocked on the door, but there was no answer. I kept knocking, hammering really. Then I saw a shadow pass the glass, and he must have heard me because everything went silent and he opened the door.' Des paused and swallowed a mouthful of tea. 'He stood there, looking down his nose at me. He asked what I wanted, and I told him we were sick of the noise. He just laughed in my face and slammed the door. I heard him run up the stairs, and I... I don't know. I was furious, and I opened the door and went straight into the house. He was in the bathroom, standing in front of the toilet, but he turned as he heard me coming up the stairs.' He shook his head. 'It takes me a while you, see, and I make plenty of noise about it. He started shouting, what was I doing in his house, who did I think I was, a lot of language. And I shouted back at him, told what we thought of them. And again, he laughed in my face, and I shoved him in the chest. I don't know why, I never even thought about doing it. It was like my hands shot out without me thinking about it. Didn't know my own strength, pushing a young lad like him over but he wasn't expecting it, you see. His head sort of bounced off the toilet and then he just lay there. His eyes were open, and I can still see them staring at me. I knew straight away that he was dead.' His voice shook and he wiped his mouth again. 'I suppose I panicked. I thought I'd better try to cover it up, make it look like something else had happened. There was a belt on the floor and I took it and draped it around his neck, I don't know why. I wasn't thinking straight.' He looked at Catherine. 'Better get the cuffs on then.'

'I don't think there's any need for that, do you?'

Irene began to cry quietly. 'What will happen to him?'

'As you might have heard, there was a fire at our station here in Northolme last night, so your husband will be taken to Lincoln and officers there will have a chat with him. I'm afraid I can't say what will happen after that.'

Des took his wife's hand. 'Can we have a few minutes together?'

Catherine and Knight stood and put their mugs back on the tray. 'Of course. We'll wait outside until the car from Lincoln arrives.'

Des met her eyes. 'Thank you.'

Catherine swallowed the lump in her throat and turned away.

As they closed the front door behind them, Catherine saw the boy who had asked how much they paid for information, the one they'd suspected of being involved in the arsons. He was leaning on his bike, waiting by their car.

'Didn't do too much damage, in the end,' he said, nodding at the vehicle.

'Not for the want of trying,' Knight said.

'Wasn't me. Blame my mate's dad for that.' He inclined his head at the Spences' house. 'You figured it out at last, then?'

'You knew?' Catherine stared at him.

'Guessed. Saw the old man coming out of the house with a face like death. I mean he's always got a face like death, but it was even worse than usual.'

'Why didn't you tell us?'

He shrugged thin shoulders. 'Why should I? No proof. I've learnt to mind my own business.' He looked away, his eyes bleak. 'And I don't like blokes who beat people up.'

Catherine looked at Knight, who pressed the fob to unlock the car doors. As he climbed into the driver's seat, Catherine said, 'What's your name?'

He was instantly suspicious. 'Why?'

'Just interested.'

'Brodie. It's shit, I know.'

'What about the arsons that have been happening in town? You were seen at a couple of the fires.'

'Saw me yourself, didn't you?' He smiled. 'Twice.'

'But you didn't wait around to talk to us.'

'Not my fault you can't run very fast.'

She laughed. 'Why were you out so late? And so early?' From what he'd already said, she thought she could guess.

'I don't sleep much. Don't always go home.'

'Why?'

He shrugged. 'Don't want to.'

She could see she was going to get no more from him on the subject. 'How did you know when there'd been a fire?'

'Obvious, wasn't it? If you're riding around town. Loads of smoke and stink, sometimes a glow in the sky.'

'You weren't there before the fires took hold?'

364

He laughed. 'Are you asking if I started them?'

'No, because we know who did. I wondered if you do.'

'Not a clue. By the time I got there, they were already putting them out.'

Catherine nodded. 'Do you have a phone?'

Brodie shook his head. 'Got smashed. Thrown against a wall.'

He didn't say who by, and Catherine didn't ask. She took out a notebook and wrote down her name and phone numbers. 'Ring me if you need help. Anytime. I mean it.'

He looked like he might refuse, but then took the paper and folded it. He looked like he might say something else, but then turned away and hopped on his bike. She watched him until he turned the corner at the end of the road then got into the car.

'Okay?' Knight said.

Catherine told him what Brodie had said.

He cleared his throat. 'Caitlin phoned earlier. I didn't want to say anything until…' He nodded at the Spences' house. 'I knew how difficult that was going to be.'

'And?'

Knight took a deep breath. 'Olivia isn't Jed's child.' His voice cracked. 'Caitlin swears that means she's mine, but she's also accepted I need another test for my own peace of mind. She took offence, but she accepted it.' He wiped his eyes with his fingertips. 'So it seems I have a daughter. When we have the final confirmation, we're going to sort out access, and Caitlin has even suggested that I'm added to Olivia's birth certificate. There's no father on it at the moment, obviously, and in Caitlin's world, that's not the done thing at all.'

Catherine felt tears in her own eyes. 'Olivia deserves a dad like you.'

Knight smiled. 'There's something else.'

'What?'

'Jo's pregnant.'

Catherine stared at him. 'You're joking?'

He laughed. 'No, I'm not.'

When Catherine thought about it, it was obvious. Jo's collapse in her mortuary, the hospital visit, Knight's concern for her.

'Bloody hell, that's great news. I'd hug you, but the gear stick's in the way.' She grabbed his hand instead. 'It's amazing, Jonathan. I'm so happy for you both.'

'Thank you. We're...' He shook his head, beaming. 'It was a surprise, because Jo thought she couldn't have children. She's been feeling rough for weeks so we've both been worrying, but the hospital say everything's fine.'

In the rear-view mirror, Catherine saw a squad car turn in at the top of the road.

'They're here. Shall we...?'

Knight nodded and started the engine. 'Yes. I don't want to watch them bring him out.'

33

Back at home, Catherine made herself a coffee and settled back onto the sofa. With their police station badly damaged by the fire, she and her colleagues would have to wait to hear where they were going to be working, but for now, she had some free time.

She must have dozed off, because when she opened her eyes, her empty coffee cup had fallen on her lap and she could hear someone at the front door.

Isla stood there, the same sports bag in one hand, and a shopping bag in the other. Catherine was horrified to find herself in tears. Isla stepped inside, lowered the bags onto the carpet and closed the door behind her.

'Quite a welcome,' she said. Catherine laughed, feeling in her pocket for a tissue.

'I'm sorry.' She knew why she was crying – the relief at seeing Isla. Her presence was calming, reassuring. It helped.

Isla shook her head, holding Catherine at arm's length. 'You're sure you're okay? When I got the message about you going to hospital, I was...' She glanced away. 'I was terrified. I got in the car, I was halfway here when you phoned me back.'

Catherine lifted a hand to Isla's cheek, looking into her eyes. 'You didn't tell me that. Why didn't you keep driving?' She already knew the answer.

'Because you said you were fine, that I should stay at home. That I had work this morning, and I needed my sleep,' Isla said softly. Catherine knew she was hurt.

'I'm sorry.' It wasn't enough.

'I just wanted to be with you,' Isla said softly.

'I know, but I...' Catherine struggled to explain her actions, because she didn't really understand them herself. 'I don't deserve you.'

Isla stared. 'What?'

Catherine turned her face away, angry with herself. 'All you've done since we got together is look after me. It's not fair.'

Isla took her hand. 'Wouldn't you do the same for me?'

'You know I would.'

'And one day, you will. It's just your turn at the moment.' Isla smiled, and Catherine knew it was true. She looked at the bags Isla had left on the floor.

'Can you stay?'

Isla nodded. 'I've taken a few days off.'

'Really?'

'I thought we needed some time, especially after the fire last night.' Isla took a breath. 'When we were on holiday, it was so perfect, and I've missed being with you. I've already said I'm not going to London so who knows where I'll end up working, and I know things are uncertain for you after the fire, but whatever happens, could we start trying to spend a few nights together during the week? Even just one?'

She looked so worried, so frightened of what the answer might be. Catherine knew she needed reassurance, that the time had come for them both to let their defences down completely. 'Of course we can.'

Isla's smile was shaky. 'Good.'

Catherine wrapped her arms around her, moving forward so her forehead rested against Isla's and closed her eyes. 'I love you,' she said.

Acknowledgements

As always, thank you to the lovely people at Canelo for everything they do to get my work out into the world. Thank you to Tom Sanderson for the amazing cover and to Federica Leonardis and Becca Allen for the copy edit and proofreading.

To anyone who has read my books, left a review or taken the time to contact me about my work – thank you.

Thank you to my amazing family and friends, and to my furry writing companions, Evie, Poppy and Alexa.

A huge thank you to the members of the Tá mé ag foghlaim na Gaeilge (I am learning Irish) Facebook group who helped me with this book's dedication. My Irish is extremely limited, though I'm doing my best to learn, and their help was invaluable in finding just the right words. If anyone's wondering, the dedication translates to: 'Although we never met, you are with me in my heart'.

Some of this book was written before the COVID-19 pandemic, but it was finished and edited during lockdown. We all know what a terrible, frightening, almost overwhelming time it has been, and still is. I will add my own thanks to the incredible staff of the NHS, and to the paramedics, police officers, supermarket staff, bus drivers and everyone else who goes out every day and risks their own safety and health to help others.

To the Lockdown Ladies – there's no one I'd rather do a quiz or reminisce about 90s music with.

And to Tracy, who keeps me steady through it all – thank you.

CANELO CRIME

Do you love crime fiction and are always on the lookout for brilliant authors?

Canelo Crime is home to some of the most exciting novels around. Thousands of readers are already enjoying our compulsive stories. Are you ready to find your new favourite writer?

Find out more and sign up to our newsletter at canelocrime.com

Lost Cause
Rachel Lynch

DI Kelly Porter has solved some of the Lake District's most gruesome murders but nothing has prepared her for the monster she's about to meet. The answers may lie with a local oddball – is he a victim, or a killer?

Lies to Tell
Marion Todd

Since she joined the St Andrews force, DI Clare Mackay has uncovered many secrets lurking in the picturesque Scottish town. When there is a critical security breach inside Police Scotland, she realises she may have put her faith in the wrong person – will it be a deadly mistake?

The Body Under the Bridge
Nick Louth

DCI Craig Gillard has spent his career hunting criminals. When a missing person case reveals itself to be far more than a routine disappearance, it isn't long before the perpetrator has another target: DCI Gillard himself. Suddenly the detective isn't just running the case – he's part of it.

A Front Page Affair
Radha Vastal

Capability 'Kitty' Weeks is determined to prove her worth as a journalist. Headlines about the Great War are splashed across the front pages, but Kitty is stuck writing about society gossip – until a man is murdered on her beat and she is plunged into a story that threatens the life she has always known.

When the Past Kills
M J Lee

The Beast of Manchester was the case that defined DI Thomas Ridpath's career, but the wrong person was convicted and only later was the true culprit put away. Now, those connected to the case are being targeted. Someone is desperate for revenge, and Ridpath risks losing more than he can stand.

Small Mercies
Alex Walters

DI Annie Delamere is off duty and enjoying a walk in the Peak District when she comes across a mutilated corpse. As the body count increases, Annie is under intense pressure to solve the case. But are the crimes the work of a deranged mind – or a cover for something even more chilling?

Home Fires Burn
Lisa Hartley

DS Catherine Bishop is dealing with the aftermath of the most brutal case of her career. Her small team is overwhelmed by an arsonist, and a new murder case provides far more questions than answers. The pieces finally fall into place, but have Catherine's demons already won?

When the Dead Speak
Sheila Bugler

Eastbourne journalist Dee Doran is investigating a woman's disappearance when the body of another is found. There are startling similarities between the dead woman and one who was killed sixty years previously. Dee is determined to uncover the connection, but sometimes the only thing more dangerous than secrets is the truth…